Praise for *Vanishing Falls*

"*Vanishing Falls* is a game of *Clue* in the Tasmanian rainforest with a rich cast of characters and a flawlessly sketched locale. Poppy Gee has written the perfect kind of mystery: a world that feels at once fresh and familiar with a story that drives at a frenzied clip."

—David Joy, author of
When These Mountains Burn

"The lush, rich landscape of the Tasmanian rain forest is the setting for Poppy Gee's *Vanishing Falls*, a novel that blends crime and women's fiction with a mystery at its heart. Gee deals with themes of class, the legacy of wealth, and a divided society as relevant to those in the US as it will be to those familiar with the razed fruit orchards and petering-out roads of Vanishing Falls. Best of all, this novel introduces us to an unforgettable heroine, Jo-jo, who will tug at your heartstrings even as you cheer for her to solve the crime."

—Jenny Milchman, Mary Higgins Clark
Award–winning author of *Cover of Snow* and
The Second Mother

"*Vanishing Falls* is an addictive, cleverly plotted mystery-within-a-mystery set in a vividly painted Tasmania. The cast of complex, secret-laden characters will draw you in and keep you riveted until the final page. Poppy Gee has created a chilling gem of a novel with a surprising heart at the center."

—Kali White, award-winning author of
The Monsters We Make

"Although this debut novel by Australian author Gee appears to unfold as languidly as a beach afternoon, she deftly creates a delicious atmosphere of mounting suspense."

—*Library Journal* (starred review)

"If you loved *The Girl With the Dragon Tattoo*, you'll like this murder mystery. *Plot notes:* Trying to get over a bad breakup, Sarah Avery is home in Tasmania for the holiday—when she finds a body washed up on shore. *Before reading:* Lock your doors. This whodunit will creep you out."

—*Marie Claire*

VANISHING FALLS

Also by Poppy Gee

Bay of Fires

VANISHING FALLS

A Novel

POPPY GEE

wm

WILLIAM MORROW

An Imprint of HarperCollinsPublishers

VANISHING FALLS. Copyright © 2020 by Poppy Gee. All rights reserved. Printed in the United States of America. No part of this book may be used or reproduced in any manner whatsoever without written permission except in the case of brief quotations embodied in critical articles and reviews. For information, address HarperCollins Publishers, 195 Broadway, New York, NY 10007.

HarperCollins books may be purchased for educational, business, or sales promotional use. For information, please email the Special Markets Department at SPsales@harpercollins.com.

FIRST EDITION

Designed by Diahann Sturge

Library of Congress Cataloging-in-Publication Data has been applied for.

ISBN 978-0-06-297849-3

20 21 22 23 24 LSC 10 9 8 7 6 5 4 3 2 1

In memory of
Ted and Margaret Embery & Donald and Diana Gee

PROLOGUE

Jack Lily

Calendar House

Late on a wet winter's night, Jack Lily arrived home to find his front door wide open and the antique carpet drenched. The hall light and the living room lamps were on. The dog dozed by a generous fire. His wife's shoes and evening purse lay neatly on the floor beside the couch. Draped over a chair was her sable coat. Her diamond necklace and earrings sat on the occasional table beside a half-drunk glass of champagne.

Celia was not in their bedroom or in the bathroom. Their daughters were sleeping peacefully in their beds. As he searched, he thought of how angry his wife had been with him earlier in the evening, and he began looking in the lesser used of their fifty-two rooms in case she had hidden herself from him. It took some time. The Calendar House had four floors, one for each season, twelve hallways, and seven staircases. Parts of the house were locked off—the northern wing on the third floor, the attic. He unlocked these doors and, with increasing concern, called her name into the darkness. There was no answer.

He hurried down the old servants' narrow stairwell and strode into his study. In this long room he kept some of his most precious artifacts and paintings, and these were untouched. Six of the seven entrances on the ground floor were secure. Nothing suggested an intruder.

Something in his chest tightened as he went out the front door and stood on the veranda. The wind made his eyes water. Lightning cracked above the poplar trees. A woman did not wander out into the heaviest rain Vanishing Falls had received that winter, for no reason. The only thing to do was to call the police.

Two young constables arrived swiftly, traipsing mud across the parquetry. They noted that earlier in the evening Jack had argued with his wife. They searched the house and spoke to his daughters. They stopped short of declaring the Lilys' grand old house, and their farm with all its outbuildings—apple sheds and hay barns, the stables and boathouse—and the pastures from the lake to the river a crime scene. They simply said they would return in the morning.

Jack did not need the benefit of the twenty-five years he had spent practicing law to understand he was in trouble.

CHAPTER 1

A week earlier
Saturday, August 19

Joelle Smithton

Vanishing Falls village

B rian said to be careful walking into the village to buy his newspaper. Even though the rain coming down was less than yesterday he thought the pavement on the main street would be slippery. As usual, he was right. Several times Joelle's gum boots slid on wet leaves or the moss growing around the cobblestones, and each time, in surprise, she cried out, "Flip."

In Vanishing Falls the winter rainy season lasted from May until the end of September. It rained every day in heavy downpours or fast sleet that came sideways and stung her cheeks or a slow drizzle or, her favorite kind, a soft billowing dampness that felt like she was walking through a cloud.

Every kind of rain gave Brian a reason to think of a warning. Since she married him and moved to Vanishing Falls twelve years ago, there was no safety advice he had not given her. It had started the moment they saw the welcome sign, with the big picture of the waterfalls tumbling into a water hole. It was a tourist attraction because there was no river or creek taking the water away. Brian said the water drained through underground creeks that emerged in the wetland kilometers away. Lots of people swam in the water hole but that was dangerous because they never knew when they might get sucked into the underground creek. Even on a hot day, when the water was so inviting, like frothy cold lemonade, she had to remember that she could get stuck inside a dark river tunnel forever.

It was hard to remember all the safety instructions. Never wander off the track in the rain forest behind their house. Don't drive on Murdering Creek Road in a heavy downpour as it could flash flood. He never ran out of advice. He even warned her about obvious things like wearing a leather apron and steel-cap boots in the butchery, or not talking when she was using the mincing machine. Her best friend, Miss Gwen, said he only spoke out of love, so she couldn't let it annoy her, but sometimes—like when he said the teapot was hot—she would roll her eyes and say, "Good advice, Brian."

It was Saturday and Vanishing's main street was starting to get busy. Joelle called a happy greeting to every person she saw, even if she didn't know them. She went past the Rosella Café, the bakery, and the hardware store. Alfred was taking a delivery outside his fruit shop and he gave her a cheery wave. She paused and carefully studied her watch. There was not time for a quick hello with Alfred.

"I can't stop," she called out. "I'm in a rush. I'm working at the school fair later today!"

Alfred smiled with his lovely straight teeth. She waved. He waved. She kept waving until he went inside. Farther down the street, Nev was standing on the steps of his news agency, waiting for her.

He looked at his watch. "You're a bit late today. I was getting worried."

She went up the news agency sandstone steps and squeezed past him. He closed the heavy door. It was nice and warm inside.

"The cat ran off again," she said, taking off her scarf. "But he came back."

"He always comes back." He offered her some licorice. "That's on the house. As long as you don't tell Mr. Smithton. Don't want him getting jealous that you're in here talking to me."

"Come off it, Nev. You talk to all the ladies like that."

"Oh!" He put his hand on his heart and pretended his feelings were hurt. "I only have eyes for you, Joelle."

Nev was her second-best friend, after Miss Gwen. She joked back, "Tell me another one."

"Have you read the paper today?" Nev asked.

She liked how he always assumed she read the paper. "Not yet."

"There's a big story on the Apple Queen Tribute Evening."

In the paper was a black-and-white photo of Miss Gwen taken in the olden days when she was crowned Apple Queen. She wore a tiara and a long gown. The evening would commemorate the town's history. Old-timers like Nev remembered when growing apples had made everyone in Vanishing Falls wealthy. Each October, at the start of spring, a festival was held, with float parades and a lovely dance, to celebrate the blossoming apple trees. For a reason no one understood, the government paid everyone to pull the trees out, and the town turned poor.

"Will you be going on Saturday evening, my dear?"

Joelle frowned. "That's going to be a crowd. I don't like crowds. It gets noisy and I can't even think. It's like everyone's shouting inside my head or something. Are you going, Nev?"

"God, no. A man only goes to something like that if his wife makes him."

"You're lucky, then."

"What?"

"Lucky you don't have a wife."

His jolly laugh made his jowls shake. "You're a pearl."

"I've got to go. I'm working on the barbecue stall at the fair today."

"Good for you, my dear."

She told Nev how, when her daughter gave her the notice for the fair barbecue roster, she refused. The twins brought lots of letters home from school about how urgently volunteers were needed. Joelle read each one carefully before putting it in the paper box beside the fireplace. But it was too late—Emily had already written her name down. Emily had said, it is only for one hour, the other mums are nice, and it will be easy.

"The trouble is that Emily is wrong. There are no other mums working with me on the barbecue stall. I wish there was. I wish I was volunteering with someone like Celia Lily—she's so pretty and nice."

"So long as she's nice on the inside, that's what counts."

"She would be, Nev. But anyway, it's not her, it's just me and two of the dads. Jack and Cliff. I don't really know them, Nev."

He stopped smiling. "Does Brian know who you're volunteering with?"

"Maybe."

He winced like his stomach hurt. "I'll mention it to him. The pair of them are bad apples—rotten at the core."

"Huh?" She studied his face, trying to work out what he meant. "Are they apple farmers?"

"Don't worry about it."

"You can tell me. I'm not stupid."

"You're not stupid," Nev said vehemently. "Don't ever say that."

"Why do you look angry?" she asked. "What's wrong, Nev?"

"Nothing. Just, look after yourself."

She showed him the recipe she had cut from a magazine for him, which was for a low-fat zucchini soup. "If you like the look of this soup, I can make it for you," she promised.

"Maybe," he said. "I'm not really into vegetarian food."

"You should be," she told him, looking at his tummy.

Breakfast was Nev's favorite meal; he often ate it for lunch and dinner and Brian said that was why his tummy was as round as a full moon. Sometimes his sweater rode up and you saw his belly button. Nev told her that at night he sat beside his fire and his cat curled up on his stomach and slept. Joelle could imagine that. Cats liked to be warm and there would be a lot of warmth on that tummy. Joelle didn't say any of these things aloud. Brian sometimes teased her, saying that there was no reason to say every single thing that popped into your head.

Nev tugged his sweater down and agreed to try the soup, as long as she made it herself.

"Who else will make it? Brian?" She laughed loudly. "That's a good one, Nev!"

She walked home with Brian's newspaper tucked under her arm. Kookaburras sat on the wire fence, occasionally swooping down to pick a worm out of the wet field. She couldn't help but think about what Nev had said about the two men she would be working with on the barbecue stall. It was not like Nev to say something mean. It worried her, but by the time she reached the stile to the forest shortcut, she had forgotten about it. There were two rabbits nibbling the green tufts growing around a fence post. She tried to creep up and pat them, but they scampered away before she could get close.

* * *

Cliff Gatenby

Gatenby's Poultry Farm

Cliff watched the dawn creep up the valley. He had not been to bed and he was not tired. He tapped his fingers on the kitchen table as thick fog slid from the rain forest. A flock of green birds—broad-tailed rosellas—rose from the canopy. A thing like that could look heavenly or apocalyptic. He was not sure which it was.

Seven of the twelve chimneys of the Lilys' mansion began to appear through the shifting mist. Three of them sent smoke upward. With all that land, the Lilys did not have to worry about buying firewood. Cliff glanced at his potbellied stove. It had burned out in the night. It was bone cold but there was no point building the fire back up yet. He would let Kim do that once the boys were awake.

The church steeple was the next part of the town to become visible. There was a truth in that, he supposed, for the Calendar House and the church were the only buildings in town used for the purposes they were originally intended. Grand buildings, both of them, built with free convict labor and inherited money. A calendar house was a showy thing, with the number of major features totaling either four for the seasons, seven for the days in the week, fifty-two for the weeks in the year, twelve for the months in the year. The ultimate vanity of the Lilys' Calendar House, in Cliff's opinion, were the 365 windows—especially considering the cost of glass when the house was built.

Decent men did not covet another man's good fortune. Cliff was a decent man. He worked twelve or more hours a day in the sheds to provide for his family. Newly hatched chicks were delivered four or five times a year, up to twenty thousand day-old chicks in each batch. It was hard, honest work.

Lately he found himself thinking back to the school holidays when he worked for his Nan and Pop. They had a contract for Ingham's to catch live chickens. They would drive in the pickup truck to farms across the state where chickens lived in massive sheds. There was a catching technique. You had to crouch down and keep your back straight. You would catch the bird by one leg and get four in each hand. The chickens were put in big cages and loaded onto a trailer and taken to Ingham's to be processed. The birds shat, scratched, pecked, and pissed all over you and the smell lingered on your skin even after you had showered. It was a horrible job compared to what he did now. But when the day ended you were done and you didn't have to keep thinking about it, jotting down ideas all night long for growing the business, worrying about how creditors were going to get paid.

Someone moved through the house. A door closed. The toilet flushed.

Cliff drank another glass of water. From the farmhouse window he looked to the west of the sheds where the fog was clearing over the pastures, revealing several gum trees and the few cows who kept the grass down. There was no time to waste. He needed to check the feeders and clean out the water lines in one of the sheds.

He pulled on a woolen sweater and then his jacket. The jacket was one Celia had bought for Jack that was too small for him. It was not what Cliff would have chosen, but it was warm. He yelled, "I'm going to work."

No one answered. They all would have heard him though.

He walked down the track between the silos, his hands shoved in his pockets and his head hunched against the freezing August morning.

* * *

Jack

Calendar House

Jack considered blindfolding Celia with one of her silk night slips that were drying on a rack in the kitchen, but the girls were eating breakfast at the table and he thought that doing so might stir their curiosity. Instead he placed his hands over his wife's eyes. She laughed and leaned back against him as he guided her into his study. It was an elegant room with tall bookshelves and six of his favorite oil-on-canvas paintings displayed on the walls. On an easel was his latest acquisition. He had positioned it by the French doors so the morning light would cut through some of the dirt on its surface.

He removed his hands and she gasped. The pleasure on her face warmed him. Celia appreciated art. It was a passion they shared.

"It's Vanishing Falls. I've never seen a landscape of the falls. How magnificent. Are you certain of the artist?" she said.

"I'll get it cleaned and appraised but I'm confident."

His collection was mostly composed of works by early Van Diemen's Land artists depicting life in the colony. He owned sixty-two canvases, as well as a collection of antique furniture and ornaments, which made him one of the most important collectors in Tasmania's art and antiquities collegiate. His hunch was that this newest acquisition was not the work of an amateur, as the signature belied, but the early work of a colonial master.

"You bought it from a deceased estate?" she said. "What did you pay?"

"A pittance."

"You've done well."

The longer he stared at it the more he could appreciate what lay beneath the grime on the surface. Inky swirls captured the deep blue of the falls, and delicate strokes depicted Pallittorre people feasting beside the water hole. Women wore possum-fur capes, the children had pouch necklaces, and the warrior men were muscular beneath their ceremonial cuts. The beauty of the work was so intense that he barely noticed the dirt. He had gently wiped away the spiderwebs. He was reluctant to clean it properly in case he ruined the canvas.

"Utterly magnificent," she repeated, and kissed him on the mouth. "You're going to be famous—an internationally recognized art collector."

He could barely breathe it was so exciting. He kissed her back and closed his eyes as her hands stroked his neck. He had never loved her more.

* * *

Occasionally, people asked Jack if he was ever inclined to sell Calendar House and his farm. He supposed they imagined that with all his wealth he could retire to a sunny seaside village.

The answer was an irrefutable no. This land was his life, his heart.

In 1828, not long after the Mersey River in northern Tasmania was mapped by the new administration, land grants were awarded to deserving men. Jack Lily's great-great-great-grandfather, Scotsman Henry Lily, received two thousand acres of wide meadows and floodplains at the far end of the valley. He named the farm village Vanishing Falls after the spectacular waterfalls nearby, and he enlisted a team of convicts to build the grand Georgian Calendar House. He planted cherries, gooseberries, apples, plums, chestnuts, English grass, and six miles of hawthorn hedges around his paddocks. The alluvial soil and favorable easterly aspect, and its location near the new road linking the garrison towns between Launceston and the prosperous northwestern coastal farms, ensured his estate flourished. He increased his fortune burning lime from a nearby limestone karst to send to Launceston for building work.

By the 1850s Vanishing Falls village was a thriving hub near a major stagecoach road. It had a chapel, a schoolhouse, an inn and two taprooms, a blacksmith shop, an apothecary, a town hall, and more. In the early 1900s the orchardists moved in and Tasmania became known as the Apple Isle. Orchards swathed the hills as far as the eye could see and a festival was held each October to give thanks for the apple blossoms.

It would not last. In the 1960s, the state exported more than six million boxes of apples a year to Britain and Europe. In the 1970s, the Europeans turned to Argentina and Canada for apples. Growers' financial difficulties forced the government to sponsor a tree-pull scheme. Almost all orchard owners took advantage. The government was quick to reinvest in building a meatworks and extending the mill. Sadly, these could not sustain themselves without government subsidies. Three years ago the mill closed; eighteen months later, the abattoir. In a district with a population of 2,000, 150 breadwinners losing their jobs was a tragedy. Some people left, most had nowhere else to go.

From any window, Jack Lily looked across a bucolic landscape. His father had not pulled out their apple trees. The fruit orchards rose and fell over the hillsides like a dappled, emerald ocean. Sheep and dairy cows grazed on lush green pastures. Rising above the valley were the Great Western Tiers, a series of rocky benches covered in smoky-indigo-colored eucalypt, beech, celery-topped pine, blackwood, and stringybark forest. Across the river, Jack could see some of the village—a church steeple and the old jailhouse.

On Jack's farm, time stood still.

* * *

Joelle

Vanishing Falls village

Overnight, the paddock beside the school had been transformed into a wonderland. The black-and-white cows had been moved to make way for the fair tents: food, secondhand goods, crafts, a carousel, a jumping castle, and a stage where the school choir was singing.

Back the other way, she could see her house, the last in a row of weatherboard cottages backing onto the creek. The houses huddled beneath the leatherwood and gum trees, as though their peeling facades left them unprotected from the cold. She could see her washing line and the old outhouse where Brian kept the lawn mower and garden tools.

If she hurried home now, she would be safely inside in five minutes. She could make a marble cake or work on her recipe scrapbook or the appliqué rainbows she was sewing onto her new sweater. These were things she liked to do.

The heels of her gum boots sank into the sodden ground as she walked toward the barbecue stall. A well-dressed man gave her the money tin and said, "I'm Jack. And this is Cliff."

"I recognize you." She beamed. "You're the PTA president and you drive a green sports car with your name on the number plate—JACK759. The number is the hectares of your farm. Everyone knows you. We met in the supermarket car park. You helped me move a shopping cart that someone left near my car."

"Did I?" He looked uncertain.

The other man, Cliff, made a funny sound as he checked the weight of the gas bottle.

"It was a few years back," she clarified.

Jack's smile was wonderful. Now, just like in the car park that day, his smile made her cheeks heat up.

"I've been to your house too," she added. "I go on the tour every year."

She listed all the things she liked about the Calendar House— the old furniture, the windows that looked out on the river and gardens, the musty smell of the wallpaper, and the fresh flowers in every room. She was about to ask him who played the grand piano when a customer interrupted, asking for a sausage.

A long queue had formed. It took her only a minute to realize it was awful working on the barbecue stall. She wished
Emily had not volunteered her. It was tricky handling the
money. At the butchery where Joelle worked, the cash register
told her how much change to give. Here, there was nothing
but the cash tin with all the money muddled in together.

She recognized the sly grin and hooded glinting eye of
someone who had been given too much change. A thin man
wearing a yellow-and-brown-striped football club beanie tried
to give her some money back. His wife, who towered over him
and wore her hair pulled tightly into a tiny bun on top of her
huge head, yanked on his arm. He followed her reluctantly,
like a big sulky child.

A boy about her twins' age said loudly, "You ripped me off
two bucks fifty."

"Sorry."

Joelle fumbled in the cash tin to find the correct money. As
the boy walked away she looked at his neatly plaited red rat's
tail. It reached halfway down his back. She felt Jack standing
beside her.

"Is everything okay?" he asked.

She nodded.

"Did you see that kid's hair? If I saw that on my land, I'd
take it for vermin and shoot it."

Joelle giggled. He laughed. It was a funny image and she
laughed louder. They were getting along so well.

At half ten Miss Gwen stopped by. She didn't want a sausage. She put her walking stick under her arm and opened her

dilly bag to show Joelle the seedlings she had bought from the plant stall.

After she left, Jack said, "She looks like a good friend of yours."

"We're best friends," she said, watching him toss onion rings onto the barbecue hot plate. "I am always so happy to see her. We see each other almost every day. Sometimes when I get upset, it's because everyone, all my friends, are always getting worried about me all the time. She doesn't ever worry about me. Not like lots of people."

"Have you got lots of friends?" Cliff asked.

"Yeah. Nev is my second-best friend, after Miss Gwen." Joelle re-tied her apron as she considered the question. "If I had to say who my third-best friend is, I would probably say Alfred Cheng from the green grocer's, because he is so kind. He looks after his dad. That's what people should do . . . they should do nice things for their families. That is the point."

"I thought the old man was dead," Cliff said. "I never see him."

"Well, Alfred Senior has a weak heart so now he only ever comes downstairs for funerals. It was love that nearly killed him," Joelle remembered. "His wife ran off with a lantern lighter from the circus."

"The circus?" Cliff said doubtfully.

"Mate, it might be true," Jack said. "Several circuses came through town in the 1930s and '40s."

Joelle continued. "Alfred's dad is so mean and that's why Miss Gwendolyn twice refused to marry Alfred." She stopped herself. "Miss Gwen says that is confidential. It's not my business to talk about it. Brian thinks it's good to save some topics for the next conversation."

"Who's Brian?" Cliff asked. "Is he your fourth-best friend?"

"No, silly. Brian is my husband. Brian Smithton. He's very tall with black hair and his hands are bigger than any T-bone steaks we sell, and we get the big ones from Cape Grim."

"You're married to the butcher, are you?"

"Twelve happy years, the best years of my life."

"That's lovely," Jack said.

Joelle grinned. She recalled something else to tell him.

"You know your mum came into the butchery one time last summer. She was with another old lady. They couldn't agree on what to buy," she said. "Your mum wanted quail and the other lady said, 'Don't be silly, the little girls prefer chicken.'"

"I remember," Jack said. "It was my birthday. That was Celia's mother, Martha. She's the only person brave enough to take on my mother. We had quail."

"They both wanted to pay but Mrs. Lily insisted. Martha wanted to know about the best cuts of meat to freeze. She wanted to take some home because you can't get meat like ours in Launceston. And Mrs. Lily said, 'Make your mind up, Martha.'" Joelle remembered Mrs. Lily rapping her hand on the glass counter. "And Martha said, 'Don't rush me, Victoria.'"

Jack stared at her. "That sounds like them."

The air smelled delicious with barbecuing sausages and onions, cotton candy, and waffles. Her bones felt rigid with cold, but the sun was starting to warm things up. She sipped Sprite through a straw and tidied up the stall table. She was actually having fun, she realized; it wasn't so bad after all.

She served some children, who took a long time to decide what they wanted. By the time she had finished with them, a crowd of people were clustered around the serving table, shoving one another, trying to be the person at the front. One lady even used her handbag to block the woman next to her. That woman, in turn, used her elbow to knock the bag away.

"Calm the farm," Joelle announced cheerfully. She pointed at an elderly man. "Everyone line up behind him. Don't worry; we are not about to run out of sausages."

Later, when the queue had reduced, Jack said, "Good work. I was worried we would have to call security."

"I'm happy with how this is going," she said. "It's a good fair. Even though it's probably going to rain later. But I love the rain. I could watch it for hours, running down my windows, making the fields all wet and mushy."

She had said too much then. She could tell by the way the two men looked at each other, then back at her. Neither knew what to say in reply. That was the trouble. People wanted to hear something they were expecting. It wasn't easy trying to remember what those things were.

"Sausages are burning," she said, sniffing the air, and they turned back to the grill.

The mist had almost lifted when Celia Lily arrived. She held the leash of a giant black dog. Behind her came her friend and lots of children holding balloons, cotton candy, and buckets of popcorn. Joelle stopped cutting tomatoes so she could stare.

Celia Lily didn't look like the other townsfolk. She was like a Hollywood movie star. Her hair was golden and tumbling over her pink fluffy sweater. She wore brown leather knee-high boots and she was tall and thin, not skinny like the scabby-faced people always smoking in the park rotunda, but nicely thin. *Athletic* was the word—Joelle often saw her jogging along the trail on the forest side of the creek.

"Cliff and Joelle, it looks like our relief has arrived." Jack pretended to take off his apron.

"No chance." Celia laughed.

Joelle chuckled too, pleased to be included in the joke. There were customers waiting to be served but Jack and Cliff ignored them as they greeted Celia and her friend and talked to the children. Jack kissed Celia's friend on the cheek. She ducked her head shyly.

"Not in front of my face, mate. Kim is my wife," Cliff's voice cut through.

There was a hardness to his tone. Kim hung back, tugging her tracksuit jacket down over her bottom. Joelle felt sad for her.

Joelle was extra careful as she squeezed the ketchup onto the sausages Celia bought for the children. Celia paid with a fifty-dollar note, shaking her head at Kim, who was counting silver coins out of a battered red purse. Joelle double-checked the change before she handed it to Celia.

"Thank you, Joelle," Celia said.

Buoyed that Celia knew her name, Joelle leaned across and pointed at Celia's French polished nails. "I had it like that for my wedding. So nice."

"Thank you." Celia looked Joelle over. "I like your sweater. Kim, have you seen how cute this is?"

"I made it. It's just appliqué. So easy."

Joelle explained the process of appliqué—how she cut out

the butterfly and flowers from different pieces of floral fabric and sewed them onto her sweater with the sewing machine using a zigzag stich. Celia was very interested. Kim stood quietly by, watching and listening but not saying anything. As they wandered away, their arms linked, Joelle wondered if Kim felt lucky to be friends with Celia. People talked about Celia a lot—the mums in the canteen, customers queuing in the butchery. They talked about the parties Celia held in her beautiful Calendar House and how they often saw her children cantering their horses along the river path. Joelle had heard that Celia shopped for her clothes in Melbourne twice a year. She wasn't sure if that was true. Once, Joelle had overheard someone saying that Celia didn't mix well with ordinary people. That definitely wasn't true—she was on Miss Gwen's Apple Queen Tribute committee. If an Apple Queen got to be crowned today, it would be Celia for sure.

"You didn't grow up here," Cliff said. "Where were you before?"

Joelle froze as she tried to think of how to fill the awful silence.

"I lived with my flatmate. It was a group home and I answered an advertisement." She could probably remember the ad word for word. "They wanted someone who was neat and tidy, who put their things away when they're not being used, who turned the lights off when they went to bed. It described me perfectly. What else? I'll try to remember. It was more than twelve years ago but I've got a good memory. You had to like cats, be friendly, wash your own dishes . . . Let me see . . ." She wasn't sure if he was smiling or smirking.

"Put the rubbish bin out when it was full."

"Yes, but that wasn't on the ad."

"Put some more burgers on, Cliff," Jack said.

Thankfully, that ended the conversation. Joelle studied the rise of the forest on the ridge. These were people who spoke a language she had never learned: a language of gestures, innuendo, and hidden meanings. No matter how hard she tried to talk like they did, people didn't understand her.

That was what made Brian different. When they first met, in the salon, he had asked her so many questions about herself that finally she had to tell him to pipe down or she wouldn't be able to finish washing his hair. He was one of a handful of clients who had let the salon owner know that they were happy for Joelle to trim their hair, even though she wasn't qualified because she could not pass the TAFE written exam. Officially, she was still a third-year apprentice, even though she could cut hair as well as anyone else.

Brian had organized help for her to get her driver's license. He said there was no reason why she couldn't have the same kind of help to sit the TAFE exam again. Joelle was not worried about it. No one at the Vanishing Falls nursing home, where she did most of her haircuts, had ever asked to see credentials. They could see she did great work.

When the hour ended, and the next group of volunteers arrived, Joelle was tired. She took off her apron and picked up her bag from where she had hidden it under the table. Taking a deep breath, she turned to say goodbye. She always tried to be polite, even when she suspected people were making fun of her.

There was no one left to say goodbye to. The men had gone.

Across the fairground, near the jumping castle, she could see Brian holding Emily's and Baxter's sneakers. She turned in the other direction, walking past the rides and the clowns. She needed a moment to try not to feel upset before they saw her. It felt like a puppeteer had tied strings to all parts of her—her cheeks, her shoulders, her heart—and instead of tugging the strings upward he was pulling them down.

There was a toilet block near the kindergarten classrooms, and she headed toward it. Away from the fair, the music of the merry-go-round sounded creepy, like the sound of a broken musical jewelry box. The empty classrooms with their dark windows unsettled her. Her footsteps sounded hollow on the shadowed concrete. She didn't like being alone in the schoolyard. It didn't feel right.

The girls' toilet gate was padlocked. She tried a door marked Staff Toilet. It too was locked. At the other end was the disabled toilet. Able-bodied people were not supposed to use it. There were no other toilets nearby. She needed to go, badly.

Perhaps, just this once, and she would be quick.

She opened the door. The room was not vacant. She gasped, embarrassed and surprised. Her eyes adjusted to the dim light and she saw Jack and Cliff. Jack held a glass pipe to his lips. From the delicate bulb came a milky white smoke, like that which would come out of a genie's lamp. Cliff snatched up a clear plastic bag that had been placed on the toilet lid and shoved it into his pocket.

"Fuck off," Cliff said.

He said it again, louder.

The rough concrete wall grazed her hand as she spun around to leave. She clutched her bag to her chest and hurried across the oval. A line of port-a-loos was set up near where the rain forest walk began. She had not noticed them earlier. She thumped up the steps of the closest one and slammed the door. Her shaking fingers fumbled with the lock. It was a relief to be alone.

CHAPTER 2

Saturday afternoon, August 19

Jack

Calendar House

Celia invited a group of friends over for drinks following the fair. It was the usual crew—Margo Wheeler, Annabel and Roger Fotheringham, Nick Gunn. It was a boisterous and fun afternoon, but Cliff and Kim began to relax only after everyone else had gone. Their old friends were warm toward the Gatenbys, but Jack could tell that Cliff and Kim were not comfortable. They were quick to smile and slow to laugh, listening carefully rather than talking freely.

Once the others left, Jack turned up the music and opened another bottle of champagne. If he was honest, he also felt better once his old friends had gone. Roger and Nick were like family but lately he had more absorbing conversations with Cliff, who had a broader view of things.

"Celia says you've got a new painting," Kim said. "When are you going to show us?"

"There's no point until it's been cleaned," Jack said.

"I wouldn't mind seeing the painting," Cliff said.

"Not today," Jack said firmly.

"You're like a little boy with a secret, Jack," Kim teased him. "It's sweet."

Kim took another serving of Celia's Peking duck pancakes. She had eaten most of them. Jack watched her with interest. After a few glasses of champagne you could see what she had been like when she was younger, or the lighthearted woman she might have been if she had married someone else.

"You know these two got themselves into trouble today," Kim told Celia. "I saw them leaving the fair, and Jack, in particular, looked as scared as a naughty kid who is about to be sent to the headmaster's office."

"Don't go there, Kim," Cliff said.

"What happened?" Celia asked.

Jack said quickly, "Kim, we don't need to talk about this."

He would tell Celia himself, later, and put the incident into context.

"Kim," Celia demanded. "Tell me."

Kim would never refuse Celia. "They were 'partaking' in the disabled toilets and another parent walked in."

"You've got to be kidding."

"She didn't see anything," Jack lied.

He thought of the pretty young woman's surprise when she saw them. With her dimpled cheeks and easy laugh, she had a childlike innocence. But she had seen what they were doing, and she knew what she saw. His years as a lawyer discussing options with his clients' wives and mothers had taught him to never underestimate their understanding of any given incident.

"I think she got dropped on her head as a baby or something," Cliff said.

"Was it Joelle?" Celia surmised. "She's married to Brian Smithton, the butcher. The one who caused the problems with the signage."

"He's the one you had the skirmish with?" Cliff said.

Jack shook his head. "Hardly a skirmish." It was a small disagreement over Jack's decision to rename a creek on his property.

"I remember it differently." Cliff grinned. "You had to send your missus in to sort it out for you. She had to go and give Brian Smithton a hug."

"I didn't give him a hug," Celia said, softening. "I simply spoke to him. I apologized for how everything had happened. He's reasonable. He didn't want to break the law. He understands the sign is on our land. He needed to feel that he was being listened to."

"Lucky Jack's got you to calm down his enemies," Cliff said. "You're the gun."

"It sounds like he's going to need me again." Celia's expression remained neutral. "I don't understand what happened at the fair."

Jack sighed. "Joelle walked in, Cliff told her to leave, and she did. That's it."

"I keep thinking, what kind of man marries a girl like that?" Cliff said. "She's a stubby short of a six-pack. Two stubbies short."

"I don't know," Jack said, watching his wife.

"You do know." Cliff pointed his beer at him and laughed.

Celia said nothing more. She reached up and twirled her hair into a messy bun. Her smile was icy. She had decided not to make a scene, and Kim and Cliff would not realize how furious she was. They would have another glass of champagne, turn up the music, and enjoy the afternoon. Later, she would let him have it.

"I'll talk to Joelle," Jack suggested. "I got along well with her. I'm sure I can calm any concerns she might have."

"You'll stuff it up more," Cliff said.

"He's right, you will make it worse," Celia said. "You've done the wrong thing. You don't need to drag her into it any more than she has been."

"Maybe she didn't even know what she was looking at."

Celia stared at the ceiling. No one spoke. She cleared her throat, and when she started talking her voice was smooth and cool, the voice she used when she was trying to contain her emotions.

"That sweet woman has seen more of the harsh realities of life than all four of us put together. Do you remember the Pieman's Junction Murder?"

Jack did, for the crime had saturated the news at the time. He could not recall the exact details, except that a young woman had been murdered in an abandoned hut in the western mining country. Judging from the sorrowful expression on Celia's face, Joelle must have been related to the woman somehow.

Cliff was confused. "Huh?"

"Joelle was there," Celia said.

"A witness?" Cliff asked.

"It was terrible. Look, I don't want to talk about it. It's

none of our business. But I do think you both should leave her alone."

Cliff started to speak but she cut him off with a charming smile.

"It's not something she would want people to know," Celia said gently. "That's why I've never mentioned it before."

"It amazes me that someone can change their life so dramatically," Kim said. "It's magical, in a way."

She sounded loopy, like she had drunk too much champagne. Jack filled glasses with sparkling mineral water for everyone.

For the rest of the afternoon, Celia was particularly attentive to Cliff—refreshing his drink, playing his favorite songs. As night fell, Celia and Cliff shared a cigarette on the veranda. There was nothing odd about it—it was something they usually did after a few drinks—but Kim sighed and began to gather her things. Jack helped her find the boys' jackets and shoes. In the space between songs they heard Celia and Cliff laughing loudly. As Jack and Kim watched through the kitchen window, Celia dusted her fingers down Cliff's back.

Jack looked around the room, at the dirty glasses and empty bottles, plates of half-eaten food everywhere. Celia's new pink silk scarf had fallen to the ground and he placed his foot on it, grinding it into the floor. It was childish, but his wife frustrated him.

"One day," Kim said tightly, "they'll wake up to themselves."

"No, they won't."

"We should behave like that for a change."

He laughed.

"I wasn't suggesting that," Kim snapped, and began stacking the dishwasher. "I just don't know what to do."

He didn't know if she meant Cliff's drug problem or that Jack had encouraged it today by having some with him or that Celia was being flirtatious. Ordinarily he was good at reading people, but he could not tell if she was angry or sad. He tried to recall if he had ever seen Kim cross. In social situations, she was wary. She smiled and drank the wine, told a few stories, laughed at the jokes—she behaved exactly as the other women did—but always with a quiet watchfulness.

"Do you ever wish you had a life other than your own?" she said. "I guess you probably wouldn't."

He didn't blame her for feeling like that sometimes.

"I'm sorry." He hoped that covered everything.

He helped her pack the leftovers into a container. No one ever commented on Kim's habit of taking home food from the Lilys' house. He couldn't imagine Celia packing a lunch box of uneaten chicken wings from the Gatenbys' table. Helping Kim was the right thing to do. Some people needed more help than others—that was one thing he and Celia always agreed on.

* * *

Cliff

Calendar House

Cliff tapped his jeans pocket, reassured to feel the thin outline of the pipe and, to the side, the small bulge of the little ziplock bag. His last hit was a quick one in the bathroom. Jack had asked him to be discreet and he had. Cliff might not know which of Jack's couches had once belonged to Tasmania's first premier, or whether it was the carpet or the wall light that was made in France, but he possessed a high level of social intelligence. He was well tuned to smaller details, such as Jack's reluctance to show off his new painting.

Jack knew how Cliff felt about art. Despite this, Jack often liked to brag about the latest addition to his collection of dull depictions of gum trees and bush huts, bushrangers on horseback, and naked Aboriginal people hunting possums. It was odd he was being precious about this painting. Cliff was not interested in seeing it. The interesting part of the story was how Jack came to have it.

He watched Jack help Kim put her jacket on. Everyone thought Jack was the perfect gentleman—but he wasn't. Gambling was not one of Cliff's shortcomings—he didn't see the point of it—but he would happily have put money on it that Celia did not know how Jack acquired that painting.

* * *

Joelle

The Smithtons' house

In winter, Joelle was the only person along the creek who used her outdoor clothesline. She liked smoothing the sheets so they hung broad and white. Later, she would drape each one over a door inside the house so it would dry properly. Here in the high country, washing never dried completely on the line. You had to *look on the bright side*—the washing stayed clean at least.

Her birth mother's house was near the Pieman's Junction quarry and the washing got covered in grit. Those flannel sheets of her mum's were so old and faded, Joelle couldn't remember what color they had been in the first place.

No grit blowing in from moonscape hills here. In this garden the air was sweet and clean, like the cool water running in the creek. Beyond the garden was the rain forest, a damp cathedral of fragrant myrtle and sassafras, sprawling mosses, and ancient lichen. The forest rose up and up around Vanishing Falls valley like the walls of a giant fortress. The first time she came to Vanishing she didn't think she would like it so much. There was only one road in, a narrow set of hairpin turns cut into the mountain above a churning river. Looking down at that water unsettled her and she wanted to leave. But past the Cutting, the road meandered through hilly green pastures where black-and-white cows grazed, past pretty weatherboard farmhouses with splendid man ferns out front, hedges, and rose gardens.

Looking on the bright side was something her foster mother, Darla, had encouraged her to become good at. Darla also liked to say, *You've coped with worse and you will cope with this.* She said it when Joelle found a kitten but couldn't keep it because Darla's husband was allergic to cats. If Joelle told her what the man in the bathroom at the fair had said to her, she would say either of those pieces of advice. Joelle could just hear her.

The year Joelle turned fifteen, when she moved to Darla's sunny house in Launceston, she had finally learned to read. For hours and hours, she had sat beside Darla on her pretty yellow bedspread reading aloud from the illustrated readers. Joelle's husband, Brian, had learned to read before he even started grade one. He was a businessman. He belonged to the Chamber of Commerce and Rotary. He knew the geography and history of the area, even things that no one else knew, like why the pretty estuary at the edge of the Lilys' farm was really called Murdering Creek, not Hollybank Creek like the new sign said, and why everyone in the car had to be silent each time they drove past it.

Brian had a hopeless brother who lived way up north in Cairns. On the illustrated map in the twins' bedroom, Cairns was a small speck at the top of the Australian mainland. It was decorated with a picture of a palm tree and a rainbow-colored fish. Beside the town the ocean was dotted with tropical islands. That was the end of the line, Brian often said, as far as you could get from Tasmania without needing a passport. His brother had a drug conviction. Brian hated drugs so much he had not been able to invite his brother to their wedding. Luckily his sister, Nicky, hated drugs too, so she was allowed to be a bridesmaid, and because she had never worn a dress in her life, she wore a nice three-piece suit. If Brian had seen what Joelle saw at the fair today he would report it to the police. Questions would be asked. Brian would be distressed if he knew the answers to some of those questions.

She stopped pegging the sheets, frightened at the thought. Darla had lots of wise words. Joelle repeated some of them:

Some things are meant to be kept private. Especially from an intelligent, respectable man like Brian. *You mind your own business and people will leave you alone,* her foster mother had said.

It was true.

Brian was an educated man; even so, Joelle knew more about some things than he did. She knew it would not be smart to tell him about men doing illegal activities on school grounds. You had to look after yourself first. That was common sense—life experience—that counted more than any high school test.

He was standing on the back doorstep, looking down at her with a soft smile.

"Something smells delicious in the kitchen," he said.

"Curry. And it tastes even better than it smells."

"I bet it does. I'm about to have a beer. Can I make you a drink?" he asked.

"Sure."

"And then I want to tell you a funny story."

"I love funny stories."

"Come on, then," he said, opening his arms to her.

He cupped her face and kissed her softly. She hugged up against him and they stood there, looking up at the vaulted branches of giant blackwood and sassafras trees in the rain forest. The rain had stopped hours ago but the sound of running water was everywhere as tiny waterfalls sprang out of the forest and bubbled into the creek.

CHAPTER 3

Sunday, August 20

Cliff

Vanishing Falls forest

At dawn, on the way up to the Vanishing Falls car park, he hit something. A potoroo, most likely, the possum-like wallabies who were small enough to cope with the freezing highland winters. He wasn't stopping to find out.

In winter, this was one of his favorite places to get high. No one came up here when the mist clothed the forest thickly; only the most dedicated jogger. When he was done, he double-checked that the leather bag with the pipe and such was well hidden under the seat. When this gear was gone, that was it. He would be more like Jack, who only dabbled with the drug socially.

Over the past year he had watched one of his dealers decline and it was ugly. This kid was nineteen and he looked a decade older. He could not hold his cigarette steady. There were small fleshy craters in his face where he had picked the skin away. His teeth looked like they had melted into black stumps and his breath was foul.

Cliff was considering going home, so he would be there when they all woke up and wouldn't have to answer questions, when a flutter of pink appeared. He thought it was a rare bird. It disappeared between the trees and he wondered if he had imagined it. Sometimes he saw things that weren't there.

A moment later Celia Lily emerged from the forest. She was wearing her pink tracksuit. She jogged with a long stride, her chest thrust upward. This was not the first time he had watched her run through the forest up here. Up close, you could see the pinkness of exertion coloring her face and the perspiration beading. Even from this far away you could tell she was a spectacular-looking woman.

Yesterday, when Jack was fawning over Kim, packing up a doggie bag for her like she was a child, Celia had caught his eye and raised an eyebrow. It was a brazen look, and he was smart enough not to react. Earlier, as they swapped a cigarette back and forth, on his turn he found that it was wet from her lips. Smiling, watching him, she had given that husky laugh and said, "Anyone watching would think we're having an affair."

He mulled this over as he watched Celia jog down the horse trail that led to the river and the apple orchards surrounding the Calendar House.

* * *

Joelle

The Smithtons' house

Everyone had piled into Brian's butchery pickup truck and gone to church. The house was wonderfully quiet. She hung out a load of washing, peeled the vegetables for dinner, and sang as she made cupcake batter.

Her foster mother, Darla, had taught her to cook. In Darla's kitchen there was always something simmering on the stove or cooling on a rack, ready for all those kids. Some kids were there for only a few nights or weeks. Others, like Joelle, were lucky to stay for years and call Darla's house their home.

She could hear Darla's voice as she made marble cupcake batter. *Divide the mixture into three bowls and color each: vanilla, chocolate, and strawberry. Swirl them gently together into each cup.* Joelle tidied as she worked, putting each ingredient back in the fridge or on the shelf before taking down the next item the recipe required.

While the cupcakes baked she took the scrap bucket out to the rabbit hutch. Brian was building a new one, as the rabbit had been pregnant when they brought her home. There were six black-and-white fur bundles hopping around in the old cage. They needed more space.

The washing had blown off the line. A pair of her underpants was draped over the garden gnome. That made her laugh.

Her bra hung from the birdbath. Down near the creek her sunflower sweater was tangled in a muddy heap in the bulb garden. She collected everything and paused at the rabbit hutch.

She gave the silky mother rabbit a long cuddle. "You have to be grateful it's just my stuff and not Brian's work whites," she told the rabbit. "I'd never get his clothes washed and dried by tomorrow."

Behind the rabbit hutch, in the dirt beneath a row of bony lavender plants, lay her undershirt. She picked it up, particularly annoyed that it was the shirt that had one of her favorite appliqué designs—a four-leaf clover. To her surprise, she noticed a huge footprint in the wet earth. It was truly enormous.

She put her foot on it. It dwarfed her shoe. The imprint was far bigger than any of Brian's boots. For a horrible moment, she looked around, wondering if the owner of the big shoe was still in her yard. But that was silly. Brian would say, Don't get carried away.

"Don't worry," she told the rabbits, "it was probably someone who wanted to see how cute you are."

* * *

By the time Brian brought the twins home from church the cupcakes were ready. She had decorated them with candy. There were pink spiders and a sticky spiderweb, a prince, a princess, yellow ducks, and green frogs.

She was playing with the cat in the bedroom when she heard her children laughing. Baxter could barely speak he was laughing so hard.

"The wonky princess looks like she swallowed a firecracker," he said.

"This lumpy green one shot out of a crocodile's bum," Emily added.

The cruel words repeated in her mind and she clenched her hands, pressing her fists into the bed. She was fed up and exhausted and so sick of everyone. She ran into the kitchen.

"Why are you being so nasty?" she shouted at her children. "It's not nice."

Brian hurried in from the lounge room. He took her flapping hands and held them tightly.

"Deep breath."

"The green one is a frog. They know that. Anyone can see that. People always tell me how colorful they are. It makes me feel really sad and angry when Emily and Baxter say those things."

She could barely speak she was crying so hard. Brian hugged her and wouldn't let go.

"You don't need to get so upset. We've talked about this. They were teasing."

"It took me two hours to decorate those cupcakes. The entire time you were at church I was working on them."

"I know."

"I get sick of it."

He stroked her hair. "You haven't got worked up like this for a long time. I'm going to make us a cup of tea. When you've calmed down, the kids will come and say sorry. You need to tell them that you accept their apology, okay?"

Later, when the twins apologized, she could see their sorrow in Emily's downcast eyes and Baxter's flushed cheeks. That made her feel sadder and she wished for their sake that they had a normal mum, not one who couldn't count money properly and made wonky cupcakes.

* * *

Jack

Calendar House

C elia ignored him all morning. He found her in the stables, brushing her horse down with long, regular strokes. He asked her if anything was bothering her.

"Bothering me? You bet. You aren't two schoolboys caught smoking a cigarette behind the bike shed. You could go to jail. I'm horrified by what other parents would think. They wouldn't let their children come here for a playdate; I can tell you that right now."

Celia knew how to build him up; she also knew how to tear him down.

"Don't overreact," he said.

"You are an idiot."

"Don't shout at me."

"I'm barely raising my voice."

"It will all blow over," he said hopefully.

"She's probably already told the school principal. I would. And if the school knows something illegal happened on their campus, they have an obligation to report it to the police."

"Do you think she has?"

"How would I know?" Her angry flush made her even more beautiful.

"I'm really sorry, Celia. We made a mistake, a bad choice,

and it's not going to happen again." He stepped closer, reaching out for her hand.

She moved her hand away from his and gave him a withering look. "You're as thick as mud if you think there won't be a consequence for what you and Cliff did."

She handed him the brush. He watched her walk her horse out of the stables and across to the paddock. The mare tried to toss her head and sidestep at the gate. Celia led her with a firm grip.

* * *

She uttered only necessities to him for the rest of the day. He retreated to the hothouse, where tending to his orchids assuaged him somewhat. A new blue orchid's tessellated petals reminded him of pieces of sky growing on a mossy trunk in alpine treetops; a brown orchid had an exotic chocolate-and-vanilla scent. Alone with the fragrant, delicate flowers, there was no world outside the hothouse door.

At dinner Celia spoke to the girls only, skillfully excluding him from the conversation in such a subtle way he almost thought he was imagining it. When the meal ended, he told her he needed to visit a client urgently.

"On a Sunday evening?"

"It's hard for some of my clients to see me during the week, dear."

He turned on the car radio and drove away from town, past the padlocked gate of the timber mill and the abattoir. Jack felt like he was the only one unsurprised when the government reneged on their promise to subsidize these facilities. He wished he'd been wrong—the closure of the abattoir and the mill had made Vanishing Falls a ripe market for drug dealers. A secret study of sewage, via water samples in wastewater treatment plants, showed the rain forest region was one of the areas with the highest drug use in Tasmania. It wasn't just methamphetamine. OxyContin, or hillbilly heroin, also presented at high levels. Cliff had mentioned that people from every walk of life were getting hooked, many of them decent, hardworking, good folk. Jack was grateful his daughters were still too young.

It was raining heavily, and he was mindful of the deep ditches either side of the road. This was old farming land and the ditches had been dug when the road was cut for a horse and cart. They saved the crops from ruin when the river flooded, but it was not uncommon to see a vehicle upended in one. If that happened to him, it would be difficult to explain to his wife the reason for his being this far up the valley. No one who lived out here could afford his legal advice.

Twenty kilometers from the town was the Cutting, the one road that linked Vanishing Falls with the outside world. Just before the Cutting was a sign so faded the destination seemed like a whisper: Marsh End.

He turned onto a gravel road. There used to be two farmhouses along here but six months ago one had burned to the ground. There were rumors of an explosion, but the police had never been able to make an arrest. Everyone was glad the man and two children sleeping inside had managed to escape. The man refused the usual offers of help and went away without telling the school that the children had left town for good.

Jack was glad that he had not been visiting the second farm-house when the fire began.

A barbed-wire fence contained a vast paddock of twisted scrap metal. Vehicles were piled two or three high—old cars or those that had jackknifed on the black ice. Concealed by the junk was the farmhouse. As he drove up the lane toward it, he told himself that today was the last time.

* * *

Gatenby's Poultry Farm

On the way home from the junkyard Jack visited Cliff. He knew Cliff would be in the office, an old timber shed with a rusted red tin roof that once provided accommodations for apple pickers. It was out near the chicken sheds, but Jack stopped by at the back door of the main house to say hello to Kim.

She answered the door wearing two bulky pullovers. In the lounge room, Cliff's three gangly sons sat watching television, all wrapped in blankets. The fire was not lit.

"How is he?" Jack asked.

"You know."

She gave a tired smile. Her eyes darted to the outbuilding behind him.

In the house, the boys laughed. You didn't often hear them laugh like that. Celia had once remarked on how well behaved the Gatenby boys were compared to the Lilys' chattering, impulsive girls. Jack knew the boys' subdued behavior indicated something about Cliff's nature. He pushed the thought out of his head as he crossed the yard toward the office. It was not his business.

Cliff's office was as cold as his house. He closed his laptop as Jack entered. Cliff's desk held a pen, a calculator, an exercise book, the kind children used at school, and the laptop. Every five seconds a CCTV screen on top of a filing cabinet flicked to a new image: the tall metal doors of the chicken sheds, the silos stark against the night sky, an empty paddock, Jack's Jaguar on the driveway, a shot of the front door of the house, and one of the back. There was Kim, still standing in the back doorway, her hands bunched inside the arms of her woolen sleeves, lost in her thoughts.

Cliff took two beers from the bar fridge and handed Jack one. They clinked the beers.

"Celia's put the fear of God in me," Jack said. "She hasn't spoken to me all day."

Cliff made a sound that could pass for sympathy. "That woman, the butcher's wife . . . she's hiding something."

"I doubt it."

Cliff's pinprick eyes glistened. He lowered his voice. "We need to know who we're dealing with. I googled her. Joelle Smithton does not exist. There's no Facebook for her, no Instagram, no email address."

"Lots of people don't have social media."

"Yeah, sure. But she's not on the Smithton's Fine Meats web page. She volunteers at the nursing home and the Country Women's Association and she's not listed on either of their volunteer pages."

"How do you know she volunteers there?" Jack said.

"She told us yesterday. Weren't you listening to her rab-biting on?" Cliff flicked a pen off and on. He never sat still. It was exhausting to watch. "Smithton is her married name. What was Celia saying yesterday?"

"No idea," Jack said firmly.

Cliff eyed him keenly. "She said Joelle was involved in something. I can't remember what she said."

Jack thought of Kim, alone in her house with her sons, while her husband was over here in his office doing Google searches on a woman who had the misfortune to walk into the wrong bathroom at the wrong time. It was not hard to follow Cliff's train of thought, and sometimes it was sport to play along, but Cliff did not need to know about Pieman's Junction. God only knew what he would do with that kind of information.

"Do you think she's in witness protection?" Cliff asked. "Or maybe she's a police informant."

"If she's ratted on you, you'll be the first to see the police coming to arrest you." Jack nodded toward the CCTV.

"Not funny. The fact that she walked in on us is stressing me out. She saw me holding the bag of gear."

Jack tried to think of some advice to calm Cliff down. "Keep telling yourself you did nothing wrong. You did nothing illegal. You have to believe the lie."

It was the wrong thing to say.

"*We* did nothing illegal." Cliff stood up with one smooth ath-letic movement. Sweat shone on his upper lip. "I'm going to—"

"Don't get emotional," Jack interrupted, and then hesitated. "There's no need to do anything. We just deny it. Our word against hers."

Cliff sat down and began picking at the torn rubber on the bottom of his boots. The soles were almost worn through. Jack had made the mistake once of offering to give his friend a secondhand pair of shoes. It was better, he had learned, for Celia to give Kim a bag of stuff they no longer needed.

"I hope you're right."

"I usually am," Jack joked. "Anyway. Brian Smithton will set his sights on me, if anyone. Look what happened with the Hollybank Creek sign. There was a moment there when I thought I wouldn't be allowed to change the name of the creek—and on my own farm! Why would anyone want to live near something called Murdering Creek?"

Cliff stared at him. "You change the name, you're acting like that shit didn't happen to those people."

"It was a long time ago. They'd barely cleared the land."

"I think you'll find this valley was fire farmed a long time before the government started carving it up as land grants," Cliff said. "That's why the settlers chose this area. It's been a treeless valley for thousands of years. Treeless valleys don't make themselves."

Sometimes Cliff surprised him with his knowledge.

"Maybe," Jack said.

He was thirsty and he drank most of his beer while Cliff talked about the anti-battery hen activists who were lobbying against him for keeping his birds in sheds. Cliff wanted to transform his poultry enterprise into a free-range chicken farm. This plan was threatened by neighbors who objected on the grounds of noise and smell.

"You're damned either way," Jack said.

"Did you know this island imports most of its free-range chicken from the mainland because of the protestors?" Cliff said.

Jack leaned back in the chair as Cliff wound himself up. He felt himself relaxing somewhat. Celia had once asked Jack why he enjoyed spending so much time with Cliff. His answer was simple—they got along. But he knew what his wife was really asking. Jack had other friends, men with whom he played golf, went sailing, or had long business lunches. Some were farmers he had known since he was a boy, others were friends from boarding school or work connections. They were friends who required something of him, a level of either intellectual or professional engagement. With Cliff he could relax. It wasn't so much that he could be more himself. Rather, with Cliff, he could be nothing.

Jack took another beer out of the fridge and held it up. "Do you mind?"

"Fucking drink it."

Cliff began listing the various neighbors who were trying to ruin his plans for the free-range chicken farm. He claimed to have dirt on them, and he boasted to Jack that he wasn't afraid to use it. Jack nodded and listened to the rant without comment.

Before he left, Jack told Cliff he needed help chainsawing some trees that had fallen near the river.

"If you can use the firewood, you'd be doing me a favor," he said.

"Always happy to help a friend."

* * *

Calendar House

His daughters were asleep. Frannie, Josephine, Alice, and Harriet. From the doorway of each of their bedrooms, he watched them and wondered at their beauty. He would not kiss them tonight.

In the bedroom, Celia also slept. She was curled on her side, her hair spilled across the pillow, her shoulders bare. He thought of pulling the blankets up, but he didn't want to wake her.

The shower was too hot, and he did not care. There was no soap he could see so he scrubbed his body with Celia's expensive geranium extract shampoo. Guilt gripped him. He closed his eyes and cursed himself. Each visit he made to the farmhouse at Marsh End sickened him. The knowledge that he had been there repulsed him. He hated himself, for doing this to Celia, for lowering himself.

In a dark recess of his heart, he knew the truth.

He would go back.

* * *

Joelle

The Smithtons' house

Sunday night was their special night. They made love to each other on other nights too; she liked Sundays best because they were planned. They only ever missed it for a good reason like when Brian had his wisdom teeth pulled out, and when the twins were newborn.

Once they had checked that the kids were asleep, they had a ritual. Brian put on music—Neil Diamond and Paul Kelly were his favorites—and Joelle lit three candles that flickered on the dresser. He never touched her until she touched him first. He never undid her nightgown—she always did that for him. Making love with her husband was something she looked forward to. When she pressed her body against him, it made his breath come from deep in his throat. He was well built, and strong, but here in their bed, he was as cuddly as a kitten. She knew what he liked, and he definitely liked it a lot.

Afterward, he placed his cheek against her heart. She ran her hand up his neck, feeling the bristles on his chin, and then the soft hairless patch just under his lip. She pressed that smooth spot with the tip of her finger.

"Joelle, I love you."

"I love you more."

"All I ever want is to take care of you. No matter what. Forever."

"I know."

"I would do anything for you."

She wriggled around and touched her lips lightly on his.

"No more talking."

CHAPTER 4

Monday, August 21

Joelle

Vanishing Falls village

Loose straw blew like shredded tumbleweed up the empty main street. Outside the café, two police officers were speaking to a man who had uncovered hay bales piled on his truck. Joelle crossed the road so she wouldn't have to go past the policemen. Seeing uniformed police officers always turned her legs watery and gave her a sudden urge to pee.

From the butchery steps she glanced back. The policemen were not looking in her direction. She went inside.

Her hands were shaking as she washed them, and they would shake for a while yet. There was nothing she could do about that. She scrubbed the back-room table and set up the mincing machine. When Joelle had first begun to make the mince, she had told Brian that the chunks of white beef fat were not going in. Fat made you fat; everyone knew that, even her stepfather used to say it. But Brian had taught her that fat was good for the mince and gave it the flavor. Their beef came from pastures at Cape Grim on the northwest coast. Huge winds blew off the Southern Ocean and coated the grass with salt and salt water. The farmers let the cattle graze for longer than was usual in other areas, letting them fatten up, giving time for the meat to absorb the flavor. Brian told their customers they would be able to taste the ocean in the meat.

She held her hands up. They were steady enough. It was dangerous to have shaky hands when you worked in a butchery. She shoved a hock of fat into the mincer and added a small side of beef. The mince that came out was bright and even, as it needed to be. When she had filled a large container, she put it in the front window. The sign said, "*100% Grass-Fed Beef, $9.99/kg.*"

The door swung open and Celia Lily entered. Everything about her was perfect, her green eyes and white-blond hair. Even her wrinkles seemed to be etched onto her face by a deft-fingered craftsman intent on hinting at the happiness that had caused this lovely creature to smile and laugh. You couldn't help but grin when you saw her. She was so pretty.

"That's a better price than the IGA," she said.

"Cheap mince brings people into the shop."

"Don't tell me all your secrets. But that's a great marketing ploy. Now, did you enjoy the school fair?"

"Yes. Well, parts of it."

She wiped her palms on her apron. Blood rushed to her cheeks.

"I know what happened." Celia rested her hand on the counter. Four rings. Joelle noted the different colors of the stones—red, yellow, blue, and green. "I'm so sorry. It's unforgivable that they put you in that situation. I was really cross with Jack when he told me."

Joelle began to say it didn't matter but Celia continued.

"We're really worried about Cliff. It's so difficult. He's addicted to methamphetamine. It's that terrible drug that's ruining so many lives."

Joelle thought of something Nev had said one day when a noisy pack of motorbikes hammered down the main street. The men parked their huge machines outside the pub and acted like they didn't notice everyone staring at their leather vests and muscular, tattoo-covered arms. "The bikers brought it here."

"It's a toxic drug," Celia said. "Jack was trying to help Cliff when you saw them. He was intervening."

"No, Jack was doing it too." Joelle could see the pair of them in her mind: Jack held the pipe to his lips and white smoke came out of it. Cliff was flicking the lighter. A clear bag of something white sat on the toilet lid, which Cliff had quickly tried to hide. "I saw Jack with the glass pipe in his mouth."

Celia frowned. Joelle realized she had made a mistake.

"You should be careful saying things like that."

Joelle tried to think of the right thing to say. It was like looking for a certain stone in a muddy creek: the harder you looked, the murkier everything became.

"I wouldn't like it if anyone heard you say that. People in this town talk too much."

Joelle nodded. A truck holding sheep moved slowly up the main road. They could hear the lambs crying.

Celia winked. "Us girls have to stick together, don't we?"

A sound like the ocean rushing remained in Joelle's ears after Celia closed the butchery door behind her. Joelle held the cold counter tightly, worrying that if she let go, she would sink onto the floor. At the rear of the shop Brian flicked his knives on the sharpening stone. He was focused on his task.

Celia's wink was the kind of falsely conspiratorial wink people gave to children. Joelle had seen that fake wink before, always on people who did not really like her.

* * *

Cliff

Vanishing Falls village

Behind the hotel and the hardware was an alley that smelled like pigeon shit. It was a good place to watch the butchery without being seen. He saw Celia go in and come out without buying anything. He considered following her and asking her what her business was in there. Fortunately, he saw the sense in not doing that.

When he was high, he had to remind himself to resist the urge to participate in actions that made him look dodgy, such as taking fifteen minutes to choose which brand of energy drink to buy from the IGA or giving the checkout lady a dissertation on how he had been spending the day. He had a mental checklist of things to remember: always wear sunglasses; don't press your tongue to your teeth as it results in painful sores that take days to heal; don't scratch; don't adjust your watchband more than twice during an encounter; if a fascinating topic is raised, don't pull out your phone and research it on Google excessively; and never, ever stop on the street and pick up what looks like a discarded meth bag—it won't be, and doing so looks very suspicious in the eyes of the average passing pedestrian. All these things made a tweaker look tweakerish. For Cliff, the hardest challenge was to stop talking once he had begun.

A solution to this was calling his wife whenever he felt chatty. Today Kim was not in the mood to listen.

"Pull your head in. She's not a police informer, you idiot."

"You're complacent, Kim, that's your problem. Other women sort shit out for their husbands."

"Good for them."

"I've given her a warning."

"What have you done?"

He had deliberately ripped only Joelle's clothing off the clothesline. He had not touched the kids' clothes or the butcher's uniforms. However, it would not be smart to discuss these details on the telephone. "Let's just say that I have sent her the message that someone is unhappy with her and that person knows where she lives."

"The only message you're sending is that you're deranged."

Her lack of respect angered him, and he ended the call.

Across the street, he saw Joelle arranging her slabs of expensive meat in the window display. She looked up and met his eye. He gave the peace sign and she scurried to the back of her shop.

* * *

Gatenby's Poultry Farm

H is youngest son, Cooper, needed some information for a school project. Appreciative of the boy's company, Cliff took his time explaining the afternoon's job. He was setting up rodent eradication units in the sheds. Cooper watched and wrote everything down.

First, Cliff mixed a small amount of vegetable oil into a portion of feed grain. Next, he put on gloves and carefully measured in the poison. It was a gray-black powder that smelled like garlic.

"I'm using two percent zinc phosphide with ninety-eight percent feed grain."

"Yep."

"There are other poisons you could use, but this is single use." Cliff read off the container, "'An acute toxicity rodenticide.' It turns to phosphine gas in their stomach. It'll kill them after one feed."

Earlier, he had cut two rat-sized holes in a twenty-liter drum. In a corner of the chicken shed he placed the bait and a water bowl. He turned the drum upside down and covered them.

"I've seen six rats during daylight. That's just the ones I've seen. There are a shitload more at night."

"Is it expensive?"

"The pellets are cheaper." He considered the question further. "The powder works better for me. Nothing comes for free.

Something might come for free; you'll pay a price on it later. Don't forget it." He inspected his work and nodded with satisfaction. "Every time the rats soil a bag of feed it's a costly kick in the guts. We can't afford to have even one rat in the chicken shed."

"Is that the only poison you use?"

"What are you talking about? You know I fumigate the silos to get rid of insect vermin."

Seeing Cooper's face fall, Cliff regretted his gruff tone.

"There's no such thing as a stupid question. Write this down: aluminum phosphide fumigation tablets get rid of any beetles, weevils, and moths that could threaten the bulk stock feed. Forty tablets are required per twenty-seven cubic meters. It's also used to control rabbits. You dog the field first, make sure the rabbits are in the warren, then drop the fumigant in and seal the burrow. Voila. I know some people think I'm a dumb chicken farmer, but there is a fine science to managing these pesticides. You need to be smart to do this job."

"I know, Dad."

If he wasn't wearing contaminated gloves, he would have patted his son on the head. "I'm telling you, son, ask questions. As many as you have to. It's only stupid people who don't ask questions because they can't think what to ask."

"Yes, sir." Cooper finished writing something down and gave Cliff a cheeky grin. "There's a teacher at school . . ."

"Yeah."

"Mrs. Bugwhistle, the PE teacher. She always says, 'Stupid question,' no matter what the question is."

"Mrs. Bugwhistle?"

They both started laughing. It felt good to share a joke with his boy.

"That's her name, Dad."

"You couldn't make it up."

* * *

Miss Gwen

Calendar House

The front columns of the enormous house cast cold shadows. Miss Gwen pulled her cardigan around her as she waited for her knock to be answered. Across the lawn were the familiar rosebushes and the birdbath. Even the branches of the poplar trees beside the lake swayed in the breeze as she remembered: blissfully out of time, like children dancing. It was more than fifty years since she had stood on this doorstep, and nothing had changed except the modern car sitting in the driveway.

Celia Lily appeared, looking disheveled. Behind her a small girl with long yellow plaits rode down the hallway on a scooter. She rang the scooter's bell as a younger girl dashed in front of her. Celia welcomed Miss Gwen with a quick embrace.

"I've been going through all the boxes," she said. "Come into the library, please."

The library, too, was unchanged. It smelled waxy and Miss Gwen wondered if they still used the same lemon-oil furniture polish. She had an odd sense of déjà vu as she looked around at the walls clothed in a familiar white-and-gold antique paper, the marble mantel above the fireplace, and the dog and irons in the grate. It had once been her task to clean those.

Celia introduced her to her two eldest daughters, who were sitting at the table, Frannie and Josephine. They were sorting old newspaper clippings into piles.

"They've been very helpful getting everything ready for the Apple Queen Tribute Evening. Jack's mother kept every newspaper article, every photograph," Celia said. "Here is one of you both on the float."

"Oh, we were so beautiful," Miss Gwen exclaimed. "These are lovely."

The photo showed a group of young women waving from the back of the decorated truck. It was a black-and-white photo, but in Miss Gwen's mind she could see the pastel yellow, sherbet pink, and cornflower blue of their dresses, and the apple blossoms hanging in festoons all over the float.

"What was Granny like back then?" Frannie asked. "It's hard to imagine her being young. She's so . . . formal."

Miss Gwen cast her mind back. Victoria Lily was a confident girl, organizing picnics and bushwalks for large groups of young people, practicing dressage on her pony, dancing to Elvis Presley and Nat King Cole records. Victoria was generous too; she spent hours trying to teach Miss Gwen to ride a horse.

"She was jolly," Miss Gwen said. "Always ready for an adventure. I worked for her mother-in-law, yet she always treated me like I was a friend. She was kind."

She was wonderful as long as everyone did what she wanted, Miss Gwen thought. Celia reminded her of Victoria, in some ways.

"She never won the crown, did she?" Celia said mischievously. "I imagine she never forgave you!"

"I was crowned Apple Queen in 1958," Miss Gwen admitted. She added diplomatically, "The prize was a trip to Coffs Harbour. I think they wanted to give it to one of the village girls, rather than someone like Victoria. She was disappointed. The next year she said we were both too old to nominate ourselves for such a silly competition."

They spent the next hour sorting through boxes and albums, finding the memorabilia they could use for the upcoming celebration evening. There was a lovely pile of photos—black-and-white and color—and even a postcard Miss Gwen had mailed Victoria from Coffs Harbour, when she was doing her tour to promote the Apple Isle.

They had almost finished when Josephine pulled out a series of early photos taken of people picnicking around the Vanishing Falls water hole. Celia checked to see if they were related to the Apple Queen history and, deciding they were not, placed them out of the way. Miss Gwen was curious. She arranged them on the table in front of her. The photos captured the water rushing down into the deep swirling pool. The bushwalkers leaned back, enjoying the wild splendor of the secluded rain forest waterfall. They were close enough to the falling water that spray would have coated their faces. The namesake of the town was a tragic and ominous place, Miss Gwen thought. It always seemed odd to her that tourists and locals alike experienced such carefree pleasure in a place that was haunted by nameless people from the past.

* * *

Jack

Calendar House

That evening, Jack sat on the end of their bed, watching Celia brush her hair. She was keen to talk about the historical event she was organizing, and he encouraged her.

"Is Kim helping you?" he wondered.

"She doesn't have time. Cliff has her working around the clock on that chicken farm." She set the brush down and pinned her hair back. "It's not fair, a bright woman like her, sweeping manure all day."

"Is she smart?"

"Very intelligent. When she was young, she was selected by one of the big Launceston banks for their management program. They wanted to pay for her university."

"What happened?"

"She fell in love." She smiled. "Happens to the best of us."

"Does that mean I'm forgiven?" he asked as she applied lotion to her face with dainty fingertip strokes.

"No," she said cheekily, but her expression was tender.

He lay back on the bed and thought about Kim. He remembered Celia telling him, many years ago, that Kim had

had a baby when she was only sixteen. Her parents had forced her to put the baby girl up for adoption. Apparently, afterward, no one reacted how Kim thought they would—the boy fell in love with someone else, her friends shunned her, and her parents remained ashamed.

"We need to help Kim," he said. "It's not fair, what she has to deal with."

"Don't worry about Kim," Celia said. "She's a survivor. But you're right. I'll talk to her. I'll remind her that we are here for her."

CHAPTER 5

Tuesday, August 22

Joelle

The Smithtons' house

When she woke up, Brian was dressed for work and sitting on the end of their bed drinking a cup of coffee. His green work tie hung undone around his neck. A posy of small starry pale-pink flowers from the garden had been placed in a glass of water on the bedside table.

"My favorites. Is it my birthday?" Joelle asked.

"No. I just like making you smile."

She sat up. "Where are the kids?"

"Getting ready for school. You slept in. Joey, is everything okay?"

"Yep."

"Are you happy?"

She looked at the flowers he had picked for her. "Of course I'm happy. I'm here with you. And I love daphnes. Do you know why?"

He touched the end of her nose with his fingertip. "Tell me again."

She told him the story, how there were daphnes in an old-fashioned cut-glass vase next to the bed when she first arrived at Darla's. Darla got only an hour's notice from the department that Joelle was coming. So many times, Joelle had imagined Darla hurrying to prepare: making the bed, choosing a soft pink towel that smelled like fabric softener, and dashing out into the garden with a pair of scissors to cut a bunch of flowers to brighten the room.

"A small act of kindness that lasts a lifetime," Brian said.

Almost everything he knew about her came from then, as though she had been born into Darla's family at the age of fifteen. Sometimes even Joelle forgot that there had been another family, her birth mother and her stepfather and his sons, in that rickety house at Pieman's Junction so close to the tracks the plates in the cupboards rattled every time the train went by. Before that place, she had vague, uneasy memories of lots of different homes and schools. School was not easy for Joelle. Storytime was the only time she relaxed in the classroom; most of the time she was never certain what the teacher wanted her to do.

Like Darla said, there was no point thinking about the past. You had to get on with it.

"Sit still, my big, lovely man." She set to work doing up his tie.

* * *

Jack

Coast Road

On Tuesday, Jack collected his mother from her home. She lived a few hours away in a cozy cottage on a headland overlooking rough ocean. It was once the family's summer house and Victoria Lily had moved there after Jack's father died. Jack was always grateful to her for letting his family have the Calendar House to themselves.

Jack and his mother spent a pleasant morning on the Fotheringhams' property, viewing a pony that was for sale. This was halfway back to Vanishing Falls, but Jack knew his mother would appreciate the outing. Victoria Lily had been close friends with Roger Fotheringham's mother. As they walked across to the stables, Victoria squeezed his arm with pleasure. It did her good to get back to the countryside.

Roger's adult children had moved away from the farm, and the dozen or so horses he had accumulated were no longer being ridden. He showed Jack and Victoria a young chestnut mare. She had competed in novice dressage and was an 80 centimeter show jumper with potential to go higher. He wanted nine thousand dollars, which Jack thought was a lot, but before he could negotiate, Victoria told Roger it was a deal. She insisted the mare would perfectly suit any of Jack's young daughters.

The men shook on it.

On the way home, Jack wondered if they had paid too much.

"I think I know what a horse is worth," his mother said confidently. "I'll write the check if you're that bothered."

"Don't be silly," he said. "Celia will be pleased. She's been wanting a new pony for the girls."

"How is Madam?"

"She's very busy with her historical committee."

"She needs something to keep her busy. She doesn't work."

"You didn't work either, Mother."

"I didn't have half the appliances she has. I didn't drive. I used to walk into the village every day."

Conversations with his mother could be exhausting. He tried to be patient. He was her only son. He had a sister, but she lived far away and claimed to be too busy to provide emotional support to their mother. Apart from him, Victoria was quite alone.

"I have something exciting to tell you." He lowered his voice to pique her interest. "I've come across a rare painting."

She perked up. "Oh?"

With one hand on the wheel, he reached into his pocket and passed her a photo he had taken of the painting.

"It's a beauty," she said. "My first thought, seeing the wide blue sky and the pastoral scene, is that this is a Glover."

"I haven't had it appraised yet, but I think so too." His thoughts strayed from the hurtling cattle trucks on the highway. "Can you imagine?"

"Goodness gracious," she said. "Remember, in 1835 John Glover sent sixty-eight paintings to be exhibited in London, from his home in Van Diemen's Land. Fewer than five of these have ever turned up. It's baffling how so many paintings could vanish."

Together they listed the general features of Glover's work—the warm and cool greens contrasting with the hint of pink luminosity in the hills; the gum trees with their regrowth close to the trunk, a characteristic unique to the species as it regenerated following bushfire; and the hedonistic attitude of the Aboriginal people, at odds with the gravity of the landscape.

"We'll unveil it at an exhibition soiree at the house," he said. "You can pull back the curtain."

When the news of this find became public Jack would credit her with nurturing his love of art. The *Garden of Eden*, as he had been calling it, would be an outstanding piece in his collection. The respect he would garner would extend beyond the island's so-called art circles, to the mainland, and internationally too.

As he kissed her goodbye in her front hallway, she clung to him.

"I wish you didn't have to leave. How is the house and the farm?" she said. "I miss it more and more."

"Come and stay," he said. "Let me talk to Celia and see when will suit."

Victoria gave a cold laugh and crossed her arms.

"Mother. You're always welcome."

"Over Celia's dead body." She stroked a pearly fingernail across her neck.

"Mum."

"I am a great one for not mincing my words," she said. "Never sweep outside your hut until you have swept inside."

"That doesn't even make sense," he said.

But his mother's words resounded in his head as he drove home. The road burrowed up into densely forested high country. He kept the window down and the wet air flushed his face. Over the years, he had accepted that no matter what Celia did, in his mother's view, she was wrong. She was ruining the house if she replaced soft furnishings; she was neglecting the house if she did not.

Thoughts of his new painting helped him forget his mother's judgments.

An open home would not suffice for a painting of this caliber. Instead, he would lend his collection to the Tasmanian Museum and Art Gallery in the capital. They could display it with a sign stating, "Collection on Loan from Jack Lily." The premier, heads of business, art scholars, and other collectors would attend the opening night. Finding one of John Glover's lost paintings was a once-in-a-lifetime occurrence.

There was traffic on the main street of Vanishing Falls. Horses—not theirs—were crossing the road. As he waited Jack looked up at the hotel. At the turn of the nineteenth century it was built for a new tourist industry, as people traveled on improved roads to view the falls and hike in the forests. At the peak of the commercial hunting boom, the pub hosted adventurous and brutal men whose legacy was the extinction of the Tasmanian tiger. The old redbrick building was now clad with beer and meal deal advertisements. The garden out back was the only thing that never changed. As a boy, he had played there with local children, beneath the huge English magnolia tree. They had spent hour upon hour poking around in the creek, which had eels, trout, and the occasional platypus.

In the pub's glowing window, he recognized the couple who owned the junkyard at Marsh End. They were having lunch. Her hair hung thickly down her wide back. Her husband had tied a red bandanna around his head for the special occasion of their midweek pub meal. It had not escaped Jack that they now ate lunch or dinner at the pub weekly. A few years ago, before he started visiting them, he only ever saw them buying fried chicken and chips at the takeaway shop.

* * *

Cliff

Gatenby's Poultry Farm

He lay on his bed, trying to rest his eyes. The noise of Kim vacuuming was like razor wire thrusting in and out of his ears. He strode into the living area. Kim was bent over, vacuuming under his weight bench. She glanced up at him. He detested her then, with her beady, resentful eyes, like the broilers as they were loaded into crates for the slaughterhouse.

"Shut that thing off. Wait until I'm at work and you can do it all day."

She turned it off.

"You look like shit," she said.

"Look at yourself."

"I'm worried about you."

The trouble with Kim was that you couldn't trust her. She lied all the time—she said things that she thought he wanted to hear, when what he really wanted to hear was the truth.

"I'm exhausted," he said. "From working too hard."

It was true. There were never holidays. No wonder he felt so prickly. His wife acted like he spent his days wandering around dreaming up schemes for free-range chickens and picking thistles out of the pasture when in fact he was up to his armpits in chicken shit, hosing out the sheds, wheelbar-rowing broiler carcasses to the incinerator, and breathing in the dusty fibers of the feed until he coughed up chunks of muck whenever he lay down.

"I'm on your side, Cliff."

She touched his arm.

"Come here," he said.

She glanced toward the boys' room.

"They'll cope without you for ten minutes," he said.

In the bedroom dirty thoughts peppered his mind. It started with him imagining he was having sex with some-one else, and then that person started looking a lot like Celia. Afterward, he felt a pang of guilt, like he had cheated on his wife. The thing was, there was too much of Celia, those ob-scenely luxuriant breasts; long, tanned legs; and all that silky hair. You'd never know where to start.

What no one realized was that Celia Lily had a crush on him. It was surprising they didn't know given the way she fawned over him. She didn't care who saw. She knew no one would dare tell her what to do.

Saturday at the fair, she had pressed her breasts up against him as they greeted each other. It was no accident.

She was too flirtatious. Give him a decent, sensible woman like Kim any day.

While Kim was in the bathroom, he took two diazepam, got dressed, and stepped outside onto the porch. The dog shiv-ered in its kennel. He strode across the muddy yard, the rain slapping his face.

* * *

Miss Gwen

The Smithtons' house

Miss Gwen walked the Smithton twins home from school along the creek path. There was a lot of water moving rapidly in the creek and she urged Baxter to be careful lest he fall in. The little boy kept dashing from the track, his attention caught by a platypus slipping through the reeds into the water.

"Why can't you just hold my hand like Emily does?" Miss Gwen said ineffectually.

"Miss Gwen . . . I think Mum needs your help," Emily said. "She told me something was wrong last night when she kissed me good night."

"I wonder if it was anything in particular?" Miss Gwen searched Emily's face for information.

"Someone was mean to her."

"Did she say who?"

"Nope."

The conversation ended abruptly because the children noticed a large stray cat watching them from a thicket of hawthorn.

Miss Gwen pondered on it as she gave them their afternoon tea at Joelle's kitchen table. Later, as she helped Baxter clean out the rabbit cage, Miss Gwen asked him if he had noticed anything bothering his mum.

"No." He laughed. He had Joelle's dimpled smile. "Mum doesn't worry about anything except doing nice things for us."

"Sweet boy."

It was good that the children did not know any more details. In the past, there had been incidences when Joelle overshared her concerns with the twins. Miss Gwen and Brian had explained to Joelle that it was not fair to burden the children with adult worries. Joelle understood.

Nine years ago, Joelle had raced down Old Dairy Road to Miss Gwen's house.

"I've got two exciting secrets to tell you," she had said, her hands resting protectively on her stomach.

At the time, Miss Gwen had struggled to show genuine happiness about Joelle's pregnancy. She was worried about how on earth this joyful, vulnerable woman would cope. At first the government provided formal support. It was a terrible solution. The professionals looked for problems. They talked about things that might happen in two years, five years, or maybe never. Eventually, Brian and Miss Gwen, and Joelle too, convinced the Department for Child Protection that the little family was doing fine. There was enough kindness in Vanishing Falls village to provide Joelle with the support she needed.

A clap of thunder startled Baxter and Miss Gwen.

Baxter wiggled his fingers up in the air like a ghoul. "Ooh." He grinned.

They were safely inside just before the downpour began. The twins turned on the television. Miss Gwen watched the rain beat the garden. Fog blew across the forest, shrouding the village. In weather like this, it was clear how old stories about Vanishing Falls became entrenched in local folklore. An obsession with the idea of the harsh Australian bushland swallowing innocent children was not limited to artists and writers. Tragically, from what she understood, stories burgeoned from fact. She had learned the hard way to keep these views to herself.

* * *

Joelle

Vanishing Falls village

Brian was in another part of the supermarket when Celia and Kim approached her in the cake decorating aisle. They were wearing exercise gear, although they didn't look sweaty or disheveled. They pushed their shopping carts right up to her.

"How are you?" Celia said like she thought Joelle had been unwell.

Joelle reassured her that she was indeed feeling good. For a moment she thought they wanted to buy piping nozzles or silicone molds, but Celia was so friendly, she wanted to know what Joelle was up to that week. It took a while to list everything: Joelle had baking to do, there were several haircuts booked at the nursing home, and, importantly, she had to select a color for the new rabbit hutch to be painted.

"Well . . . we'll catch up soon," Celia said.

"We should have coffee at the Rosella Café," Joelle said. "That's supposed to be the best coffee in Vanishing. Better than the art gallery and definitely better than the gas station."

Joelle had often seen happy groups of school mums enter the cheery café with the green parrot on its sign. She had been there with Brian, and Miss Gwen, but it wasn't the same as going with friends her age. Before they had a chance to reply, Kim stepped aside to let a heavyset woman steer her shopping cart past them. It was Karen, a lady who Joelle occasionally delivered dog bones to. In her cart were two large cartons of Coca-Cola cans.

"Is there a limit on how much soft drink a person can buy?" Celia asked.

"Hush," Kim said.

"She can't hear me," Celia said.

"You probably don't realize how loud your voice is. The same thing happens to me, especially in church or at the movies." Joelle looked worriedly down the aisle where Karen had gone. "You have to be careful because there's no point hurting someone's feelings."

They stared at her. She tried to think of something else to say, to keep the conversation going. She looked in their carts. Kim didn't have much, but Celia's was piled high.

"Did you know there's no difference between the home-brand flour and the Four Roses flour?" Joelle said.

She explained about how basic products were the same beneath the packaging, but some things, like chocolate or cola, you could tell the difference on.

Neither woman said anything.

"Close your eyes and you wouldn't know what toilet paper you were using," Joelle went on. "It's all the same."

Kim was staring at the canned food on the shelf. Celia nodded encouragingly.

"Look at everything you're buying," Joelle told Celia. "You could make some savings."

"That's good to know. Thanks, Joelle." Celia's ponytail swished as she turned around. Her pink tracksuit clung neatly to her figure. Inadvertently, Joelle's hands went to her own hips and pressed the swell of her curves.

When she was gone, Kim said in a soft, kind voice, "You seem really sweet. But . . ."

Joelle thought she was going to say something else when Brian called out, "You okay, Joey?"

"I'm catching up with some friends," Joelle called.

She turned back to Kim, but she had gone. Instead, Karen, the woman who bought the butchery's off cuts for her dogs, was coming toward her.

"Watch out for them two. They're not as nice as everyone thinks." Karen paused. "If you ever need to chat, you know where I live."

Joelle turned away from her, wishing she would go to another part of the supermarket. Brian put the eggs in her basket and frowned. "What did they want with you?"

"We're friends."

"I've never seen you talk to them before."

She could tell Brian disapproved. "Brian, I don't like it when you look at me like that. Did you ever think that I might want friends my own age? Nev and Miss Gwen are so much older than me. There's things they can't do, like walk up to the falls with me. Those girls really like me, I can tell, Brian. We're going to have a coffee one day, real soon," she said proudly.

Brian did not look happy. He had the same expression as he did when he realized she had accidentally put the "*Organic, Free-Range!*" chicken sign on the normal chicken and it had been there all day.

All he said was, "Sweetheart."

CHAPTER 6

Wednesday, August 23

Joelle

The Smithtons' house

Wednesday was one of the days Miss Gwen came to help. She was waiting in the driveway in her little blue car when Joelle returned from walking the children to school. Walking the kids to school used to be Miss Gwen's job, but since the twins turned eight, the arrangements had changed.

Miss Gwen was very happy with Joelle. The washing was done, the kitchen was tidy, and when Miss Gwen checked the twins' bedroom, she said it was spick-and-span. Joelle beamed.

"I love spending time with you," Miss Gwen said as they cut up some vegetables for dinner. "I always have. But lately I think that you might not need my help as much."

"No!" Joelle said. "I love you coming."

"Have a think about it. Especially now that the children are getting more independent."

"I'll always find something for you to do," Joelle said kindly. "Don't worry."

Miss Gwen turned to Joelle's daily schedule chart. It listed every task, in the order that they needed to happen. Miss Gwen liked structure; she did not like it when Joelle fell out of routine.

"I hear you might be adding a coffee date to this chart soon," Miss Gwen said. "That's lovely, dear. Don't forget to let Brian or me know before you do that. It's not that we don't want you to go. We do. But we like to know where you are," she added firmly.

"Why do I have to?" Joelle said. "You just said that I might not need you anymore. Sometimes I get so sick of being bossed around by you and Brian."

"It's annoying, I can only imagine," Miss Gwen said. "You do understand it is because we care about you."

"I know that. Brian says that all the time." She thought of how she sometimes saw Brian and Miss Gwen speaking to each other in hushed voices. "I just feel like you're ganging up on me."

"No, we're not. If you want to have coffee, you have coffee. We just want to keep you safe."

Joelle supposed it made sense . . . but still . . . a tiny little voice inside of her said, *Why do I have to ask them?* It was hard to find the right words. Some people—not really Brian and not really Miss Gwen—got annoyed when she misunderstood, and they got really annoyed when she understood more than they wanted her to.

"Celia Lily is on your Apple Queen history committee," Joelle said. "Do you like her?"

"Sometimes I do find her difficult." Miss Gwen faltered. "I suppose her heart is in the right place. She stands up for people. She asked the school to ban peanut butter sandwiches, years ago, before everyone knew about nut allergies. It was not her child who had the allergy either. I heard it was a family she didn't even know. And Kim . . . well, I don't know much about her."

Joelle sighed happily. "They both seem nice."

Miss Gwen tapped her wristwatch. "Is that the time? If we don't leave now, we'll be late."

On the way to the nursing home they fell silent as they drove across the first bridge and turned left along the creek. They never spoke when they drove along here. People had died here. Brian said there were lots of versions of what had happened but the only thing everyone agreed on was that the people who passed away were Aboriginal and the people who killed them were the sheep farmers.

It had snowed in the night and the onion paddock next to the nursing home was covered in white. They had seen the farmer put the onion seed in a week ago. Miss Gwen supposed they would be all right, tucked under the soil. On the hill the black-and-white cows were running and bouncing like children excited to wake up to snow.

Miss Gwen parked the car and adjusted her headband around her hair.

"I'll see you in an hour, more or less."

The first haircut was for Mr. Keith Porter, an enormous man who had been a dairy farmer since he was fourteen. Joelle set up her portable mirror and tools on a table in the common room. He was unsure on his feet and one of the staff helped him sit down in the hairdressing chair. She thought of the first time she met him: his wobbliness, and the fact that he was so friendly and loud, made her think he must have been drunk. He had roared with laughter when she asked if he had been drinking, and told her, "I wish."

"Sit still," she told him now.

"You're a bossy one."

"Manners. Remember you're with company, not in the milking shed."

"La-di-da," he said, and laughed loudly.

Joelle laughed too. "You have the kind of laugh that makes me want to laugh, even if I don't know what's funny."

She sprayed water on his hair and combed it.

"Have you managed to convince that husband of yours to take the children hiking?" he asked.

"Not yet," she said, pleased that Mr. Keith remembered their conversation from a few weeks ago. "Brian said they'll get tired and complain, and he'll have to carry them on his back. I love hiking. I want my children to love it too."

Before the twins were born, when she and Brian were a new couple, they had gone hiking almost every weekend. From Cradle Mountain to Wineglass Bay, Maria Island to Mount Field; they had hiked and picnicked and taken photos of beautiful views. Best of all, they had talked. There was something about being in the forest that helped quiet men like Brian want to share their thoughts.

"A good walk never hurt anyone. Keep asking Brian about it," Mr. Keith advised. "That's how my dear Anita got what she wanted. She would go on and on about something until I said yes. That's why we had five children."

He laughed so hard she had to pause the scissors. He spent

the rest of the time talking about his wife. One of Joelle's favorite things about Mr. Keith was that he didn't mind how many questions Joelle asked—he loved to talk about the olden days on his farm. He never said anything was off-limits either, the way some people did.

On the way home, Miss Gwen sighed. "I don't know about that place."

"Why? We like going there."

"The manager didn't want Mr. Keith to have his appointment with you. Apparently he wasn't following instructions."

Joelle looked out the window at a drift of wild daffodils growing beneath a wall of golden wattle. She hoped the cold nights would not hurt them. "Did I tell you what happened in the hospital after I had the twins? The social worker at the hospital said that mothers like me would not cope with raising children. She wanted me to hand the twins over for adoption. There was a form I had to sign. She put it on the table next to my bed with the pen on top. That's why I never breastfed. The nurses gave my babies bottles because they thought they were going to someone else. Some people who worked at the hospital said that partners of mothers like me struggled with the responsibility and probably did not stick around."

Miss Gwen was driving so slowly Joelle could see burrs of wool on a barbed-wire fence where sheep had tried to escape.

"Maybe the midwives were worried there would not be enough breast milk for two babies. It's normal for twins to be given a bottle as well as breast milk," Miss Gwen said.

"I felt like they were watching me, all the time, waiting for me to mess up." Joelle glanced at her worriedly. "The social worker was wrong, wasn't she?"

"Oh yes." Miss Gwen took her hand off the wheel and reached out as if to comfort Joelle, but she returned her hand to the steering wheel before she made contact. "Very, very wrong. You've got a lovely family, my dear. You should be very proud."

Miss Gwen sounded so sad. Joelle felt a rush of sympathy for her because she had never married or had children. Joelle could not imagine how lonely she would be if she did not have Brian, Emily, and Baxter. For the rest of the way home Joelle got Miss Gwen talking about the Apple Queen historical evening. It was Miss Gwen's favorite topic. The lovely lady had perked up by the time they reached Old Dairy Road.

* * *

Cliff

Vanishing Falls village

He spent a few minutes watching the residents come and go from the housing commission flats. A pregnant girl pushed a stroller heavy with plastic shopping bags. She held a red-faced toddler on her hip. It was the middle of the day, freezing cold, and the child was wearing pajamas and no shoes or socks. She entered a unit that had an Australian flag pinned up as a curtain. An old man smoked a cigarette on his doorstep. His hands shook as he bore down on the smoke. A sex offender, probably. No one lived here unless they had nowhere else to go.

Vanishing Falls had not always been so impoverished. Even when they began bulldozing the orchards, people were optimistic about the future. The mill was expanding, the government was throwing money at improving equipment at the abattoir. The flow-on effect of this was immeasurable—local meat processing meant farmers saved on livestock transport; people moved here for the good jobs; the school started growing. Fast-forward thirty years, the government stopped funneling money into local industries, and only one out of three pubs remained open. The only neighborhood where business was thriving was the housing commission street.

Two boys who should have been in school lurched past on skateboards. Neither of them paid any attention to Cliff.

All day he had felt like he was moving through thick honey. When he had tried to work that morning, he could not concentrate on the monitor. The smell of the chicken sheds made him feel ill.

There was so much work to do.

He had no choice.

The old man dropped his cigarette butt onto the concrete. Cliff walked decisively toward the flats, as though he were a landlord seeking rent. Unit five had overflowing rubbish bins out front, and an abandoned shopping cart holding, among other things, a soiled duvet and a broken chair. He knocked once and was let inside.

An hour later, Cliff stood on a stump at the falls car park

and threw his arms up to the sky. Warm tingles rushed beneath his skin. Everything had a reason—you just had to think about it, and the answers would be clear. There were people who went places, and people who stayed. He was moving, had been going somewhere all his life. He could hear the creeks brimming and flowing out of the national park, and when he planted his feet apart and stood still, he could feel the throbbing of underground springs. Silver birds weaved through the dark gray sky. The greenness was palpable; it shone. It was good to be alive.

He got in his car and started the engine.

Driving home, he realized he needed to stop at the Lilys' place and collect the money Jack owed him from Saturday.

Celia was sitting in the gazebo, watching one of the girls ride around their dressage arena. A jug of iced tea sat on the table and she poured him a glass. It was like she had been expecting him.

He settled in and sipped his drink and told her about playing cricket for the Tasmanian school boys' team and how he had missed out on a place in the first eleven after injuring himself at training. He talked about his plans to pioneer Tasmania's most progressive free-range poultry project. He confided that he wanted to spoil Kim. When he first met her, way back when she was a bank teller in Launceston, they had planned to drive around Australia in a camper, but she became pregnant before that happened.

"I suppose you better be going," Celia said after a while. "She'll have your dinner ready."

"I'm not hungry. Did Jack tell you there's nothing about the butcher's wife on the internet?" He slapped his leg to emphasize. "Nothing. Do you think that's odd?"

"I don't know."

"I think Joelle Smithton is in witness protection. What's her story? I need to know, Celia."

"Forget about her. You both are lucky she hasn't reported you. As far as we know."

"You've been chatting to her. I saw you go in there. Did my name come up?"

She shook her head. "We have other things to talk about than you, Cliff."

"Will you be so ambivalent when the drug squad hauls Jack in?"

"For goodness' sake."

Of course she'd have no comeback to that.

Beyond the horse ring, one of the Lily girls cantered across the paddock, jumping fallen trees and white picket fences. He glanced at Celia. She was staring at her daughters. Paranoia rippled through him. He suspected he'd been speaking frantically, so he feigned a big yawn and added, "I'm so tired from work I'm probably not making sense. I might use your bathroom before I go, if that's okay."

Celia insisted on escorting him there.

Obediently he followed her across the lawn and into the vast house; down the hallway, past the billiard room and bar. She walked like a flight attendant, swinging her hips, shoulders back.

The study door was open. He saw the easel right away. It

stood in the middle of the room and was covered in a big white sheet.

"Jack's latest acquisition," he said.

He strode in and tugged at the sheet. Celia said, "You'd better not."

The cover sheet tumbled to the ground and Cliff gasped.

* * *

Jack

Calendar House

He skidded the Jaguar to a stop when he saw Cliff's car parked in his driveway. He ran inside. He could hear Cliff's loud voice coming from the study. He hurried down the hall. The *Garden of Eden* was uncovered. The calico cloth lay on the floor like a crumpled nightdress.

Cliff whistled in appreciation. "It's Vanishing Falls."

Cliff reached out to touch it. Jack understood the urge. The paint was applied thickly and was bubbly like congealed blood.

"You can't touch it."

"Worth a lot."

"I don't know."

Every time Jack looked at the painting, he saw the scene differently. The blue sky, the curving trees, the Aboriginal children playing on the banks of the water hole—that was still there. It was a mood, he realized, of sadness or hope or joy, that the painting prompted within him as he studied it. Today he could see something in one of the women's expressions. She was looking over her shoulder, beyond the gilded frame of the painting. There was a glimmer of terror on her features.

Jack's habit was to keep his cultural interests separate from those friends who did not truly appreciate art. You couldn't blame him. He looked his friend over. A broken feather was stuck to his work shirt. His hands and his nails were dirty. Apart from that, he looked healthy. His teeth were not decaying, his skin did not have ulcers or sore patches, and he was as muscular as he'd ever been. It was the intensity of his eyes that unsettled Jack. The word *rabid* came to mind. It was clear he was high.

"Time to go," Jack said.

Celia gave Jack a grateful, helpless smile as he ushered Cliff out.

They reached the pickup truck and Cliff spun around. He shoved his hands in his pockets and eyed Jack. "I need that two hundred dollars you owe me."

Jack ignored him. He called out an encouragement to his girls, trotting on their ponies. He felt Cliff shifting beside him. Silence was how Jack dealt with needy, desperate clients. No one had taught him that; he had always known it was the smoothest way to get the result you wanted, particularly when dealing with volatile, emotional people. When he was a young solicitor, a distraught client had turned up at his office with a carload of her children. Sobbing, she told him she was frightened to go home, and the domestic violence shelter was full. She asked if she could use his spare room for one night. Celia would have skinned him alive. Patiently, he had asked a few generic questions until eventually she remembered a friend who had a caravan she might be able to use. The key was to let people solve their own problems.

Cliff shoved his hands in his pockets. "Don't pretend like you don't do it."

Jack felt himself color. He had never given Cliff money for drugs, for the very reason Cliff was implying. Paying for it confirmed his intention, as opposed to just going with the flow when the situation got loose.

"You can afford it," Cliff said. "You're collecting million-dollar paintings."

Jack was unable to hide his shock. "Did Celia tell you that?"

"I took an educated guess."

"Listen. The painting will generate a substantial degree of attention. I don't need any mud thrown at me right now. Last Saturday was . . . unfortunate."

"It's all good. Lucky I'm just a chicken farmer with no reputation to worry about."

Jack took out his wallet and handed Cliff two fifty-dollar notes. "That's all the cash I have."

After Cliff left, Jack went inside and found Celia in the kitchen. She was leaning against the counter with her arms crossed.

"He scares me," she said.

"He's gone now."

"He turned up unannounced. I couldn't get rid of him. I'm worried about offending him. He wouldn't stop talking. He went inside to use the bathroom. I tried to keep him out of your study, but the door was open, and he pulled the cloth off before I could stop him."

"It's not your fault, darling."

"I know. He said that the police are going to haul you in. . . ."

"That won't happen."

"Will you listen to what I'm saying? Joelle saw you with the glass pipe to your lips. She actually told me that."

"When were you going to tell me that?"

"Don't you dare get angry with me. I tried to talk to her. I tried to help you. I'm trying to help Joelle too. I should never have mentioned the Pieman's Junction Murder in front of Cliff. He keeps asking me about it. I feel like I've got everyone's back, but who's looking out for me? I've got a lot to lose here too."

Celia bit her lip. Her eyes scrunched. He thought she was about to cry but she steadied herself and said firmly, "If the police ask me, I'm not lying for you."

* * *

Joelle

Vanishing Falls village

It was always a delight to shop in Alfred Cheng's old-fashioned green grocery store. It was one of the original village buildings and since it was built in 1855 it had been used as a steam flour mill, a bakery, a bus depot, and a bicycle factory. Alfred lived in the quarters at the rear comprised of three tiny rooms. His father lived upstairs in an attic bedroom.

For a few minutes she forgot about her children, who were waiting in the car. The cool, dark aisles were full of crates of cabbages and carrots, new potatoes still covered in dirt, parsnips and turnips, and red apples. Bunches of drying vegetables hung from the timber beams: clusters of chilies, squash, onions, and garlic. It smelled so deliciously fresh.

She collected what she needed and placed the basket on the counter. While Alfred calculated the bill with a pencil on a piece of scrap paper, she walked quickly outside to check on the twins.

Beside her yellow station wagon in the parking bay outside was a white truck. It had a goat's skull tied to the bull bar. Above the bumper bar was a sign that made her stomach twist: DO YOU WANT TO PLAY CHICKEN? The big headlights came on and she blinked, blinded by their brightness.

Alfred shuffled up behind her holding a cardboard box containing her vegetables.

"My kids are in the car," she said. "That man . . . why is he there?"

"That's Gatenby's pickup truck."

"I'm scared."

"I'll carry this out to your car, love. If anything happens, I'm here."

She looked at his skinny arms and how his overalls were draped over his thin body. She said, "You'd be no good to me."

"That doesn't mean I'm not coming."

As they neared her car, the pickup truck started up with a horrible roar. It slid on the wet road as it reversed out. Joelle hurried, panicking that he had done something awful to her children. Thankfully, they were lying against each other, reading peacefully.

Alfred put the grocery box in the back of the car. "There's a few of them like that, love. I find their mess in the alley behind the store. It's ruining every town. You can't help them." He wiped the rain from his brow. "You wouldn't know about that rubbish."

She got into the car, put on her seat belt, and turned the ignition. Ten deep breaths. She couldn't drive. Not yet.

Alfred was mistaken about her. She knew something of what lured people into back bedrooms, garages, and garden sheds. It could happen in the most normal-looking houses. When she was growing up at Pieman's Junction, it was not just her stepbrothers. Even Joelle's own mother smoked a joint. It was a secret. Her mother's husband, Trapper, always said if Joelle told anyone, it would be the last thing she did. Joelle believed him.

A knock on the window caused Joelle to scream.

It was only Alfred. He was drenched, the rain battering his face. "Do you want me to call Brian?"

Joelle shook her head no.

She started driving home.

"Mum, when you were in the shop, Cooper Gatenby's dad asked us what your maiden name is. What's a maiden name?" Emily said.

"That man talked to you? He opened the door?"

"It's okay, Mum," Baxter said. "We know him."

"Don't . . . don't ever talk to him again. Never ever. And I don't know what a maiden name is. A maiden is . . ."

"I think it's a girl. Are you going to tell Dad?"

"No one tell Dad. That would ruin everything. Cross your heart."

They kept her secrets—when she lost her house keys or mistakenly fed the cat sirloin. Her kids were good kids. She told them so, repeating it over and over until they turned onto Old Dairy Road.

*　*　*

The Smithtons' house

On Emily's dressing table was a plaited cotton bracelet. It reminded Joelle of one she used to own. She remembered the red-and-blue symmetry so clearly, as though she still wore it. A girl from her school in Pieman's Junction, Milly Dakin, had given it to her. It was an Aztec design, Milly had said. She had taken it back afterward—after everything that happened.

Joelle folded it up and held it tightly inside her clenched fist. In the mirror, she saw herself, and she looked like her birth mother when she came home from stacking shelves at the supermarket, tired and mean. Quickly she flung the friendship band back onto the dressing table and rushed out of the room.

CHAPTER 7

Thursday, August 24

Cliff

Gatenby's Poultry Farm

He had an old foam mattress for those nights when he knew he wouldn't sleep. For a few hours before dawn, bored with trawling his usual internet sites, he lay the mattress on the floor of his office and rested his eyes.

It felt like he was on a treadmill. He could speed up or slow down, but he could not get off. He knew he was smart and strong-willed enough to handle any course he chose. And he would, just as soon as he got on top of his work and sorted out the free-range poultry farm deal.

The work never ended. The broilers had been trucked out ten days ago. The next batch of day-old chickens would arrive in two days' time. It was not enough time to clean properly. The shed floor was covered with litter and you could smell the stink of feces and urine from outside. Lack of sleep was making him sick. He sat up and put his head in his hands.

He had a reserve dose buried in the dirt beneath the boys' bedroom window. It took several attempts until his trowel tapped the glass jar. He tucked the stash into his pocket and went inside to the bathroom. The house was silent, everyone asleep. Afterward, he felt half-normal.

It was a surprise to see Kim sitting at the kitchen table when he came out, looking at old photos.

"You didn't answer your phone yesterday," she said.

"I was busy."

"I'm worried about you."

"You're like a dog with a bone, Kim."

Silence.

"Look at all this." He feigned enthusiasm at the memorabilia she was sorting. "This stuff is for the Apple thing?"

"The Apple Queen Tribute Evening on Saturday."

She laid each item out on the table. The front page of a brightly illustrated promotional brochure for the Apple Festival, 1956, depicted his house and the farm before the orchard was bulldozed. In the peak of an apple season the weatherboard farmhouse overlooked picture-book hills awash with pink- and peach-colored blossoms. The farm was so prosperous and picturesque he barely recognized it.

Now the same view was of sheds and mudded tracks, concrete silos and broken farm vehicles Cliff was yet to repair. The few remaining apple trees were codling moth–infested. The orchard floor was a rubbish dump containing broken white goods, busted mattresses, old bikes, the springs of a couch, and several flat tires.

Soon, he told Kim, he would obtain the free-range chicken rating. He could charge more for the eggs and birds, but also, he could sell the property for a solid price to an investor from the mainland. A farmer up north had done it and made a surprising profit.

"If my old man was alive, he would've been happy with that."

"Nothing made your father happy."

"You have to move with the times if you want to survive."

In the 1970s, when the original orcharding enterprise was subdivided, Cliff's father's lot included the original weatherboard farmhouse, a picker's hut, and the old apple-packing shed. Only a smattering of trees remained: Cox's Orange Pippin, French Crab, and Granny Smith. Sheds that were used to grade and pack crates for the steamer now stored tools and the tractor. Sometimes, as he rummaged through the drawers for a spare part or a tool, he fancied he could smell the apples' sweetness over the diesel fumes and dust.

It was not too late to change their lives. "Twenty grand, Kim. That's the total amount we need for the required upgrades. It's not a hell of a lot of money."

She didn't answer.

"What? Say whatever you're thinking."

She stared at her folded hands.

"Spit it out," he urged.

"How much are you spending? I have to ask you."

He gave her a look of disgust. Without the gear, he couldn't work or think or do anything. "Do you know how hard I'm working? No man can work eighteen-hour days without help."

He looked at the illustration of his house again. He did not need Kim to remind him about his failings. He was trying to improve their cash flow. Of any woman he knew, she deserved more from life than what she had ended up with. All the hard work he did, it was for her. He wanted her to have nice things, take a holiday, or treat the boys to a decent meal in town now and then.

"Come here," he said.

She walked over to him. He put his arms around her and kissed her cheek. "We'll get back there, Kimmy. If this farm gets the free-range go-ahead, everything is going to change."

* * *

Jack

Calendar House

Another unsealed letter arrived in the mail from his mother. She lived only a few hours away but she wrote to him regularly. Often the contents were dreary—questions about the whereabouts of obscure pieces of furniture, notes on the funerals of her elderly friends, instructional advice for his daughters. Once she had criticized his daughter Frannie's handwriting. Celia said the old lady should be simply grateful for receiving a birthday card from a grandchild. Jack agreed.

In the early days he and Celia read the letters together. They laughed at how eccentric and awful his mother could be. Celia said she felt sorry for Jack.

Troublingly, not long after his wedding, his mother had written to him listing the reasons why he had made a mistake in marrying Celia. At this point he stopped sharing the letters with his wife.

The top flap was tucked inside the throat of the envelope, an invitation for attention. His stomach cramped each time he saw his mother's pale blue stationery sitting on the little side table in the hallway. He always wondered if Celia secretly read any of the correspondence.

In the afternoon, while Celia was gardening, he telephoned his mother. He planned to tell her that she must stop putting troubling thoughts down on paper. Words failed him. Instead, he listened as his mother detailed the urgency of trimming the pine trees behind her house.

"We trimmed them last year," he reminded her.

"I don't think so, Jack." Her voice rose as it did whenever he disagreed with her. "They're a menace."

He took a breath. "I'm more worried about a different kind of menace," he began. "I received your letter. Thank you. However, I found the contents very unhelpful."

He spoke calmly and kindly. His mother was a good woman—she did not mean to be cruel. Outlined in this letter were updates to her will, based on an outlandish set of conditions. He feared she was losing her mind. There was a long pause when he finished speaking. He heard her sniff. Surely an apology was forthcoming.

But the line went dead.

He shoved the letter inside his desk, closing the drawer so hard his stationery rattled. He stood at the window, where he could see Celia's straw hat rising and falling as she weeded a flower bed. He had a memory of his mother working in the same garden, thirty-odd years ago. His mother and his wife had so much in common and their similarities gave him no comfort.

When he was eight years old his mother had walked him to the river. She demonstrated how to do freestyle, then tied a rope around Jack's waist and instructed him to jump off the jetty. When he refused, she had struck him with a willow branch.

Frightened of what she might do next, he jumped.

He had almost drowned.

The bracken-steeped smell of river water still made him gag. His father had been furious with his mother. It was the one time he could remember them arguing. His mother had wept and begged Jack's forgiveness—she had only been trying to help, she had explained. It was the way her father had taught her brothers to swim.

Years later it was Celia who had urged him to forgive his mother. She said people showed their love in different ways. Considering Celia had never gotten along well with his mother, he was impressed with her empathy. It was one of the things he loved about his wife. She was not perfect—she could be cruel—but she did not judge. Other women he knew would have enjoyed mocking Joelle Smithton and her dubious background. Not Celia.

During dinner his wife was quiet. She stared at the water pooling against the window. The heavy rain obscured the view of the river. He could see her reflection in the glass. Her throat quivered; she had been crying. Stricken, he kept eating and hoped the girls would not notice and make a big deal out of it.

He wanted to ask her if she had read his mother's letter or if it was the incident at the school fair that had upset her, but he knew that asking such a question would be a mistake.

He looked at his daughters—blond heads bent together, chitchatting like a nest of contented birds—and he hoped they married a better man than him.

Later, when the girls were asleep, and he had the fire blazing in the lounge room, Celia stood in the doorway to tell him that she was going to bed early to read her book.

"Is anything wrong?" he asked.

"Of course there is."

"What do you want me to do?" He didn't mean to sound so angry.

"Stick your head in the sand, Jack. What's new?"

He knew it was cowardly, but he couldn't bring himself to ask her what she meant. It was too late in the evening for arguments.

He was staring into the flames when she lunged at him. She seized him by his shoulders and shook him, shouting, "It's your fault. Take responsibility."

Stunned, he lay against the back of his chair, letting her shout until her voice turned hoarse and she fell away sobbing. "I won't let my daughters' lives be ruined by you."

"Darling," he said.

"No," she said, her eyes dark. "You want me to fix this, don't you?"

He nodded, feeling a rush of sickening relief. She would sort it out; he did not doubt her capacity to make things right.

* * *

Miss Gwen

Creek Cottage

She placed the hot water bottle in her bed and spread out an extra blanket, for the night was cold. She poured a cup of tea and sat in the kitchen as the last of the warmth faded from the heater. This was her nightly ritual, a quiet moment to reflect on the past few days and to think about what she was doing tomorrow.

She was worried for Joelle's daughter, Emily. Recently, the little girl had asked Miss Gwen what to do if someone was mean to her. Apparently, some girls were not letting her join in the games at lunchtime. One of them had offered her a dollar if she would go away. Miss Gwen had been relieved to learn that Emily had not taken the dollar.

"There will be someone else in your class who is looking for a friend," Miss Gwen had advised. "You need to find that person. It might even be a boy."

Emily looked doubtful. Even Miss Gwen was not sure this was good advice. Little girls could be so mean. Their tactics of exclusion and subtle rejection were hard for even a vigilant teacher to police.

Emily had said, "I'm not playing with a boy. They'll say I have a boyfriend. That's disgusting."

Later in their conversation, Emily had asked Miss Gwen if she ever had a boyfriend.

"Disgusting!" Miss Gwen said.

They both chuckled.

She finished her tea and rinsed the cup, setting it on the dish rack. She did have a boyfriend once. No one would remember. Her engagement to Alfred Cheng had ended scarcely after it had begun. There had been a few sweet kisses; at times it felt unbearable that that was all she would ever have.

When she realized the relationship was over, she escaped to Launceston and lived with an aunt, but homesickness for Vanishing Falls made her heartbreak more painful. She returned after a year of her self-imposed exile and took a job at the newly built nursing home. Caring for people was what she did well.

Many years later, she and Alfred resumed their Sunday strolls by the river. From her window she could see the back of his store. She waited until his bedroom light went off. When his house was in darkness, she too turned off her lights.

* * *

Joelle

The Smithtons' house

Joelle sat cross-legged on her bed, trying to choose a color to paint the rabbit hutch. She was looking through the brochure of paint shades that Brian had brought home from the hardware store, when she heard a car stop outside the house.

She waited to hear the doorbell ring. There was nothing.

Her mind raced. Her children were safely in their beds.

Snowcat was stretched out on her bed. Brian was doing his paperwork. What about the rabbits? They were out there, tiny velvet creatures in their hutch. She thought of the big boot print she had seen last week, when her washing blew off the line.

She ran into the kitchen. "I'm worried about the rabbits," she told Brian.

There was a gentle knock on the door. Brian got up straightaway and put his glass of beer in the fridge.

"It's late for a visitor," she said.

"It's okay."

To her relief it was only Nev, dropping off some tools he had borrowed from Brian.

"Oops-a-daisy, I'm in my pj's," she called to Nev. "Don't look!"

She was wearing a long, pink frilly nightdress and she ran and hid in the bedroom, giggling, until she heard his car leave.

CHAPTER 8

Friday, August 25

Joelle

Smithton's Fine Meats

B rian made two cups of Russian Caravan tea, using just the one teabag, for they liked their tea not too strong. Most days, once the shop was set up and before they put out the open sign, they sat in the kitchenette and talked.

It was her favorite time of the day for it was when Brian gave her his undivided attention. They talked about the children, and what they might do on the weekend. He repeated an anecdote he had been told by Alfred Cheng. Recently, in a restaurant in one of the coastal towns, a waiter taking Alfred's order had spoken excessively slowly, as though English was not Alfred's language. Alfred had quipped, in a true Aussie accent, "Bangers and mash, thanks, mate." Alfred said the embarrassed expression on the waiter's face was priceless.

Joelle laughed. "I can see why they thought he was Chinese," she said. "But that's still a funny story."

She asked Brian's opinion on a range of pies a salesman had approached them about stocking. They decided to order several to try at home first. Brian confided that he wanted to do more exercise if he was going to be taste-testing pies.

"That reminds me. I want to go hiking again," she said. "This time I want us to take the kids."

He nodded reluctantly. "They could do a two-hour walk."

"No, a nice long day walk. They could do any of the walks we've done, Brian."

"I love hiking with you, not that we've had time to hike lately," he said. "It's one of the reasons I fell in love with you. Remember the first hike we did? It was one of the best days of my life. But can you imagine taking Emily and Baxter? Someone will get sore feet. Someone won't like the sandwiches. I know I'll have to piggyback one of them home. Can't we just send them to my sister's, and you and I go by ourselves?"

"Brian," she urged. "Where's your sense of adventure? How about Wineglass Bay? There's only one hill."

"A big hill."

"Please."

He relented. "In early summer. After the rainy season. Before it gets too hot."

"Deal." She made him shake on it. "We can swim on the way."

They finished their tea and she stood up to wash the cups.

He said, "Darling."

"What's your problem?" Smiling, she searched his face for a clue.

"I think you forgot something. . . ."

She felt her chest. He was right and she giggled. "Don't worry. I'll put my apron on."

"Darling . . ."

"It digs in."

"Can we buy you a new one that fits better?"

"A sports bra. That's what I want."

"What sport are you playing?"

"Brian. It's activewear. This is what people wear when they go for coffee. And it looks like I'm going for coffee real soon. With the girls."

"All right."

She sighed. "I've had these since I was ten years old. Big boobs that people stared at. The mums at netball training used to tell me to put a sweater on, even in summer."

He had the helpless, stricken look that he always got when she told him anything about living with her mum and Trapper at Pieman's Junction. It was partly why she never liked to talk about it.

"Brian, I hope Emily doesn't get big boobs."

"Whatever happens, we will help her with it."

It was reassuring to hear him speak like that. He was such a big, handsome man, with his wide shoulders and dark ruffled hair. She reached across the table and touched the tip of his nose with her finger. "You treat us like treasure."

He nodded. "I love you."

She thought about how much she loved him. "I love you to the moon and back. And back again another loop too."

* * *

Not long after opening, two policemen came into the butchery and asked to speak to Brian. Joelle stood in the kitchenette and counted the daffodils growing in the garden next door.

She kept losing count and having to start again, so she had only reached seventeen when they left. There were hundreds of daffodils, probably.

She returned to the front of the butchery only when she heard Brian saying goodbye to the policemen. It turned out there was nothing for her to worry about; the hardware store had been broken into.

"Why do people think they can take what's not theirs?" Brian slapped his hands on his apron, making a horrible sound. She cringed.

"They tore the place apart trying to find cash. Absolute junkie scum. They didn't find any."

"We keep ours in the freezer."

He looked at her worriedly. "You wouldn't tell anyone that, would you?"

"I told everyone at the nursing home." She clapped her hands over her mouth to try to hide her laughter at tricking Brian. "I'm joking, Brian. Cross my heart and hope to die, I can keep a secret."

Later, she stood at the butchery window and watched the people of Vanishing Falls going about their business in the rain. Cars moved in and out of the parking spaces. It was a funny feeling to be glad that the police were here to investigate a robbery at the hardware store. She knew she should feel sorry for the hardware man and his wife but the strongest feeling she had was relief that the police were not here to talk to her. She knew that was mean of her.

A bunch of people got off the bus. Some elderly folk went into the café. A family of tourists stopped to read the historical plaques outside the hotel. You could tell they were tourists because of their clothes, which were new and not that warm-looking. Three times a police car drove past.

Joelle was arranging the parsley garnishes when the door chimes rang, and Celia Lily came in.

"Good morning," she called, with her lovely wide smile. "Did I see police in here earlier?"

"Yes."

She stopped smiling. She was upset about something; even Joelle could see that. Joelle watched her walk up and down, jabbing her finger at the meat as she ordered sausages, lamb cutlets, quail, brisket, and sirloin.

"Are you going to pack them for me?" she said.

Joelle hurried. Panic flooded through her and she had to ask Celia to repeat the order, slowly this time. She weighed each item, wrapped it in butcher's paper, and stuck on the sticker.

"I'm not happy, Joelle. I thought we had an understanding," Celia said. "But now you're talking to the police. I feel rattled."

Joelle blinked. Adrenaline, bitter and sickly, coursed through her body, like when she was a child and an adult told her to do something and she knew she could not refuse. It was impossible to look away from Celia's eyes—it was like seeing a snake on a walking track.

"They talked to Brian. . . . I didn't talk to them," Joelle said.

"They were in here for a while. I was in the café, watching."

"They were talking to Brian about the hardware shop break-in."

"For a crazy moment, I thought you might be telling them about what you saw at the fair."

"No."

Celia smiled and Joelle felt instant relief. Then she said, "I always meant to ask you. Where did you live before you moved here?"

Joelle's skin felt blisteringly hot. A tremor rushed through her body. She patted her cheeks.

"Launceston."

"Before that?"

Joelle pushed the meat across the counter toward Celia. She didn't take it.

"Who is Joanne Sparrow?" Celia said.

"Never heard of that name in my entire life." The words sounded wooden and rehearsed, even though that was the first time Joelle had said that sentence.

The thing was, Celia did not have to worry about Joelle keeping her mouth shut. If anyone knew how to keep their mouth shut it was Joelle. She could barely breathe and there was a pain in her chest.

"I didn't . . ." Joelle began.

Celia held one hand up, demanding silence. "It's okay. Only I know about it. As long as everyone minds their own business, no one needs to worry."

"I will," Joelle said desperately. "I promise I will. Cross my heart."

Celia handed her a credit card. Joelle rang up the order and processed the credit card payment. It was more than three hundred dollars. Celia shook her head when Joelle held out the receipt.

"I trust you," she called as she walked out.

* * *

In the bathroom, Joelle felt like vomiting. Her underpants were damp and she realized she had wet her pants a little bit. To make it worse, Brian knocked on the door and asked if she was okay.

"Go away."

She ran the tap and held on to the basin. It wasn't often she let herself cry.

She had cried every day when the twins were babies. Missing all that sleep doing double feeds had made her crazy. Someone told her about postnatal depression, but it wasn't like that. She didn't worry that she would hurt her babies or hurt herself. What worried her sick was that someone was going to take them away from her—that they would be sent to a foster home, and not a good one like Darla's, but one of the bad ones where they took in more kids than they could handle.

In the twelve years she had lived in Vanishing Falls, no one had mentioned Pieman's Junction to her. Even Brian did not know why she left that place. One night, Joelle was watching television by herself—the kids were in bed, Brian was at one of his local business meetings—and a program had come on about the Pieman's Junction Murder. They showed photos of the woman who died, Wendy Field. They interviewed Wendy's family, the pub owner, a teacher, even Bev from the purple house who sat on her porch all day in summer, yelling at kids for riling up her sausage dog. Wendy's sister said she would never forgive the four people in the car for what they did. She said that any of them, at any time, could have chosen to save Wendy. She cried the way her sister cried, with breathless gulps, like she couldn't get enough air.

In the car that night the crying had made Joelle angry. These were only teenage boys. It was like Wendy had never had to put up with blokes pawing her, ripping at her clothes like they didn't care if the buttons broke off.

The presenter said the three men were unemployed drifters who had come to town to do concreting work. Bev said they were pure evil. She said Joanne Sparrow was "the little girl who got picked on. Some of the school kids pushed her onto the train track once." Joelle had not known that Bev knew about the flying stones and sticks flicking dog shit. Bev added, "There was nothing Joanne could have done to help Wendy. That girl is lucky to be alive herself. Those blokes only let her go because they thought she wouldn't talk about it." Joelle did not know if that was true. The only thing she knew for sure was that her mother and Trapper agreed with Wendy's sister.

She splashed cold water on her face. She would try not to cry any more. Like Darla said, there was no point feeling sorry for yourself.

* * *

The Smithtons' house

The horrible feeling that something terrible was about to happen lasted all day while she did some deliveries, and into the evening when she tidied up her sewing room. It had stopped raining. The sound of the ball bouncing to and fro on the driveway told her that Emily and Baxter were okay, they were right there, smacking the handball to each other. Still, she went outside and checked on them. Brian was right; they were lucky children. They would never have to worry about horrible stuff. That was how it should be for all kids. She washed the lunch boxes and prepared the dinner and did some laundry and the whole time she could not stop thinking about Celia.

Later that night, she lay on her bed and stared at the ceiling. It was worse when she closed her eyes. The edge of her sunflower sweater was fraying. Her fingers kept plucking at the loose woolen thread. Brian came back from kissing the kids good night. The bed sank as he sat beside her. He brushed her hair back from her face.

"I need to know what this is all about."

Joelle blurted, "At the fair, I saw something really bad. Now everyone hates me."

She described the glass pipe with the smoke coming out of it and the plastic bag holding the white crystals.

"They told me to fuck off. In a real nasty voice. You know, like 'Fuck off.'" She tried to mimic Cliff's harsh tone. She said it a couple of times, trying to get the sound right.

Brian became very still. "Is that what Celia was talking to you about at work?"

She nodded.

"Cliff Gatenby is a thug. The Lilys are bullies," he said.

He stood up and swore. He never lost his temper. The one time she could remember Brian being truly furious was when he first heard the Lilys were changing the name of the creek.

One of the customers had told him that Murdering Creek would soon be called Hollybank Creek, and the same with Murdering Creek Road. Brian had shouted about how the creek should be called by its indigenous name if anyone could find out what that was. Then he had apologized to the customer for raising his voice.

Joelle stared at Brian.

"You're all puffed up like the cat gets when he sees something scary. You've gone red." It made her laugh and she pointed at him. "Brian's cross!"

"We're calling the police, Joey."

Horrified, she shook her head. "Don't do that."

"That's the only thing to do. I knew something was up, but I had no idea. Alfred said something was going on."

"No." She raised her voice; he wasn't listening. "Brian, you know about farming, meat, cricket, and the school stuff, but there are things you don't get. I'm thinking of your brother. . . ."

"Scott gets no sympathy from me either."

"There's nothing worse than a narc. You don't get it because you were raised proper. They won't let someone like me drag them down."

"The pair of them think they can do whatever they like. What else did that woman say to you?"

Joelle pressed her lips together. She would never tell him about Joanne Sparrow. He knew she had a mother who had given her up to foster care, but when she said she didn't want to talk about her, he had accepted that decision with a wise nod. He really loved listening to her talk about Darla. She liked it here in Vanishing Falls. People were happier in this farming district than the ones she remembered whose lives revolved around the digging up of iron ore and piping it as slurry to the port.

Everyone in Vanishing liked her too. Good things had always happened to her here. When she brought the twins home from the hospital, baby presents and home-cooked meals were delivered for months on end. A few weeks ago, the cricket club held a fund-raiser in the town hall and Joelle won first prize in the raffle, which was a meat tray donated by Smithton's Fine Meats. Of course, she donated it back. The next day, the people who were at the function chipped in and organized for flowers to be delivered to the butchery.

If Brian found out the truth, it would break his heart, and that was almost as bad as thinking about her children being taken away.

He steered her hands away from her damaged sweater. He tried to tuck the loose wool back together. It was hopeless. His big fingers only made it worse.

CHAPTER 9

Saturday, August 26

Jack

Mile Road Inn

Nicola DeIonno was a private art appraiser and restorer who had worked for Sotheby's. Her studio was in the township of Deloraine, an hour from the Vanishing Falls range. He liked her immediately. She had a motherly smile and a strong handshake. There was something familiar about her, he thought, as she led him inside.

Her studio was like an old apothecary shop. High shelves held hundreds of glass jars and bottles, brushes and tools, canvas rolls. A ladder stood by to reach them. A wall was covered with paintings, including several dot paintings and some amateurish contemporary pieces.

Under a bright light, Nicola examined Jack's painting with a magnifying glass. She took several books from her shelf and compared illustrations. The whole time, she made copious notes in small, neat handwriting. Her credentials were impressive—she had studied art history in Paris and had a degree from a New York university. Her opinion mattered to him and he waited impatiently.

Finally, she took off her white gloves. "How did you come across this?"

"Deceased estate on the mainland. I bought a crateful of paintings and this was one."

"Paper trail?"

"Nothing, I'm afraid."

"That might not matter." She exhaled. "This is . . . possibly . . . miraculous."

He waited. It was important to hear her say it.

"I am convinced that we are in the company of an original John Glover. Most likely this is one of his lost paintings that were sent to the 1835 London exhibition. Only a few of them have turned up, and most historians understand that the bulk of the shipment was lost at sea," she said, repeating the theory he and his mother had discussed. "Don't be deceived by how dirty it is. It's superficial grime. There are ways to clean it delicately."

"What kind of value would you place on it?"

She whistled. "Let's see how it cleans up. When are you coming back?"

"I intended to watch the cleaning process."

"I'll be here for five or six hours."

"I know."

She wiped the surface and they discussed simply giving it a new varnish. He suspected, though, that if they could remove the old yellow-tinged varnish, the result would be beautiful.

He directed her to take a small sample and test the solvent.

She nodded. "If that doesn't work, we'll have to chip the old varnish off. It's time consuming."

"It's important that we do it properly."

She dabbed the solvent onto the edge. He watched closely; he was right. The removal of the old varnish allowed the dark colors to saturate, and once the new varnish was applied, the transformation was startling.

Several hours later Nicola's work was complete. Jack was transported. It gleamed. The colors—olive greens, misty grays, ochers, and intense blues—were striking, as though a light shone from behind the painting. They viewed it in silence.

After a while, she said, "The noble savage."

"Yes," Jack said thoughtfully. "But Glover was sympathetic to their plight. He knew what their fate would be. He presents the Aboriginal people very respectfully."

"I don't know. They come across, to me, more strongly as curiosities."

He nodded, considering this. "To be fair, he does make mistakes," he said.

"It's not just that the shields and boomerangs weren't used by Tasmanian Aboriginal people. Rather, the expressions on the faces of the indigenous people during corroboree annoy me." She smiled ruefully. "Anyway. What do you think it's worth?"

"You're the expert."

She gave him a shrewd look. "A collector in London paid around three million for a John Glover a few years ago. That too was one of the few 1835 exhibition paintings that have been recovered."

"What was the painting called?" he asked.

She opened her laptop and did a search. "It was called *Ben Lomond from Mr. Talbot's Property—Four Men Catching Opossums.*" With a tape measure, she checked the dimensions of the painting and wrote down 2 feet 6 inches by 3 feet 9 inches. "This canvas you've found is Glover's standard Tasmanian size. The subject of the fugitive Aboriginal people is like the paintings he completed at his Patterdale property in the 1830s. The artist mixed the oil with copal varnish to increase the translucency, particularly effective with the bright double-primed background. . . . This is all technical stuff. It bears scrutiny, is what I'm saying."

Jack nodded; she was confirming what he already knew.

"What will you do for insurance?" she asked. "Fire and water damage are one thing. You can cover yourself for the cost of restoration."

"I've never insured anything against theft," he said.

"It's complex, isn't it? I don't think it's worth insuring artworks worth less than five hundred thousand for theft. If a painting is worth five million, of course you would insure it. If it is stolen, you use the insurance money to hire a private investigator to find it."

"I know."

"Keep it safe until you decide what to do. You must have a good alarm system; you live in the Calendar House, don't you?"

He didn't want her to know where he lived. "Why would you think that?"

"I recognized your name. My brother lives out that way."

He could have asked who her brother was, but he was not in the mood for a diverting conversation about mutual acquaintances. Now that she had confirmed what he suspected, he wanted to leave.

With the painting wrapped in a muslin sheet and stored in his car, he drove home, resolving to make sure his security alarm worked. He had installed the system years ago, when his art collection had begun to be discussed in art journals and blogs. It used to go off accidentally, if the dog was left inside or an open window caused the drapes to sway. It had not gone off, accidentally or otherwise, for at least a year.

Visibility was poor as he descended into the valley. The ditches were overflowing, and several times the Jag lost traction. A wallaby bounded out from the thicket that divided the wooded part of his estate from the Vanishing Falls state forest. For a split second, he thought about hitting it. Instead, he swerved.

The car slid across the long grass on the side of the road, smashing through the bracken and ferns growing on the bank of Murdering Creek. Jack thought the car would roll, in which case he would be dead. Finally, the Jag fishtailed back onto the road.

God damn, he was lucky no vehicle was traveling in the other direction.

He reached home and felt himself swaying as he entered the kitchen. He dropped his keys onto the kitchen table. Celia was talking on the phone. She took one look at him and ended the call.

As she embraced him, he realized how rattled he was.

"Sit down," she said. "What happened?"

He didn't move, just closed his eyes as she hugged him, and

pressed his face into her fragrant hair. Lately, he felt like happiness was always just out of reach.

"I lost control of the Jag. I nearly ended up in Murdering Creek. I mean, Hollybank Creek," he said. "It took me two years to organize that name change and I'm still thinking of it as Murdering Creek."

"Don't let Brian Smithton hear you say that." She laughed. "It goes to show, even you can't rewrite history, Jack."

He grinned, feeling his customary confidence return. "It's my land. I'll do what I like."

She placed a bowl of potato-and-leek soup in front of him. Gently, she brushed her hand across his cheek.

"I like it when you're nice to me," he said.

Her smile faded. "It's not over. If Joelle is blathering to me about it, like she did when I was in the butchery on Monday, who knows who else she has told?"

"I don't know."

Celia placed the salt and pepper shakers in front of him. "Is there anything, anything at all, you want to tell me?"

"You know everything about me."

He ate the soup, wondering what she was getting at. The people at Marsh End were discreet. However, it was a small town and most people knew each other. He wondered if anyone had noticed the frequency of his visits to the isolated farmhouse.

Celia picked up her spoon and began to eat. Her beautiful face revealed nothing—no accusation or sign of betrayal. A feeling of déjà vu made him think of the first time he was invited to Celia's family home for dinner. He was twenty-four

and had just joined a Launceston law firm after traveling over-
seas. Celia's mother, Martha, had questioned him about his
travel, demanding to know his favorite destination. Wanting
to impress her, he claimed it was Fès, an ancient city in Mo-
rocco. He had spent two days in Fès, mainly drinking beer at
a backpacker hostel. When she wanted to know why he was
drawn to Fès, he could not think of any reason except to say it
was beautiful. "Oh," she said; his answer had underwhelmed
her. Then, like now, he felt inadequate.

An hour later, in the living room, he had the fire crackling
and a bottle of red wine airing on the blackwood star-topped
table. She burst in wearing a pink silk dress and carrying one
of his mother's fur coats. Her hair was pinned on top of her
head and held in place with a diamond pin.

He groaned. He had forgotten about the Apple Queen event.

"Would anyone notice if I don't go?"

"I know why you don't want to go," she said. "You're worried people will be talking about what you and Cliff did in the
bathroom at the fair."

"I am worried. Of course I am. But that's not why I don't
want to go to another dreary function."

"I don't believe you. And I wish you would man up." She
tightened her diamond earring and glanced at the clock. "We
have time for a drink. I need to talk to you about something
else."

He fired the bellows and swept up some stray ash while she
poured herself a glass of red. She dragged a chair closer to the
couch and sat so they were facing each other.

"I'm not going to beat around the bush. We need to turn

Cliff in to the police," she said. "Reporting on someone is sometimes the best thing you can do for their family."

The fire cast a rosy light on her cheeks and hair as she described a *60 Minutes* program she had seen on people whose lives were ruined by their meth addiction. It was graphic, showing the white crystals of methamphetamine, known on the street as ice, that users smoked through a pipe. These were people who tried it once and then could not quit. Their skin was ruined, their teeth fell out, they betrayed family and friends and had criminal convictions from stealing sprees to fund their addiction. One man had almost beaten his own mother to death.

He interrupted. "They shoot up, darling. Cliff smokes it."

"These people were smoking it. I'm worried about Kim and the boys. I don't know half of what goes on in that house, but it's a matter of time until he hurts someone."

"Maybe he won't." Jack stared into the fire. Her suggestion was not simple. The consequences would be catastrophic. "Try talking to Kim first."

"I can't talk to Kim about it; she stonewalls me if I try. She's naive or in denial."

He nodded. "She wants to believe Cliff's problem is that he's working too hard."

"I've lost count of the times I've seen him parked up at the falls car park. He's not there for the fresh air."

"Darling, reporting him to the police won't resolve the situation."

"I don't trust Cliff or Joelle Smithton. Brian Smithton was so angry with you for changing the name of the creek, why wouldn't he use this opportunity to cause trouble for you? If he tells the police that people are doing drugs on the school grounds, and you are implicated, you will lose your license to practice law. There's a lot at stake, Jack." She eyed him darkly and he looked at the floor, at her bare toes, so white against the pink floral flat-weave Aubusson-style rug.

"Throw Cliff under the bus to save myself?" He searched her face for reassurance. "I can't."

"You'd smoke methamphetamine in the school toilets, but you wouldn't alert authorities that a woman and her children are at risk?"

He felt like a helpless boy. It was ironic that her haughtiness—one of the things that had initially attracted him to her—had become a weapon with which he found himself frequently attacked.

"I'm sorry I did that. I promise you I'll never do it again."

"It's a gutter drug."

He nodded. "Reporting on Cliff will backfire, Celia. Cliff is not a meek little lamb. He'll take me down with him."

"Listen to me, Jack. Cliff is going to take you down anyway. People know what he's doing. They don't like it. It will be interesting how loyal he'll be to you when he's in the hot seat. We have no choice."

"I know you didn't mean to," he began softly, for she did not cope well with being criticized, "but while we're on the subject, I do wish you hadn't shown Cliff the painting. He's got a chip on his shoulder about money. I try to keep these things private from him."

"I didn't do it on purpose."

He shifted under the fire's heat and drew a shallow breath. "You took him into my study."

"I was escorting him to the bathroom."

"He won't see it like that."

He was trying to lighten the conversation. In the past, they had joked about how Cliff might have a boyish crush on Celia.

She stood up and glared. "Don't you ever say that."

He rose and tried to take her hand. She pushed him in the chest. He staggered backward. Wine spilled from his glass onto the antique carpet.

"The rug!" he cried.

"I'll get it dry-cleaned. I'm good at cleaning up the messes you make." She picked up her coat. "Maybe I should report you both. I know you gave him money. You're no better than him."

"Why is everything always my fault!"

"Bring out the violins for Jack."

She rushed out of the room, yanking the door so it closed with a loud bang. He followed her.

"Don't slam the door," he shouted down the hallway. "I've had enough of you telling me what to do. You treat me like I'm . . . your servant."

It was an observation his mother had once made about Celia and he was surprised to hear himself repeating her words.

"If you were my servant, I'd sack you."

Her heels clicked across the floorboards. For a moment he thought she would come back and apologize. He looked out the window and saw the lights of her taxi retreating into the rain.

In the next room, he heard the babysitter tell the girls to sit down in front of the television. Mortified, for they seldom argued so bitterly, and never had they had such a heated exchange in earshot of another person, Jack grabbed his car keys and left.

CHAPTER 10

Saturday, August 26

Joelle

Smithton's Fine Meats

S he heard their laughter as she emptied the mop bucket into the flushing gutter in the alley beside the butchery. Across the street, on the upstairs veranda of the Vanishing Falls Hotel, Celia Lily and Cliff Gatenby were sharing a cigarette. Celia wore a fur coat and Cliff was in a dinner jacket. Standing by the ornate wooden balustrade, they looked old-world, a couple from a bygone era. Joelle could not take her eyes off them.

There were posters up all over town advertising the function they were attending: *"A Tribute Dinner to the Vanishing Falls Apple Queens of the 1950s."* Miss Gwen was making a speech about her memories of being an Apple Queen. She had traveled to Coffs Harbour and Brisbane, with a chaperone, to visit the pineapple and banana plantations and talk about Tasmanian apples.

"I already know all your stories by heart," Joelle had said when Miss Gwen invited her to come.

In truth, she would have happily listened to those stories all over again. But big events, crowded rooms, and making small talk in all that noise—these were the things that made her unravel like a ball of wool and get twisted up as though the cat had been playing with it. Luckily, she and Miss Gwen agreed they both had more fun when it was just the two of them.

Celia dropped their cigarette over the railing. The burning ember fell slowly to the ground like snow.

The mop bucket slipped from Joelle's fingers. It clanged down the wooden steps and rolled loudly into the concrete alley. She glanced back up at the couple on the veranda. They were watching her.

Celia wiggled a finger at Joelle. Through the rain, she could not tell if it was a wave or if Celia was pointing at her. Just in case, she gave a little wave back, but Celia did not smile. Cliff held open the door to the pub and music and chatter filled the night. And then they were gone.

Alone in the store, she rushed through her final tasks. The butchery was not a friendly place at night. The knives and hooks gleamed, and the steel counters distorted the light. Grating and scratching sounds came from the alleyway. Brian called this time of evening the gloaming. He said it like it was a good thing but in Joelle's mind the gloaming sounded like a world of shadows, where evil goblins and bad men lurked.

She thought of Brian's repeated safety warnings. It was easy to stay on the track in the forest or wear a leather apron and steel-cap boots in the butchery.

It was people who scared her. It was people who did bad things. Everyone thought something bad would never happen to them. They were wrong. Bad things could happen to anyone.

* * *

Cliff

Vanishing Falls Hotel

T hat's as cold as a witch's tit," Cliff said as they stepped back inside the pub.

Celia ignored him, which made him grin. She didn't like crass language. Over near the memorabilia table, Kim stood with a group of former Apple Queens. They were animated, talking and laughing and showing each other various souvenirs on the table. They mostly wore color, blue silky scarves and billowing rainbow tunics. Kim, in her old black woolen dress, looked so plain. She deserved a nice dress, and decent shoes and some earrings too.

A waiter offered them a tray of drinks and he took a beer for himself and a glass of champagne for Celia.

"Kim never takes her eyes off you," Celia said. "You've got a good woman there."

He didn't need to look at Kim to know he was in her line of vision. It didn't matter where they were—a mate's backyard barbecue or a crowded room like this—she was always aware of him. Even if she was in the middle of conversation, with her timid, gentle watching she was like a sparrow keeping an eye on a mountain eagle: part admiring, part nervous. A different woman would not stand for the way Celia Lily was shimmying around him tonight, but Kim knew he was trustworthy.

"We're all a bit worried about you," Celia continued. "Specifically your health."

"Don't go there." He used the blunt tone with which he spoke to hired hands on the farm, lazy no-hopers who he paid to catch the broilers and load them in transport crates. They often cost him more than they helped him. "Where did you say Jack was?"

"Out of town."

He leaned on the windowsill, wondering if Jack was avoiding him. Down on the main street, the butchery was the only shop with its lights on.

"That's who you should be worried about. Big mouth down there."

"I'm not worried at all." Celia raised an eyebrow. "Why would I be?"

He chuckled. "She knew what Jack was doing. It was clear as daylight. And she's not going away."

She regarded him with her green eyes. "I know how we can encourage her to keep the secret. She has her own secrets."

"The Pieman's Junction Murder? You told me to leave it alone."

She took a breath and exhaled. "I won't let anyone compromise my family, Cliff."

He waited. He wouldn't give her the satisfaction of hearing him ask about Pieman's Junction again.

"I was in the last week of year twelve," she said. "I was living in the school boardinghouse, studying for exams, and it was all anyone would talk about."

He drank some beer. It had been sitting too long in the jug and it was going flat. "Go on."

"A young barmaid was abducted by three men. They drove her up to one of the miners' huts in the mountains. Joelle was with them. She's changed her name now. She used to be known as Joanne Sparrow. She was fourteen and she was dating one of the men. The stuff that came up in the court case was appalling."

He'd driven through the Pieman's Junction district a few times. There was nothing up there except scattered boom-and-bust mining towns with their abandoned huts, rusting machinery, and untended graveyards. The iron ore mine at Pieman's Junction was the only one still operating.

"Nothing surprises me about people from the northwest corner," he said.

Celia smiled. "They might say the same about the people from this valley."

He laughed. "Nothing wrong with us."

"Anyway. The victim's family and the locals wanted Joelle prosecuted for the abduction, along with the men. They say she could have stopped it. It was the kind of lynch mob behavior you see when nice people learn they have a convicted pedophile living next door. Joelle's family received death threats."

"So that's why she changed her name. There's nothing on the internet about her." He was irritated that Joelle Smithton had stayed one step ahead of him. A tiny thought occurred to him—Joelle was fourteen at the time, the same age as his eldest son, Chris. "She was only a kid."

"I've always felt sorry for her too. She's so eager to be everyone's friend. I can only imagine how easy it would have been for those rotten men to coerce her into accompanying them."

"Imagine if your daughter was the barmaid. You wouldn't feel sorry for anyone."

"The point is that Joelle is very happy maintaining a low profile. Do I need to break it down further?" Celia took off her fur coat and swung it over her arm. She leaned toward him and the fluffy fur encased his free hand. It gave him a pleasant shiver.

He didn't pull his hand back. He stepped forward, so they were almost touching. He expected her to be skittish at their proximity. She held her ground.

"I'm fairly confident her husband doesn't know about it. And I think Joelle wants to keep it that way."

She stalked away before he could reply.

* * *

From the hotel hallway, he watched the door of the gentlemen's bathroom. When he was certain it was empty, he excused himself and crossed the room. There was only one cubicle and the toilet had the old-fashioned pull-rope flush system. He didn't have his leather toiletry bag that held his accessories, so he had to snort it. He took the tiniest bit. It burned, like taking a shot of bourbon through his sinuses. It slid from the back of his nose down his throat, warming him with a delicious tingle that made him feel like he could dance over water or play a Beethoven concerto loudly on the church organ. The idea made him laugh out loud.

* * *

He enjoyed the rest of the function. The speeches were colorful, and he liked hearing old Gwendolyn Lancaster talk about her time as Apple Queen. He sat in a comfortable chair, drinking beer and adding interesting comments for Kim's benefit. She shushed him a few times half-heartedly. He had loosened his tie—a strip of green silk that Kim had given him for Christmas years ago—and she leaned over and tightened it for him.

"Behave," she said.

"You love it."

Near the front, Celia shifted in her chair. Pink fabric stretched tautly across the round haunch of her backside. He had overheard Celia and Kim talking about sex last summer. They were drinking champagne in his kitchen and Celia's buttery voice had drifted through the open window and across the yard to where he was putting fuel into the lawn mower. Celia had said, "Sometimes it's just easier to give Jack a blow job, especially when he's tired from work."

Those words had tortured Cliff for a long time. The generosity of the gesture . . . and how Jack would have to hold all that hair out of the way.

After the function he offered to pack up the chairs, and then he helped Kim carry the memorabilia out to the car. She told him that Celia had drunk too much and so Kim had offered her a lift home. Celia was already sitting in the front seat, her fur coat plumped up around her like a lion's mane. Kim climbed into the back without complaining. Cliff turned on the heater and the music, then took off his tie and tossed it over the back to Kim.

"Hurry up, I'm freezing," Celia said.

He didn't know how Jack put up with being told what to do.

The back route to the Lilys' was via an unsealed farm road. It took a few minutes longer but there would be no random police checks. He prompted Celia to talk about the new painting.

"It's a John Glover. A famous colonial artist." Her words ran together. "It's worth a million or something stupid. I said I don't want it in the house. He has no paperwork for it, so anyone could steal it."

"How would a thief sell it if it has no paperwork?" Kim asked.

Celia twisted around to face her. "The art-collecting world has a sordid underbelly. Ugh! Sitting backward makes me feel sick."

"Don't throw up in the car," Cliff said.

The Calendar House rose up before them. Tall white pillars and a Georgian facade, illuminated by spotlights hidden on the wide, green lawn. Celia blew Cliff and Kim a kiss as she staggered up her front steps.

"She's going to have a headache tomorrow," Kim said. She sighed. "That painting would solve all our problems."

They sat in the car looking at each other. The rain drummed the roof. A vehicle came up the driveway.

"That will be the babysitter's parents," Kim said. "Let's go."

* * *

Gatenby Poultry Farm

When they got home, he didn't waste any time. He slid one hand inside her underpants and felt her smooth warmth. She was hairless, how he liked her. She kept herself that way for him.

"I'm tired." She tried to move away. "Exhausted."

"Don't be like that."

He could sense her relenting, and he pushed her back onto the couch. Eventually she told him she needed to get a drink of water. He shrugged. When he first started getting high, the sex had been excellent with Kim. Lately it was like trying to scratch an itch and not quite reaching it. It was a lot of effort for not much payoff. He preferred to sit in his office watching porn.

She switched on the kettle and put a tea bag in a cup. He watched her add water to the milk carton so there would be enough in there for the kids' breakfast cereal in the morning. She closed the fridge door, lifting it to accommodate the warped hinge.

"I wonder where Jack was," he said.

He told Kim how flirtatious Celia had been on the veranda, begging him for a puff on his cigarette, touching him with those bejeweled hands.

"She's inappropriate. If my wife carried on like that, there's no telling what I'd do."

"I know."

"Celia told me an interesting story about the butcher's wife." He cracked his knuckles, eyeing Kim. "She changed her name, created an entire new life for herself," he said. "I would not have known about her connection to the Pieman's Junction Murder until Celia started talking about it. I didn't even know that's where she came from."

Kim shrugged. She looked tired. He decided he was bored of the conversation. His high was plateauing. He still had a few hours before he would be ready to lie down. There was plenty to do. The internet. Xbox. Other stuff. "I've got to do some work."

"You live in the office."

"It doesn't end, Kim. We've got endless bills. What are you doing about them?"

He grabbed his coat and went out into the rain.

* * *

Jack

Vanishing Falls farming district

After the argument with Celia about Cliff's addiction, he drove around the valley aimlessly. The rain turned to hail and wet fog collapsed across the lower pastures. It was like sailing with only the instruments—he could see the road in front and not much more. Occasional landmarks peeped through the mist. The empty meatworks factory was lit up with security lights that showed new graffiti sprayed on the concrete wall blaming the government for killing jobs. In the high pastures dilapidated farmhouses sank in their paddocks like marooned and scuttled boats.

Fleetingly, he thought of driving over to the Fotheringhams' or the Wheelers'. They were good friends; he could easily pop in unannounced to say hello. But the mere thought of sitting by either of their fires, drinking red wine, and holding another predictable conversation about the people they knew made him feel exhausted.

They would wonder why he was not attending the Apple Queen Tribute Evening. He considered going to the function. It would make Celia happy. But wasn't that what he always did, kept other people happy? His mother, his wife, his clients—he was always the one who acquiesced.

His chest felt hot where Celia had shoved him. He forgave her. The reality was, she could do anything she liked, and he would never complain.

He took the Cutting and ended up in an old stagecoach pub in the next district. He ordered a chicken parmigiana and a beer. It was busy, mainly with farm laborers playing darts and pool and watching football. A plain-faced girl, no more than eighteen, wearing a bra and lace underpants, tried to sell him raffle tickets for a meat tray. Pink sausages, a bundle of graying mince, and two dry T-bone steaks. He declined. The girl pushed through the crowd with the meat tray balanced on one hand above her head. He thought of his own four girls and felt pathetic for being in a pub like this.

On the way home he saw the gravel road marked by the familiar wooden sign and he did not think twice. In the rutted yard that served as a turning circle, he parked between a broken tractor and a monstrously overgrown blackberry bush. Dogs barked and tugged on their chains. The farmhouse door opened, and he hurried toward the dim light.

CHAPTER 11

Late Saturday evening, August 26

Jack

Marsh End

Three cats slept on folded washing on a sofa. Another small black cat sat on a pile of newspaper beside the toaster. Jack was not allergic, but standing here made his skin itch.

Keegan's wife sipped Coca-Cola through a straw.

"He's not home yet," she said.

Jack did not offer to leave.

"You can sit there till he gets here." She yanked a chair out for him. "I'll fix you a drink."

She took a glass off the drying rack and opened the fridge. He couldn't see what was inside. Presumably it was cask wine, for soon enough she plonked the glass in front of him. He took a small sip. It was sickeningly sweet.

A postcard was stuck to the fridge. It showed Niagara Falls. With a jolt, he remembered his painting, still in his car. All day he had been driving around with a million dollars' worth of artwork. He needed to get it home.

An engine hummed outside.

"That's Keegan now," she said, and left the room.

Jack wiped his clammy hands on his jeans.

Keegan greeted Jack with his usual friendliness. He looked at the glass and smiled. If they knew each other differently, Keegan might have made a joke about Jack drinking cask wine. Instead he led Jack down the narrow hallway. All the doors were closed except the last one. In the bedroom, the wife—Jack never uttered her name—was sitting on the bed. She had unbuttoned her dressing gown; he did not need her to take it all the way off.

She was fatter than any woman he had known. Her huge breasts were more than he could hold. He was not rough with her, but neither was he gentle, and she seemed to like it for she slavered and sighed and touched him back in her awkward way.

The husband watched, standing in a dark corner by the wardrobe. Jack closed his eyes, feeling himself sinking in her softness, like falling into a deep warm sea. He forgot about his wife at home and his work, and concentrated on the delicious rhythms coursing through him, this foul pleasure.

The husband shuffled to the edge of the bed almost shyly. Jack instructed the woman to turn over. She heaved herself onto her stomach, and he splayed open her legs, parting her copse of pubic hair, and shoved himself back in, this time roughly, for it would soon be over, and he could no longer contain himself. Across from him, the husband delicately smoothed his wife's hair back from her face. She heaved herself onto one forearm and opened her mouth.

Afterward, Jack went into the bathroom and washed his

hands. The bin was full, the basin stained with toothpaste and mold. There were broken tiles on the bathroom floor and the plastic shower curtain was moldy. He scooped handfuls of water from the running faucet and splashed his face and neck.

He glanced around the bedroom as he went out. He suspected Keegan did not sleep in the room with her. There was no sign of a man's presence—no clothes, shoes, or toiletries. The dressing table was a clutter of nail scissors, a hairbrush exploding with hair like a small electrocuted animal, a tub of Sorbolene cream, a pink scrunchie and burred hair ties, and several tatty magazines.

In the kitchen the man had set out a plate of fruit cake and a teacup for himself, a glass for her soft drink. It was their ritual, Jack supposed. She had wrapped herself back in the fluffy orange dressing gown and she had even tied a pink ribbon in her hair. He could scarcely stand to think of them sitting there after he left, eating cake. He counted out the money and dropped it on the table.

"The rain has stopped," Keegan said.

Jack nodded. "At last. I feel like it hasn't stopped raining for months."

"That's because it hasn't," she said. "That's why Vanishing Falls is the rainfall capital of Tasmania."

That was not strictly true—there were other places that received more rain—but Jack did not want to correct her. Inexplicably, Keegan started talking about greyhound racing. Jack had once had a client who was in the industry, so he knew enough to make small talk. The woman paused in flicking channels on the television and listened, turning her face from one to the other as they spoke. He felt a rush of sorrow for them, with their awful lives.

"I wonder, would you like to see something interesting?" Jack said.

The evening was cold and clear. As he carried the painting from the car to the kitchen, he thought how the valley became incredibly pleasant whenever the rain stopped.

There was no clean surface on which to rest the framed canvas, so he dragged a chair out from the table and propped the painting on it. In layman's language, he listed the noteworthy aspects of the painting: the technique, the colors, the scene. Finally he asked their opinion, for he wanted to give the impression that he regarded them as equals. The truth was, he didn't give a fig what a man like Keegan, or his wife, thought about art.

"Is that one of them ones you took from the back of the wrecked car?" Keegan said.

"It is. It's a common piece, not worth much. There were many people painting like this in the 1800s," he lied. "It's interesting to me given my family's long connection with the area."

He had discovered the painting on a recent afternoon visit. Keegan had asked Jack to identify an unusual plant that had sprouted up in the junkyard. Jack followed him through the broken car shells and scrap metal, feeling annoyed that Keegan knew him well enough to understand he was an avid gardener.

Despite himself, Jack was intrigued by the junkyard. The air was scented with a combination of moss, rubber, and rusted metal. Mushrooms sprouted in heady colors in the grass between each vehicle stack. A mature man fern grew in the middle of a gutted car. On a tractor dashboard was a nest of chirping infant crows.

Keegan pointed at some orchids growing beside a wooden cartwheel. Indeed, they did appear to be the rare gaping leek orchid. Jack explained to Keegan that since the local area had given over to dairy, rather than crops, the land was less fertilized, and orchids had been reappearing.

"Thank you for showing me," Jack said. "It's a marvelous find."

They walked out past a partly dismantled mustard-colored Kingswood station wagon. A gilded frame glinted in the back seat. Jack stopped to examine it. In the trunk were several paintings, boxes of books and photo albums, crockery, and suitcases of clothing.

"You'd be doing me a favor," Keegan replied when Jack asked to buy a few things. He refused to take the fifty dollars Jack offered him. "We got enough stuff to go around."

Jack took three paintings that day. Two of them he tossed in the farm skip bin as soon as he got home.

In their kitchen now, Keegan and his wife looked indifferently at the painting. The woman poured more Coca-Cola into her glass.

"We're not really art people, are we, love?" she said.

A clap of thunder sounded. They jumped. Winter rain hit the tin roof with a strength that made Jack stare at the discolored ceiling in dismay.

"How will I get this back to the car?" he said. "Can I borrow a garbage bag?"

The woman clucked sympathetically. "We don't use them.

Most of our rubbish we incinerate. Or feed it to the goats. Some towels?" she suggested.

She dug through a washing basket and held up a torn purple towel. He tried to wrap the painting but the towel barely covered it. In any case, a towel would be soaked in an instant out there tonight. Keegan held out three plastic supermarket bags. Jack tried to wrap the small plastic bags around the painting. He shook his head at the pathetic makeshift cover. It was not worth the risk of damaging the painting. "I'll run home and get some heavy-duty garbage bags."

"Have we got an umbrella or a raincoat?" Keegan asked.

She left the room and returned with a large black umbrella. Unfortunately, when she tried to open it, the ribs were broken.

"Don't worry. We'll keep it safe until you come next time." She said it the way she said everything—without conviction.

As he returned to his car, he tripped on a plastic dog bowl. He fell on his knees on the wet ground. He glanced back at the house, hoping no one had noticed. Red mud stuck to his hands and his trousers. When he tried to brush it off, he made it worse.

Driving home, he thought of Keegan's wife, and the lingerie waitress, and other women he had known. These women were all someone's daughter. They were born with potential. Yet they would never reach it. The fault lay with men like him— men who corralled those less fortunate into lives of few options. He vowed that after he collected his painting, he would never return to the farmhouse at Marsh End.

* * *

Joelle

The Smithtons' house

On Saturday night they were in bed, cuddling, when Joelle had what Brian called one of her meltdowns. There was no place in the world she would rather have been than there with her husband. Tonight, his kindness pried open that rusted memory box inside her that sometimes felt too heavy for one person to carry.

"It's not that easy for me." Her voice rose into a wail. "When my babies were born, none of the other mums had to stay in the hospital for three weeks. There was nothing wrong with me. I wasn't sick." She suspected the midwives were making up excuses—extra blood tests, further weigh-ins—in order to make her stay. She overheard a nurse telling another that the poor little babies might not be safe with Joelle. It was only when Brian asked Miss Gwen to promise to help that the hospital staff let Joelle go home. The memory of that time made her cry even harder. "I don't want to give people reason to think I'm a bad mother."

Brian held her tight against his big chest.

"No one is taking our children away." He kissed her hair.

"All I ever wanted was to be a mum."

"You're a great mum. There is no better mum than you, not anywhere. They only take children away who are in harm's way. Your mother didn't cope, and things were different. We would fight for our children."

He was speaking slowly, like he was worried she would not understand. He was the one who didn't understand anything.

"You don't know anything," she said. "You just think everything will be all right and it won't. It's different with women like Celia Lily. She wouldn't care if my children were taken away. As long as her life didn't get upset."

"My darling . . ." he started to say.

"Stop treating me like a child," she shouted.

Disappointment crumpled his face.

Instead of saying sorry, she yelled, "Leave me alone."

He got out of bed and she could hear him doing something in the kitchen. The meltdowns felt like she was drowning in the ocean on a dark night. They had begun happening when she was a teenager living at Darla's house. When she was a child, even when things got bad, she never used to get so wildly upset. She tried to do some breathing exercises to calm herself. Miss Gwen had taught her these—deep breath in through the nose, and slowly out through the mouth—and sometimes the technique helped.

Brian returned with a glass of water and a sleeping pill.

"No," she said.

"Yes."

"It makes me dopey the next day."

"Better dopey than both of us exhausted because you keep wriggling around."

After she took the small pink pill, he kissed both her cheeks. When Brian held her, she always felt calmer. She stroked his hair and touched the tips of his long lashes. The twins had his lashes. It was funny. People who had known Brian for a long time, such as his sister, thought the twins looked more like him than Joelle. Joelle's best friends—Miss Gwen, Alfred, and Mr. Keith—thought the twins looked more like her. She supposed they saw what they wanted to see. She wondered if she looked more like her mother or her father. It was impossible to know what her father had looked like. She couldn't remember ever seeing a photo of him.

Soon the medication began to work, and she felt her limbs growing heavy and her thoughts slowing down. She matched her breathing to his and pressed herself against his warm, solid body.

In the middle of the night something woke her up. She lay in darkness wondering why she felt strange. She could hear the rain and the apple tree's branch scratching on the roof when the wind blew. She rolled over and realized Brian wasn't there. She patted her hand across his side of the bed, feeling the warmth from the electric blanket. She was alone.

For no apparent reason, she thought of the motel room where she had last seen her real mother. The authorities had taken Joelle and her mother there. They sat on the green bedspread, side by side, and her mother kept saying, "You little idiot," until the lady told her to stop saying that. Mum started crying then. Strangely, that comforted Joelle. Another memory interfered, from earlier that same day. She could see Trapper in his blue undershirt that stretched over his enormous stomach, standing in the doorway at the house, telling the authorities that he didn't want Joelle's mother leaving with her. The people were not scared of Trapper. The main lady told Joelle's mother to get her handbag.

As Joelle got older, and had her own children, she wondered if things could have been different. She had thought about inviting her mother to their wedding or letting her know when the twins were born. Brian's sister, Nicky, knew what Brian knew—that Joelle's mother had given her up—and she said Joelle was crazy to even think about it. Nicky thought Joelle's mother was bad for giving her child up, but Nicky didn't know what Joelle had done.

She opened her eyes and looked at the time. The digital clock was on the nightstand but it was not lit up. She slid out of bed. It was so black she had to feel her way across the room, touching the bedside table, then the chair and the dressing table until she reached the open doorway. The wooden doorframe was sturdy beneath her grasp.

The house was silent. No fridge hum, no crackle of the electric heater. Brian said storms sometimes cut the power.

She took too many steps, and her knee knocked the couch. Disoriented, she felt the heavy fabric of the curtains and guided herself up. She pressed her face to the cold window glass. The light from the neighbor's driveway lamp shimmered in the sheets of rain. The one streetlight on Old Dairy Road was working. She let go of the curtain and stood with her back to the wall.

A horrible feeling shook her. It was like being caught between some enormous creature's sharp teeth. This feeling was one she had not had since she was eleven, twelve, or thirteen at Pieman's Junction. A cold room and damp sheets, walls that shook when the train went through at 3 a.m., and the constant sound of machinery groaning in the ravine. Downstairs, men swearing, the fridge door slamming, cans crunching, the creaky floorboard in the hallway outside her room. Never shut your eyes. What was hidden in the darkness was worse when your eyes were closed.

Two hands landed on her shoulders. She screamed.

It was only Brian.

"The power has gone out," he said, leading her to bed. "A tree fell on the lines."

Safely beneath the blankets, she considered his explanation.

Brian was wrong this time. She had seen the lights of the other houses on Old Dairy Road. Only her house was in darkness.

* * *

Cliff

Gatenby's Poultry Farm

Something was coming up from the river toward his yards. It could have been one of the huge wildcats that occasionally came in from the scrub hunting chickens. He studied the CCTV. Whatever it was, it was not trying to conceal itself.

In the past, trespassers had cut the lock off the door. Last year someone broke a window, costing him two hundred bucks. They released the broilers and took photos and footage. A video montage of chickens being reunited with nature had been circulated on social media. They called themselves eco-warriors but they were idiots—if the birds didn't die from exposure, they would die within days without antibiotics and nutrients.

The rifle was stored in the ceiling above the bedroom. If he told Kim he needed his gun, she would tell him he was psychotic. He took his fishing knife out of the tackle box and clipped it to his belt. It was long with a serrated edge. He had once used it to gut a feral pig.

Outside, the night echoed with running water. Overflowing gutters splattered into the mud and rivulets sluiced down through the grass. A squall flapped his moleskin coat against his thighs as he cut between the silo and the chicken shed. The intruders were cunning, coming on a foul night like this. Visibility was poor. The relentless rain ensured there would be no telltale footprints in the morning.

From a crest at the top of a paddock, he surveyed the cold dark curves of his land. His anger surged. He marched toward the shed. Rain cut sideways across the hill. Far away, in the house yard, he thought he saw Kim standing at what remained of the wood heap. The wind twisted her coat around her legs. It was hard to be certain. When he looked again, there was no one there.

* * *

Jack

Calendar House

It was close to midnight when he arrived home. The house was lit up. The front door was wide open. He wondered if Celia was entertaining, but when he walked inside, there was no music or conversation. The floor runner carpet was soaked.

He noted the glass of champagne. His first thought was that she had passed out and let an eighteenth-century carpet get destroyed.

Annoyed, he called out for her.

No answer.

He strode from room to room. He called her name, quietly at first, and then loudly. The dog woke up and rubbed its head against his hand.

Her coat and bag were here, so he knew she had come home at some stage. But now she was gone. Uncertainly, he wondered if he should call the police now, or search the house again, in case anything was out of place. He tried to suppress his rising panic, knowing that the next few hours were vital.

CHAPTER 12

Sunday, August 27

Cliff

Gatenby's Poultry Farm

At dawn Cliff retraced his steps down the boggy track behind the silos where he thought he had seen the trespassing vigilante. The fences remained intact and the padlocks were secure on the shed and silo doors. His head hurt and his mouth was dry. His skin felt taut and itchy, like he was sunburned. He could barely recall what had happened last night.

In the house, Kim sat at the table in her dressing gown drinking a cup of tea. Her wet hair was wrapped in a bath towel. She had a small scratch on her cheek. He thought of them making love last night and wondered if he was to blame. Better not to ask, he thought, as he sat across from her.

"Want some eggs?" she asked.

"No, thanks."

The kettle's shrill whistle was painful. Kim added steaming water to the teapot, swirled it around, and poured tea into his cup. She stirred in his sugar. He took a sip, looked at the tea with distaste, and filled a glass with water.

A ball bounced down the hallway. He frowned.

"Don't say anything," she said, and then called to the boys, "No balls in the house."

He watched her drink her tea.

"I was thinking about lighting the fire," she said. "It's so cold."

"Put a jacket on."

The landline rang. They stared at the phone. It was early. No one telephoned the house at this time of the day.

"Can you answer it?" she said.

"Don't tell me what to do, Kim," he said, picking up the phone.

It was Jack. He was mumbling and Cliff struggled to make sense of what he was saying. "Slow down."

"Celia is missing. She's not here. I got home last night and she's gone."

"We dropped her home"—he tried to recall when exactly—"maybe between ten and eleven."

Kim nodded. She spread butter on a piece of toast. Because she was listening, he said, "Remember Kim nicked off once, to her brother's place. They always come back, tail between the legs."

Kim gave him a filthy look.

"I need your help," Jack said. "Please."

Cliff had planned to spend the day beginning his weekly withdrawal process. This involved locking the office door, drinking protein drinks, and sleeping. He needed his drug to help him work, but he was smart enough to know that he could not keep doing it without a break. In any case, Celia would turn up, probably at a five-star hotel.

"I don't know what to tell the girls," Jack said.

"Don't tell them anything yet," Cliff advised. "You know, I did see something odd on my CCTV last night. I'll check it out. We'll search the farm now. If she hasn't turned up by this afternoon, you and me should go for a drive."

He hung up the phone and looked at Kim.

"Celia's missing," he said. "What do you know about that?"

She made him repeat everything Jack had said.

Kim pressed her hands to her cheeks. "I'll ring everyone. What else can we do? Are you going to look for her?"

"I've got a few things to do first. The boys can search our land. Tell them to get dressed and come over to the office for instructions," he said. "I don't know what I saw on the CCTV. So lock the doors, Kim."

"I don't want the boys out there if you think there's a psycho wandering around."

He shook his head, irritated. "Stop mollycoddling them."

* * *

Joelle

The Smithtons' house

Two magnificent orange cakes steamed on the cooling rack when Brian and the kids came back from church. She clapped her hands as they came in, eager for them to smell the nutty, citrus aroma.

"I've got cream cheese frosting," she said.

"You wouldn't have heard." Brian took his sports jacket off. "Celia Lily has disappeared."

Joelle felt a rush of confusion.

"We drove past the Calendar House and there was a police car going up the driveway," Emily said. "Everyone was talking about it."

"There were lots of police cars," Baxter added.

Late last night, when Jack Lily arrived home, he discovered that his wife was missing. It was a baffling mystery, Brian explained, because their children were safe and sound in their beds, and even the dog was still asleep. Apparently, nothing was stolen so it wasn't a break-in. Jack had spent all night searching their farm, and at first light he had begun door knocking their neighbors.

Emily added, "Nev was delivering papers early this morning and saw Jack Lily."

"What happened to Celia?" Joelle asked.

"She's gone," Brian said.

"Forever?" Joelle felt frightened. "Is she dead?"

"She's missing."

"We saw Mr. Lily outside church," Baxter said.

"He was rattled, talking to everyone," Brian said. "He knows he'll be the number one suspect, unless there is someone else with blood quite literally on their hands."

"Oh no."

"It's usually the husband."

He was excited, in the unkind way people were when recalling a tragedy that did not affect them.

"You're all hyped up," she observed.

"I am not."

"I don't think Mr. Lily did anything to hurt her. He's nice—"

"It's raining!" Brian shouted.

Startled, she followed him out to the clothesline and began pulling the clothes down.

"I wish you wouldn't shout at me like that," she said. "It makes my stomach hurt."

"We had to bring the washing in. Why do you even hang it out in this weather?"

"It was sunny for a while."

They brought it into the laundry, and he helped her peg it on the clothes rack. When the job was done, they stood at the small window. They could not see past the garden fence. The rain forest and the mountains were a blur of green and gray.

"The police will have their work cut out," Brian said quietly. "The rain muddies anyone's tracks. If you wanted to get away with murder, Vanishing Falls is the place to do it."

* * *

Cliff

Gatenby's Poultry Farm

He had planned to start a detox. He really had. The trouble was there was so much work to do, so he gave himself a small serving of his medicine. He could get a lot done when he focused. He checked the feed and water and cleaned out the sheds. He incinerated six dead chickens and scattered the ash in the back paddock. The rain wet down the grit, preventing it from getting in his nose and mouth.

At lunchtime Kim came out. She was pale and she had not gotten dressed for the day.

"What's going on?" he said.

"Everyone's ringing everyone. No one knows where Celia is."

"I guarantee she will turn up."

"I hope so. Those poor little girls will be beside themselves." Kim was waiting, wanting his reassurance about Celia.

"She's probably rooting someone," he said.

Her face fell. She gave him a hateful look. "Sometimes I can't stand you."

*　*　*

Jack

Calendar House

His mother-in-law was sitting in his kitchen when he returned from the Vanishing Falls loop walk. Martha Gardner was a tall, imposing woman who did not bother with artifice. Her long hair was tied back with a plastic clasp and it hung bleakly down her back like a long, brittle horse's tail. She dressed in plain, practical colors—green, brown, maroon—and wore sensible, flat lace-up shoes. She looked more like an organic mushroom farmer than one of Launceston's senior obstetricians.

Today she had his daughters clustered around her and she did not stand up to greet him or offer him a hug.

"What on earth is going on?" she said.

"I've just been up to the falls again," he said. "She runs there three times a week. I went up at dawn. It was so dark in the forest I couldn't see."

"Where else could she be, Jack?"

His daughters had been crying. He had no intention of voicing his fear in front of them.

"Mum will come home," he told the girls, ignoring Martha's intense gaze. "She might be staying at a friend's. We will find her."

He took off his mudded boots and put them in the laundry to dry. He switched on the coffee machine. He wanted a stiff drink. He wouldn't have one in front of Martha. She'd never let him forget it.

"You shouldn't have left the girls alone in the house," she said. "They were terrified when I arrived."

"What else was I supposed to do?"

"Tell me again what happened last night." Martha tapped the table with her finger. "None of this makes sense."

The evening before was a blur. He had suspected something was wrong when he saw the front door open. His first thought was that the house had been robbed, but in the living room Celia's expensive jewelry was on the table in plain view. Surely a thief would have snatched the diamonds? Nothing else was disturbed. He supposed that the door had accidentally blown open and that Celia had drunk too much and was asleep somewhere. This was what he had hoped as he strode around the house, searching for her.

The operator who answered his emergency call questioned whether an intruder remained in the house. Fearfully, he ended the call and hastily shepherded his daughters into the study, which had a lockable door. The dog started barking and the little ones, Alice and Harriet, clung to him, sobbing.

The police arrived and agreed that there was no intruder. Jack telephoned the babysitter and learned that she had been collected by her mother just after 10 p.m. The babysitter's mother confirmed that Celia was relaxed and happy. There was nothing more the police could do, so they said. They told him to call the station in the morning if she had not come home.

At first light, Jack searched the farm buildings closest to the house. It was freezing and the rain was relentless. If he found Celia asleep in a barn, he would be furious. But as the sky lightened, and Celia did not turn up, disheveled and defiant, Jack had no choice but to leave twelve-year-old Frannie in charge of her younger sisters. He walked the back roads and laneways of the farm, visited the closest neighbors, and called every local person in his phone. With reluctance he called his mother-in-law, Martha, to find out if Celia was there. She was as scathing as he expected her to be, and two hours after the call, here she was, sitting in his kitchen.

"You need to continue your search. Are there unsecured wells nearby? Or one of the caves in the national park?" She listed other places for him to look.

"I just don't think she would wander off. . . ."

Martha raised an eyebrow. In her obstetrics work, she was not used to being questioned.

Later in the morning the police returned in three vehicles. Jack gave them permission to search his home and land without warrants. A team trawled the house and he wondered what they might find. He could hear their boots thumping the floorboards upstairs. Several times they moved a piece of furniture carelessly, making a horrible scratching sound.

Martha watched them search the garden from the window. She had less to say. He knew what she was thinking, that police did not ordinarily investigate a missing-person scenario until the person had been missing for forty-eight hours.

Martha looked out the window for a long time. When the glass fogged from her breath, she wiped the pane with her sleeve. Eventually she instructed her four granddaughters to each pack a bag.

"This is a shit show, Jack," she said. "They don't need to be here."

Watching a police dog snort its way through the vegetable bed, he could only agree.

CHAPTER 13

Sunday afternoon, August 27

Joelle

Vanishing Falls village

The boxes of fresh baby carrots, cucumbers, cherry toma-toes, lettuces, containers of berries, and huge peaches on the back seat of Miss Gwen's Datsun filled the car with a sweet scent. The unsold produce from Alfred's green grocery store would help families in need. When Joelle first moved to Vanishing Falls, she remembered it feeling busier, more pur-poseful. Now there were lots of people who sat in front of the supermarket or the hot chip shop all day long. After the mill closed, Brian said there was not enough work to go around. When the meatworks shut down last year, he worried it could be the death of the town.

Delivering the boxes was a job Joelle always enjoyed, but today Miss Gwen was not in her usual good mood. She barely added anything to the conversation.

As they reached the next address, Miss Gwen stopped the

car beside the mailbox of a long driveway. "I don't like some parts of this job. We drive onto someone's property and . . . we don't know what we're going to find there."

"If the dog isn't tied up, we won't get out of the car."

"I don't think we should get out of the car at all."

"They need their box. We can't just leave."

Miss Gwen steered the Datsun up the driveway. In the paddock a big green sign stated, *"Gatenby's Poultry, Trespassers Prosecuted."* A moment later Joelle saw the white pickup truck with the goat skull and horns tied to the bull bar.

"Oh no," Joelle said. "Turn around. I know who lives here."

"That's what I was talking about," Miss Gwen said. "We're not stopping."

She began a lengthy three-point turn. Joelle glanced around. The yard looked normal—the grass was mowed, and the dog was tied up. The back door opened, and Kim came out. In her faded jeans and dirty white shirt, she was almost the same color as the peeling weatherboard. She waved and Joelle waved back.

"Kim's there," Joelle said. "She's seen us."

There was no choice—they had to get the box out of the car and carry it into Kim's house. Like some of the people who needed help, Kim seemed a little bit angry. She pointed with her thumb at the kitchen table, indicating that was where Joelle should place the groceries.

"Your house is so clean and tidy," Joelle said as she heaved the box onto the table. "You should see my kitchen. It's crowded with stuff. Everything is about cats—cat tea towels, cat fridge magnets, even a cat tea cozy that I made myself. I've got a cat-shaped cookie jar. I love cats."

Joelle looked around for something to admire about Kim's kitchen. There were no photos or recipe books, and no ornaments or bric-a-brac. It smelled a bit like cleaning products. A blue-and-white tea towel was folded neatly on the sink and it reminded Joelle of the motel kitchenette at Boat Harbour where she had spent her honeymoon.

"We're so worried about Celia," Kim said. "My sons and my husband are searching our farm right now."

"She'll turn up," Joelle said. "Our cat runs off all the time. Just flits off. He always comes back."

"Oh."

"She bought a lot of meat from us on Friday. Enough for a week at least. Three hundred dollars' worth."

"It makes no sense," Kim said. "That's what worries me. Celia would not leave her children alone in that house. She's a beautiful mother."

Joelle thought of how nasty Celia had been to her in the butchery the other day. "I thought I liked her. But that was before she—"

Somewhere in the house a door closed.

"All right, then." Miss Gwen moved toward the door.

Kim placed a hand on Joelle's arm. "Did you still want to catch up for that coffee?"

Excitement bubbled through Joelle. "Yes. When?"

"I'll text you."

They swapped numbers. In the car Joelle's cheeks almost hurt, she was smiling so hard.

"Why are you grinning like a Cheshire cat?" Miss Gwen asked.

"I can tell that Kim likes me," Joelle said. "I hope Celia is safe, but I also hope she stays missing until after I have coffee with Kim."

"Do you think that's being unkind?"

"I guess." Joelle felt a tiny bit bad. "But I can't help thinking it. I wonder where Celia is. The situation is *peculiar. Peculiar* is a funny word. Saying it feels nice in your mouth, like sucking on a barley sugar. It was one of Baxter's spelling words and we looked it up in the dictionary. Peculiar: *weird, strange, uncanny*. Miss Gwen, would you call it peculiar?"

"Everything about that house is peculiar," Miss Gwen said.

"I can't believe Kim and I are going to have coffee."

"Hmmm."

"Are you excited for me?"

Miss Gwen did not reply for a long time. Finally she said quietly, "I question Kim's motivation."

"You know . . . you know . . . Brian says people like to help me and it makes them feel important and when they realize I don't need help they get annoyed."

Joelle turned her body so she faced the side window. It was true, Miss Gwen was a little bit jealous Joelle might end up best friends with Kim.

After a while, Joelle added, "You should be happy for me."

"I hope she wants to be your friend. I really do."

* * *

Cliff

Gatenby's Poultry Farm

Midafternoon, as he swept the shed, he heard a car coming up the driveway. It set the dog off. From behind the silos he watched two cops knock on the back door. Kim was a good woman; she didn't open it. He could see her on the other side of the house, hovering on the closed-in veranda. She would be freaking out. He grinned as he washed his hands in a trough.

He was in a good mood and decided to save them a return trip. By the time he walked down the track, Trixie was riled up. A raised hand was all it took to settle her.

A visit from the cops did not bother Cliff, not one bit. That tiny bit of smoke he had taken earlier was just enough to perk him up without being silly about it. He was freshly shaved, his hair was washed, he didn't have sores on his face or sweaty skin or any of the giveaways of the meth users who lingered outside the IGA on dole day. Confidence was key. You followed the rules, answered their questions without being too talkative, made good eye contact but not too much, and gave them information they hadn't been expecting. Simple.

Both the police officers were women.

"Can I help you, fellas?"

They turned around.

"We're investigating a missing person."

"It seems a bit early to call her missing," he said.

"There are unusual circumstances."

"Yeah?"

"We can't tell you any more than that."

"I suppose you're going to tell me I'm the last person to see her alive," he said.

"A babysitter confirmed her arrival home."

"Okay."

"Where did you go after you dropped her home?"

"Back here. My wife was with me. She's in the house. She'll confirm that."

"We will need to talk to her." The woman glanced at her partner, who was looking across the paddock. "Jack Lily says he was here last night."

"Did he now?"

The policewoman nodded.

"He does some paperwork for me," Cliff said smoothly. "He knows where the key is. Even if I'm not home."

So Jack had lied to the police. What was that fool up to?

He opened the back door and was about to follow them inside, when the older officer said they would prefer to speak to Kim alone.

"It's a free world," Cliff said.

Paranoia began nuzzling him. He walked around the yard pulling out Scotch thistles. It was a job he had tasked his sons with, and they had neglected it. He had pulled out thirteen thistles, refreshed the dog's water, and was filling in some of the potholes around the tool shed when the police finally finished with Kim.

They came out holding their hats like they had been visiting the Queen herself, not Kim in her kitchen. The older one had a buzz cut like a 1950s astronaut. Neither needed to speak to him again.

He watched them drive away. The kitchen window curtain shook, and he knew Kim had been watching too. He went inside and frowned at the open biscuits on the table.

"Don't get fooled by their friendliness," he said. "What did you tell them?"

"We dropped her off and came home."

"All right."

"I'm going to go for a drive to look for her."

"Let the police do that. It's not your job."

"I'm real worried, Cliff." Her voice wavered. "Jack keeps calling. He keeps asking if she's here."

"Why would she come here?"

"We're best friends."

"You say that. Have you never noticed that everything is always on her terms? Does she ever ask you what you want to do? Celia always has a sidekick."

Kim tugged her woolen cardigan around her shoulders. "Why can't you ever be nice?"

He felt mean then and he gave her an awkward hug. This time she clung to him.

"She'll be all right," he said gruffly.

A cardboard box of food sat on the table. Written on the

side was the Country Women's Association logo. The cops would know what it was.

"That's embarrassing," he told Kim. "Put it away."

"If that's the worst thing the cops see when they come here, you should be grateful."

"I don't want people turning up here unannounced. You drive down there and pick it up."

"We can't go on like this," she muttered.

He almost didn't hear her. "What did you say, Kim? Say it to my face or don't say it at all."

She nodded and began wiping the table down.

* * *

Toward the end of the day, as he moved through the last shed, he noticed a chicken caught in the wire at the bottom of the cage. Her skin was worn and her tiny feathers broken where she had tried to free herself. She was exhausted. Her head hung limply. She didn't object when he eased her out of the accidental snare. She lay on her side on the ground, occasionally lifting her head and opening the blunt hole of her beak like a baby mewing for milk. Judging from how weak she was, she hadn't had any feed or water for a few days.

When the boys were younger, he used to collect the injured chickens and put them in a cage in the garden. His sons would nurse them back to health and, just for fun, he would buy them back when they were fattened up.

He looked at the chicken. The bird's queer brown eyes watched him. She had life left in her. But it wasn't worth the feed it would take to save her. He lifted his heel and crunched it down hard on the bird's neck, grinding it into the cement floor until he felt the tendons break apart. He tossed the dead bird into the bin.

* * *

Jack

Calendar House

At dinnertime he telephoned Martha. She refused to let him speak to his daughters.

"They're in the bath."

"All four of them at once? What have you told them?" he asked.

"Nothing," she said. "Have you found my daughter?"

"I'm doing my best."

"Celia would not walk out on her children. Find her, Jack."

It was obvious she thought he was complicit. He began to cry. She did not say anything. His sobs slowed and quieted, and he felt embarrassed.

She excused herself politely and ended the call.

It was horrific being in the empty house. Never had he imagined that his wife would leave him or that the notion of her leaving him would be a best-case scenario. His footsteps sounded loud as he walked through each room, looking for something to direct him to her whereabouts. He rummaged through her drawers and in her bedside table. On the family wall calendar, he looked at the week ahead. She had a beauty salon appointment on Monday and a friend's birthday lunch on Wednesday. She had arranged a playdate for the little girls. Everything indicated that Celia was planning to continue her life as normal.

It was a matter of time until the police showed their cards. He probably had a few days until he heard via the media that he was "helping police with inquiries." A few more days, perhaps, and the police would quietly let him know he was under suspicion. He had seen it play out this way with his clients.

With a start he recalled his mother's recent letter. In her beautiful handwriting Victoria Lily explained that she had amended her will for Jack's protection. In the sad event that he was widowed, she would leave him all her properties: the farm, his house, her summer cottage, and another old farm in the north. Otherwise, him being married at the time of her death, apart from a small financial gift to be bequeathed to Jack and his sister, all Victoria's properties and possessions would be donated to the National Trust. This was an organization for which she claimed she felt immense respect.

He tried to remember where he had left the envelope. Damn, he should have tossed it in the fire as he usually did with any of her volatile correspondence. He went to his study, closed the curtains, and opened his drawers. This was where he had placed it, in the top left drawer. He was a neat man; everything was as he had left it. Pencils, pens, leather-bound notebooks. The one item he was looking for was not there. He pulled everything out of the drawer and stacked it on the desk. Then the next drawer, and the next. He clutched the back of a chair to steady himself and glanced around the room.

It was missing.

He could not believe that someone as thorough as he had overlooked something as crucial as this. He opened the curtains and looked down at the lake. Wind creased the surface with black ripples.

He telephoned Inspector Kanton.

"What can I do for you, Jack?"

"I thought of something," he said.

His mind began racing, the possibilities unfolding neatly like a deck of cards shuffled and fanned out on a table. He would tell the police about the letter eventually. The risk of redirecting their investigation was too great if he told them now.

"You should search the dam. And the lake." Saying the words sickened him.

"That is happening first thing in the morning. We've talked to a lot of people today. More tomorrow. We will locate her."

"Locate her? Find her safe and sound."

"Of course we want to bring her home safely. That's our job. One more thing," Inspector Kanton said. "Have you engaged a lawyer?"

"Why would I do that?"

"Some people in your situation do."

"I won't be. I've got nothing to hide. Nothing."

The call ended and the evening loomed. He paced along the veranda. The fog was so thick the rain was invisible. You could hear it, clattering on anything in the way, the tiled roof of the stables, the gravel driveway, the lake.

He thought of the men he had represented over the years who had been accused of murdering their wives. There were four. Two were convicted—the evidence was solid. Crucial to the prosecution's case had been the movement of the men in the hours and days following the death or reported disappearance. One had gone straight to his mistress's home and had not joined the search. Another had disposed of his wife's mobile phone.

Jack successfully argued against a murder charge for two other men. Public opinion sided with the men, both of whom had been vocal and active in the chaotic days following their wives' tragic demise. They both appeared to be devoted husbands. The client whose wife was found drowned in a swimming pool had worried Jack. It was his reaction in the private chamber following the acquittal that was troubling. The man had winked at him and said, "We did it."

There were several colleagues Jack could call for discreet legal advice, but he did not feel he needed it. Jack had as much experience dealing with this kind of case as anyone he knew. He certainly was not going to engage a lawyer—that would make everyone assume he was guilty.

A man suspected of murdering his wife could not make a mistake. Jack grabbed his car keys.

* * *

Cliff

Gatenby's Poultry Farm

O n the plate was diced carrot, mashed potato, and a casseroled chicken leg. He looked at it closely and sniffed it. He dipped his finger into the potato and tasted it. The trouble was, there were poisons and other medications that were odorless and tasteless. He told Kim he needed to send some emails and would eat at his desk. He crossed the yard, toward the office, and veered over to the kennel. He scooped up a small portion of each food and tossed them to Trixie. Better her than him.

In the quietness of his office he avoided the blaring television, the boys arguing, his wife sidling around him like a needy cat wanting affection.

Whenever he was tweaking—those difficult hours between the last high and when he passed out—he understood he was prone to paranoia. Fortunately, he had enough willpower to ignore the relentless voices in his head.

Half an hour later, Trixie was still tugging on her chain. He managed to eat some of the casserole, pushing each mouthful down with a drink of water. He felt stressed. His jaw hurt, his skin felt incredibly tight. It didn't help that he had been awake for more than thirty-six hours. Thoughts snapped in and out of his head. When he read his notes, he couldn't recall why he had written them.

Something was wrong. He was not an addict. An addict

could not say no to the drug. Cliff could take it or leave it. It wasn't the drug itself that made him feel bad, but rather the lack of sleep and nutrition. Addicts couldn't recognize that. Right now he knew he needed to rest, rehydrate, and recuperate from what he had done to his body this weekend.

He lay on the floor and shut his eyes. The sensor beeped and he jumped to his feet. A car was approaching. The CCTV showed Jack's Jaguar. The vehicle stopped. Jack got out. Kim ran over and threw herself into his arms.

It gave Cliff a funny feeling. He didn't like seeing his wife touching other men, even one whose wife was missing. He opened his office door and positioned himself casually, leaning against the wooden frame. The moment she noticed him, Kim led Jack over to the office.

"Off you go," Cliff told Kim.

Once she left, he took Jack inside his office. "I don't know if I should be talking to you. Where is Celia?"

"You've got to help me." Jack's voice cracked. He rubbed his face with his sleeve and Cliff looked away. "She was there when the babysitter went home, then she vanished. She's gone. But she's taken none of her stuff. Nothing is missing. Not her wallet or phone or anything. I'm so worried."

"Who was the babysitter?"

"A girl who's been babysitting for years for us. Her parents picked her up. They said Celia waved to them from the doorstep. There was nothing unusual."

Cliff nodded. He could barely think straight.

"I don't know what to do," Jack said. "I thought she would come home by now. They're sending divers into the dam tomorrow. I can't bear it." His weeping was the silent, shaking kind that Kim did when Cliff lost his temper.

Cliff went into the bathroom. This was an extreme situation. A weaker man would send Jack on his way. Not Cliff. He was a mate and he would help. He just needed something to help him process all this information.

He splashed water on his face. When he emerged, Jack was texting someone. Thankfully, he was no longer crying.

"The first thing that comes to mind is someone broke in to steal the new painting," Cliff said.

"There's no sign of a break-in. And the painting . . . is with a colleague."

"Did you tell the cops you were here?"

"Yes. Did you say I wasn't?"

"I haven't told them shit."

Cliff opened the window and breathed in the cold, damp air. He wanted to put some space between him and Jack. "What's really going on?"

"We had an argument. I went out and she went to the function. The babysitter heard us arguing. It looks bad."

"Where were you?"

Jack was wild-eyed. "It doesn't matter."

Cliff could not resist baiting him. "Are you having an affair?"

"No."

Cliff stretched one arm, then the other. He thought he knew where Jack had been. It wasn't the first time he'd seen a mate try to hide a dirty secret. This was Vanishing Falls; people talked about each other because there was nothing else to talk about. Years ago Cliff had heard that the Keegans were involved in some kind of swingers network. He dismissed it as ridiculous gossip. But then one of the truck drivers delivering his hatchlings had asked him about a local prostitute. This time Cliff paid attention.

A bloke like Jack, with all his education and importance, thought he was smart enough to deceive everyone. Not Cliff though—he might not have fancy degrees, but he was highly intelligent, and he could smell bullshit from a mile away. It would be amusing to bring it up again later.

"Where are your kids?" Cliff asked, changing the subject.

"Celia's mother took the girls to her place in Launceston. The cops are treating the house like a crime scene—they have gone through every room. I had to let them. It's a nightmare. Believe me, I didn't kill my wife."

Cliff had never seen Jack unhinged. His clothes were dirty, he hadn't shaved, and his confidence was gone. An unnatural wave of sympathy came over him.

"Take it easy. Don't say it like that."

"What?"

"Don't say, 'I did not kill my wife.' It sounds suspicious. You say, 'I'm going to find Celia.' Use her name. Keep positive."

"Okay."

"Nothing was stolen, and there was no sign of a struggle, so why are the police treating it so seriously? Maybe she's gone to stay with a friend."

"I don't know. They won't tell me anything."

"All right. Let's presume she's gone for a wander and had an accident. She had quite a few drinks Saturday night. If she's incapacitated out there . . ." Cliff shook his head and didn't finish the sentence.

Jack tried to light one of Cliff's cigarettes. His hands were shaky. Cliff snatched the lighter and ignited the smoke for him. Jack inhaled slowly and coughed.

"You need to tell the truth about where you were," Cliff said.

"I don't want to make things worse."

"Jack, it can't get much worse than if your wife's gone. Cops are going to work out you weren't with me."

Jack coughed again and stubbed out the half-smoked cigarette. "So, I tell them where I was, she comes home, I'm in the shit."

Cliff glanced at the wasted cigarette in the ashtray. "We're not doing any good sitting here talking about it like housewives."

They decided to drive every road within a twenty-kilometer radius of town. There was no other traffic and they kept the spotlight switched on. Driving along the edge of the national park, Cliff said, "Do you think she's gotten lost in there?"

"She's not going to walk into the rain forest in last night's storm."

"Unless someone forced her to. Who hates your guts?"

"Take a number."

Jack explained that there were countless people whom he had sent to jail when he worked as a prosecutor in Launceston in the years before his children were born. Burglars, violent men with mental problems, drug dealers, grubs who beat their wives; the list of people who might have a reason to seek revenge on Jack was substantial. It was unlikely, though, that one of these criminals was responsible—Vanishing Falls was a two-hour drive from Launceston.

"There's people who might like to throw a punch at me if we saw each other in the street, but why would they come all the way out here to hurt Celia?"

"Yeah. Celia's a lovely lady but she's not harmless. We've got to keep an open mind. On Saturday night Celia told me she had a go at the butcher's wife."

"I didn't know."

"She went into the butchery and told Joelle to keep her mouth shut. It wouldn't have been nice. Celia can be a bitch."

Jack didn't deny this. "Do I tell the police to interrogate Joelle? It will bring to light what happened at the fair."

"Who cares? No one will believe her."

"You should hear the way the police speak to me. Like I'm scum."

They fell silent as Cliff drove through state plantation forest where pine trees grew in tall, thin rows. There was nothing unusual to see out here. They returned via Murdering Creek, where sheets of water gushed across the road. The new Hollybank Creek sign glowed beneath the spotlight. Somewhere among the aged gums, leatherwoods, lantana, and ferns were the ruins of the old flour mill.

Cliff cleared his throat. "If she's been disposed of in there, someone's trying to give you a message."

"Good grief."

Cliff turned off the ignition. "Get out of the car," he said.

"Huh?" Jack said.

"What you need to remember is, as you rightly said, you're the number one suspect. You fought with your wife, which was overheard by a witness, then a few hours later you've reported her missing. You don't have time to be stupid. You need to bring Celia home. Tomorrow, tell the cops you searched up here. Mention the butcher and his vendetta against you."

"Brian Smithton?"

"Walk in there and take a look." Cliff took out his provisions and began to prepare a hit. If he was honest, he was starting to enjoy the search. "The cops aren't going to help you, mate. But I will."

* * *

Jack

Hollybank Creek Bridge

Jack was shocked to see Cliff unzip the dirty toiletries bag he carried everywhere with him.

"Are you out of your mind? Celia is missing and you're getting high?"

"I'm having a tiny amount. No different to a shot of coffee."

"You're crazy. We're probably being followed."

Cliff glanced in the rearview mirror. "No one is following us. I would have seen their lights. This looks like a cigarette anyway. Want some?"

"No." Jack was aghast. "Never offer it to me again."

Jack opened the door. The creek sounded like a person

choking. The spotlight made long starving arms out of the leafless branches.

In daylight, the bridge over Hollybank Creek was a pretty spot. He had chosen the name because of the bright green trees, with their pink, orange, yellow, and white berries, that Great-great-great-grandfather Henry Lily had planted on either side of the creek.

"Get on with it." Cliff flicked his lighter.

Jack walked into the rain. Mud sucked at his boots. He pushed fern fronds, heavy with water, out of the way and walked up to the water mill ruin. A high rock wall remained on one side and crumbled piles of stone on the other. The last time he had stood here was with Celia when the sign got changed. They had admired the council's workmanship. He shone his flashlight across the long, wet grasses and called her name.

There was no sound except the slap of rain and the rushing creek.

Jack was soaking wet when he returned to the vehicle. Cliff started the engine.

"Don't take this the wrong way, but if she's been abducted, why didn't they steal something?" Cliff mused. "It makes no sense."

There were many things a thief could have taken from his house. Everything was insured. Except the painting. And that was in the farmhouse, completely insecure, and he had no way of getting it back without drawing attention to his connection to the Keegans.

"Don't know," he said.

On Old Dairy Road, Cliff slowed near the cattle chute. He

pointed out Brian and Joelle Smithton's house, at the end of a row of quaint weatherboard cottages that backed onto the stream.

"Old mate was pretty upset when you changed the sign," Cliff said.

Jack nodded. Brian Smithton had written to him initially, badgering him to leave the Murdering Creek sign unchanged. But Jack hated the name. So did Celia. Jack wrote back, explaining that a member of his family had farmed the land around the creek since the first land grants in the 1830s. He said it was his legal right to name his land however he wanted to. They met on-site, with some local officials, and Jack did offer, kindly, to be open to name suggestions from Brian. The man was unbending. A few days later Brian approached him in the main street, where they had a heated argument. It was not physical, of course, but Jack had raised his voice. Brian did not care that a small group of passersby had stopped to watch. It was Jack who had to walk away from the argument.

"Brian could have suggested an indigenous name for the creek if he wanted to. But he insisted it remain Murdering Creek. If his long-lost ancestors were killed there, you would think he would like not to be reminded about it every day. In any case, it's a big jump to go from objecting to signage to abducting a woman."

"Whatever," Cliff said. "I don't know how the criminal mind works."

"Really?"

Cliff braked hard. Jack slid forward and almost cracked his head on the windshield.

"You need to start counting your friends, not saying stuff like that," Cliff said.

He sped up. They flew past a gorse hedge, and a wide paddock where sheep huddled beneath a lone tree. Jack hated to admit it, but Cliff might be right.

* * *

Joelle

The Smithtons' house

The goat skull strapped to the bull bar was unmistakable in the glow from Old Dairy Road's one streetlight. He was down near the cattle chute, like he had been three times since the fair. Sometimes the pickup truck did a U-turn and returned toward town. Other times it continued where the road turned to gravel and entered the forest.

She tried hard to concentrate on Brian's voice as he read to the children. He read with lots of expression from a book he had been given when he was a boy. It was so long ago, the last time she had read the twins a story. They knew more words than she did. When she struggled to sound out a word, one of them would go ahead and say it, which annoyed the other one. It turned into a squabble. It was much better for Joelle to make up a story from scratch. They loved her tales of the imaginary witches and wizards who lived in the forests around their home.

To distract herself from peering out the window again, she

turned on the television. A cooking show was on. The cook was making golden syrup dumplings. She tried to concentrate on the program, but her gaze kept returning to the window.

Brian wandered in and changed the channel.

"What did you do that for?" she said.

"I didn't think you were watching it."

"Do you know the man who has a goat's head tied to the front of his truck?"

"Lots of people around here have those." Brian grinned. "And it's called a skull, not a head. Someone came into the butchery just the other day asking for a bull's skull for his bull bar. I said, We don't butcher bulls here. I offered him a lamb skull and he said no." He chuckled. "Why would anyone want to put a dead animal's skull on their car?"

Joelle considered this. "A decoration?"

"A pretty miserable decoration, I'd say."

"I think the man who just drove past was Cliff Gatenby."

"Oh." Brian kept watching television, unperturbed. "They're all out there searching for Celia."

"What do you think happened to her?"

"In eighty-five percent of cases, the killer is either the last person to have seen the missing person alive or the person who reported the person missing in the first place. The last people who admit to seeing Celia alive are the babysitter and her mum. Assuming it wasn't them, that leaves the person who reported her missing—Jack Lily."

She snuggled beside him. He took off her slippers and began giving her one of his special foot massages.

"Jack Lily is not the kind of man to do that."

Brian gave a weak smile. "I know you think he's handsome."

"I do not!"

"I just wouldn't put anything past that man."

Years of loving him had taught her to keep quiet whenever certain topics came up. Jack Lily was a topic that made Brian emotional. Sometimes he used what Darla called *colorful language* to refer to him.

Not long after they moved to Vanishing Falls they had hiked up through the forest to the lookout. It was a clear day and they could see the Calendar House and its surrounding estate like a patchwork of different shades of green. Above the farmlands were the Great Western Tiers, rugged dolerite mountains.

In his quiet, confident voice, Brian explained that these were the Mountains of the Spirits. The Gog Range was where three different Aboriginal tribes had found ocher, traveling huge distances to obtain this valuable material. When the settlers came, Brian said, there were wars, for the people had not given up their lands freely. There were places around here where unspeakable crimes had occurred. Two Pallittorre women were camping by the creek when they were killed by a farmer. They had children with them, who were chased up to Vanishing Falls. Brian said it was understood that they drowned in the water hole.

Brian wasn't certain, but he thought he was a Pallittorre man.

His grandfather Ted Flowers had grown up in the children's home just outside Launceston in the 1920s. Ted's mother was a house servant unable to accommodate him. His birth certificate said "Father Unknown." Ted investigated his family history and he did not like what he found. There was more prejudice back then, Brian noted. Years later, Brian pursued his family history all the way to the foothills of the Gog Range. Through the Tasmanian Aboriginal Heritage Register he met people whom he felt he had a connection with. They tried to help him piece together the fragments of the past. It was almost impossible.

Brian's trouble, he confided to Joelle, was that he would never be able to work out how he belonged. That day, he talked about the mountains and the valleys, and things that happened long ago. These things made him feel hopelessly incomplete. In particular, he felt he had failed his grandfather. As he spoke, she could hear birds calling in the treetops. In the cool mountain air, their notes were sweeter than in the valley, and lasted longer.

Sensing his sadness, Joelle held him, this liquid heaving man. It was exciting to be the person giving comfort. She had felt like she was finally doing the one thing she had been preparing her whole life for, and she had felt very close to him right then, but also scared—like how she imagined a snake shedding its skin might feel.

CHAPTER 14

Monday, August 28

Jack

Vanishing Falls valley

Snow was expected. The roads were slick with black ice and several times the wheels slid. He drove slowly up and down every road in town, including the narrow service lanes behind the main street stores. A man was unloading a van at the rear of the hardware store and a woman walked her dogs near the park—neither had any information about Celia's whereabouts.

He drove the lonely roads in the industrial estate and out to the swampland. Here the land was not farmed properly. The rain forest was gradually reclaiming the pasture. Hidden among the stringybark and blackwood trees were homes of those who were content being left alone. Their deprivations appalled him. Large extended families lived in run-down shacks and malnourished dogs growled from homemade kennels. Teenagers who should have been in school sauntered out to look over his car. There was no power or town water. Neglect was everywhere—the dirty toddlers, rusty water tanks, and piles of rubbish. He was not welcome—one man threatened him with a four-by-two wooden plank. Still, he showed a picture of Celia and left his card and a plea for people to call him if they heard anything.

It was the same everywhere. No one had seen her.

He waded through ditches and traipsed across the wetlands. At each bridge he peered into the river's bracken-dark depths and in the reeds growing in the cold waters. At a riverside picnic ground he called her name. He felt like he was drowning in the middle of the dark ocean—inevitable, terrifying. You could scream but it was pointless.

From a bridge near the Cutting, the view took in the turnip field and the Keegans' farmhouse. It was the only hovel he did not visit.

He knew she wasn't there.

Returning to town, he saw a long line of volunteers moving through a paddock, hitting the grass with sticks. His stomach turned.

* * *

Rain turned to hail. He parked outside the café, for once not caring if his Jaguar got damaged. He thought he might buy a coffee and a toasted sandwich and sit in the café for a while. It was company he needed. A few friends had texted today, but the messages were all meaninglessly open-ended: let us know if you need anything, know that we're thinking of you.

The main street was as busy as it got for the monthly farmer's market. People were everywhere, mostly walking toward the town hall. Jack followed the crowd. He had spoken to the police four times that day. No one had told him there was a gathering.

The hall was a lovely stone building that had once been a theater. Today the main open space was chaotic with what seemed like the entire district, all wearing raincoats and mud-slicked boots and trying to find his wife. Lots of people smiled at him, but no one approached him. Across the hall he saw Kim. She nodded, but even she remained in a tight bunch of women. He wondered if this was how it would feel to have a contagious terminal illness. Everyone was sorry for him—but they didn't want to get too close.

Inspector Kanton stood near the front, speaking on her phone. Jack waited beside her until she ended the call.

"What's going on?" he demanded.

"In these extreme weather conditions, every hour makes a difference in a search-and-rescue endeavor. We're trying to rally up as much help as possible from civilians," she said. "If we don't find her today, I'm going to recommend we open a major incident room."

"Why wait?" he demanded. "Open it now."

"Usually we wait longer."

He told her where he had been looking. She nodded patiently, like the information was inconsequential. Her phone rang but she didn't answer it.

"I need you to account for your whereabouts on Saturday night." She sounded unsympathetic. "I know we've been over it, but it needs to be put in a statement. Normal procedure."

They arranged for him to go to the police station the following day.

She said, "Your wife has got a lot of supporters."

"It's a close-knit community."

"Let's talk about your greenhouse."

"The hothouse? I grow flowers. Orchids mainly. Some lilies and hibiscus."

"That would require some heat."

"There's a gas heater. What is your point?"

"We need to look in there."

"I thought you would have done that already."

Kanton gave him a hard look. "It was locked."

Her phone rang again. This time she answered it.

Jack had a quick look at his own phone and tried to compose himself. Of course his hothouse was locked. The flowers in there represented years of work—painstaking hand-pollination using a toothpick to transfer a seed between flowers. It was more than a hobby—it was his passion—and he rarely let anyone go in there. The key to the hothouse was on his key ring. For a crazy moment he considered handing it over. Things were moving too fast though. He would check the hothouse himself first.

He looked around the room. No one was coming over to talk to him, but they were not ignoring him either. He wasn't used to feeling anxious in a crowd. At the refreshment table were several older ladies, including kind old Miss Gwendolyn Lancaster. She had been a friend of his mother's.

When he reached the table, she was no longer there.

He put a tea bag in a cup and added water. He couldn't see the sugar, and the tea ladies didn't try to help him. These ordinary people, who had known him and his family all his life, suspected him of doing something awful to his wife. He could barely breathe; the realization made him dizzy, as though someone had driven a knife into his guts.

Carefully, he placed the cup of tea on a nearby table and turned to leave. Keegan and his wife stood alone under the framed photo of the Queen. They wore baggy tracksuits and he could tell from the mud splattered up their legs that they had joined the search.

Keegan was not a lithe man, but he moved fast enough, dragging his wife by the hand toward Jack. Despite their unspoken agreement not to acknowledge each other in public, they intercepted him at the doorway. Keegan put his arm around his wife.

"Thank you for being here," Jack said politely.

Keegan's wife smiled. Her receding gums made him think of an angry old horse who wanted to bite someone.

"If we can help, we will," she offered.

"There are plenty of helpers," Jack said, not wanting their involvement.

Keegan eyed Jack. "I imagine we might not be seeing you for a while."

Jack was appreciative of Keegan's subtlety. Everyone was watching. He lowered his voice. "I'll stop by soon. To pick up my item."

"We don't want no trouble," Keegan's wife began.

"There's not going to be any trouble," Keegan said.

Keegan gave a sly smile. Jack suspected the value of the painting was distilling in Keegan's sludgy brain. He suppressed an urge to swing his fist and land it smack in the man's mouth.

Cliff's hand clamped down on his shoulder.

"Let's go," Cliff said quietly. "I'll walk you to your car."

Outside, a television camera crew was taking footage of the people coming and going from the hall. They asked him how he was feeling and he gave a quick statement before excusing himself. A newspaper journalist pressed her card into his hand. He thanked her and kept walking. As Jack and Cliff reached Jack's car, he noticed that the camera operator was still filming them.

"Those people," he said. "They all think I did something to Celia."

"You should get a lawyer."

"I don't need a lawyer. I've done nothing wrong."

"If they don't find her by tomorrow morning, get one." Cliff lit a cigarette. "Don't talk to scum like the Keegans. Everyone is watching everything you do."

Jack nodded. On the porch of the town hall, people were watching him curiously. There was no malice, not yet, but there was no empathy either. It was like they were waiting for him to do something. Confess? Beg forgiveness? Lash out at them?

"Be straight with me, Cliff."

Cliff cupped the cigarette in his hand so it wouldn't get rained on and sucked on it. "Most people around here lost their job either at the abattoir or the mill, while the Lilys are driving their shiny new horse float through town every weekend. She's gone, you're still here. Yes, they think you did something to her. She came to the Apple Queen Tribute event without you. Everyone's asking where you were on Saturday night."

"I told you. It's not something I need her to know when she comes home."

Cliff blew smoke to the side. "I wouldn't be a mate if I didn't speak my mind to you. It's not looking good for Celia. If she's dicking around and comes back, it doesn't matter where you were Saturday night. If someone saw you Saturday night, can you trust them? You're a lawyer, mate. Stop being stupid. They're going to stick it on you. There's no one else."

"The policewoman asked me about the hothouse."

Cliff looked interested. "Perfect place to dispose of a body."

"They're trying to rattle me."

Perhaps he should have handed the key to Kanton just now. It would show them that he had nothing to hide. But before he convinced anyone of that, he needed to convince himself.

Jack sank into the soft leather driver's seat of his car. He turned the ignition.

"They've probably put a tracking device on your car." Cliff leaned in the window. "Sometimes they fall off by themselves. Look under the hubcap."

"I've got nothing to hide."

"That doesn't matter. Don't give them enough rope to hang you."

On the drive home, Jack reflected on how lucky he was to have a friend such as Cliff. Here he was in the worst situation, and Cliff's advice was the most practical he had received. Other so-called friends had offered their kind thoughts but no concrete support. Cliff was right in telling him to get a lawyer, but it was a double-edged sword. As soon as people knew Jack had legal representation, they would be suspicious of him. He would react the same way. However, it went against his instinct to remove the tracking device. That was tampering with police work. If he got caught doing that, it would look worse than enlisting a lawyer's assistance.

Don't give them enough rope, Cliff had said.

Something about the rope comment niggled Jack.

His mother's letter.

Yesterday, while Inspector Kanton's team dusted for fingerprints and used a laser device to look for blood, she had made Jack sign their evidence inventory. It included Celia's laptop, phone, address book, handbag, shoes, and coat. There was no correspondence listed.

The letter had to be there somewhere—if not in his desk, then where? Perhaps Celia had found it and squirreled it away. He had agreed with Celia on several occasions about the need for a frank conversation with his mother's doctor about her diminishing mental capacities. The letter arguably demonstrated that. Or perhaps one of the girls had snooped in his study and accidentally taken it. In the past, they had taken his stapler, his magnifying glass, and a large amount of his carbon copy paper without asking.

Halfway up his driveway, where the poplar trees circled the lake, a police car was stationed. For a fleeting, horrible moment he thought it was a barricade and they were there to arrest him. Then a young constable waved him through, and a fresh wave of despair washed over him; clearly they had no news for him.

* * *

Joelle

Vanishing Falls Nursing Home

Joelle spent the morning at the nursing home. She and several of the residents were halfway through a game of charades when they saw a large tabby cat walking across the garden with a bird in its mouth. The ladies screamed. Matron hurried outside and caught the cat. They watched through the window as she pried its mouth open and the bird was released. It was a red robin. It flapped around on the grass for a while, then flew off.

Everyone clapped when Matron returned.

"Get me some strychnine and I'll sort that cat out for you," Mr. Keith said loudly, raising his glass of orange juice to Matron.

Many of his fellow residents protested.

"That's a horrible thing to say," Mrs. Bester said. "You don't mean it."

She was the head of the gardening club. Her friends were quick to agree with her.

"I've killed more feral cats than you've had rolls in the hay, Leslie," Mr. Keith told Mrs. Bester. "My dairy farm was teeming with them."

He laughed loudly. That made Joelle chuckle a little bit too, even though she knew she shouldn't. Mrs. Bester was a regular client who liked a classic updo with curls on top and a soft wave fringe that required a lot of hairspray.

Matron frowned. "This conversation is over," she said.

Mrs. Bester was annoyed. "He should be careful no one puts strychnine in his juice," she said, and her friends laughed.

"It tastes disgusting, so I wouldn't drink it," he returned. "You soak the cloth—"

Matron intervened again. "Joelle, please take Mr. Keith to his room."

When they were back in his room, Joelle closed the door. He was upset and wringing his hands.

"They don't understand what I'm trying to tell them," he said.

"I might understand," she said. "Tell me."

"Strychnine-soaked cloth tied to a metal trap," he rambled. "That does it. Rat poison pellets. Always wear a mask. Phosphine fumes from wet pellets is a painful death. Bloody cats and rodents. You got to sort them out."

Joelle sat beside him. "You know I love my cat," she said. "Remember, I told you about Snowcat. He's a good cat."

Mr. Keith sighed. He smiled sheepishly. "I'm sorry."

She patted his hand. "Let's play cards."

* * *

The Smithtons' house

After lunch the doorbell rang. It always took Joelle a long time to unlock the front door. First she undid the dead bolt. Then the top lock, and then the bottom lock, and then finally the main lock. She left the Crimsafe door locked. On the other side of the mesh stood a tall woman with a nice smile.

"That's a lot of locks," the lady said.

"Brian says you can never be too careful."

Joelle pressed her face against the mesh and scrutinized the woman. She looked friendly.

"Are you selling Girl Scout biscuits?" Joelle asked.

"No. My name is Inspector Kanton. I'm with the police force."

"I thought police had to wear a uniform?" Joelle blurted as anxiety swept over her.

"Plain clothes today." She held up a shiny badge.

Nauseous, Joelle hugged herself as Inspector Kanton explained she was visiting every house on Old Dairy Road to ask if they had any information about Celia Lily. Joelle hoped she did not want to come inside. Brian always said she was never to let strangers or authorities into the house unless he was there. That was an easy rule to remember.

"Did you know Celia?" the inspector said.

"Everyone knows her. I'm better friends with Kim though. We have more in common. She's upset. They were best friends. I don't understand why Fergus did nothing."

"Who is Fergus?"

"He's a big black dog about this tall." She held her hand near her waist. "Celia brings him to the school gate. All the kids are scared of him. He can't bite anyone because he's got a muzzle. . . ." She lost track of what Kanton had asked her.

She felt very sick in her stomach and her head. She blinked, but her vision was blurry.

"I have to go." Joelle closed the door.

When she opened her eyes, she was lying on the couch.

It had been a long time since she had reacted so badly to stress. One summer when the twins were still in the double pram, Joelle had been walking along eating an ice cream. The Vanishing Falls Hotel had all its doors and windows open to let in the sunshine. The distinctive pub smell of sugary wheat had caused her to vomit in the rubbish bin outside the take-away shop.

Around the time she got engaged to Brian, her foster mother, Darla, had taken her to see a counselor. The woman talked to Joelle about things that might happen once she got married. Some of those things had happened already and the counselor said that was okay so long as Joelle was happy about it. She had also taught her to anticipate posttrauma triggers. This was the technical name for things that caused panic to rush through her like noxious gas. The solutions were simple—she crossed the street instead of walking past the pub, especially in summer when the window was open and the smell of the hops made her think of the Pieman's Junction Hotel and Wendy Field walking tentatively toward the car. Whenever she thought about Pieman's Junction she had horrible nightmares in which she called out to Wendy, *Run away, don't let them pull you into the car with us, just go.* The worst bit was waking up knowing that in real life Joelle had snuggled up against Trent and watched silently as Wendy walked toward the car.

Police were another trigger.

Next time a police person came to Old Dairy Road she would pretend she wasn't home.

* * *

That night Joelle did all the things that calmed her. She made a nice dinner of lamb chops and vegetables, she ran a big bubble bath for the children, and she sang to them while they settled into bed. When she came back to check on them, Baxter was already asleep. He had kicked his duvet away and Joelle tenderly folded it around her little boy. She kissed him, touching the silky lock of hair fallen across his brow.

"Why aren't you asleep?" she asked Emily.

"I'm worrying about something."

"School stuff?"

Emily nodded. "Sometimes I don't have anyone to play with," she said in a small voice.

Joelle tried to think. She looked around the room and noticed a handball. She picked it up. "Put this in your bag. If no one will play with you, you just play. You can bounce it against the wall or something."

"I'll try," Emily said. "Thanks."

Pleased she had helped Emily with her problem, Joelle sighed happily as she closed the twins' bedroom door.

It was Monday night, card night, and Brian and Nev were in the kitchen. They spoke in the rough voices they used when women weren't around. She sat down in the living room and stroked the cat. He yawned extravagantly and rolled onto his back. Hailstones rattled the roof and windowpanes.

"The weather is clagging in," she told Snowcat, rubbing his soft fluffy tummy. "You can hear that hail scraping the mountaintops."

She could also hear Brian talking to Nev in the kitchen. "If you think about where murderers hide bodies, it's bound to be an area they know," he was saying. "You wouldn't drive to a new place. Too risky. It would make sense for the place where you dispose of the body to be close by. You would choose a place that you've been before, even if it was years ago. Obviously you wouldn't hide a body in your own backyard. If Jack Lily killed his wife, he would leave his house, take a main highway or road, so no one notices him."

She crawled to the end of the couch so she could peep around the corner. There was a large road map spread across the kitchen table. It usually lived in the center console of the car. They both had their backs to her.

Nev chuckled. "I'm interested to see where you're going with this."

Brian tapped on the map. "Then he might take a secondary road, a dirt road, for a certain distance. Then he would walk into the bush and dispose of the body. It's heavy though, so not too far off the track. Hypothetically, Jack Lily murders Celia in their house, puts her in his car, drives down his driveway, and turns left, away from town. He's on the main road. Then he turns onto a secondary road—our street—drives to the end. What's there? A dirt road—the old stock route they used to move the sheep to fresh pastures. He could dump the body on any of the farmland along there, but he wouldn't. He'd go all the way until it joins the national park."

"Why did you highlight this section?"

"These are tracks going up the eastern escarpment toward the falls. My money is that Celia Lily will be found around here."

A horrible feeling crept up inside Joelle. Her fingertips left damp patches on the leather sofa.

"It'll be hard for the police to prove what happened," Brian continued. "If she's lying in some shallow grave her vital organs will be disintegrating. By now they won't be able to tell whether she was strangled or suffocated. If there are bullets in her or if her bones are chipped by a knife, that would reveal something more useful."

"They won't find her," Nev said. "Even if the weather cleared and they could use the helicopter. Burying a person in the rain forest is like throwing a body off a boat into the ocean. It's too dense to search, and before you know it, the person is mulch."

There was a long pause. She heard one of them clear his throat.

"Someone knows what happened," Brian said.

"What I don't like about all this is that Vanishing Falls is going to be known as the place where someone got away with murder," Nev said.

"People have gotten away with enough around here," Brian said. "Joey saw something at the fair that would blow your mind. I won't go into it, but I don't mind saying Jack Lily is sketchy."

Brian was wrong about Jack Lily, thought Joelle. Brian didn't like him. That didn't mean he was a murderer.

The person she was scared of was Cliff Gatenby. When he told her where to go, you could tell he didn't care about anything. His eyes were dead. She had seen that look in a person's eyes before and it was something you never forgot.

* * *

After Nev left, Brian was surprised to see she was still awake.

"I'm worried you're going to tell the police about what I saw in the bathroom at the fair," she said.

"We need to, honey."

"No. Brian, you don't get it."

He took both her hands. Since they met in the hair salon all those years ago, his hair had grayed, and his face was chubbier. The one thing that never changed was how kind he was. He expected everyone to be kind too.

"I get it," he said. "If he's done something wrong, justice needs to occur."

She was too exhausted to argue with him.

When Brian went to have a shower, her mind turned electric. He was the thing that kept her steady. Without him nearby, her thoughts dipped and shot sideways, scattering and re-forming worse than before.

No one listened to her.

Her mother had not. Joelle thought of her, lying in bed watching television with Trapper most weekends, or endlessly cleaning when he was out driving trains. Everything had changed when they moved to Pieman's Junction. Her mother laughed a high, screechy laugh when Trapper's sons were mean to Joelle. She agreed with Trapper when he said Joelle was stupid. She told Joelle to go upstairs and keep out of everyone's way, especially when Trapper's friends came over. She cut Joelle's hair short because it was always knotty. They never even watched cartoons together anymore because her mother said the sound got on Trapper's nerves.

It wasn't always like that.

Before they moved into Trapper's house, her mother liked to brush and plait her hair. She took her late-night shopping at Kmart and afterward they had cinnamon doughnuts. On hot days her mother took her to a park by a river and they would dip their feet in the cold water. Joelle never understood why her mother always said that living at Trapper's in Pieman's Junction was the best thing that ever happened to her.

After Wendy Field went missing, a customer at the supermarket told Joelle's mother she saw Joanne Sparrow in the car outside the pub that night. A few days later, someone graffitied about Joelle on the front path. Joelle's mother gripped her arms and said in a hard, mean voice, "What have you done?"

She didn't want an answer though.

Joelle had met Trent outside the takeaway shop. He stuck up for her when the school kids teased her. The attention he gave her felt so good. Joelle went back to the takeaway shop several times, hoping to see him. She was waiting there, eating fries, the night Wendy would die. Thinking about the past was like being sucked into a deep, black hole. Bad memories came to life in your brain. Joanne Sparrow, a horrible girl who smoked cigarette after cigarette, tossing their hot remains out the car window. It was summer and high fire danger and she didn't care about anything except Trent being nice to her and drinking the green ginger wine even though it made her want to throw up.

That night, when the crying on the back seat got too loud, Joelle said, "Shut up." She said that herself, not anyone else.

They drove too fast on roads weaving through thickly planted pine forest and they were all close to dying. They all said it: *What happens up here, stays up here.* What happened, happened to Wendy, so she had to stay.

It made sense at the time.

* * *

Jack

Calendar House

K anton had lied to him. The police had been inside his hothouse. He could see the remains of their efforts—an African violet had been shoved carelessly to the side, and the stem of a pale orchid was freshly snapped. Bags of potting mix had been moved from their usual spot. The hothouse had just a regular lock on the door. It wouldn't take much fiddling with a special key to open it.

There was nothing in here that would interest the police. However, they were right about one thing: if one wanted to dispose of a body, this would be the place to do it. It was perfectly warm. Anyone walking past would not notice the smell of decomposing flesh; the air was pungent with compost and living soil.

They did not trust him, but he didn't trust them either.

He could not shake the feeling that somehow, he was being set up.

* * *

Miss Gwen

Creek Cottage

In the middle of the night Miss Gwen heard a car doing a burnout on Old Dairy Road. Unemployed youths, she thought, with nothing better to do. Knowing she would not get back to sleep, she turned on her light and read for a while.

She was too tired to read, and her thoughts kept returning to Joelle and her desire to make a new friend. There were mothers from the school who Miss Gwen had seen Joelle chatting to at the school gate. Emily and Baxter were often invited to parties and playdates. However, Miss Gwen had never seen other children playing at Joelle's house.

She heard the screech again. Slowly, she slid out of bed and stood at her window. It was Cliff Gatenby's truck. She recognized the horrible goat's skull and horns on the bull bar. That man was an oaf. You should not judge a woman based on her husband, she thought, but there was something tricky about Kim Gatenby that made Miss Gwen uneasy. There were better friends to be had for Joelle.

CHAPTER 15

Tuesday, August 29

Jack

Latrobe Police Station

The district police office was a ninety-minute drive away, longer in heavy rain that made Jack cautious on the narrow, winding road. It was a nondescript redbrick building surrounded by cracked concrete. He was shown to a cramped room where the curtains were drawn shut. With a strained smile, Jack dismissed his right to have a lawyer present as he gave Inspector Kanton his statement.

"I want to do this quickly so we can all get back out there and look for Celia," he said.

He told the police that he had argued with his wife, gone for a drive, had dinner at the pub, and then gone straight to Cliff Gatenby's office, where he had done two hours' work on behalf of Cliff. He had not seen Cliff, and he had traveled home via his eastern paddocks to check on cattle that had been escaping onto the road. The extra white lie explained why he had not passed the Gatenbys' car en route from his house to theirs.

As the interview was ending, Kanton mentioned Celia's dog, Fergus.

"Where was he when you got home?"

"Asleep by the fire."

"What's his temperament?"

"Fergus is a gentle giant. He's very old. We keep him inside a lot."

"Is he protective of Celia?"

"Very. And of my daughters."

"A few people I spoke to yesterday said he was a bit snappy. He wasn't upset when you arrived home?"

He kept his expression neutral, a perfect poker face. "If the dog was in the living room, he wouldn't have heard the front door open. He's old and deaf."

The truth was they usually tied him up when visitors came. Fergus jumped and barked and frightened people, even those who knew he was gentle.

Kanton's lips twitched in a satisfied smile and Jack realized his mistake in admitting that the dog was asleep when he got home. It was unjust; telling the truth gave Kanton further reason to suspect him. Likewise, as soon as he admitted he had spent part of the evening with the Keegans, the depraved nature of their relationship would provide another reason why a man might dispose of his wife—to preserve his reputation.

Jack did not realize how unnerving the interview was until he got into his car. He placed his arms on the wheel and leaned his head back. He wished there was someone he could talk to.

When he got home, he heated up some soup and tried to

call his mother-in-law, Martha. There was no answer. Frustrated, he called Kim.

"She won't let me talk to the girls," he explained.

"She's always been a tough woman," Kim said.

"And the police are not searching properly. They won't use the chopper."

"It's too dangerous in this wind."

After they ended the call, he sat for a while by the fire, wondering what to do. More than forty-eight hours had passed since she had been seen. The whole town had been looking for her—yet no one had found a single trace of her. He walked from room to room. The house was too big, too silent.

Outside it started to snow.

He put on his thick coat and considered taking Fergus with him. In the end, he left him sleeping by the fire. It was cruel to let a dog out in such bitter weather. The wind picked up as he trod across the frost-covered paddock. He realized he had forgotten his gloves when he opened the first gate.

The route zigzagged steeply toward the falls and his breath came in short gasps. His bones ached from the cold and his feet slipped on the track where it was eroded by the record winter rainfall. Exhausted, he imagined running a hot bath and pouring himself a whiskey.

He reached the open glade by the falls. Spray coated his face. He called her name, his voice cracking over the gushing torrent.

He knew one thing, almost for sure. Kanton knew it too, although the police had arrived at a different conclusion. If Fergus was peacefully asleep, it was someone Celia knew who had been at the house on Saturday night.

* * *

Joelle

Vanishing Falls village

J oelle dropped the laundered tea towels and aprons at the butchery. On the corkboard was one of the postcards that Nev sold in his news agency. It showed Wineglass Bay: a perfect curve of white sand wrapped around turquoise water. She extracted the pin and turned the card over. In Brian's handwriting it said, "Can't wait." Joelle clapped her hands. Brian grinned.

"I'm looking forward to taking our kids there," he said. "You're very good at talking me into things, such as being more adventurous with Baxter and Emily."

She stood on tiptoe and kissed his cheek. "I guess you would be lost without me!"

"I would," he said seriously. "Life would be boring."

When she came back out there was a group of women she recognized standing beside her car. Kim was among them and she waved at Joelle.

"You don't normally wear makeup," Joelle said, admiring Kim's lipstick and blushed cheeks. "You look real pretty."

"Celia always encouraged her friends to dress up." Kim's voice wavered. "I was thinking of her when I was getting ready this morning."

"You're doing well, Kim," said Margo Wheeler.

She was a strong-looking woman who always wore riding

boots and often walked her dog along the river path with Celia. She gave Joelle an appraising nod and told Kim, "As I was saying. When I saw his face on television last night it was not the man we know. He's lying."

"I can't think that about Jack," Kim said. "He's a friend. We need to focus on hoping that she went for a walk and twisted her ankle and soon someone will find her and bring her safely home."

"That person will be a bloody hero," Margo said. "If someone brings Celia home, I'll carry them through town on my own shoulders."

"That's a great idea, Margo. I can just imagine it," Joelle said.

"It won't happen, will it? Trying to find anyone in the forest around here is like trying to find a needle in a haystack."

"I told Brian they should hike up to the lookout," Joelle said. "He took me there because it's his favorite place. You can see for miles."

"You won't see anything in this fog," Margo said.

"That's right. You wouldn't see your hand in front of you up in the forest today. If they don't find her soon it will be impossible to know what happened to her," Joelle said. "Brian says her vital organs will all disintegrate, and the police won't be able to tell how she died."

The women stared at her.

"Unless she died from a bullet or knife," Joelle clarified. "That's different."

She swallowed and pressed her fingers on her heart, as though that might stop the babble rising up. Nothing helped. The more they stared, the more her thoughts wanted to explode. "Brian says she'll be close to home. If you look at it statistically, it's someone that knows her. They'll hide the body in a place they know really well."

It wasn't like anyone was mean to her. But people didn't have to say something for you to know what they were thinking. Gradually, like a wave seeping out to sea, the group dispersed until only Kim and Joelle remained. Distressed, Joelle clapped her hand over her mouth.

"I get nervous and I talk a lot," she said.

Kim patted her on the arm. "Don't worry. Let's go get that coffee."

* * *

Rosella Café

Joelle dipped the last bit of carrot cake in the cream and put it in her mouth. Her happiness hummed so hard she looked at her arms to see if they were vibrating. This was, without doubt, the best coffee date ever.

"You're a great listener, Kim."

Kim wanted to know all sorts of things: the recipe for scones, how to cut out appliqué patterns, what were the best types of meat for the cheapest price, what hairstyle Joelle thought might suit Kim if she cut her hair.

"Do you think it's true what Margo said? Would she really carry someone through town if they were a hero and brought Celia back?" Joelle asked.

Kim laughed. "Margo's tough. She could do it—she shears

her own sheep. I think she meant everyone just wants Celia to be found."

Joelle licked whipped cream off her cake fork. "I probably shouldn't say this, Kim . . ."

"You have to say it now."

"A tiny part of me is glad Celia is gone because now you and me are friends."

Kim reached across and squeezed Joelle's hand. "I know what you mean. And yes, we are."

At the end, Joelle insisted on paying for their coffee and cake.

"It's a pleasure," she said grandly. "It is my pleasure. A very big, enormous pleasure."

Kim took her hand. "I'm curious about you."

"Huh?"

"I'd love to know more about you, that's all."

Walking back to the butchery afterward, Joelle was expecting someone to say, *What are you smiling about?* Her cheeks ached from happiness.

* * *

Cliff

Gatenby's Poultry Farm

Kim walked Trixie across the paddock to where Cliff was loading straw bales onto a tractor. In one of the sheds, the broiler litter needed urgent refreshing.

"Can I ask you something?" she began. "Did you think Jack was acting odd yesterday?"

Sometimes she was smarter than he gave her credit for.

"What do you mean?" he said.

"He was too calm. I feel terrible saying this . . ."

"Just say it, Kim."

She took a deep breath. "What if Jack hurt Celia?"

"I've had the same thought," Cliff admitted. "But you never know how a person is going to behave when they're under that kind of pressure."

"I know they had huge life insurance policies for each other."

Cliff climbed off the tractor. He wished she would leave. He was feeling irritated. He had no gear and his skin was crawling. Soon, he knew, he would be remembering the buzz and forgetting the comedown. That's how meth got its claws into people who were weak-minded. He walked around the tractor to get away from her. She followed, oblivious to his irritation.

"Then again, he doesn't need life insurance money," she continued. "The painting is worth over a million."

It wasn't fair. Jack Lily over there boning Keegan's wife and stumbling across a piece of treasure. Cliff stopped working and looked at her.

"You know how Jack got that bit of artwork? He found it in a wreck at Keegan's junkyard. By rights it belongs to the Keegans. They wouldn't have a clue what it's worth."

"He's a talented con man." Kim gave him one of her hope-less looks. "He'll get away with it. Celia was saying that there is no paper trail with the painting. It doesn't exist. That means anyone could sell it. We could sell it."

Cliff plucked a piece of loose straw from his hair. "It would solve a lot of problems. But it wasn't there the night she went missing. Jack told me he left it with someone."

"Who? Where is it, Cliff?"

"Don't know."

"Find out, Cliff. That might explain where Celia is." Kim shivered and tucked her hands into the sleeves of her jacket.

"Find the painting," he said, imitating her. "Like I need another thing to do. I work eighteen hours a day. Where's my million-dollar painting? Where's my Jaguar? Where's my Mercedes?"

Head down, shoulders slumped, she started walking back to the house, the dog trotting faithfully beside her. Then she turned around and said, "You're never going to drive a Mercedes. Suck it up."

He stared, astonished by her rudeness. Damn, that woman was lucky he had a thick skin.

* * *

Joelle

Vanishing Falls School

I n Mrs. Duncan's grade-three classroom Joelle cut out cardboard squares, pasted a child's drawing onto each one, and pinned the artwork to the wall. Usually she was good at cutting and pasting, but twice already she had accidentally cut the edge crookedly, and then, trying to trim it straight, had made it worse. She could not stop thinking about Celia and how to bring her home.

She put the scissors down and looked at the boy delivering a talk to the class. It was Kim's youngest son, Cooper. Joelle smiled encouragingly.

"One pair of rats and their offspring can produce up to eight hundred baby rats within nine months," he read. "On a chicken farm, they use the barn rafters, beams, walls, and fences as a roadway to move around. They eat thirty grams of food each day. Worse, they ruin much more by spilling it or using the food storage areas as a toilet. They carry infectious diseases that can spread to poultry and to humans. They carry parasites such as lice, mites, and fleas. Sometimes they can eat the chicken eggs. They are hard to get rid of because they burrow deeply under the dry matter and nest in hollow walls and holes. We bait them using zinc phosphide. It makes them thirsty so they run out into the open, looking for water, instead of dying and rotting in the chicken sheds. Historically, rat catchers were heroes because they saved the town from plague and diseases brought in by rats."

As he began talking about the fumigation of insects, Joelle's thoughts drifted. She wondered what Baxter and Emily would talk about when it was their turn. She had not known that they needed to prepare a class talk. Lately they had been going to Brian with homework-related questions. It made her sad to think that she couldn't help them.

Margo had talked about someone being a hero. It would

be whoever brought Celia home. Joelle gazed out the window at the rain forest escarpment. Being the woman who found Celia Lily would be so much better than being the girl from Pieman's Junction.

Her daydream was interrupted by the sight of Jack Lily. He was deep in conversation with the school principal. Some of the children pointed him out to each other. Mrs. Duncan began closing the blinds. She said, very quietly, "He's got nerve."

* * *

Cliff

Gatenby's Poultry Farm

Past the turnip paddock was a huge round bulldozer hole he had dug out of sight of the house. It was where they tossed the household and farm waste. He reversed the pickup truck to the edge. He was about to unload rubbish from the tray when an unusual object caught his eye.

He walked over to take a closer look. Nestled on top of the rubbish pile was the goat's skull and horns he had wired to his bull bar. He had no memory of removing it from his vehicle or of bringing it here to his dump. In fact, he had not even realized it was missing from the front of the truck.

Like most men who lived around here, Cliff's pickup truck was pimped-out. The sign above the bull bar said, DO YOU WANT TO PLAY CHICKEN? It was a joke. The stickers on the rear window said worse than that. Kim hated everything about it—but she knew there was nothing she could do.

She was hovering in the yard under her umbrella when he returned. He drove up beside her and asked her what she knew about the goat's skull. She stared at him and shook her head in disbelief.

"That's a problem," she said, "that you don't even know what you're doing from one day to the next."

"You sound like a broken record," he said, and drove away.

* * *

Vanishing Falls Hotel

It was happy hour, yet the pub was dead. He sat at the window drinking beer and watching the cars cut through the rain. He jotted down ideas as they came to him. He wrote long lists of numbers, adding them up and scribbling the total. No matter what he did, it came up short.

The café closed. A customer came out of the butchery. The newsagent walked slowly to his car, an old Chrysler that was always parked right in front of the news agency. That annoyed Cliff. No one should feel entitled to park their car on the main street, every day, all day, just because they arrived at work early.

The butcher brought in his sign. Smithton's Fine Meats always had a steady stream of people coming and going. It was the neatest shop on the main street, with new paint and a huge glass window. If he had his time again, Cliff would open a butchery. Brian Smithton should put a gag on that daft-headed wife of his. Kim said she'd been telling everyone that Brian was speculating on the whereabouts of Celia's body.

He swirled his beer and looked around. The pub couldn't give their beer away. The pub owner hated locals and treated weekend tourists like royalty. Right now the owner stood behind the bar fiddling with the till; he couldn't even be bothered to come and collect the empty glasses on Cliff's table. Apart from the old bird sipping wine while she slid coins in the slot machine, Cliff was the only customer in the place.

A man wearing a hoodie paused outside the pub. Cliff nodded. They had exchanged several texts, which Cliff had already deleted. He had not used this guy before. An accumulated debt with his usual contact had forced him to pursue this new relationship. He stood up and tucked his wallet into his pocket. A sweet tremor of anticipation ran through him.

The owner acknowledged Cliff's thanks with an unfriendly nod.

"See you next Tuesday," Cliff called nastily.

* * *

Gatenby's Poultry Farm

He locked the office door.

It was a relief to sort himself out.

He felt it slide down the back of his throat, like swallowing warm, thick treacle, the kind his granny used to give him when he was sick. Heat rushed through him, from his brain to his face, and all the way down to his toes. The familiar chemical taste soured his tongue and his skin tingled deliciously.

Inspired ideas spun kaleidoscopically through his mind. Celia appeared and reappeared—playing tennis, chasing the children around the lawn, tossing a salad in her kitchen. Her silky hair and those tanned, lithe legs. She was talking to him, telling him something about Pieman's Junction and Joelle Smithton.

When the rush ebbed into an energy more controllable, he set to work. A Google search brought up old photos showing a very young Joelle Smithton and three blokes who looked like they had been kicked in the face by a steel-cap boot when they were babies.

Back then the butcher's wife was called Joanne Sparrow.

The details made his skin crawl.

On a summer's night in 1999, Joanne Sparrow and her boyfriend, Trent Campbell, drove past the Pieman's Junction Hotel as a barmaid called Wendy Field was ending her shift. Trent's two mates cajoled her into the back seat of the car with the promise of a lift home. They took her up to a disused mining village and tied her to a bunk.

Cliff gritted his teeth at the details. All the time those fiendish things were happening, Joanne Sparrow was copulating on the other bunk with her boyfriend.

No wonder she changed her name.

He expanded the image on the screen. Joanne Sparrow, at fourteen, was better-looking than the victim, who was too skinny, with short hair. Joelle had dimples and plump lips and a big curly hairdo. She had already developed that impressive rack. If she didn't wear wacky outfits with bright pictures sewn everywhere, Joelle Smithton would scrub up all right.

His recollections of the night Celia disappeared were messy. Now, like scattered seed that was beginning to shoot up, things started to make sense. He could see Celia sitting beside him in the front seat, giving him that cheeky smile of hers that promised the world and delivered nothing. There were other images: his wife sitting quietly in the back seat looking out the window; the spray as he drove steadily through the flooded Murdering Creek crossing; and on the veranda of the hotel, Celia flicking the cigarette into the darkness. He had watched the ember slowly falling to the street, where the butcher was sitting in his car watching them.

* * *

Jack

Calendar House farmland

He spent Tuesday afternoon on horseback, riding the farm boundary. For the second time he checked the potato storage and drying sheds, and he walked through the hay barns and the old milking sheds. At the bridge he dismounted. He leaned over the parapet and surveyed the river below. The water moved with heavy surges, thrusting with the debris it had picked up along the way. This was the deepest part of the river. Farther down, it split and formed Murdering Creek, the waterway that had once serviced the old mill. There was a lot of water moving down. The police divers had not bothered with the river. A person who fell in here would be gone forever. Sucked out to sea or wedged beneath a tree root in the muddy depths. If you wanted someone to disappear, the river would do the job for you.

From a hilltop above the river bend Jack called Inspector Kanton. She reminded him police had already searched in all the places he had just looked.

"Except the river," he said.

"Do you think she's in the river?"

"No. Maybe. We need to check everywhere."

Flustered, he wondered if she was baiting him. Without thinking, he mentioned that the dog was helping him search.

"Nothing has disturbed Fergus except a family of rabbits."

"That's a long distance for an old dog to cover, especially if you're on a horse."

Jack hesitated. "He's used to it."

A huge crack of lightning lit up the sky and the horse jumped. The mare tugged on the bridle and he ended the call. He gave her some slack and she trotted toward home.

* * *

It was dark when he settled the horse in the stable and went into his house. He lit a fire, fed the dog, and poured a drink. It felt obscene to be warming himself while his wife was God knows where.

Two drinks in, Kim telephoned. Her familiar voice soothed him. They talked over the events of their day and then Kim said, "I have to ask you . . ."

"No, you don't."

"Have you considered that she might have run off?"

"Oh. Well. I can only hope she has."

"Celia is smart enough to orchestrate a thing like that."

"The police don't think it's likely." Since she had left, he had checked their bank accounts online several times a day. Nothing had been touched. "She wouldn't leave the girls."

A long pause.

"Are you quite certain she hasn't staged her own disappearance?"

"Yes," Jack said.

"You don't sound convinced."

The implication offended him, and he would have confronted her about it, except he could hear Cliff saying something in the background. There was a crashing sound and one of the boys cried out. That house was always chaotic.

"I've got to go," Kim said. "Talk tomorrow." She hung up abruptly.

His anger at Kim's suggestion faded. Indeed, he had wondered if his wife had pulled off a great deception. Perhaps Celia had followed him to Marsh End and sat down the road in her car while he went inside that house where the dinner dishes piled up in the sink, the television blared, and the woman wore an orange dressing gown covered in cat hair. Celia had the temperament to bide her time.

She had left him once, before they had children. They had argued at a friend's wedding. She had not said goodbye, nor had she returned to their hotel room. Jack had found her days later at her mother's house, two hours' drive away in Launceston. She never apologized for the stress she had caused him. If anyone could orchestrate their own disappearance, Celia could.

It was not likely, no matter what his mother said. In his heart, he knew she would never leave her children behind.

Folded on the couch was Celia's gray cashmere blanket. He pressed his face into its softness and closed his eyes. The fabric smelled of her. It was spicy, like sandalwood or cardamom. He could see her lying here, reading a novel, her hair fanned out around her shoulders.

So many times, her gladness to see him had filled him with a sickening shame. He hated that as he ate the dinner she had cooked for him or watched her fold his laundry, he was compelled to question her incessantly about her day. Despite all his lawyer's tricks to find out otherwise, it was clear her days were filled with simple pleasures—coffee with Kim or other women, taking the girls to ballet, watching riding lessons, grooming horses, cooking, gardening, and jogging. He was the one with something to hide, yet he always needed to know where she had been and whom she had spoken with. He both feared and hoped he would catch her out. He wondered if he loved her too much.

There were times when he wished that she would guess what he was up to. She could have stopped him going to Marsh End.

CHAPTER 16

Wednesday, August 30

Joelle

The Smithtons' house

Apavlova decorated with strawberries, kiwi fruit, and passion-fruit seeds was on the front cover of *The Australian Women's Weekly Basic Cookbook*. It was Joelle's second-favorite recipe book and had been a wedding gift from Darla, along with the *Dinner Party Cookbook* and the *Children's Birthday Cake Book*. She liked them all, but the birthday cake book was the best. Without saying anything, Darla had made it clear that she expected Joelle to have kids. The pages were splattered and there were only three cakes she had not yet made—the piano, the castle, and the log cabin.

Joelle had never used the *Dinner Party Cookbook*. Teatime was best when it was just her and Brian and the twins. Once, they had invited one of Brian's suppliers and his wife to have dinner at their house, but it had been hectic with Joelle so busy making sure everyone had drinks and something to talk about that the roast lamb had burned. Everyone laughed about it. But when the supplier made a good-natured joke about a butcher's wife not knowing how to cook meat Brian had stopped laughing. Knowing that Brian could not bear someone being unkind to her, Joelle said, "It's just a joke, Brian."

Baking was something she preferred to do alone. You needed to set your mind to it, if you wanted to do it right. Joelle was very good at it. She made the same treats, again and again: melting moments, chocolate chip cookies, marble cake, and delicious cinnamon banana loaf. Brian said her sponge cakes were as fluffy as if she had whipped white summer clouds into the mixture; her lemon meringue pie made him close his eyes when he tasted it. Usually, her cakes did not look like the illustrations, but Brian said it was how they tasted that mattered. It was a mystery to both of them why her cakes never won a prize at the Vanishing Falls Royal Show baking competition.

She liked the process, the order of taking out the flour and measuring it into the bowl, melting the butter, folding the wet mixture into the dry mixture. She liked scraping the batter into the baking dish or pressing the damp balls of dough flat onto the baking tray with a fork. First Darla, then Miss Gwen, had helped her to make each recipe a few times. After that, she never had a problem remembering how to make each item. The list of ingredients helped remind her what to do. So long as you followed the recipe, nothing went wrong.

She opened the *Basic* book for inspiration. Trying to choose between the kiss biscuits and the melting moments was a big decision. Once a month Miss Gwen asked her to bake something to sell at the Country Women's Association shop. It was one of the places where Miss Gwen volunteered and they raised money to help farming families. Miss Gwen had said the kiss biscuits sold better. Joelle knew that meant she should bake them, but the melting moments looked so much more special.

She was still trying to decide when Brian telephoned.

"Don't get upset, but I told Nev what you saw at the fair. Hush, I want you to listen to me. Nev was not surprised. He agrees with me, especially given Celia's situation as a missing person, we need to tell the police."

"No, no, no."

"It's about doing the right thing."

"Please, Brian. Don't talk to the police today. I need time to think. I can't think, Brian."

There was a long pause. She could imagine him biting his lower lip as he considered his position. Brian did not take decisions lightly.

"Fine," he said. "Let's talk it over tonight."

"Thank you. I love you. I just want you to be proud of me."

"I'm already proud of you . . . so proud, my love."

He would not be proud, though, once he talked to the police and they told him who she really was.

She sat at the kitchen table, turning the pages of her recipe book from melting moments to kiss biscuits and back again. It was all too complicated.

She put her head in her hands. The troubling thing was, she wanted to tell Brian all the things that were worrying her. He always helped her fix her problems. If Darla were alive, she would shake her head. Darla had made her promise never to speak of Pieman's Junction, not to anyone. *Brian is a good man,* she had said, *but even good men don't need to know everything about everyone.*

* * *

Vanishing Falls village

With no baking for Miss Gwen to place on the cake table, Joelle walked reluctantly along the main street to the Country Women's Association shop. Miss Gwen was sitting inside with Alfred Cheng the grocer. They had been friends since they were teenagers. Back then the pair of them had been in love, Miss Gwen had told her. Every Saturday night they went out together—to a barn dance or a cocktail party or sometimes to the Princess Theatre. In those days, when a special play came, the queue stretched down to the old apothecary shop.

Sadly, Miss Gwen had explained, it was not to be. Mr. Cheng Senior, an invalid who lived above the green grocery store and banged his walking stick on the floorboards when he needed something, had suffered a broken heart when his wife ran off with a lantern lighter from the circus. He said his son, Alfred, could only marry a Chinese girl. So Miss Gwen and Alfred never married but remained the best of friends. Miss Gwen never met anyone else she wanted to marry. Fortunately for her, there weren't many Chinese girls in Vanishing Falls, so neither did Alfred.

Joelle's thoughts stalled as she realized what was taped to the glass door of the Country Women's Association shop. It was a missing-person poster. There was a big photo of Celia Lily, beautiful and smiling. Around her was endless ocean and sky, and under her outstretched arms were the blond heads of her daughters. Their faces had been cropped out of the photo.

It made Joelle think of the missing-person posters that had been everywhere that week in Pieman's Junction. Even after Wendy's funeral, you still saw them in gutters and rubbish bins. There were too many.

Miss Gwen and Alfred waved from inside, beckoning her to hurry up and come in.

Joelle's body felt as heavy as the granite statue stuck to the concrete platform in the park. Old memories surged up in her throat, threatening to turn into words and sentences, a bilious, rushing story that no one would want to hear.

Alfred opened the door for her. She had to go in. There were more pictures inside, showing Celia riding her horse and standing in front of a garden of snapdragons and tulips. There was a wedding photo of her with her handsome husband, their arms looped, holding champagne glasses.

"You're very pale, dear," Miss Gwen said. "You need to warm up."

Joelle took the teacup Miss Gwen handed her. She tried not to look at the posters, but she couldn't help it.

"What have you baked?" Alfred asked.

"I didn't bake." Joelle felt worse remembering this. "I'm not my usual self."

"We all have days like that," he said.

"Tonight, when Brian comes home from work, he'll try to guess what's for dinner and there will be nothing." Joelle put the cup of tea down. She held her hand to her mouth, squeezing her lips to stop herself from crying. It didn't work.

"Hush, dear," Miss Gwen said. "If I know Brian, he won't mind. Nothing wrong with eggs on toast for dinner."

That made Joelle cry more. She leaned against Miss Gwen, conscious of the older woman's dainty shoulders and her motherly way of patting Joelle's arm. Soon Joelle's sobs lessened, and she could hear Alfred slurping his tea. It was a horrible, gurgling sound. She looked over at him.

"Is that you making all that noise?" she asked.

"Now, now," Miss Gwen said. "I wonder who can help me arrange the jams? They're all wrong."

Joelle knew what needed doing. It was simple. She lined them up in a different order, the apricot jam to the left, and the dark red raspberry jam and applesauce to the right.

Alfred didn't help. He kept chatting in between slurps of tea. He remembered how his grandfather ran cows in the high pastures. A few animals went missing. The grandfather accused his neighbor and they had a fistfight, which was reported in the evening paper. Weeks later, the carcasses of the cows were found, twenty-five kilometers away, in the wetland. They had wandered into the forest, fallen into the water hole, and got flushed down through the underground river.

"The Vanishing Falls water hole is a dangerous drainpipe. Thinking about Celia Lily, my money is on that water hole. That could be it." Alfred's brow furrowed as he elaborated. "The underground river comes out in the wetland bog. They should look there."

Joelle nodded. What he said made sense. He wasn't excited talking about it, like how Brian had been the day she disappeared, but more matter-of-fact.

"Brian thinks she's been killed and dumped in the forest."

Miss Gwen put down a pot of jam with a thud. In her loud, huffy voice, the one she used when she thought the nursing home manager was getting too big for her boots, she said, "No more of this talk. I've got too much to do and you're not helping, Alfred."

"Yes, she's right." Joelle nodded. "You always sit back and watch us do all the work."

"Hang on." He grinned. "I don't even work here. I've got my own business to run."

"Have you ever thought that maybe if you were more helpful, Miss Gwen might have accepted one of your marriage proposals?" Joelle joked.

"Third time's a charm, they say," he said.

"Enough of this rubbish," Miss Gwen said.

Joelle offered Alfred the plate of marshmallow-topped biscuits Miss Gwen had set on the table.

"Try an Iced VoVo," she said.

"They look stale." Alfred took one.

"Now, you're saying that because you know Miss Gwen made them." Joelle took one of the larger biscuits for herself. "You're a tease."

"Watch him. He'll have two at least," Miss Gwen said.

Everyone ate their biscuit and looked at each other.

"A comfortable silence," Joelle said, and they all laughed.

Friends made you feel better, no matter what the trouble was. Plus, Alfred had just given her an idea. A really good idea that would make everything better.

Miss Gwen began clearing up the tea things. Alfred pushed

himself onto his feet. He put his hat on and took a second biscuit. Miss Gwen stood at the window as he walked slowly back to his green grocer's store.

* * *

Vanishing Falls wetlands

Her anticipation and excitement increased as she drove away from town.

Before Brian went to the police, she would find out what happened to Celia. Like Margo Wheeler said, Joelle would be a hero. She would never be the girl from Pieman's Junction. There would be a special program about the Celia Lily Mystery, hosted by Oprah. Joelle would sit on the couch with Oprah and she would wear her tropical frangipani dress with the off-the shoulder ruffle. She saw it when they were Christmas shopping in Latrobe last year. Brian thought it was too cold for Vanishing Falls. He had bought it for her anyway, but he was right. It still had the tag on it.

Alfred did not realize it, but he had told her exactly where to look.

The wetland was a twenty-minute drive out past Marsh End. She walked around the edges of the springy peat bog. The damp air smelled faintly unpleasant, like rotten eggs. She tried to remember if it had smelled so bad when she came there with Brian. He had said the Aboriginal people had used it like a supermarket, collecting eggs, birds, fish, plants, and water.

There were deep pools between mossy pathways. Ducks sat

cozily on a pillowy green island. Wallabies grazed on the edge of the button grass moorland. They weren't frightened. She looked into each pool but all she saw was her own reflection. It wasn't that she hoped Celia was dead. She just wanted to go back to town and tell Brian, *I found her!*

Across the wetland and the button grass the pencil pines stood in a long, unflinching line. There was nothing else to see. On the other side were the floodlands and the road. A car moved slowly, like the driver too was looking for someone, and then disappeared into the pines.

She looked around her. The birds and the wallabies had gone. The only movement was the water, shivering as though it knew a storm was coming.

* * *

Jack

Vanishing Falls village

J ack was having a phone conversation with one of the reporters who kept calling him when Kim came out of the Rosella Café flanked by several ladies he knew. He answered a few more questions, watching the women as they kissed each other goodbye and wiped their eyes. Eventually, he told the reporter to call him back if she had any new information, and he ended the call. It seemed the media were as useless as the police.

Kim crossed the street toward him with a length to her

stride that was at odds with her usual shuffle. He wondered if she was enjoying the attention that came with being the best friend of the missing woman. On the footpath outside the café, the women of Vanishing Falls continued hugging each other.

One of them gave him a half-hearted wave, which he returned. They were Celia's friends and he had known them for years. He had telephoned each of them on Sunday. Their reactions were shock, distress, concern, and, in one case, hysterics. They had all agreed Celia would be found. No one accused him of being instrumental in Celia's disappearance.

Country women were good at making their feelings clear. When Celia had her cancer scare, she and Jack were inundated with wine, flowers, and frozen containers of home-cooked meals. Jack had complained that he was sick of eating spaghetti Bolognese, curry, and pumpkin soup. Generous displays of support were normal in this town. But now no one had dropped off even a bunch of flowers, let alone a spaghetti Bolognese for Jack. Their indifference was ferocious.

A cold wind tugged at his scarf.

"Just ignore them," Kim said as she reached him. "You know what they're like."

He was startled to recognize her dress. He had bought it for Celia on a business trip. It was a dark blue silk wraparound that had cost nearly five hundred dollars. What on earth was Kim thinking?

In Celia's dress, she looked like a weather-beaten sparrow wearing a peacock's finery. He supposed she wore it as a tribute to Celia. It was getting harder and harder to know what was right. She gave him a long, heartfelt hug and he regretted thinking uncharitable thoughts.

He knew Kim tried to be a good wife, a loyal friend. Her constancy was never rewarded. He recalled Celia feeling sorry for Kim. It was not fair, Celia said, that life could be so generous to some people, and so harsh on others. He thought of the baby Kim had been forced to give up for adoption, the university degree she had never been able to pursue, the husband who let himself be crushed by drug addiction. Celia was probably the only person who had never let Kim down, and now she was gone.

"Those friends of yours all think I did it." Jack framed it as a statement, but he was curious as to how Kim would respond.

"They barely looked at me."

"No one knows what to think. Cliff and I have your back." She took a breath. "I hate to be the one to tell you this. But at lunch, someone said you . . . might be seeing someone."

"That's ridiculous." He was indignant for a moment; then a grotty image of Keegan's wife swam into his mind.

"I told them it was rubbish."

He nodded, although he did not believe a word of it. Kim was the kind of woman who agreed with everyone, all the time. He could not imagine her defending him. Jack frowned at the women across the road.

"Who am I allegedly having an affair with?"

"Around here, if people don't know what's going on, they make it up. I'm no better. I feel like Celia has had a sudden mental breakdown but that she is okay and living somewhere beautiful. She's taken the colonial painting and sold it and is living off the proceeds."

"It's a nice idea, Kim. She hasn't touched her credit cards. Her passport is here."

"If she sold the painting—"

"She doesn't have the painting," he snapped. "It's in storage at the Keegans'."

"The Keegans'?"

He regretted speaking harshly to her. "He's a client. I had it cleaned and was showing it to him, and then I couldn't get it back to my car because of the rain. The moment this rain stops, I'm going to get it. It's in a storeroom on their veranda. It's safe." He was blathering. "How is Cliff?"

"It's a nightmare." She gave him a tedious look. "He's obsessed with Joelle Smithton."

"He told me that Celia threatened Joelle. But Celia is not that callous."

"Yeah," she said, but she didn't sound convinced.

He surveyed the street. It was now empty apart from some teenage girls sipping soft drinks outside the takeaway shop and two elderly people walking with their grandchildren.

"All the bad things that happen around here—robberies, domestic situations, child neglect—it's all related to the meth epidemic," he said. "That house fire out near the swamp was a meth lab exploding."

An ordinary woman would rebuke him or dissolve in distress. Not Kim. Beneath her frail, meek exterior was a steel backbone.

"What are you saying, Jack?"

"Crystal meth is a dangerous drug—"

She raised her palm. "Stop with the advice."

He didn't blame her for her anger. In the past months he had promised her he would help Cliff, yet, from where she viewed it, all Jack had done was try to distance himself.

* * *

Joelle

The Smithtons' house

The house was empty. She went into the kitchen and checked the calendar. In Brian's handwriting it said that he was picking the kids up from basketball training and would be home at six o'clock. The weird thing was that there was food in Snowcat's bowl. It looked like the food she had put there that morning.

She stood at the back door and called the little orange cat's name. The wind tossed her voice. Even if Snowcat was close by, he might not hear her. It was so wet you couldn't see where the rain met the creek. The night echoed with the gurgling sound of flushing mud, rushing creeks, and a thousand dripping leaves. Wild animals and birds knew how to shelter in the rain forest. Snowcat would not survive a night out here.

She rang Brian at work to tell him the bad news.

"You're not going to believe it," she began. "The cat's run off again."

"He'll come back."

"Brian, are you taking this seriously?"

"I always take Snowcat seriously."

He had to serve a customer, and they ended the call before she had a chance to ask him if it was okay for her to walk along the creek. Brian did not like her walking in the forest at night.

The first time she had broken one of Brian's rules was when she did a cannonball into the water hole. On a hot January day, she had hiked up to the waterfall on her own. Some local kids were daring each other to jump off. Joelle was the first to run and jump. It was a long way down. Her eyeballs almost froze when she opened them under the cold water. A stranger pulled her out and she lay on the bank for ages. Brian was waiting for her when she got home. He told her that the rules were there to protect her and that he would always find out if she broke them. Someone would tell him, he said.

But what was worse? Breaking a rule, or letting your cat drown in the rain? Brian would probably say, "Go have a quick look for the cat." She looked out at the rain for a few more minutes. The day after Celia went missing, searchers had walked up and down the creek. They never returned. Brian said if they didn't come back, they weren't doing their job properly. Water moved and moved things, he said. He didn't elaborate; she knew what he was thinking. Celia might be lying dead in the creek, right in everyone's backyard.

Joelle put on her raincoat and walked through the backyard and across the little creek bridge. The rain nipped at her face with small, cold teeth, and it made her tuck her head down and shove her hands in her pockets like a kid. She thought back to when she was little. They lived in lots of different places until her mother married Trapper and they moved into his house. Often, Joelle imagined being grown up and how she would live in the same house forever. It would be a sunny house with a flower garden, and she would cook a nice meal every night for a husband who came home and kissed her on the cheek. They would sit at the table to eat like people did on television. She would be a kindergarten teacher or a lady who worked in a fashion boutique and wore high heels and pretty dresses.

They remained at Trapper's place for longer than they had lived in any house before, but it was not as good as Joelle hoped. At Trapper's, you had to be quiet whenever he was home because he was tired from driving the coal trains. If he was reclining in his chair—the blue undershirt he always wore stretched across his mountainous gut—she kept out of the living room, especially if her mother was not home. It was an old house that made a lot of noise—grinding taps, rattling windows, and every time a coal train passed the walls shook. Trains were long and took ages to go by and the loudness could hide the warning sound of the squeaky hall floorboard that told you he was coming.

At Darla's she feared being sent back to Pieman's Junction. She thought that would be the worst thing that could ever happen to her. But now she knew there was something far, far worse . . . and that would be to get kicked out of Vanishing Falls.

She reached the fork and stopped. The track vanished into the dark hollow beneath the clasped branches of giant trees. The falls bellowed like a giant baby crying in the forest. Scared, she hurried back down the way she had come. At the section of path that ran along the barbed-wire fence of the Lilys' farm stood a man. He was dressed in a black raincoat and beanie and he was calling out to her.

"You shouldn't be out here," he shouted.

She stepped to the side of the trail, hoping he would pass her by.

He moved toward her slowly, never taking his eyes off her. "Where are you going?" he asked.

"I'm looking for my cat."

"A cat?" He sounded like a person who didn't like cats.

"He doesn't catch wildlife."

"That you know of." He was missing a few teeth and his face was red. "You're Brian's wife. I saw you going up the hill. I was coming to get you."

She stared at him in horror.

"Take it easy." He spoke with the local drawl, where the words came out flat, like his voice box had gone rusty from lack of use. "I wanted to help you."

"I'm not supposed to talk to strangers."

"That's okay. I'm Brendan. I used to play cricket with Brian, a long time ago. So I'm no stranger."

"Okay."

"Tell me about your cat," he said. "I might have seen it."

They set off together. It was slippery walking toward the creek cottages. He offered her his arm. She refused, politely, not wanting to offend him, but not wanting to stand too close to him.

It turned out he liked hearing about her cat.

"Orange, friendly, pink nose, long tail. White fluffy stomach. He dribbles when he's asleep and he snores too. He even snores when he's having his throat stroked."

"He sounds like a character."

"He is! I'll tell you something else. I'm going to find the missing woman." She looked down the deep grassy bank at the creek, trying to see something in its black crease. "Her name is Celia."

"Ah well. The police won't find her because they're fools. They searched my land yesterday. No one even bothered knocking on my door. The night she went missing I was called to a job. Someone got himself bogged up near Myrtle Bridge. When I got there, no one was there. Maybe they got themselves un-stuck and drove off. Coming back down, my tow truck nearly got wiped out by a white pickup truck flogging up the middle of Myrtle Bridge Road. He was lucky I was well over on my side. You'd think the cops would want to ask me about that. They're idiots, all idiots. That's all it is."

He sounded angry. She did not speak in case she said some-thing that made him even more cross.

After they walked in silence for a while, he started the con-versation again. "Anyway. Cats are tough. Nine lives. You got more chance of finding your cat."

At the crest of the hill he pointed through the rain at the row of cottages along the creek. He wore yellow fingerless gloves.

"That's you," he said. "Go."

She ran.

*　*　*

When Brian was cross with her it felt like she was shrinking, or maybe it was more like he was getting bigger and bigger like the cat did when it saw something scary in the bushes.

"Tell me again," he said. "You went looking for the cat, and a strange man walked you home?"

"The cat, Brian. The important thing is that we find the cat."

"Who was the man?"

She couldn't remember his name. Brian's mouth was set hard, like it had been carved on his face. She closed her eyes and cast her thoughts back until she could hear, in her head, the odd man saying his name.

"Brendan. That's his name."

"I thought so. I don't want you talking to him."

"Why?"

"It's not safe anymore."

She closed her eyes again. It never was safe to start with.

From her bedroom, she could hear him locking the back door. He walked to the front of the house and pulled the dead-lock into place. She knew he was trying to protect her and the children. Still, she couldn't help but think she was as locked in as anyone else was locked out.

* * *

Jack

Calendar House

At twilight Jack fed the horses, then took Fergus for a walk along the river. It was ground he had covered several times. The shifting river was full. It moved with a gleaming stillness that concealed its strength. When Fergus scampered into the bushes, Jack waited.

Across the river, where the hiking trail entered the forest, he saw Brendan Keegan and Joelle Smithton. Side by side, they came down the hill from the forest, chatting like the oldest friends in the world. He stepped into a gum copse so he could observe them unobtrusively. They walked down to the creek cottages. Joelle went ahead, and Keegan remained on the track, watching. Marsh End was at least an hour's walk from here. He was a long way from home.

Late that night Jack drank a glass of port and stared into the fire. Celia had said that Joelle Smithton lacked intelligence, and that this was an advantage. He was no longer sure. He could not help but wonder if Keegan and Joelle were colluding. Were they friends? Jack did not know, but in a small community such as Vanishing Falls anything was possible.

Perhaps Joelle had told Keegan about the drug use she had witnessed in the school toilets. Keegan was crafty; he could use that information to blackmail Jack into walking away from the painting. If that was Keegan's strategy it would work.

With his hands shoved in his pockets, a stance all too familiar to Jack, Keegan watched Joelle until she went through her garden gate, before returning the way they had come. Crucially, he had remained out of sight of the cottages. It was the behavior of a man with something to hide.

Jack's theory was a long shot but that was no reassurance.

He had made many mistakes—his visits to Marsh End, his carelessness with the painting, the way he had underestimated people. These loose ends needed to be tied up.

* * *

Cliff

Gatenby's Poultry Farm

The most striking photo of Brian Smithton depicted him standing beside a heavy butcher's hook with sausages slung on it. He held a cleaver. The accompanying story was about his secret ingredients for beef sausages, which weren't so secret after all—just top-quality beef, no additives or gristle. He made the casings and stuffed them on-site, the old-fashioned way. It was the kind of information that usually warmed Cliff to someone.

He took a black pen and circled Brian's face. There were many people in town who had a grievance against the Lilys. The butcher was the only one who would have the know-how to dismember and dispose of a carcass.

Cliff's dossier was impressive. Every article on the internet concerning itself with the Pieman's Junction Murder was now printed and glued in the scrapbook. For background, he included several unrelated pieces. There was the sausage story, three news stories on the spat over the name change from Murdering Creek to Hollybank Creek, and a series on the

Vanishing Falls Historical Committee showing Celia smiling like the Apple Queen she thought she was.

There were connections here. They weren't all clear yet—but they would be. He'd work it out.

* * *

The boys leaned over the table like salivating dogs, waiting for the whistle granting them permission to eat. The smell of the shepherd's pie steaming on their plates turned Cliff's stomach.

Kim tried to kiss his cheek.

"I'm filthy," he said, leaning away.

He took his time washing his hands in the kitchen sink. Soaping each finger and rubbing at the printer ink stains. The boys watched him quietly. Three sandy heads. They had inherited his looks but not his disposition. Their mother was spoiling them.

"Are you eating?" she said.

"I think I've worked something out."

He began to describe the contents of the dossier to her. She shook her head, indicating that it was something the boys should not hear.

"What's your problem, Kim?" he shouted. "You've got your head in the sand. You think you don't have to worry about anything because I'll do everything for you."

The boys were hunched over, staring at their food. He could not sit down with them. He dried his hands on a tea towel and whipped the towel toward them, making them flinch. He threw it into the sink and returned to his office.

CHAPTER 17

Thursday, August 31

Joelle

The Smithtons' house

Her dreams were about Celia—drowned in the water hole, hanging from a noose in the lone tree in the paddock where the Lilys' horses lived, curled up and shot dead in a ditch. In each dream she kept begging Joelle to do something. In the worst dream, Celia and Joelle sat in the back seat of a car looking out at tall trees rushing past.

After the twins were born, she had terrible dreams followed by hours of sleeplessness. It was exhausting looking after two tiny babies, even though Brian's sister had moved in to help with the nights, and Miss Gwen was there almost every day. At night, after each feed, she would try to match her breathing to Brian's, or count the many reasons why she loved him, but her thoughts often betrayed her and she worried about how she would cope if he no longer wanted her, or if the twins were taken away, or who would look after her young family if she died. Darla had said it was because she felt she had so much to lose. At times it felt like the night would never end.

Come spring a small brown bush bird rescued her. He made his nest in the leatherwood outside her bedroom window. His curious voice called out in the quiet hours before dawn. His song brought the happy news that the long night was almost over. By the end of the summer she counted three nests and a big family of bush birds living among the leatherwood's fragrant rosy blossoms. In the winter the birds left. She told Brian why she missed them, and he bought her the clock radio.

She thought of that man, Brendan, with his ugly fingerless gloves. On the night Celia went missing he had seen a white pickup truck zooming down Myrtle Bridge Road. There was nothing much up that road. It went above the falls and was usually just used by logging trucks.

Brian's big arms held her tightly. She watched the bedside clock as it flicked to a new number. It was nearly time to get up, but not quite, and she didn't want to wake him. Nights were long in the rain forest.

"I know you're awake," he whispered.

"I'm thinking about Celia."

He kissed her neck, in behind her ear where it tickled nicely. "Hush."

"The man I was talking to saw a pickup truck coming down from the mountains that night. A white one."

"Give me a break." Brian rolled out of bed and switched the light on. His face was red. "I had my problems with Jack Lily but that's a stretch."

"I wasn't thinking about your white butchery truck," she said, but he had already gone into the bathroom and closed the door.

* * *

Jack

Calendar House

Victoria Lily's pale blue car arrived unannounced as he drank his morning espresso. Her driver circled the turning area slowly before stopping beside the house. The car door opened, and a black umbrella popped out. Jack placed his cup down and frowned. His mother turning up now was the last thing he needed.

His mother, Victoria Lily, was a small woman who dressed immaculately. Today she wore navy slacks with a matching blazer. A brooch was pinned to her lapel. She raised her hand and waved in the style of the Queen.

"Darling boy," she called. "It's so good to be home."

He kissed her cheeks and escorted her inside. The driver followed carrying two suitcases.

"This is a surprise," he said. "How long are you staying?"

"I'm not leaving until we sort this out," she said reassuringly.

"Great." Jack tried to hide his disappointment.

Her heels clicked across the entrance hallway floorboards. She went straight to the formal sitting room. It was a large room, containing late-eighteenth-century furnishings and papered in the original blue botanical wallpaper chosen by the first owner of the house. The stiff chairs and precious collectibles meant they rarely used it.

"Tell me what happened." Her smooth hair bobbed on her

shoulders. She indicated he should sit beside her on the chaise longue. "I don't understand."

"I don't know what to tell you."

She studied him closely. "We need a cup of tea first."

He did as she asked, setting up her favorite tea set on a small blackwood table. He poured her tea, and then his own, and passed her the sugar bowl.

"Why are you really here?" he said. "You're not a detective, Mother."

"Did you receive my last letter?"

"You know I did. And now I can't find it."

"Where is it?"

"Maybe the police took it as evidence."

"I can't recall what I wrote."

"Yes, you can."

"Did Celia see it?"

"I don't know."

"Oh dear." She patted his knee. It was almost an apology, and the affection unspooled him. His composure slipped and he began to cry. "Mother, I'm scared. They think I did it."

From her handbag, she took her handkerchief and offered it to him. Reluctantly he took it and wiped his nose.

"Stop being hopeless," she said. "You must find the person responsible."

He tried to control himself. "There's no one."

"Anyone who hated Celia—there must be lots of those."

"Enough, Mother. Otherwise you can leave."

"It's my house."

They stopped talking as a policeman walked past on the veranda. He did not disguise his interest in staring in at them.

"So this is how it feels to be a freak at the fairground," she murmured. "Have they been doing their job?"

"They were thorough," he admitted.

He told her how the police had searched the garden sheds and stables, the garage, the hothouse, the crop fields and horse paddocks, the dam, and the hay barns, as well as every laneway and road on or near his farm. They came through the house at odd times and left disposable coffee cups and takeaway wrappers in the kitchen bin and cigarette butts on the driveway. Inspector Kanton said if their presence bothered him, they would leave.

"She knows I can't request any such thing," he said.

"They're going to pin this on you, Jack." She dropped a sugar cube into her teacup. "Unless you hand them the perpetrator on a platter."

"The police have no suspects."

She surveyed the room. When her hooded gray eyes finally rested on him, they were as cold as those of a bird of prey. "Think of the most despicable person in Vanishing Falls and point your finger at them. There must be ripe pickings."

He had once asked Cliff how he could bear to eat chicken when the stench of chickens surrounded him all day. Cliff said it made no difference to him. He was used to it. It was the same for Jack with his mother. When he was with her, inhaling her musky perfume, he found himself agreeing with her about things that would otherwise seem completely crazy.

* * *

Cliff

Gatenby's Poultry Farm

Thursday morning arrived like a coward punch to the back of the head. He had no idea where the week had gone. It felt like five minutes had passed since he was sitting in the local pub, planning to get high. That was two days ago. Sometime last night he had taken a sleeping tablet and he had the blurry sensation of being awake but not lucid. It was always that way—but it was better than not sleeping at all.

Kim stood in the shed doorway, her hand blocking the ripe rancid smell from her mouth and nose. On the soiled straw were too many carcasses to count, piles of feathered bodies covered in hay and shit.

"Cripes," Kim said. "What has gone wrong?"

He supposed he had failed to give them the right amount of antibiotics. The shed stank more than usual of feces and ammonia; maybe they had succumbed to a respiratory illness. He was uncertain when he had last checked the birds. It was his fault, and he would pay for it. This was a thousand-dollar mistake, maybe more, particularly if they didn't sterilize the shed pronto.

"We have to hurry," he told Kim. "Let's get these birds into the incinerator. Then I'll brush the floors; you scrub the feed pans and flush out the water lines. And clean the fan blades. Then I'll hose it out and disinfect."

First thing in the morning, a shipment of one-day-old hatchlings would arrive. He had two other empty sheds, but both had problems with ventilation. It was too late to cancel the order. A few years ago, he employed three men. They left for full-time work at North-West Poultry. Cliff could not compete with holiday pay and sick leave. He could not recall the last time he had cleaned the sheds the way they needed to be.

"I need to modernize this business," he said angrily. "I need employees. I can't do this on my own."

"You're not alone." Kim put her gloves on. "This is bad, Cliff. If we get a random inspection—"

He interrupted. "I know what the fucking fine is. Just do your job and let me worry about the rest."

"Don't speak to me like that."

He strode over to her. Anger surged through him. She had no idea how much pressure he was under. He frowned as she braced herself, her small gloved hands clasped in front of her chest.

"Listen," he said, his breath coming quickly. "I could spend all our money hiring lackeys to scrub out these sheds, or you could just fucking help me and save the sermon for your sons that you're spoiling. When I was their age, I helped my old man. They should be down here helping."

And if he hadn't helped his old man, he would have copped a hiding.

"They're at school, Cliff."

He tried to control his breathing. *Walk away*, he reminded himself. *You are not that kind of man.*

He took the wire broom and began to sweep, pushing the

sludge out the door. Later, he would get one of his sons to fork it onto a trailer and take it down the back to dry out and eventually burn.

"Cliff . . . I'm on canteen duty at school this morning."

He turned his back and counted to ten. He heard the metallic *tink* as Kim began to scoop the leftover feed out of the trays.

* * *

Joelle

Vanishing Falls School

"There's a fly," she called. "It's getting into the sandwich meat."

The school canteen manager, Judy Button, was cooking hot dogs at the other end of the kitchen and she shrugged.

"Free protein." She laughed. "You know they're all saying it was her husband that did it."

Joelle shook her head. "Not Jack."

"I'm just repeating what people have told me. And that's what the newspapers think too. Read between the lines for yourself."

"Don't say that when Kim gets here. They were like sisters."

Judy Button made a snorting sound. She put her hands on her hips and said, "They weren't best friends. Celia worked here sometimes—and she wasn't very helpful, she liked to tell me what needed doing—and Kim would be waiting outside, like a faithful little puppy. I never saw Celia waiting for Kim.

I'll never forgive Celia Lily for reporting on me to the office for not keeping this place clean enough. I do my best, and I'll tell you, they don't pay me that well."

Judy Button took boxes of frozen pies and sausage rolls out of the freezer and slid them down the counter to Joelle. "Stick them on the trays, please. What do you think about all those stories about Celia and Cliff Gatenby?"

"Don't know," Joelle said quickly.

"It's funny. I've been running this canteen for ten years. I see the mums, and who is friends with who, and who's not. I always expected Kim to rear up and bite Celia. But now . . . Celia's gone, and she's—"

A knock at the door stopped her. Kim came in.

"Good morning, lovely," Judy Button said. "We were just wondering where you were."

"I've had one of those days," Kim said. She washed her hands and put on an apron. "I didn't want to let you down, Jo-jo."

"You're here now." Joelle beamed.

She placed frozen sausage rolls and party pies on a tray and put them in the oven. Kim heated up the soup and they chatted as they worked.

"I had one of those days yesterday," Joelle admitted. "The cat nicked off again last night."

She told the whole story, of how she searched for the cat until she ended up in the forest, and then met a man who used to play cricket with Brian, who insisted on walking her home.

"Brian went off his brain when I told him I was talking to Brendan."

The other women nodded sympathetically. All wives knew what it was like to have overprotective husbands.

"It comes from love," Kim said.

"It's when they don't care where you've been you have to worry," Judy advised. "Brendan who?"

"I don't know. He drives a tow truck."

"I know the one," Judy said. "I haven't seen him in years. What did Brendan have to say for himself?"

Joelle tried to think. "Well, he told me he nearly got hit by a speeding white pickup truck on Myrtle Bridge Road the other night."

Kim stopped stirring the soup. "I wonder who nearly hit him. Did he say?"

"Nope."

At morning teatime Judy Button went for a cigarette in the teachers' car park. They watched her run across the asphalt in the rain. Kim sat down on a stool.

"I'm not working if she's not," Kim said. "She's paid to be here; we're volunteers."

Joelle giggled. She sat on the other stool. Rain streamed on the window. Fog smudged the rain forest, so the view was like a poor watercolor of green hills below a gray sky.

"How did you do it, Joelle?"

"What?" Joelle blinked.

"How did you do it?" Kim said each word very slowly.

"I don't know," Joelle whispered.

"You don't have to tell me. But I'm your friend. I admire you for your courage."

Kim stood up to check on the soup simmering on the

stovetop. Joelle did not want to lose her attention. For the first time she spoke the words Darla had made her promise not to say.

"I changed my name when my foster family adopted me. I never really liked being called Joanne. Then I changed it again when I married Brian."

Nothing bad happened. Kim nodded like it was no big deal.

After the shift ended, Joelle walked down to the main street to visit her friend Alfred. She felt dreamily happy, like a balloon that had escaped its tether and was floating up into the sky at the mercy of a summer breeze.

Real friends accepted you for who you are—Brian had said that more than once. Kim and Joelle (*Jo-jo*, Kim had called her!) were at the start of a long, lovely friendship.

* * *

Cliff

Vanishing Falls village

C liff hummed as he sat in his truck, preparing his things. The anticipation before the high was almost as good as the high itself.

He had done as much as he could in the poultry shed until he realized that it made sense to get some gear. It was about being efficient. Kim had rewarded him with a wide smile when he told her she better get down to the canteen. As soon as her car was on the road, he got in his own pickup truck and drove into town. After he picked up the gear, he didn't have time to go up to the falls car park, so he parked behind a stand of huge oak trees on a wide street of magnificent Federation homes. It was sufficiently private. To compensate for how sick he felt, he carefully measured himself a generous amount.

He flicked the lighter, put the pipe to his lips, and closed his eyes. His heart began to race before he had blown out the smoke. All the blood in his body shot into his head. Calm washed over him, from his head to his feet, as the initial hit lodged warmly at the back of his throat. It was so delicious he decided to give himself a second serving.

* * *

No longer did the morning feel so bitterly cold. The church bells began in all their glory and he jumped out of the truck to hear them better. Dappled sunlight broke through the rain and stroked his skin. He walked past picket fences. Early tulips bloomed in clusters of yellow, pink, and purple. As he approached the busy part of town, he reminded himself not to scratch his face or use his phone to ask Google endless questions, and not to stare at people. These were things he had made the mistake of doing in the past. The last one was harder than it sounded. Too much eye contact, especially with strangers, would give away that he was on a good one.

He entered the park where scores of birds darted through the sky like confetti. Joelle Smithton and Alfred Cheng sat on the park bench. They were feeding the birds with seed from a brown paper bag. As he approached, his feet made a decisive tapping sound on the concrete pathway and the pigeons cleared.

"We need to put a bell on you," Cliff joked to Joelle. "You're always just turning up."

She didn't laugh, just stared at him with those big eyes.

"You helping Alfred feed the chickens?" he said, grinning hard.

"What are you after, mate?" Alfred asked.

"You just worry about yourself," he told Alfred. To Joelle he said, "I know your old man gave Jack Lily a hard time about the name change at the creek. For the record, I agree with your husband, but that's not what this is about."

"What is this about?" Alfred asked.

"There is business I want to discuss with her."

Cliff knew he needed to stop the words convulsing from his mouth. They probably couldn't recognize what was causing his intense behavior. But maybe they did. He looked from one to the other.

"I want you to know that you're messing with the wrong man," he said. "You've spied on me. Well, now I've been spying on you."

Very quickly, he told her about the dossier. It made sense to explain it chronologically, counting each event off on his fingers—Wendy Field's murder, Joanne's role as a witness, the manhunt, the men's trial, and Joanne's expulsion from Pieman's Junction.

"You are Joanne Sparrow, aren't you? Don't lie to me. I worked it out."

She stared at him with her big blue eyes. He wondered

how much of what he had said she even understood. The birds jumping around on the grass drew confidence and darted in toward the bag of bird seed.

The grocer stood up. He thrust his hand into the paper bag and threw a handful of seed high into the air above Cliff's head. Yellow and brown seeds colored the sky, scattering like a mushroom bomb. Cliff stared upward, amazed by the spectacle.

The filthy pigeons descended on him in a burst of warm, dirty air. He batted at them, but it was no good. They flapped and squawked around him, pecking grains out of his hair and off his shirt. He yelled, shielding his face and chopping his arms in the air to scare them away.

"Piss off!" he shouted.

A soggy slew of bird shit splattered on his cheek. He ran.

* * *

Joelle

Vanishing Falls village

S he wiped at her eyes with her sleeve.
"He's got a mean streak," Alfred said.

They sat looking up the hill, where a double-file line of schoolchildren was passing the memorial statue.

"He drives down Old Dairy Road all the time. There's nothing down my street, only the old forestry road. It makes me anxious when I see his truck. It sounds crazy but I think he's coming to get me."

"Don't worry," Albert said gently. "He's all talk."

"It's silly." She tried to laugh at the silliness but the noise she made sounded broken. "I saw an enormous footprint in the garden near the rabbit hutch. The washing had blown off the line—only my clothes, just my luck!—and I was trying to get it out from under the lavender when I saw it. And the other thing, our power switches off in the night. It doesn't happen to anyone else on the street. Alfred, do you think Cliff would do that?"

"I won't lie to you. He's disturbed." Alfred patted her leg. "He's the kind of lunatic who would rip a woman's washing off the line. I don't trust him. What does Brian say?"

"I'm not telling Brian."

She thought of the god-awful things that Cliff had just shouted about. Explaining those things would break Brian's heart.

"Dear girl, you should talk to your husband about this. He needs to know."

"I can't tell Brian. I'd rather die."

* * *

Jack

Calendar House

Rugged up in a sensible gray woolen cardigan and matching scarf, his mother sat at a table on the veranda, reading the newspaper. Her toast and condiments were arranged on crockery from the bone china tea set that was usually displayed on a sideboard in the formal sitting room. He watched her, this old-fashioned woman with her long pearls and girlishly pinned-back hair, wondering why it so often felt like she was a stranger to him.

"It's not good," Victoria said. "You've dealt with the media wrong, Jack. You sound guilty."

"They've printed errors." He sat down with her. "For one, this farm has no debt. Secondly, I'm a lawyer, not a doctor, and I collect colonial artwork and furniture, not just any kind. Thirdly, Celia didn't run off following an argument. Dozens of people saw her that evening and by all accounts she was happy."

"Yes. Everything attributed to you in today's newspaper mentions those corrections," she said. "The implication is: here's a man who is more concerned about his reputation than his wife." Victoria examined her polished nails. "Why is there confusion about where you were that evening?"

"I was at a friend's house, doing paperwork, alone."

She shook her head.

"You never seemed that happy with Celia," Victoria said.

"Don't," he said unsteadily.

"Who would do this to her?"

"No one I know of."

She opened her handbag and he wondered if she was going to give him something—written instructions, a key to one of her houses, or a bank account she had set up in his name. These were her weapons of choice. Instead, she took out a lipstick and slicked pale pink on her lips. The intimacy of the gesture made him look away.

"You need to sort this situation out," she advised. "You are the wounded beast left behind by the herd. If you want to rejoin the herd, you need to cleave off the weakest member."

"Can you hear what you're saying?" he said.

Startled by her callousness, he walked away without excusing himself. He retreated to the hothouse and his orchids. Thankfully, she did not follow him. He needed time to think.

He added fertilizer solution to the soil of the older plants. The most dubious person he knew was Cliff. He had debated telling the police about getting high with Cliff at the fair. There was a chance the police would find out at some point. He could use a partial truth—he was with Cliff but not smoking, for instance. The trouble was, Cliff was not a meek lamb who would sit quietly and take the blame. Cliff had never outright accused Jack of having a sordid relationship with the Keegans, but he had made many veiled comments and asked annoying questions, and Jack wondered if he knew more than he let on. If he betrayed Cliff, things could get worse for Jack.

He could hear Kanton summarize: *You take illegal drugs, you're having an affair, you argue with your wife, and now she's missing.*

The thought was horrifying.

Truth be told, he enjoyed the rush Cliff's gear gave him on the three or four occasions he had tried it. Addicts said meth was Goliath to cocaine's David. Jack could believe it. It was so good he had made a point of declining Cliff's offers more times than he had accepted. Celia hated him doing it. On the afternoon she disappeared, she had told him it was a gutter drug. Jack had promised her he would not touch it again.

With the firelight coating strands of her hair in gold and lighting up her porcelain skin, she resembled an exquisitely beautiful Dresden doll. He was glad he agreed with her. There were other things he wished he had said, and he wondered if he would ever get to say them.

* * *

Joelle

The Smithtons' house

Alfred insisted on coming home with Joelle. Apparently, a long time ago, he had promised Brian he would plant some lettuce seeds in the vegetable garden.

"I need to plant the seeds right now," he said. "Before I forget."

"He wouldn't remember," Joelle said kindly. "He doesn't even like lettuce."

Clearly, Alfred felt terrible for breaking a promise. He locked his shop and drove her to Old Dairy Road in his rickety van.

Planting the seeds took him ages. The ground was hard, on account of the cold weather. First, Alfred turned the soil, puffing each time he plunged the spade in. When the soil was loose, he used a ruler to measure the exact spot he wanted to plant each seed.

"You're taking your time," she said.

She offered him some suggestions of several ways he could

do it faster. He just smiled and kept working, poking his finger into the soil to measure the depth.

"Don't let this go to your head," she told him, "but I'm glad you had to do this job. I don't feel good about being home by myself today."

"There's nothing to worry about," Alfred said, but he looked up and down the road, like he expected someone. Maybe he was hoping Brian was on his way.

"Brian never gets here until after five," she said.

"I know."

Joelle walked around her front garden, yanking out weeds and tossing them over the fence onto the vacant land next door. Mist had settled over the village. Damp air coated her face and a raindrop kept forming on the tip of her nose. A car came up Old Dairy Road and slowed outside her house.

It was Kim's old station wagon. She parked on the nature strip and honked the horn. She got out waving, holding out a parcel wrapped in pink tissue paper.

"Are you mad at me?" Joelle asked.

"No. I'm sorry for you. I know what Cliff said to you." Kim offered Joelle the parcel. "It's a scented soap. Put it in your lingerie drawer and everything will smell nice."

"Oh!" Joelle took the parcel. She sniffed it. "I can't smell anything."

"Open it."

Joelle hesitated. She tried to think how to say what she wanted to say. "I want the present. But it doesn't change that I think he's a bad man. He's not a nice man."

Kim nodded. "Can you keep a secret?"

"Zipped." Joelle mimed zipping her lips. "Buttoned up." She mimed buttoning them.

"I'm leaving him. But . . . you can't tell anyone."

Alfred came up the side of the house. He saw Kim and stopped, way back near the kids' cubbyhouse, and leaned on his spade.

"You don't have to go," Joelle said, as Kim climbed back into her vehicle.

Joelle opened the passenger door and leaned in, so they could continue chatting. "Come inside for a cup of tea. Flip! You need to clean this car."

There was a lot of rubbish on the floor. Newspapers, lunch wrappers, and drink containers. Joelle grabbed a few pieces to put in the bin. That's what friends did for each other. Among the rubbish was a neat package that had a skull and crossbones on it. Curious, Joelle reached for it.

Kim slapped her hand away.

"Leave it, Jo-jo. That's aluminum phosphide fumigant and it's toxic." She started the engine.

"I wish you could stay. Alfred has nearly finished," Joelle said hopefully.

Kim shook her head. "I can't right now, sorry."

"Oh, well," Joelle said. "Another time. Thank you for my gift. You are such a nice friend. God bless you."

"I don't go to church, but I need all the blessings I can get."

After Kim left, Joelle watched Alfred measure and plant. Brian said that going to church could help lost sheep. The lost sheep, he said, were people who had hit rock bottom or had struggles in their life. It was never too late to turn things around. According to Brian, you had to remember that God created challenges for people to help them find their right direction. She wondered if God had sent Cliff to her for this reason.

Brian genuinely believed that prayer could help. He said you could hear God talking if you listened hard enough. It wasn't true. She didn't have the heart to tell him. Brian went to church every Sunday and had done so all his life. Joelle imagined that he secretly found it incredibly dull. She had attended church with him a few times. She suspected that her voice was too loud. Even when she whispered, the ladies and gentlemen in the front rows of the congregation turned around.

She looked at the soap Kim had given her. Kim knew her secret and she didn't care. "Kim is a great friend," Joelle told Alfred. "A friend accepts you for who you are. Tonight, when Brian gets home, I won't keep any more secrets from him."

"Just remember . . ." Alfred rubbed his jaw and left a dirty streak on his face. His damp black hair gleamed like a crow's glossy sheen. "Brian is very protective of you. Go easy on him."

When the butchery truck drove into the driveway, Alfred hurried over to greet Brian. They shook hands and Brian thanked him several times. It was generous of Brian, considering Alfred had wasted a lot of time digging holes for the seeds. Brian even pretended he was looking forward to eating the lettuce. Joelle gave him a secret wink when Alfred was washing his hands at the tap.

Once Alfred had left, they sat down at the kitchen table.

"Where are the kids?" she asked.

"My sister came and got them from after-school care. They're staying the night with her. She's excited to be taking them to school in the morning."

"Lucky them." She took a deep breath. "I want to tell you something about me. It will give you a shock and I am sorry."

"I know Cliff Gatenby gave you a hard time." He wouldn't look at her. "Darling, you don't have to worry about that anymore."

"He is bad and mean. But . . . it's true what he said." She thought of those last, frightening days in Trapper's house. "The people from Pieman's Junction have a really good reason to hate me."

"No one hates you. How could anyone hate someone as lovely as you?" Brian gave her the same smile he gave Alfred when he said he was looking forward to eating the lettuce.

"People threw rocks at our house and the teacher sent me home from school for my own safety," she said. "No one wanted me there."

"Hush," he said.

Frustration welled up in her. She pressed her fist into her mouth and bit on it. This was not the time to cry. "Listen, please."

He pulled tissues out of the box for her, more than she needed. The cat door rattled. Brian jumped up.

"Look who's here." Brian was excited. "Where have you been, big boy?"

The cat made Brian sneeze, so it was a surprise to see him pick up Snowcat like he'd never had an allergy in his life. He rubbed the cat's orange furry head all over.

"You have to stroke the way the fur grows, Brian. That's how he likes it."

"He looks happy to me."

She pressed her face onto Snowcat. He smelled like cut grass and rain. She crossed her fingers, on both hands, and looked at the ceiling and sent a prayer up to God.

She waited.

All she could hear was the rain battering the tin roof like tumbling rotten fruit on a too-hot January day.

Brian was watching her.

"I'm a monster," she told him.

It was the only way to begin the story. She thought of the day they had moved into their new house. It was summertime and they opened all the doors and windows and a warm breeze filled the rooms. Tonight the air was cold and biting. She had finally outstayed her welcome in Vanishing Falls.

CHAPTER 18

Friday, September 1

Joelle

Latrobe Police Station

For the first Friday since the twins were born eight years ago, Brian did not work. The police station he took her to was in the nearest big town. They sat at a table across from Inspector Kanton, the lady who had door knocked at the start of the week. Inspector Kanton explained that there was supposed to be a counselor present, but that person did not work Fridays.

Joelle was glad about that. The more qualified people were in mental health, the less they understood her. They tried to explain things to her in their complicated language that made all the things that had happened sound repairable, so long as you went through the stages they outlined. Sometimes they made big statements that were supposed to help her, like how they said that her challenges were only one part of her personality, which seemed to imply that there was a better part of her locked inside that was trying to get out. Joelle had stopped looking for that imaginary person a long time ago.

Joelle told Inspector Kanton what she saw at the school toilet block. She repeated what Celia had said to her in the butchery. It was harder to repeat what Cliff had said yesterday, but she did. Brian closed his eyes when she spoke about Pieman's Junction. He held her hand so tightly his knuckles whitened. She wanted to tell him that he was hurting her hand, but big tears were already rolling down his cheeks.

"You're a brave person, Joelle," Kanton said.

"I'm scared," she said.

"What scares you the most?" Kanton asked.

Joelle looked at Brian.

"He knows now. The threat is worthless," Kanton said.

When it was over, and they were back in the car, Brian sobbed and hugged her. He cried for a long time, as if all those things had happened to him.

After a while, he said, "Don't worry about doing the deliveries today. Do whatever you like."

"I always do deliveries on Fridays," she said. "I don't want to sit around doing nothing. And besides, what will the pets eat if their meat doesn't come?"

* * *

Marsh End

It was not easy carrying the big bag of necks and trotters up Karen's back steps. Karen always took a while to answer the door. You could tell her house used to be nice. Someone had once loved the place and planted rosebushes along the driveway and beside the curving pathways that led to a birdbath and a fountain full of slime. The roses were dead from lack of pruning. Lantana had swallowed the gazebo. An explosion of ferns grew beside the tank stand where it was leaking water. If Joelle had liked Karen a bit more, she would have offered to help her, for the real thing the garden needed was love.

She tried not to look at the kennels because they made her shudder. They were built from broken bits of wire and crooked sheets of metal. The dogs had a long trough that was filled by a spindly pipe running from the tank. Another pipe went from the tank back to the house. At the rear of the kennel area were several grimy sheds where the dogs sheltered from the harsh weather. The whole setup looked like the science experiment of a psychopath. The dogs never stopped barking, and sometimes they lunged at you from inside their chicken-wire fence.

"Terrible about the missing woman," Karen said as soon as she opened the door. "What's everyone in town saying?"

"Everyone says the husband did it."

Karen's mouth dropped open, showing her chalky-white tongue. "That sends shivers up my spine, hearing you say that. Wait till I tell Keegan."

"I don't think he did it. I didn't mean that," Joelle said, trying to backtrack. "I don't even know them."

"We know him," Karen said. "Through business."

Joelle wondered what their business was. Brian thought they were unemployed. There was nothing unusual about that. Plenty of people were unemployed in Vanishing Falls. She thought of the goats that lived in the paddocks around the house.

"The goat business?"

"No," Karen said dismissively. "I'm talking about our main game."

"I didn't know you have a main game."

Karen frowned and shoved her thumb toward the paddock of broken cars and piles of tires. "We sell spare parts. Scrap metal. That's a gold mine."

"The rubbish pile?"

"Don't let Keegan hear you call it that. He'll have you."

In all the years she had been coming to Karen's house, she had never met Keegan. She imagined an obedient man, hard-working and willing to be bossed around by Karen.

Joelle counted the money Karen gave her.

"It's all there," Karen said.

Joelle didn't like delivering the dog food to Karen. The older woman made her uneasy. You could never predict whether what you said would offend her. The only time she was friendly was when she admired the appliqué designs on Joelle's outfits. She had once confided that she too liked to sew.

"I'll show you something before you nick off. And I'm only showing you because I trust you."

Reluctantly, Joelle followed Karen inside. Karen tapped a switch and the light flickered like a candle before showing the squalor, the stained carpet and dusty framed photographs on the sideboard. Karen took a key from a drawer. They went out onto the veranda and Karen unlocked a storeroom.

Grunting with exertion, Karen dragged out a large square wrapped in fabric. She tugged the heavy cloth away. It was an old-fashioned painting. In dark oily swirls the artist had painted an enchanted garden, with pretty Aboriginal children standing beside a cascading waterfall and shimmering pool. Trees of various heights and shades of green were reflected in the water.

"I'm no art expert but I can tell you this is worth north of ten grand." Karen put her hands on her hips and waited for Joelle's reaction. "What do you reckon?"

It was beautiful. Joelle gazed at it. She reached out to touch it and Karen slapped her hand away.

"No, you don't."

It was the most beautiful picture Joelle had ever seen.

"I don't even know what I'm thinking," Joelle said. "I feel funny all over. Is it Vanishing Falls?"

"Sure is. Jack Lily left it here for me to look after." Karen threw the cloth back over the painting and locked the store-room. "Weirdest thing. He left it here the day his wife disappeared."

"Poor Celia Lily."

"Stupid bitch," Karen said. "She never bothered saying hello to me."

"Maybe she didn't know you."

Karen shoved her tongue behind her bottom lip and made an idiotic guttural sound. Her mouth hung downward like there were weights attached to her jowls. Joelle thought of the few times she had seen Karen in town. She slouched low in the passenger seat of her car, glaring out like she was in the middle of complaining about something. Sometimes she parked in the disability car spot on the main street. Her car didn't display a disabled parking permit. Nothing much annoyed Brian except people using the disability spot incorrectly.

They had returned to the kitchen when they heard a sharp knock at the back door. Karen looked out a window and muttered, "Better not be the God botherers again."

Jack Lily stood on the back doorstep. He looked disheveled. His shirt was crumpled, and he had not brushed his hair.

"Shit," Karen said. "Speak of the devil. Here you are. How are you holding up?"

"Well enough."

"Everyone says they blame you, Jack," Karen said.

He looked horrified. Joelle fumbled with her keys.

"I didn't mean it like that," she said. "That's not what I said."

Karen smiled widely. "Jack, you're the number one suspect in your wife's disappearance."

"That's a terrible thing to say," he said.

She wasn't being mean, Joelle realized. She was joking around. Flirting even. She had brightened up since he got here. She looked much nicer when she smiled.

"I'm playing with you," she said. "I was just telling Joelle we're business associates. Is that how you'd describe us, Jack?"

Jack cleared his throat and glanced at Joelle. He looked wretched. She almost apologized for everything she had said about him to Inspector Kanton. Common sense told her to leave.

"I have to go," Joelle said.

She rushed past him. It was a relief to reach her car. She drove so fast the wheels skidded in the gravel as she turned out of the driveway.

* * *

Jack

Marsh End

To what do I owe this pleasure?" Karen smiled at him horribly. "I would have thought you'd drive on by as soon as you saw there was another visitor here. Or were you hoping Joelle was part of the package? She's very pretty."

"Stop it."

The sun was out, briefly, and it highlighted a jade-colored clip she wore in her hair. He had to remember what he was there for. "I've had a terrible week, as you know, but I've come to get my painting."

"No can do," she said.

"I beg your pardon?"

"I don't have the key. Keegan's gone and locked it away. Keeping it safe for you."

He looked at her helplessly. The trouble was, this uncouth woman knew him too well. Indeed, he had almost done a

U-turn when he saw Joelle Smithton's yellow station wagon parked in the Keegans' turning circle.

"I'll have to come back," he said.

"You better. Old mate wouldn't like you being here when he's not."

Her implication embarrassed him. There was a flicker of something intelligent in her eye, more than you ever glimpsed on her husband's broad features. Karen's type of intelligence was cunning. He had mistaken her long silences for docility.

"Is he going to be long?"

"He's out on a job. No idea how long he'll be."

"I'll be in touch," he said.

"I'll tell him."

On his way home, he told himself he did not feel bad for taking the painting from them. The Keegans deserved no credit—they had allowed the precious artwork to fester in a wrecked car in their junkyard. This was a national treasure and they could have ruined it. Jack was not going to profit financially—after he had enjoyed showcasing it to interested parties, it would be loaned to an art gallery, for everyone to enjoy.

For two years the lure of the farmhouse had pressed on him, like heavy rain drenching freshly tilled fields. He told himself that going there was not a choice he consciously made. Most times, as he drove across the wetlands near Marsh End, he intended to drive straight home.

On one occasion he had driven past the turnoff and then, with no rational thought, done a jagged three-point turn and gone straight there. The rusted roof of the old hay barn, the sphagnum bog, the curving hip of river where the willows clasped each other from opposite banks: each familiar landmark gave him a rush of excitement as he passed by.

Each time he left the farmhouse he hunched over the steering wheel, sickened and revolted by what he had done. Each time he vowed never to return. Weeks would slip by, and it was no trouble to pretend that Keegan and his wife did not exist. But the feeling would creep up on him, a desire to stand in that stifling kitchen, feeling their dull eyes on him. They were nervous around him. They wanted his grubby dollars; they were an addiction he could not shake.

He felt the same when he was sailing. When he was alone on an eighteen-foot skiff in Bass Strait, every thought left his mind while he focused on the exhilaration at hand. Ejaculating inside Keegan's wife was maddening, like rushing down a freakishly huge wave, not caring about the impact of reaching the bottom.

* * *

Joelle

The Smithtons' house

It was frustrating; Joelle kept messing up the appliqué she was working on. Twice she had had to unpick a pair of red cherries. Since leaving Karen's, Joelle could not stop worrying that she and Brian had made a mistake going to the police. A powerful man like Jack Lily would not let a woman like

Joelle cause trouble for him. She knew he had a good heart, but it was obvious he was bending under the pressure of being a suspect in his wife's disappearance. It would be terrible if he started another argument with Brian.

The phone rang. It was Kim, a very welcome distraction.

"I am so happy to hear your voice," Joelle said. "What a nice surprise."

"I'd come over, but I can't get away right now." Kim spoke quietly into the telephone. "Can you hear me?"

"Loud and clear," Joelle said.

"I need to know you're okay. Cliff is . . . troubled. This has been the worst week of my life and I couldn't have coped without your kindness, Joelle."

Joelle beamed. "You're welcome, Kim."

"I thought they would have found her by now. I could list lots of places where I don't think the police have even looked."

"Like where, Kim?"

"Well, how about under all the bridges. Myrtle Bridge . . ."

"Brian says it would have been hard for anyone to drive up there, given all the rain that night."

There was a long pause.

"Are you still there, Kim?"

"A four-wheel drive would go fine on that road. All the way up to Myrtle Bridge. Have you ever been up there?"

"Probably. With Brian. Do you want me to go look, Kim?"

Another pause. "No. I don't want you endangering yourself. It's not worth it. We don't know what's out there."

"Yes, Kim," Joelle said, but she was grinning—whoever found Celia, dead or alive, would be a star. It would be worth it.

* * *

Miss Gwen

Cheng's Green Grocery Store

Miss Gwen was standing at the counter, talking to Alfred, when she heard a very familiar voice asking the young grocery boy if he had any crab apples. Her voice was frailer than Miss Gwen remembered, but the mellow, confident tone remained. She peered down the aisle and saw a petite, well-dressed lady carrying a wicker basket.

"Is that who I think it is?" she whispered to Alfred.

"She's been in here the whole time." He grinned. "She's seen you."

"I should go. Or I should tell her what I think about how disgracefully she treated me."

"She's coming," he whispered. "You look like a deer in headlights."

In the past fifty years Miss Gwen had glimpsed her old friend on the odd occasions Victoria visited Vanishing Falls. She saw her from a distance—when Victoria was with her son or attending the Christmas carols in the park with her grandchildren. Once Miss Gwen had seen her, through the shopwindow, buying a birthday cake from the bakery. In all that time, they had not exchanged a word.

Victoria stopped short of the counter holding a basket of pink apples. She regarded Miss Gwen with interest.

"I thought that was you," she said.

Miss Gwen stepped forward and held out her hands. For an awful moment she thought Victoria might snub her. Instead, Victoria set her basket down and they gave each other a stiff little hug.

They laughed awkwardly.

"It's been too long," Victoria said.

"Far too long." Miss Gwen nodded.

"I don't even know how this happened," Victoria said. "Come and visit me for morning tea tomorrow."

Miss Gwen agreed. After Victoria left, Alfred chuckled.

"You sure told her what you think," he said.

"Stop it." She smiled. "It's not that funny."

* * *

Vanishing Falls School

She met the twins at the school gate. As they walked to her car, a quarrel began. Emily was bouncing a ball and Baxter kept trying to steal it. This went on and on, and as the children piled into the back seat, arguing between themselves, Miss Gwen clapped her hands in frustration.

"Stop bickering, you two," she reprimanded. "Whose ball is it?"

"Mine," Baxter said.

Emily burst into tears as he snatched it and zipped it into the top of his schoolbag.

"It's just a ball," Miss Gwen said.

"It's Baxter's ball but I need it. When I have it, I always have someone who wants to play with me. If I don't have the ball, I'll have to play by myself. Baxter doesn't understand—he has lots of friends."

The little girl collapsed sobbing against the seat. Miss Gwen tried to think what to do. She knew Emily had struggled with the other little girls in the class. She turned around just as Baxter removed the ball from his bag and gave it to his sister.

"You can have it," he said kindly.

"Thank you." Emily sniffed.

"Crisis averted." Miss Gwen sighed, and started the car.

* * *

Cliff

Gatenby's Poultry Farm

At the end of a mammoth fourteen-hour shift, the shed was ready for the one-day-old hatchlings to be released. Cliff slept well and woke up at Friday lunchtime feeling like a reincarnated version of his former self. He jogged along Old Dairy Road and up the steep, slippery rain forest track to the waterfall. He knew the trails well. There was a horse path that followed the river toward the Lilys' mansion and he ran home along it, enjoying the fresh scent of the uncut fields. It was where Celia ran and he kept looking for her, even though he knew she was not going to appear.

Even before she disappeared, he had found he could not stop thinking about Celia. On Saturday night at the Apple

Queen Tribute Evening she kept touching him with feigned casualness, and once, she wiped her lipstick off his cheek with a firm thumb. He pretended not to notice, but a small, secret part of him liked the attention.

Last month he saw Celia's car on a narrow section of road that cut at right angles around the Lilys' fields. Tall hawthorn hedges grew on either side of the road and it was tight when two cars had to pass each other. The hedge gave a feeling of complete privacy and this was not lost on Cliff as he stopped his pickup truck in the middle of the road, blocking Celia. He walked over to her vehicle and placed his hands on the roof of her car. Her blouse was buttoned loosely, and he could see the rise and fall of her cleavage. He suggested they drive up to the falls and share a cigarette.

"No one needs to know."

"No one will know because it's not happening, Clifford. Now fuck off and let me through."

He laughed. That was the humiliating bit, when he recalled the interaction later. He wished he had delivered a sharper response. She made him feel like a dim-witted farmhand.

Now she was gone. Dead, everyone said.

Cliff had figured it out, pretty much. Jack Lily would be forever grateful that Cliff was about to hand him his "Get Out of Jail Free" card. It was surprising that no one else had been able to join the dots.

When he reached home, he did fifty sit-ups and fifty push-ups, and then ate a meal of bacon and eggs washed down with a protein shake. He showered, dressed, and drove to the Lilys'.

* * *

Jack

Calendar House

His mother answered the loud knock on the front door. Jack hurried down the stairs. He could hear Cliff trying to charm her.

"It's a pleasure to see you again, Victoria," Cliff said. "Although I can only wish it was in happier circumstances."

"Hi there, Cliff," Jack said.

"Wait until you see this," Cliff said. "I've collated everything there is on the internet. There's a connection. When you changed the name of Murdering Creek last year, Brian Smithton wrote three letters to the newspaper. Then he met you on-site, and you had an argument, witnessed by a local politician and a journalist. And you had the heated exchange in the street. You told me people saw that too?"

Jack flipped through the pages. It looked like a messy school project. Cliff had glued or stapled newspaper article printouts, all about Pieman's Junction, Joanne Sparrow, and the three men who made up the Pieman's Junction Trio. The headlines alone were enough to turn his stomach.

He stopped at a newspaper story about Murdering Creek and how a prominent farmer had made an application to the local government to have the name changed to Hollybank Creek. Cliff tapped the picture of Brian Smithton standing in front of the old Murdering Creek sign. "How angry does he look?"

"What is the point of this?"

"A butcher knows how to dispose of a carcass."

Jack studied Cliff's eyes, trying to work out if he was high. "Saying things like that . . . it's not helpful."

He glanced at his mother. She was listening carefully.

Cliff understood. "I apologize, Victoria. I shouldn't have spoken like that in front of you. You must be so worried."

"Terribly upset," she said. "I agree with Jack; that is a long bow to draw. Regardless, I'd like to see that scrapbook for myself."

She held out her hands for the scrapbook.

* * *

Cliff

Gatenby's Poultry Farm

Kim clapped her hands when he told her he was taking the family fishing for the weekend. Her excitement reminded him of how she used to be when they were young.

She had clapped like that the first time she saw the farm. They were married with a child and had been living in Launceston, where he was working a dead-end job as a delivery driver for a bread company. Kim had quit her job as a bank teller not long before their baby was born. Cliff had encouraged her to,

but it was a financial decision he came to regret. It was for-
tuitous when his father died. There was no one else to inherit
the farm.

They returned to Vanishing for the funeral. Cliff had not
been back for eight years. Jack Lily had an office in Vanishing then, before the economic downturn forced him to close
it in favor of running just one office in Latrobe. They had met
in Jack's office to sign the transfer of ownership for the farm.
Jack had warned them that the property was run-down, but
it was not enough to prepare Cliff for the shock of seeing the
collapsed barns and moldy, damp farmhouse.

Kim was unperturbed. She rushed around the place in delight, admiring the fruit trees, the deep green pastures, and the
sweeping views of the forested mountains. She was enthralled
and he loved her for it. That day he felt like the luckiest man
on earth.

Looking at her now, with her flushed cheeks and sparkling
eyes, he felt nostalgia for those optimistic years, and a faint
pang of something else: the nasty tug of guilt.

"It won't always be like this," he said.

"I know."

"Thank you."

He didn't know why he thanked her. It came out of nowhere. As he walked toward the door he could feel her watching him. Her gaze had a magnetic pull. He turned.

"Come here," she said.

"What? I've got to get the fishing gear."

She tapped her cheek. "Kiss."

He returned and kissed her. She wrapped her arms around

him and he hugged her tightly. She was a good, loyal woman, for all she put up with.

* * *

Land of a Thousand Lakes

Between two of the sandstone garrison towns, they got stuck behind a half-dozen cyclists.

"I hate cyclists," Cliff said when it was finally safe to overtake them. "I have to rank the cost of my time versus the value of the cyclist's life. And then there's my time spent scraping bike shrapnel off my bull bar if I did hit him. It's not worth running one over."

"I guess I'm relieved to know that you would give way to a man on a bike."

He chuckled. "I'm not as bad as you think."

Something slid across the floor as they went around a tight corner.

"It's those baits you asked me to pick up," Kim said, pushing the package aside with her foot.

"Did I?" He could not recall the conversation. This was happening more and more frequently.

His mood was mellowing as they gained altitude. The road narrowed and the trees grew wider, sprawling their arms up to the sky. Like a woman's arms, Cliff fancied, the flesh white and smooth where the bark peeled back in curling tendrils. The high country was God's own with lakes brimming with trout and no one around for miles. It would be the break he needed. He glanced in the rearview mirror and corrected himself—it would be the break they all needed.

In the back seat the boys helped each other make flies using a box of materials they had collected from around the house and the farm. There were clumps of rabbit fur, chicken feathers, dog fur, colored strings of wool, plastic cut from chip packets, and an old pair of pantyhose. They twisted and tied these onto hooks to resemble the small, colorful insects that lived around the lakes. As the boys worked, they planned how many fish they would catch.

"I'm looking forward to having trout for dinner," Kim said.

"There's always a chance we might not get any bites."

"That's okay. I've brought plenty of chicken to barbecue."

"Good Lord, please let us catch a fish." Cliff chuckled.

Kim put some music on and he chatted to her, telling her about a used-tractor salesman who was coming to buy some equipment next week. There was good news from the accountant too: he had found a way to reduce some of their repayments temporarily.

"It's breathing space." She spoke without conviction. "It doesn't solve anything in the long term."

Cliff accelerated out of a corner. "What do you want me to do?"

"I don't know. Find a priceless painting. You know Jack's painting is sitting in a storeroom on the Keegans' veranda? Jack told me."

"He actually said that?"

"Yes."

Cliff laughed loudly. His suspicions about Jack's private life had been confirmed.

"Do you think the Keegans know what it's worth?" Kim said.

"You're talking about folk who deal in scrap metal and thought a lump of coal was gold. Remember that?" It felt good to laugh with his wife. The coal story had circulated about the Keegans and no one knew if it was true any more than the speculation that Brendan and Karen Keegan shared the same father.

Tea trees began to appear beneath the towering swamp gums and he knew they were getting closer.

"I bet I know why he hasn't picked up the painting," he told Kim.

"I don't want to know," she said.

"Let me just say, the cops could ask him some pesky questions."

They turned down a dirt road signed Wallaby Rocks and emerged through the trees beside a sky-blue lake. The uneven row of fishing cabins along the shore sat near the high-water mark, where driftwood and leaves had washed up on the white arch of sand. Across the water glacial mountains rose in subalpine splendor.

"It takes your breath away," Kim said.

* * *

For a brief moment in the Guest Registration cabin, the two men did not recognize each other. His mate Kane was as gaunt as the mountain gums. Cliff searched the man's face for a glimpse of his old friend. It was fleeting, like a reflection in the water. They had spent a summer working on a trawler on the east coast. It was hard physical work, pulling up the nets and sorting the fish, but they were young men, and both had been better for it.

It appeared Kane had spent most of his time since sitting indoors. His skin wasn't weathered like the men Cliff knew. His gray hair was long and stringy and tucked behind his ears like a woman's. He wore a green woolen cardigan over a rainbow tie-dyed T-shirt. Kane's purple tracksuit pants revealed the unsettling sag of his tackle.

Kane ignored his outstretched hand and came in for a hug.

"All right, that's enough." Cliff hugged him back weakly. "I hope this isn't Brokeback Mountain."

Kane chuckled. He gave Cliff a map of the campsite. He put a cross next to Cliff's cabin and next to another cabin at the end where a masseur was operating.

"My partner Lorelai had one this morning. He's only there for today—drives up from Bothwell."

"A long way to drive to sell massages. Not for me. No one puts their hands on me except my wife and my doctor, and I haven't seen my doctor for years."

"Good for you. We overmedicalize everything these days and a few are getting very rich because of it. I'm into naturopathy myself. If I can't grow it, I don't want it."

"That's right," Cliff said. He wasn't sure if he meant it, but the mountain air was making him feel agreeable.

Kane handed him a flyer. "For your wife, then. . . ."

A woman came through the back door carrying a pile of firewood. She dropped it into a basket and nodded at Cliff as she left the office. She wore a thick woolen sweater, but even so, Cliff could tell she wasn't wearing a bra. Kane saw him looking.

"That's Lorelai. My partner. We're not married. We won't marry until the law recognizes everyone can marry."

Cliff resisted the urge to make another joke.

That afternoon the boys caught three fish. These were big trout that took patience and muscle and caused them to cheer and high-five each other.

* * *

In the evening the boys toasted marshmallows on the open fire. Kim returned from her massage flushed and relaxed. She cooked the fish, which the boys ate greedily, licking their fingers when they were done. Cliff had a small portion. Kim knew better than to save him anything.

After the boys went to bed, he and Kim stayed outside by the fire and shared a bottle of wine. The night pressed cold against their backs and she leaned into him and listened to his plans.

"I'm thinking long-term. Free-range chickens will make the same amount of money as we make now, but the land will double in value. Work hard, play hard, enjoy the rewards. We might buy a block at the beach and a runabout. My boys aren't working in the sheds." He stared at the fire. "They should learn a trade so they don't have to do the shit I do. But it's all right. I'm going to buy you a house with a decent laundry and a kitchen that doesn't leak."

"Can I get a clothes dryer too?"

"Don't get greedy." He grinned and tucked the blanket around her.

Softened by the wine, she talked about the kids and he let her go on a bit. Occasionally he offered advice where he thought she was too lenient on them. They were boys; they needed firm guidance. She talked about money again, worrying that they would never save enough to make his dreams of the free-range farm come true.

Finally she poured the last of the wine into his glass and said quietly, "I think you should consider becoming an art dealer."

His skin prickled.

"It would be easy," she said. "Almost no one knows about it."

He looked at her through the darkness. "Maybe our ship is coming in."

She leaned in and stroked his thigh. It was times like this he didn't need anything else. He put the fire out, then took both her hands and led her inside to the double bed. She still wore the slender silver chain he had given her for her twenty-fifth birthday. She dressed nicely without wearing anything too revealing like some women did. With her body she could easily tart herself up. She wasn't like that.

The bunk room was quiet—the kids were asleep. He stretched out on his back and looked out the window. They were above the clouds up here and the high-country stars were as bright as fireworks.

CHAPTER 19

Saturday, September 2

Joelle

Vanishing Falls Nursing Home

The residents were restless in the nursing home. Instead of their usual card or chess games, knitting, or peaceful chitchat with their visitors, people were walking around, peering out the windows, and whispering to each other.

Near the piano, Mr. Keith paced up and down. He swatted the air in the direction of any staff who approached him.

"Don't go near him. We're waiting for the doctor," the matron said.

Joelle was curious. "Why? He's big and strong but he wouldn't hurt a fly."

"If the doctor wants to sedate him, that's for the doctor to say," the matron said. "And I hope he does. We've got a full plate as it is."

The matron strode off down the hallway to deal with her full plate and Joelle made her way over to Mr. Keith. He was making pitiful crying sounds. She took his hand and led him to the rocking chair. He sat down and she gave it a few gentle rocks. It only took a short while and he was calm.

"There, there," Joelle said softly.

"Those witches from the garden club said I fit the profile of the murderer." He pointed across the room at a group of ladies. "I bloody well don't."

The women glanced over uneasily. Joelle gave them the look she gave to Emily and Baxter when they squabbled over Monopoly or the TV remote control.

"They know they've done the wrong thing," Joelle said.

"The police should find out what happened to that woman," Mr. Keith said decisively. "That's their job—they should do it."

"They haven't looked beneath Myrtle Bridge," Joelle revealed. "My best friend told me that."

"Is Miss Gwen doing some detective work?" he said.

The idea of Miss Gwen investigating crime made them laugh. The ladies from the gardening club looked over to see what was so funny. That made Mr. Keith and Joelle laugh even louder.

"I might be doing some detective work," Joelle whispered. "A tow truck driver told me he saw a white pickup truck driving down from Myrtle Bridge the night Celia Lily disappeared."

Mr. Keith perked up. "Let me think about that. They're a dime a dozen around here."

Joelle thought about how true that was. "Doesn't Matron drive a white pickup truck?"

He threw his head back and gave a hearty laugh. "You're funny. But keep that to yourself about the pickup truck, won't you, girl?" He was no longer smiling. He leaned forward with his bright blue eyes pinned on her. "Cliff Gatenby," he whispered.

It gave her a chill.

"I saw his pickup truck go past the other day. He's taken the goat's head off," he said. "When someone depersonalizes their vehicle, it usually means they're hiding something. Tell your husband to look into it. Brian Smithton will know what to do."

Over the years Mr. Keith had given her sensible advice, especially when it came to managing Brian. She nodded slowly.

"Did that tow truck driver mention the goat's skull?" he asked.

"I don't think so."

The goat's skull had been on Cliff's truck when he parked next to her car outside Alfred Cheng's green grocery store. She remembered feeling unsettled by it. She looked through the window, across the lush field, to the road that wound darkly toward the river.

"Maybe it just fell off," Mr. Keith said. "Don't look so worried."

On Joelle's way out, the matron called her into the office. She reminded Joelle that she was always there as a visitor and that visitors had to follow the rules and instructions of the staff. It was for her own safety, the matron emphasized.

"Yes," Joelle agreed. "Matron, where were you last Saturday night?"

"Here. I haven't had a Saturday night off since March. Are you heading home now?"

"I'm going straight to work at the butchery. Brian won't cope on a Saturday without me. We get very busy, Matron."

"You're not lazy, I'll say that," Matron said.

"I would say the same about you." It occurred to her that Matron often just stood around watching what other people were doing, or spying on them, as Mr. Keith liked to say. "Most of the time," she added.

Matron laughed.

"I mean it," Joelle said kindly. "See you next week."

* * *

Miss Gwen

Calendar House

A welcoming fire burned in the sitting room. It was hot enough that Victoria had opened the window slightly and Miss Gwen could smell the cool, earthy dampness of the garden. On the table between them were the remains of their morning tea.

"There are old friends whom you do not need to see frequently to resume the friendship," Victoria mused. "I think you and I are like that, Gwendolyn. Here we are, after all these years, and nothing has changed."

"It's true." Miss Gwen nodded.

It was almost true. Since she had arrived at the big house, Victoria had made her feel incredibly welcome. They'd enjoyed dainty sandwiches on soft white bread and slices of tea cake with chilled glasses of apple cider. They'd caught up on the past fifty years. Miss Gwen had talked about her work at the nursing home and the Country Women's Association, and the rewarding task of helping care for Joelle and her children. She'd even found herself confiding that she had been lonely at times.

Victoria had understood. Her daughter, Jack's sister, lived on the mainland and rarely made the effort to keep in touch. Victoria missed her terribly. Victoria had spoken of the investigation into Celia's disappearance and confessed to not always getting along well with her daughter-in-law. She worried that Celia had spoiled her son, that he was becoming entitled and forgetful of where they had all come from. The members of the Lily family were simple farmers, she'd insisted.

Neither mentioned the argument that had severed their friendship.

After morning tea, Victoria stood up and took a set of keys from a drawer.

"I do want to apologize to you," she said, waving her hand to dismiss Miss Gwen's protest that no apology was necessary. "First, let me show you some things."

They walked up two sets of stairs and, while they waited for Victoria to get her breath back, stood at an upstairs hallway window looking across the pastures toward the blue-green mountain range.

"I can't help but think Celia has been swallowed by the forest," Victoria said. "I feel like this house is cursed."

"That's rubbish," Miss Gwen said quickly, although the thought had occurred to her.

Victoria swung the keys as they walked down a long corridor.

She stopped in front of a small door and unlocked it. Behind the door was a narrow, steep staircase. In single file they went up and entered the attic.

In all the years Miss Gwen had worked at the house, first cleaning for Victoria's mother-in-law, and then caring for Victoria's two children, she had never been up there. It was always locked. She had imagined it would be full of stored treasures—old furniture, antique toys, trunks of English linen.

On the contrary, it was a sparse, modern space, lit by downlights. A temperature control panel was installed on one wall. Dozens of colonial-style paintings were displayed, some on the walls, others on easels in the middle of the room. From the village Miss Gwen had seen the windows of this room glowing through the fog, often late at night.

"Jack's collection. I bought most of these for him. We share a passion for art from this period. Experts used to think that early colonial artists painted their Australian landscapes to look more like England," Victoria said thoughtfully. "We know now that the land did in fact look like this before colonization, with wide-open meadows and the occasional tree. By burning off the meadow, the indigenous people created kangaroo-grazing pastures. They farmed the land."

Miss Gwen nodded, wondering what Victoria's purpose was in showing her this room. She anticipated some theatrics, or showmanship, was in the cards. Victoria was a very deliberate person, but as she led Miss Gwen around the room, her motivation was not clear.

"What are you trying to tell me?"

Victoria smoothed her skirt. "That our interpretation of the past can change. There is something else," she added.

They left the attic and returned to the third floor of the house. The ground floor was where the family lived, the second floor was where they slept, but this third floor was not well used, except for a large, cheerful-looking playroom. Wide windows let the light in, showing toys, books, and puzzles scattered across the floor.

Miss Gwen sighed sadly. Life as those young girls knew it had ended abruptly. It was doubtful things would ever be the same again. She squeezed Victoria's arm, and for a moment they stood, side by side, staring at the empty room.

Victoria sniffed. "It's unfathomable."

"I am so sorry," Miss Gwen said.

Victoria led the way to the unused northern wing. There were stories around town of ghosts haunting this part of the house. Miss Gwen had always dismissed them as silly, but walking along here now she couldn't help glancing back down the hallway. Victoria unlocked another door. Reluctantly, Miss Gwen followed her in. It was dark and smelled of mildew. White dust sheets covered a bed, a wardrobe, a dressing table, and a chair.

"This was my late husband's great-great-grandfather's bedroom. They slept separately. He must have snored." She unlocked an adjoining door. "This was his wife's room. She outlived him by twenty years. They attract good genes, the Lily men."

The second room was nicer. The wallpaper, although faded,

was embossed with pink-and-green rose vines. In an alcove was a porcelain bathtub and washstand. Victoria tugged open the curtains and dust shimmered in the morning sunlight. She tapped her foot against a leather trunk sitting in the corner.

"Several years ago we found a journal in here belonging to Great-great-grandmother Alice Lily. There were several entries describing a terrible incident that occurred on this land."

"The Murdering Creek massacre?" Miss Gwen said. "Victoria, the last time we talked about this you told me I was trying to rewrite history."

Miss Gwen had been a softly spoken young woman, slightly in awe of her accomplished friend. Humiliatingly, she remembered apologizing and Victoria cruelly dismissing her.

"I regret that." Victoria looked at her keenly. "In her diary, Alice Lily wrote about two native women who were camping near the creek when they were shot dead. Two children were with them; they ran away."

"According to the legend of Vanishing Falls, the children jumped into the waterfall and were never seen again," Miss Gwen said.

"They didn't jump," Victoria said. "Alice Lily wrote that her husband, Henry Lily, accompanied by a stockman, first killed the women, then pursued the children up into the forest and shot them too. His stockman pushed the dead children into the water hole. He was hiding their bodies. It was 1829. At that time, the martial law proclamation stated that defenseless native women and children should always be spared. What the journal revealed is that old Henry Lily, his wife, and the stockman were complicit in hiding this crime."

"Where is the journal?"

"In a special storage facility in Hobart. Experts are studying it so the historical record can be corrected."

"I'm intrigued. And I'm incredibly glad the truth will finally be recorded."

Miss Gwen was skeptical. It was an argument about this that had ruined their friendship. Victoria had been scathing when Miss Gwen suggested that Murdering Creek was named after events instigated by the Lily family's Tasmanian ancestor. The venom with which Victoria had rebuked Miss Gwen was impossible to forget. Victoria had accused her of being malicious, jealous, and even cowardly. She had described Gwendolyn as being obsequious. Reading the meaning of that word in the dictionary later had mortified Miss Gwen. It was easy to decide to never speak to Victoria again.

Years later, Miss Gwen had come to understand that Victoria was offended and ashamed. On reflection, Miss Gwen admitted to herself that she could have been more tactful.

"Please accept my apology, Gwendolyn. I didn't listen to you. I want you to know that we accept those wrongdoings now. Our interpretation of the past can change," she repeated.

It was a surprise how much of a relief it was for Miss Gwen to hear the apology. Victoria stood with her hands behind her back, staring out the window.

"I do worry, though, that we're seeing a repeat of pointless violence." Victoria's eyes flickered from the window to Miss Gwen and back again. "This situation with Celia is terrible. Was she murdered? I understand there is a local butcher who can't stand our family."

"I hope you're not talking about Brian Smithton."

"His threats against my son have been well documented."

"No," Miss Gwen recoiled. "How could you make such a vicious accusation?"

"Don't overreact, Gwendolyn. Think of it from my perspective. My son might go to jail. And he's innocent. So please, calm down."

"I'm seventy-six years old. You will not tell me how to feel or what to do." It was invigorating to speak so firmly to Victoria. "Do you understand?"

"I only wanted to show you some history," Victoria said meekly.

Miss Gwen wondered if she had overreacted. She took a moment to compose herself, reviewing the strange conversation. Victoria watched her closely. When Miss Gwen spoke, her voice was gratifyingly calm.

"It seems to me that the main genetic legacy of the Lily family is the ability to pursue your ambitions, ruthlessly and heartlessly," she said.

Miss Gwen excused herself and left the dusty room before Victoria could reply. She half expected Victoria to follow her down.

She grabbed her handbag from the kitchen and, hesitating for just a moment, took back the raspberry jam she had brought as a gift. She looked around sadly as she made her way out, taking in the beautiful rooms that she used to care for so well. This was the last time she would visit the Calendar House.

As she drove her little sedan down the tree-lined driveway, her mind buzzed with everything Victoria had said.

* * *

Jack

Vanishing Falls village

Jack woke early and took a long, slow drive around the outlying farms. It was unbelievable that an entire week had passed since Celia had gone missing. Several days ago, when he drove these roads, he saw people searching the fields. Now there was no one looking for her. The assumption made his throat constrict.

He drove into town and ordered a takeaway coffee at the café. Most tables were occupied but no one met his eye. The women working behind the counter glanced at him and murmured to each other. He told the cashier to keep the change and she dropped it into the tip jar without a word of thanks.

He returned to the blustery street and stood under the post office awning drinking the coffee. Across the road, Joelle came out of Smithton's Fine Meats. In her uniform white shirt and slacks, with her peachy complexion and dimples, she looked very youthful. He tossed the paper cup into a bin and was about to get back into his car when she waved at him.

Tentatively, he waved back.

Joelle glanced at the butchery, where, presumably, her

husband was working out the back. She hurried across the street to where he stood. "We can't talk here," she told him. "Walk this way."

It was strange to be bossed around by this pretty, young woman. He went with her, recalling Cliff's theories about Brian Smithton abducting and murdering Celia in an act of revenge for the name change of Hollybank Creek. The suggestion did not bear scrutiny. In every heated dealing Jack had had with Brian, despite his anger and frustration, the butcher had barely raised his voice. It was Jack who had shouted. To which Brian had simply responded, "You're angry because you know you're complicit."

Brian would be unimpressed if he discovered Jack was walking to the river with his wife. She seemed relaxed though, especially once they were out of sight of the butchery. Her hands rested on her hips as she waited for a car to pass and she chatted away about her day and the things she had done and what she thought she needed to do. They reached the river, and the willow trees enveloped them. Beneath the draping branches the river swirled and sucked at the bank.

He interrupted her prattle. "Where do you think Celia is?"

She blinked. "Dead," she said.

He swallowed hard. In the paddock across the river two chestnut horses sheltered by a collapsing hay barn. One of them reared its head and snorted. He could see the horse's warm breath rising up on the cold air.

Emotion rushed through him. "Who would hurt her? I don't know anyone who didn't adore her. She was that kind of woman."

Joelle looked doubtful. She kicked at the earth with the toe of her boot.

"Jack, I want to tell you that the day before Celia disappeared she bought enough meat to last the whole week. That seems important, doesn't it, that she bought so much meat?"

Her confidence took him by surprise. So did her preciseness as she correctly listed the items Celia had bought. He knew what these were, for the police had asked him to read over the inventory they had made of what was in the fridge and freezer.

She continued speaking slowly, as though he were the one who had barely completed a middle school education. "It makes me think, if she could come home, she would," Joelle said. "There's something else. A tow truck driver saw a white pickup truck hammering down Myrtle Bridge Road the night Celia went missing. It wasn't one of the logging trucks; they wouldn't go up there in those conditions. Maybe it was Cliff Gatenby's pickup truck."

"I doubt it was Cliff," Jack said automatically. "Many people drive pickups in this district. It's a practical choice. Joelle, you must be careful making accusations about people."

She nudged a tussock with her boot and did not reply.

He continued. "The Gatenbys dropped Celia home from the function and then they went home themselves."

"I saw Cliff and Celia on the veranda of the hotel that night," Joelle said.

He waited for her to explain this suggestive comment. When nothing was forthcoming, he prompted, "Were they together in a romantic way?" He felt like a schoolboy asking the question, but he needed to know.

"No."

His relief was embarrassing.

"That doesn't mean anything," she added.

He searched her face, trying to understand. She returned his gaze with her usual clear expression. The conversation was becoming exhausting.

"Go back to what you were saying before. You mentioned you were talking to a tow truck driver?" he said. "Who was that?"

"I don't want to say."

"Are you worried you're implicating him? You're not. But he could be an important witness. The police want to lock me up. No one cares who took Celia. They just want to blame someone." His emotions threatened to overwhelm him, and he sounded desperate and angry. "What was this guy's name?"

Her forehead wrinkled. She put her hands over her ears and looked up at the sky. It was not a petulant gesture; her breathing was rapid and gasping. She was distressed.

Faltering, he tried to use a gentler tone. "Please, Joelle."

He thought of what Celia had told him about the terrible events of Joelle's childhood. "I know people have taken advantage of you. I know about Pieman's Junction. I won't—"

Her ample chest heaved. Heat flushed her pearly cheeks and her voice rose childishly. "I already told Brian. He says it doesn't matter because he loves me and it was so long ago and I . . . was . . . fourteen."

He touched her arm, a fatherly gesture intended to calm her. She became very still, like a small, terrified animal cowering before a predator. She didn't smack at his hand or try to step away. Somewhere in Joelle Smithton's past, she had learned that it was easier to submit than resist. Double tears ran down her cheeks.

Ashamed, he took a step back. "I'm so sorry."

"I told the police what you did at the fair. I had to tell the truth."

Jack had no rebuttal. She ran off then. Instead of following the track, she pushed through the fringe of willow branches and cut across the field. He walked along the track and watched her disappear behind the old flour mill. Since the fair, he had feared she would tell the authorities what she saw; now that it had happened, he wasn't as upset as he thought he would be. Like everything else, it became a thing he would take care of.

He was startled when her face peeped out from behind the mill wall. It looked like she was spying on him. He wondered if she really was as guileless as everyone thought.

* * *

Joelle

Vanishing Falls village

It was the nothingness of Jack's reaction that told her what she had said was dangerous. As soon as she mentioned the tow truck driver seeing a white pickup, Jack's composure became fixed. Like when Snowcat was hunting field mice, he didn't move, just watched them without blinking. The stillness had a force to it.

She quickened her step—in case he tried to catch her. When she was talking to Jack it felt like she was melting under the warmth of his smile and she could feel her thoughts building up, like a bottle of fizzy drink that was being slowly shaken.

The trouble was, she had talked too much. It was the scent of the wet earth that had rooted her to the ground, made her fill the air with her noise. It was the smell of the place where Wendy Field died. Then, like now, she could barely think.

She hurried along the main street footpath, past the boarded-up boutique, the takeaway shop, and the news agency.

Nev was standing on his doorstep.

"What are you doing? Why were you down by the river with Jack Lily?"

"I can talk to whoever I want to talk to, Nev."

"We don't want you talking to him."

He looked up and down the street, frowning horribly. He didn't resemble her good friend.

"Quick, inside now," he said.

She entered the butchery with Nev's hand on her back. Brian was serving a customer and he didn't look happy. Nev kept hold of her shoulder while they waited for Brian to finish with the customer.

"Stop it, Nev," she said. "You're annoying me."

He took his hand off her immediately. "Sorry, Joey."

The customer left and Brian came around the counter. She began to speak but he shushed her by placing his finger on her lips.

"It's not safe to talk to him," he said. "Especially since we've been talking to the police."

"I wish . . ." She let the words fade. There was plenty to wish for but wishing never did anyone any good.

"We don't want people taking advantage of you," Nev said.

"Jack Lily is not trying to do that. He just wants to find—"

Brian interrupted. "He's a bad man. Don't talk to him again, okay?"

Nev nodded at Brian, as though Brian had given him a silent message. They wanted her to trust them, but something was going on between them and they wouldn't even tell her what it was. Brian loved talking about how the world would be a better place if everyone treated one another with respect and kindness, yet here he was, ganging up with Nev, and treating his own wife like she didn't count. Unbelievable.

"Guess what?" she said. "I quit. You can find someone else to boss around in the butchery. I'm tired of being told what to do."

She went out the back, grabbed her handbag, and left through the back door before either of them could try to stop her.

* * *

Jack

Vanishing Falls village

The gas station noticeboard listed three tow truck companies operating in the Vanishing Falls area—although one had been scribbled out. The first, Barnes Tow Trucks, was owned by Matt Barnes, who also owned the gas station. His competition, Cheap Tow Company, was run by Phil Graham, an older man who lived near the river. The third tow truck company, Mr. Skid Towing, had been crossed out with a permanent pen, so presumably it was no longer operating.

Jack went inside and asked the cashier if he could speak to Matthew Barnes. The cashier informed him that Matt was on a three-week trip to Thailand.

"Due back tomorrow."

"Who's driving for him while he's gone?"

"This past week, with Matt away and Phil's situation, I've been giving people the number for a new guy who just bought the license from Mr. Skid. Turns out he is as useless as tits on a bull and never answers his phone."

"Who is he?"

She flicked through a drawer, looking for the information. "Let me think. He hasn't taken any work. Having said that, he could be taking cash jobs. They all have access to the radio. I can't find his flyer."

"Can you try to remember his name?"

She bit her lip as she thought about it. "Keeps to himself. Lives out at Marsh End. And here is the info." She held the card up and read, "Brendan Keegan."

Reeling, Jack left without thanking her. Standing out front near his car, he counted to ten and tried to slow his breaths. He was hyperventilating. He told himself to stop overreacting. There was a chance it was not Keegan who was driving up near the forest that night. There were two other tow truck drivers; Matt Barnes was in Thailand, so maybe Phil Graham was driving on Myrtle Bridge Road that night.

He drove to the river boulevard, where the houses were new. He knew where Phil lived, and the tow truck was parked along the side of the house next to a boat and a large shed. A young woman answered his knock. He asked to speak to Phil Graham. Bluntly, she informed him that her grandfather had passed away two weeks ago in the hospital from pneumonia.

Jack bowed his head, chastised. In a town this size, the death was something he should have known. In fact, he did recall that Mr. Graham had been ill. What had the gas station cashier said? Something about *Phil's situation*. If only she'd just said, "He's dead."

"Has anyone been operating his tow truck in the past few weeks?"

"No."

He apologized and excused himself.

That left Brendan Keegan.

Bile pressed up his throat. He hurried away through the drizzling rain. He made it to his car, where he vomited on the ground, kneeling so he was out of sight of the Graham residence.

A horrible scenario was taking shape in his mind.

It couldn't be the case. Keegan would not have had time. The babysitter had left Jack's house at 10 p.m., which was about the same time that Keegan had arrived at the farmhouse. Or was it? At the farmhouse at Marsh End, he was always surprised by how an hour felt like a mere twenty minutes.

Had Keegan murdered Celia, then hurried home and watched his victim's husband pay to have sex with his wife? It was depraved.

Jack stopped at the hardware store and bought several large black industrial-strength garbage bags and a roll of electrical tape. As he walked out, he looked straight at the security camera. He was so angry he did not care who saw him.

* * *

Cliff

Wallaby Rocks

On Saturday they woke to a pristine blue sky. Cliff waded out, dragging his line across the sleek water in a four-count rhythm between ten and two o'clock. His rod was light and felt like an extension of his arm, and as he let the fly fall, then the transparent leader, then the line—in that perfect order so as not to scare the fish—a calmness crept through him, quieting the usual rabid progression of his thoughts.

The boys changed the flies and debated which ones worked better.

"Fly fishermen have to be more patient than regular fishermen," he reminded his sons.

It was Callum, his middle son, who got lucky first with a large rainbow trout. Ten minutes later, Chris caught one too. Cliff raised his fist in a celebratory air pump.

"That's dinner sorted," he said. "And breakfast too."

He cast out, dragged the line, and checked the water for ripples. The air was fragrant with the cinnamon-scented sassafras bark. A flock of birds, white on the blue sky, fell like they had lost their breath in unison.

Soon it felt like ants were burrowing under his skin. He took off his waders and looked over the map Kane had given him. A hike was what they needed.

The boys quickly packed the fishing equipment away and changed into their hiking gear. The family followed the curved shoulder of the lake. Kim pointed out the tracks on the sand of a lizard, a wading bird, and a wallaby.

The path was edged with fallen gum tree boughs and veered toward a boardwalked swampy area. Soon it turned into grassland dotted with clusters of pink and yellow wildflowers. They walked up toward the saddle, through the damp green silence of old myrtle-beech forest. Cliff paused to drink from his water bottle.

The mountaintops were above the clouds. "It's a long way up."

"We can do it." Kim's brown eyes were pleading. "Where's your positive attitude? Work hard, play hard. That's what you say is the secret to success."

He stared at her. "Don't you get it? Success is luck, not hard work. If success was industriousness and hard work, I would be a millionaire, and so would every maize farmer in Africa."

He knew why he felt so angry. For days he had been clean. It was not easy. He touched the pocket of his fleece and felt the reassuring outline of his pipe.

A sign warned that the track was no longer maintained, and soon after they entered a moss-covered enclave of fallen trunks and towering swamp gums and monstrous roots. They balanced along the trunks of fallen trees where the scrub was too dense.

"These paths are called the bushmen's highway," Kim told the boys. "Did you know that, Cliff?"

His head was throbbing. "No."

They bashed their way through tanglefoot that opened onto a field of enormous dolerite boulders. The boys cheered at the sight of Mount Olympus and Cliff told them to go on to the peak without him.

"I'm waiting here for you. My back hurts."

Kim hesitated. "It's important to me that we do this as a family."

"Go."

"Please, Cliff."

He shooed her away with a wave of his hand. It was a relief to slide down behind a boulder and shelter from the blustery wind and Kim. Eventually she followed the boys, clambering across the rocks toward the ridge. Their laughter drifted back to him. It sounded like they were making fun of him behind his back.

When they were well away, he took out his pipe.

Through the trees he could see the valley below. It was dotted with hundreds of small round lakes, set like jewels on green velvet, the Land of a Thousand Lakes.

* * *

When they returned from the summit, he was ready for them. He chatted nonstop as they marched back to camp, identifying an inlet across the darkening lake where the fish would be feeding at dusk. The boys whooped and ran on ahead.

"I keep thinking about Celia," Kim said. "She would have loved it up here."

"She wouldn't have loved the plastic mattresses in the cabins."

"Poor Jack. I don't know how they'll cope without her."

He was tired of hearing Kim bleat on about poor Jack. She needed to know that no one was perfect—especially not the Lilys.

"It's time you knew the truth about him." He described Jack's visits to the farmhouse at Marsh End. "Jack pays for it. Keegan's pimping his wife. It's despicable."

Kim was not as disgusted as he'd thought she would be. "I've heard rumors about what happens at Marsh End. I didn't want to believe it. It just makes me sad," she said.

Not long after, he saw her fiddling with her phone. His jaw tightened. "You better not be texting anyone what I just told you."

"Of course not." She offered him the phone. "Check yourself."

"Not interested." He would read the texts later.

Kim took a deep breath and exhaled. "Brendan Keegan is a bad egg. Apparently, he is going around saying he saw your car in the forest on the night Celia disappeared. I heard about it while I was doing canteen duty at school."

"Why are you only just telling me this?"

"Because you react like this."

He swore. "You're my alibi. I was with you."

"Cliff, I don't know where you were."

His recollections were blurry. Something had happened after they got home from the Apple Queen event. He had taken his knife and gone on a patrol of the farm. His memory of the night felt like a dream that made no sense.

"Has Brendan Keegan told the police?" he asked.

"I don't know."

"I was nowhere near the forest that night. They can put me on a lie detector test."

"Better start doing yoga or something to slow your heart rate before you go doing lie detector tests."

"Stop being a bitch, Kim."

"Talk to Jack about it. It sounds like Keegan's on the Lilys' payroll."

Cliff stared at her. "You're freaking me out."

"Don't get angry with me. I'm not your problem."

* * *

He lengthened his stride when he saw the campsite amenity block. He locked himself in a cubicle and measured enough to calm down. He was sensible about his usage. After all, he was here with his family—he didn't need to embark on an *ice-capade*. He chuckled at his clever play on words.

When he returned, Kim had the fire going. He sat in his camping chair and drank from his water bottle while they waited for the fire to burn down to the nice, slow-burning coals that were perfect for panfrying fish.

"I'm disappointed with Kane and Lorelai," he said.

"Yeah."

"You were the only client the massage guy had yesterday,

except for Lorelai, who didn't pay for it because that was the bloke's rent for the right to set up the massage table." He stared at her until she looked at him. "Now, that is taking the piss."

"Keep your voice down." Kim glanced at the grass track that led to the reception area.

"I don't care if he does hear me," Cliff said. "He needs to be told. They should be thanking that massage bloke for driving two hours to get here. I'm going to say something to Kane."

"No point," Kim said.

He stared at her. "You're fucking gutless, Kim."

She nodded. She actually agreed with him.

"Kane and Lorelai are not hippies," he said. "They are ruthless. Fancy taking a free massage from someone who has no hope of even earning the cost of the fuel to get themselves here. . . ."

"It reminds me of how Jack just helped himself to that painting. He found it in the Keegans' junkyard. Technically it belongs to them," Kim said.

"Finders, keepers."

"You could walk in there and take it tonight," Kim mused. "You would be back here by dawn."

The idea inspired him, and he talked about it at length. Kim had some clever ideas about how to control the Keegans' noisy dogs. Soon he felt like this wasn't a game. He could do this. It made so much sense. His excitement increased. He was pumped and he walked around the campfire, adrenaline energizing him. His heart raced but his mind was clear.

He sat back down and watched his sons wandering along the shore, shining their flashlights into the treetops. Cliff should have been a military commander. He was practical and intelligent. If he was organizing an attack, the offensive would be flawless.

She curled her legs under her. "I wouldn't feel bad. That painting almost got crushed into scrap metal."

"We're not greedy people." The painting was worth more than he could spend. "We would do some good with the money."

* * *

After Kim and his kids went to bed, Cliff sat up and waited. When it was time, he poured water on the fire and watched the embers sizzle into damp sludge. A ribbon of smoke shot upward into the dark, windless sky. He took his phone and Kim's and switched them off and placed them in the fishing tackle box.

He checked his watch. Two hours down, a quarter of an hour there, and two hours back. He would return before anyone knew he had gone.

CHAPTER 20

Sunday, September 3

Joelle

The Smithtons' house

Under her pillow was a small pink sleeping tablet. Brian didn't know it was there. Last night she had sipped the water, but as he took the glass away, she spat the pill out and hid it. Surprisingly, she had slept quite well.

He had apologized for being bossy and mean when he got home from work last night. She forgave him. She told him she would consider his request for her to come back to work, so long as he stopped talking about it until she made her decision. Of course, she knew she would return. The butchery would not be the same without her. Chatting with the customers was not Brian's strong point.

She lay in bed, listening to the morning cartoons the children were watching, thinking about Celia Lily lying beneath Myrtle Bridge. Myrtle Bridge was where Kim thought the police had failed to look. There were lots of bridges around Vanishing and Joelle wondered why Kim thought of Myrtle

Bridge in particular. She went into the kitchen and spread Brian's map on the table. All the roads he thought Celia might have been taken to were circled with long oval shapes. Myrtle Bridge was one of three areas he had circled twice.

Brian had to check something at work. He wouldn't be long. The children were dressed for church. He said it would be a good idea for Joelle to come to church with them today, seeing as how she had not attended for so long. He told everyone to be ready when he got back.

Joelle paced around the kitchen. Finding Celia would fix everything. Part of her wondered if she should tell Brian; but another part of her said, No, you can do this!

Feeling excited, she told her children to get into the car. They asked her where she was going as she drove away from town and she told them to pipe down so she could concentrate. They passed a family of wallabies grazing on the juicy shoots beside the road. Usually they would tell each other to look. In the back seat, the children were quiet. The upper fork was a long winding track that led past the falls and high into the part of the rain forest where most people had no need to go. Myrtle Bridge Road led to nowhere.

The car clattered as they crossed Myrtle Bridge. She parked so close to the mountainside the ferns pressed against the windows.

Beneath the bridge, the river was a silver ribbon twirling through the greenery. On either side were near vertical slopes covered in man ferns, spiky pandanus with gray undergrowth, and the towering gums festooned with mossy lichen that looked like patches of old man's beard. Overnight a dusting of snow had fallen, and the foliage was decorated. Far below, a blackwood wattle grew in the middle of the stream. Its frosted branches reached up toward the sky.

She climbed over the barrier. It was steep and she slid down the first bit, stopped by the wide trunk of an ancient swamp gum. A pademelon took fright and bounded away. She continued the difficult descent. Mud stuck to her hands and a tree root lacerated her ankle. The ground gave way and she was deep beneath fern fronds and looping vines. The rushing of the water rang louder at the bottom of the ravine. She climbed over a fallen trunk and there, on the other side, on a mossy crop beside the river, was Celia.

She was dead all right. Stiff and twisted grotesquely with her mouth wide open in shock, like a possum that got electrocuted on the wires and fell onto the road. Around her neck was something green. Joelle stared at it. The fabric was green like grass, like the Emerald City, like the ties she tied on Brian every morning.

Dampness soaked into Joelle's jeans. Cold air swirled through the gulley. She wrapped her arms around herself, but the shivering would not stop. High above, the bridge was alight with sunshine, a sliver of life bright enough to hurt her eyes. It was so far away. Down here the water was rushing, the eerie noises increasing in pitch and fury. Birds screeched and flapped out of the scrub. Something must have scared them.

Joelle had to run. She took two steps and fell. She landed hard and hit her head on a rock. Her face was pressed into the dirt. The forest floor was dark like a grave. This was how it ended for Wendy Field.

Joelle was fourteen, hearing a dog howl in the dark as Wendy climbed into the back seat. The vehicle was sucked through the night, beyond the cozy weatherboard homes and into the dark grip of gravelly moonscape hills. The hut they ended up in smelled like urine and shit and green ginger wine.

"Crying doesn't help," she told Wendy when the men went outside to piss. "Probably it makes it worse."

Wendy cried harder. She said she wanted to go home. Joelle crossed the floor of the hut and held Wendy's hand.

"Me too," she said.

She let go of Wendy's hand when the men came back inside.

They let Wendy run as far as the trees before they shot her in the back. Trent laughed, afterward, when someone waved the gun at Joelle and asked her if she wanted to go for a run too.

There were fifteen days between when Wendy Field got into the car and when the doorbell rang. The townspeople guessed what happened. Someone had seen Joelle sitting in the front seat.

Far away, up high, she could hear a joyous sound. Her children's voices. Golden threads floating around her, tightening and drawing her back to the world. There was another voice, and it terrified her.

Her husband.

* * *

Jack

Calendar House

Yesterday, when he tried to go to the farmhouse, he noticed a police car following him. He was too rattled to speak to the police, let alone be questioned by them as to why he was visiting Marsh End, so he drove home. He resisted the urge to call Keegan and question him about that night at Myrtle Bridge Road. He intended to record the man and he knew the conversation would work better in person.

This morning, as he walked Fergus, Jack had begun to feel more clearheaded. The longer he thought about it, the more he doubted that Keegan would have had time to abduct Celia and dispose of her before meeting Jack at the farmhouse. In any case, Jack would know as soon as he asked Keegan directly. Perhaps more important were the details of the vehicle Keegan had seen that night. He decided he would go to Marsh End as soon as he had fed the horses and checked the troughs were working.

He was making a coffee when there was a knock on the back door. Kim entered before he had time to invite her in.

"I've brought you a fish." She placed the foil-wrapped parcel in the fridge, moving some items around to do so. "The boys caught plenty."

"Was it a good weekend away?" He tried to sound interested.

"Relaxing. Exactly what we needed. Cliff caught up with

an old friend he used to work with. Beautiful place. Celia
would—" She stopped herself.

"You can mention her."

Kim looked uncomfortable. "I better go. Cliff will be waiting for me."

"How is he?"

"He didn't sleep all weekend."

"At all?"

"He said he slept by the fire."

"I'm sorry, Kim."

A clap of thunder made them both look out the window.
The sky was black except for shimmery streaks of sunlight over
the mountains. It looked like an Italian religious painting. This
was the kind of beauty Celia would have whipped out her
phone and taken a photo of.

Kim wrapped her scarf around her neck. "There is nothing
anyone can do."

There was a defiance to her tone that made him defensive.

"I don't have a magic wand, Kim. I wish I did."

* * *

Cliff

Gatenby's Poultry Farm

C liff watched the footage flick to the concrete shed.
It was a simple building, with no windows and one
triple-padlocked door. It was where he stored the poisons—

fertilizer, insecticide, rodenticide, and others. The painting was hidden in the wall cavity. It had taken him a while to locate it at the Keegans'. No one would find it here. It could remain in his shed for years if necessary. He was the only one with the keys.

* * *

Jack

Calendar House

In the bedroom, as he gathered his things, he silently rehearsed what he would say to Keegan. He paused at the window, distracted by the striking sight of the poplar trees swaying in the wind. In summer they were all long limbs and feathery leaves. Now the foliage was gone, revealing an abandoned bird nest in the spindly branches. Dark ripples roiled across the lake. A police diver stood in the reeds, waiting for his partner to emerge. It was the second time Jack had seen police divers in his lake.

Anguished, he opened Celia's jewelry box, touching the pearls, the necklaces, rings, and antique bracelets. Inside her wardrobe he pressed his face against the soft cotton of her shirts. They smelled clean, like her. A photo of the girls taken last Christmas sat on the sideboard. He felt like his heart was breaking.

He returned to the window. The police divers had gotten out of the water. They were packing up. Two constables now stood on the bank. They spoke to the divers, and then turned and ran toward the driveway.

Something had happened.

*   *   *

The house phone started ringing. A delicious salty aroma of baking fish and lemon filled the kitchen. His mother smiled as he hurried into the room.

It was Inspector Kanton on the line. There was a kindness in her voice that he had not heard before.

"I'm sorry to tell you that we have located a deceased person who we believe is Celia," Inspector Kanton said. "A local resident found her beneath Myrtle Bridge on Myrtle Bridge Road, a few hours ago."

"Did she fall from the bridge?"

"It appears so, but we can't confirm that yet."

"Who found her?"

"A lady by the name of Joelle Smithton. We have a lot of unanswered questions. Mrs. Smithton is not in a good place right now, understandably."

Jack sank onto a chair. Myrtle Bridge was several miles from Vanishing, high on the range. It was built by silver prospectors for a tramway in 1891. The project was abandoned but Myrtle Bridge remained—a narrow, one-lane bridge cutting through sassafras and giant man ferns. At thirty feet above the river, it was the highest in the area. Myrtle Bridge Road joined a network of forestry roads, one of which eventually turned into Murdering Creek Road. Hollybank Creek Road, he corrected himself.

A week in the wet forest. The animals. The damp. It wasn't Celia they would bring home but a decomposing corpse.

"Maybe it's not her," he said.

"We believe it is, Jack. You have my deepest condolences. Do you want me to send a car?"

It took a few seconds for it to sink in; he would have to go up there.

"No."

He placed the phone down. Victoria put a gentle hand on his shoulder. He couldn't cry; neither could he speak. It felt like as long as his eyes were closed, he could stop the flow of time and the inevitable nightmare that had begun.

* * *

At the bottom of Myrtle Bridge Road, a sign announced the road was closed. With his mother beside him, Jack drove up into the heart of the heartless forest. On cold, damp ground under the trees, where the sunlight could scarcely reach, lay his beautiful wife.

Three police cars including an unmarked white van were parked near the bridge. Seeing the van made his guts contract. He peered from the bridge, through the dappled light, into the black-slit gulley. Beneath fern fronds something white moved. He knew it was the men in protective suits. There was something else that didn't belong there—a stretcher cradled in the river rocks.

"Once they assess the situation, we will decide how to bring her up," Inspector Kanton said. "I'd like to call in a helicopter. It's very steep."

Jack shuddered and leaned on the railing. He felt like everything inside him was going to come pouring out, like a glacier cracking open or a dam wall breaking. His vision blurred and he felt himself lurching forward. Inspector Kanton grabbed the back of his jacket and another officer helped guide him to the police car to sit down.

"There were two vehicles on this road the night she went missing." He could barely get the words out he was crying so hard. "A tow truck and a white pickup truck."

"We'll talk about everything later," Kanton said. "You need to look after yourself, and your children."

His daughters would be having a lazy Sunday at their grandmother's house in Launceston. They would be eating lunch or playing with her golden retriever. There were no words to tell them.

CHAPTER 21

Monday, September 4

Cliff

Gatenby's Poultry Farm

His father spent six months lying on a mattress in the hospice—a skeleton with a vicious tongue. He was nastier on his deathbed than he had been when healthy, and that was saying something. The hospice staff weren't the only people who were glad when the bowel cancer was finished with him. After the funeral, Cliff called the Salvation Army, who came and packed up the old man's clothes and his bedroom furniture and took it away. Cliff wanted nothing to remember him by.

"Say something." Kim's voice shook him back to the present. "I've just told you Celia is dead and you're catatonic."

"How did she die?"

"Strangled and thrown off the bridge."

"Strangled?"

"Someone strangled her with a man's tie."

Mascara ran down her cheeks and he wondered why she had bothered making up her face this early in the morning. All she would be doing was the housework.

The slow realization came to him that she was crying. Her sobbing nudged something tender deep inside him.

"Come here," he said, and she hopped onto his knee and he hugged her.

* * *

Jack

Calendar House

It was the first flawless day since last summer. The vegetable garden glistened with diamond dew. In the sunlight everything appeared healthier, the leaf buds upturned to catch the first fleeting rays of early spring.

It should be hailing, he thought bitterly. Savage winds should be ripping up the flower beds, flooded creeks washing out roadways, the laneways muddy and unpassable, and rock slides echoing like gunshot through the valley.

He packed a bag with clothes he had carefully chosen— Celia's yellow cotton dress, underwear, and her favorite peach-colored cashmere cardigan, plus her makeup purse. No one had asked him to bring her things; he knew what was required.

At the morgue a sheet covered her. The technician pulled it back, exposing her face. He shuddered. The only thing that looked anything like his wife was her beautiful hair. Someone had brushed a middle part into it, not her favorite style. He tried to adjust the hairstyle. The technician warned him not to. It was too late; her head jerked sideways in a way he had only ever seen in a horror movie.

*   *   *

After he formally identified Celia, he was sent into an interview room. A box of tissues and a water jug sat on the table. He waited.

The door opened. In the hallway, Kanton laughed at something her colleague said. Her poker face returned as she entered the room. It occurred to him that she would be pleased her case was progressing.

"Do you want to call your lawyer?" she asked.

He shook his head. She switched on the interview recorder. First she identified herself, and then he did the same. He knew the procedure.

"What now?" he asked.

"Now we officially begin the search for Celia's killer."

"Okay. Good." He took a tissue and wiped his eyes.

"We know that Celia was dead when she was . . . when she fell from the bridge. Her cause of death was asphyxiation."

"Someone strangled her."

"We're not releasing any more specific information than that." She let out a small sigh. "I can tell you that later today, there will be a media conference. We will indicate that you are helping us with our inquiries."

He stared at her, shocked.

"I understand that you and Cliff Gatenby engaged in illegal drug taking recently."

"I know the incident you're talking about. Ask anyone.

We've all been trying to help Cliff with his drug addiction. Of course, I didn't partake. I'm happy to do a drug test to prove it."

"Thanks, Jack." Kanton spoke pleasantly, as though Jack had simply offered to buy her a drink one day soon. She scribbled something on her notepad. "If it was a few weeks ago, it's probably not in your system. Methamphetamine lasts two to ten days in the body, depending on the dose."

"Why don't you bloody well charge me with something?"

"We're examining evidence. . . ."

"Exactly. Have you actually looked for any, apart from digging up my farm? Apart from fueling ludicrous rumors about me? Pull your finger out. What about the pickup truck that was coming down from Myrtle Bridge that night, or the bloody tow truck?"

"Tow truck drivers keep logbooks." The inspector's quiet answer contrasted with Jack's angry tone. "We're looking into it."

"You should have already looked into it. It's like you're not even trying. Joelle Smithton knows about the traffic on Myrtle Bridge Road that night. Did she tell you that? Keegan from the junkyard saw a vehicle up there."

"Brendan Keegan." Kanton rolled the *r*, enjoying the sound it made.

Jack opened his lips, desperately wanting to take control of the direction in which the conversation was heading. All he could think to say was "Ask him."

"We will."

Jack hit the table with both his hands and Kanton's paper coffee cup shook. "Do that before you announce I'm the only suspect!" he shouted. "I can't believe you haven't investigated that angle."

"I said we will. I'll talk to Joelle again in a few days." Kanton made a sympathetic expression. "She's not coping so well, as you can imagine."

"Neither am I."

"You're free to go. You haven't been charged."

"Fuck off," Jack said.

He drove back to Vanishing Falls in a fury. Kanton did not care what Brendan Keegan saw on Myrtle Bridge Road that night. From the start, Jack had been her only suspect. The stupidity of the police was unbelievable; yet there was so much more at stake than a lazy accusation against him. His four innocent daughters would be left without parents. It was devastating.

His wife was dead. Yet he could not grieve. Even a fool could see the prosecutor would be able to build a convincing case against him. Extramarital sex, drugs, a priceless painting, and a murdered wife. There was also the matter of his mother's missing letter, which a prosecutor might present as a motive. A jury would be very comfortable convicting him. They would sleep well that night.

He supposed he had a day or two before the police put a set of handcuffs on him.

Someone in Vanishing Falls knew what happened. Someone was responsible for strangling Celia and throwing her off that bridge. For the sake of his daughters, he needed to find her killer and save himself. That person should consider themselves lucky if Jack simply handed them over to the police.

* * *

Marsh End

There was four-wheel-drive access to Marsh End via an old forestry trail that bypassed the main road.

The morning's sunshine had not lasted. Caramel sassafras swayed beneath heavy rain. The forest was soaked. He drove through the creek crossings without slowing. Each time, water slapped loudly across his windshield.

The Keegans' turning circle was a bog, so he parked in the center of the driveway. Passing traffic would see his car but he no longer cared. He checked his phone had enough battery to record a statement from Keegan about seeing the pickup truck coming down from Myrtle Bridge Road. He would confirm who had requested a tow from Keegan that evening. He also intended to take the painting home, no matter what the weather. In his car were the garbage bags he had bought to protect it from the rain. If Keegan needed convincing, on any of these points, Jack would do whatever it took.

He did not bother slinking to the back door, as he had in the past. He followed the garden path to the formal entrance. The front of the house was reminiscent of a more prosperous era. He climbed the once-gracious wide staircase, the curving balustrade swaying with rot. Sparrows nested in the eaves. The elegant doorbell was broken so he rapped the knocker.

Strangely, the dogs were not barking. There was a foul stench in the air, like rotten fish. It was probably a burst sewerage pipe. He waited and then knocked again, wondering if the Keegans had left town abruptly.

The door swung open. Karen glared out. She wore the fluffy orange dressing gown and she looked ill.

"Apologies for the intrusion, Karen. I need a few minutes with Keegan."

"Not happening."

"It's important."

He looked behind her, down the cavernous, dark passageway with its peeling wallpaper. Karen shoved him hard on his chest. She was strong and he almost lost his footing on the rotten veranda floorboards.

"He's dead," she said.

"What?"

"Brendan died yesterday."

"Good God."

"The dogs are dead too." She leaned toward him and gripped his arm. He could smell her sour breath. "Murdered."

"Of course they're not."

"I know what poisoned dogs look like."

She started crying in loud, wet gulps.

"Hush, now," he said. "Tell me what happened."

"On Sunday morning, he got up, had a cup of tea, went outside to feed the dogs. I found him collapsed just outside the kennels. Heart attack. Or liver failure. He's had problems with his liver. He was on medication for it. He'd probably been dead for a few hours by the time I found him. I would have come out sooner, but I thought he was over sorting scrap metal. I couldn't do anything for him. The ambulance people told me nothing. No one is returning my phone calls. I don't even know where they've taken him. They certainly didn't give a rat's about the dogs."

"Where are the dogs now?" he said.

"Still in the kennels. They're too heavy to move." That made her cry harder.

"Show me."

He followed her through the house to the back door. She pointed to the mishmash of recycled metal and wood that comprised the dogs' dwelling.

"Go take a look for yourself," she said.

Carefully avoiding the puddles, he walked to the kennels. The cage door was open. Two dogs were contorted against the wire, looking like prisoners who had desperately tried to escape. Another lay near the trough. Watery pools of vomit were splattered across the concrete cage floor. The door to the indoor section of the kennel was ajar. Presumably, the other two dogs were inside.

A hose lay on the ground. It appeared that someone had tried, unsuccessfully, to flush the cage out. Flies swarmed over small bones, the remains of the dogs' last meal. He covered his mouth and nose with his sleeve and ventured closer. It wasn't the pigs' trotters he knew Karen fed them. The carcasses lying on the concrete slab were the fine-boned sections of a bird. Yet it stank like rotten seafood.

When he got back to the house, Karen was seated on a kitchen chair, blowing her nose. He looked around for somewhere to sit. There was one other chair, but it had newspapers stacked on it. Three cats slept on the sagging couch alongside piles of un-folded washing and the broken parts of a vacuum cleaner. He shoved one of the cats aside, hoping it wouldn't bite him. After witnessing the disturbing state of the kennels, standing in this mess, it was almost impossible to gather his thoughts.

"I agree with you. They've been poisoned, probably with baited chicken meat."

"Who would be that malicious?"

"Karen. The night Celia disappeared, Keegan was called to a job. What do you remember about it?"

"What's it got to do with you?"

She looked at him with such hatred he recoiled. He thought of her, splayed on the bed after they had engaged in the act, her mouth agape as she struggled to suck oxygen into her feeble lungs. At that moment, he never recognized himself. He felt like he was a stranger, an actor in a scene. He had wondered at times if she ever felt the same. Now they had something else in common—the death of their partner.

"I identified my wife's body this morning. They found her in the gully below Myrtle Bridge." He took a moment to com-pose himself. "Someone's murdered your dogs. Keegan told a witness that he was up there that night. He said he saw a white pickup truck coming down. This is crucial. I don't believe he hurt Celia—he was here, with us—but we need to find out what happened."

Karen began sobbing loudly. Reluctantly, Jack took her hand. "Did he say anything?"

"It's your fault." She snatched her hand back. "Everything that's happened is your fault."

"Why do you say that?"

"Someone wanted the painting. You lied. You said it's not worth anything."

"What do you mean?"

She placed her palms on the table and pushed herself up. From a drawer she took a padlock and an exercise book. She gave him the padlock. It was heavy and had been roughly cut, most likely with a saw or a bolt cutter.

"It's for the old bathroom off the veranda where we locked the painting."

"Where is the painting?"

"Gone. Get that through your head. Someone wanted it. They had a good look for it too. They killed the dogs. That's given poor Keegan a heart attack." She used her thumb to point to the veranda. "Go see for yourself."

He walked to the end of the veranda. A door was ajar. Inside the dark room there was a black-seated toilet with a long hanging chain and a washbasin holding rusty tools and old cardboard boxes of nails. A junk room, in a junkyard.

Back in the kitchen, Karen had poured herself a glass of soda. She didn't offer him one.

"Keegan died Sunday morning. And the painting was stolen Saturday night?" he said.

"For the tenth time, yes." She shoved the exercise book toward him. "It's his fuel book he keeps for tax. It says he went to Myrtle Bridge at 10:25 p.m., Saturday, August twenty-sixth."

He opened the book. Indeed, Keegan had recorded his odometer readings for that evening. Under the heading "Purpose of Trip," it said, "Emergency roadside towing, silver sedan, Myrtle Bridge," and then it said, "Driver and vehicle absent."

"He was shitted off. He got a call to say someone was bogged. But by the time he got there, they had driven out." Her face flushed with indignation. "He came home. As you know."

"Yep."

She looked at her hands. "These people are the first to call for help, before they even try to sort themselves out, then they get themselves unstuck and piss off without a courtesy call. Brendan worked hard. He didn't deserve that."

"Did he mention he saw any other vehicles out that night?"

"The only other vehicle I know of roaming around that night was yours."

He could tell she was lying. "I'm the only one who's offering to help you, Karen."

They looked at each other. She wiped her eyes on her sleeve.

"You always act like you're doing everyone else the favor. You only help someone if you think it helps you." She sniffed.

"The painting is worth a lot. How do you know that whoever stole that painting isn't coming back to finish what he started? You need to work out who your enemy is, Karen. It's not me. My only intention for the painting was to share it with other art enthusiasts. No one was looking at it while it was under a pile of rubbish in your scrap heap." He tapped the book before she could reply. "This confirms that Keegan was at Myrtle Bridge that night. He has said he saw someone else; who saw him? That is what you should be worrying about."

She exhaled noisily through her nose and slumped back in

her seat. "He saw Cliff Gatenby's white pickup truck. The one with the goat horns." She stabbed the air with two pairs of fingers.

"Are you certain?" he asked.

She nodded. "We didn't want to get involved. And I still don't. We've heard the stories about him."

The loyalty he felt to Cliff withered. Since Celia disappeared, Jack had been preoccupied with preserving his own innocence and reputation. If Cliff had been in the vicinity at the time of his wife's murder, Jack was the stupidest lawyer in history. After she went missing, Jack had welcomed this man into his house, had aired his concerns to him, and had allowed him to help search.

"We need to cooperate, Karen."

"I don't care."

"We have to tell the police," he said.

She looked doubtful.

"I'll say that we're business associates," he said.

She gave him a horrible smile.

"To protect you as much as me," he added.

"We know how to keep our mouths shut, don't worry. That's how we survive. And don't think you were our only visitor."

He swallowed. "All right."

She tilted her head back and finished the last of her cold drink. "Call the cops, then. Take the book."

Before he left, he telephoned the Mersey Community Hospital. He gave them Brendan Keegan's name and described the situation as best as he could. They put him on hold while they checked the morgue list.

His mind raced.

Whether Cliff was culpable or not, he was an erratic, drug-addicted man who had not been truthful about his whereabouts the night Celia went missing. Nor had Jack been clear about where he had been. Celia would say, You're only feeling ashamed because you got found out. She was right; he was pathetic.

Eventually a doctor came on the line and confirmed that Brendan Keegan of Marsh End was indeed in the morgue, awaiting an autopsy. The doctor apologized for the lack of communication and gave Jack a direct number for Karen to call for further updates.

Jack picked up Keegan's logbook and prepared to leave. "I'm going to send someone over to bury the dogs," he said. "Are you going to be okay?"

"No. Brendan was my best friend." Her shoulders shook as she started sobbing again. "I don't know what to do without him."

* * *

Joelle

The Smithtons' house

Brian said what she had seen beneath Myrtle Bridge was traumatic. He took Monday off work to look after her. By lunchtime he admitted he had cabin fever. He took some carrots and cabbage leaves and went outside to feed the rabbits.

Joelle curled up on the couch under a blanket. Brian had said that Emily and Baxter could stay home too, but they wanted to go to school. No one said it outright, but Joelle imagined people were disappointed with her for taking the children up to Myrtle Bridge. It was a mistake. Maybe she was a hopeless mum.

Brian had been outside for a long time.

She went to the kitchen window that overlooked the rabbit hutch. Brian was not there. From the living room windows, she could see that he wasn't in the front yard either. He had told her to stay inside the house. She didn't want to be here by herself.

The back door was locked. So was the front one. Even the bathroom window, usually left a tiny bit open to let out the steam, was now locked. Brian wanted her to feel safe.

It didn't feel good being locked inside the house.

* * *

Jack

Calendar House

As soon as he returned home from Marsh End, he rang Kim. Her familiar, kind voice was comforting. She already knew about Celia. There was an awkward silence.

"It's complicated, Kim. New details have arisen. . . ."

"Go on."

"I'm about to give some information to the police, and when I do, you could be in danger."

"What is this new information?"

He told her that Keegan had passed away. He explained

that Keegan had been called to a nonexistent job and had seen Cliff's truck on Myrtle Bridge Road the night Celia disappeared, that someone had poisoned five dogs at the Marsh End junkyard on Saturday night, and that his painting was most likely stolen from the Keegans' storeroom at the same time.

"Brendan Keegan is dead?" Kim sounded shocked. "You're kidding. That's terribly sad."

He had not expected her to be so emotional. The Gatenbys and the Keegans knew who each other were, but they certainly weren't friends.

"Karen thinks he had a heart attack from the shock of seeing his dogs murdered. She's distraught. The place is like a horror movie, with dog corpses in the cage."

"I'll tell you how I see it," she said. "The theft of the painting was orchestrated. Thieves do not break into a crappy farmhouse like the Keegans' and accidentally discover a painting such as that. Whoever took it was looking for it."

"Who knew it was there?" he asked. "Just you and I."

"The Keegans could have bragged about that painting to anyone."

"Kim, I suspect the dogs were killed with poisoned chicken."

"That doesn't mean anything. I didn't tell Cliff about the painting. He was fishing at the lakes on the weekend. I can vouch for that. Unless he drove to Vanishing and back to the lakes in the middle of the night. I doubt it. Have you looked at the dossier he made?"

"I don't think that Brian Smithton is a violent man. If he killed Celia, why would he send Joelle up to Myrtle Bridge to 'find' Celia's body?"

"No idea. You need to give the dossier to the police, Jack. Maybe Brian did throw the dogs some chicken. He hates you with a passion. He would hate a painting like that too; it's patriarchal, colonizer crap."

"That's very dismissive, Kim," Jack said. "In any case, I think you're wrong about Brian."

"I've been wrong before. But Cliff's pickup truck was not on Myrtle Bridge Road that night."

"Keegan told a witness he saw Cliff's vehicle. And Keegan kept a logbook confirming he was up there."

"Did he?" she said. "You've seen it?"

"I have it. The witness's description of Cliff's pickup is quite specific."

"Did I tell you he took the goat's skull off his pickup truck? It was on the rubbish heap." Her voice wavered.

"I didn't know that. I'm about to show the logbook to the police. Kim, once Cliff realizes there's a cloud over him, who knows how he will react?" There was a long silence. "Kim?"

"I hope you realize what you're doing." She sounded deflated.

"This might be a good time for you to go away for a few days."

She went quiet again. He could hear her breaths coming in shallow rasps, and he imagined she had her hand over her mouth.

"He would kill me if I left," she said. "You know that."

He didn't answer. It was chilling to hear her say that.

"What do I do?" Her voice cracked.

"Kim, there's a poisonous snake under your porch," he said. "You can't keep pretending it's not there. This snake . . . it's not hibernating. It's time we're all honest about that. You have to do something."

"I can't do this on my own." She sniffled.

He hesitated. "You're not alone, Kim. I'll call you tomorrow."

"Don't hang up," she said.

A wave of frustration rushed over him. "Kim, you need to make some brave choices. Let's talk later."

The next call he made was to Inspector Kanton. Jack outlined everything he had discussed with Karen Keegan, apart from the secret evening visits.

Kanton sounded surprised. "We've had no reports of poisoned dogs at Marsh End. And I thought you and Gatenby were friends."

"Listen. Five healthy dogs don't suddenly die of natural causes," Jack said. "You could sit back and speculate on who you think I'm friends with. Or you could go to the Keegans' property and have a look at the mess in the kennels. You work it out; I can't do your job for you."

It felt good to hang up on Kanton.

He stood at his window. With his hands shoved in his pockets and his shoulders slumped, he stared without seeing at his fruit trees and the colossal, densely forested range rising beyond his land. Presently, he walked around his house, checking windows were locked, pulling curtains, closing doors to rooms he did not need to use. His mother was in the kitchen, stirring pasta in a pot. He kissed her cheek and told her he would be ready to sit down for dinner shortly.

From the gun safe in his bedroom, he took the smallest firearm. It was Celia's handgun. She had shot a possum with it once and then vowed never to use it again. It was clean, for he looked after his equipment properly. He was reluctant to select any of his larger rifles, feeling that this was an overreaction, but holding the smaller weapon gave him some reassurance. He went downstairs and slid the gun under the couch in the lounge room and placed the ammunition in a drawer. On second thought, he loaded the gun and stowed it high on the bookshelf. From the other side of the room he surveyed the placement. The gun was concealed behind a framed photograph. No one would know it was there.

* * *

Cliff

Gatenby's Poultry Farm

Cliff could not shake the feeling that a snake was sliding up his back. Soon it would coil around the vertebrae at the top of his spine and tighten. With his tongue, he probed the stinging cut inside his mouth. It was deepening. Six hours was all he had slept in the past few days. He needed to stay awake, keep hydrated, and hopefully tonight, if he took a sleeping pill, he would crash for a decent stretch.

A rush of cold air blew through his office as Kim entered. "Can you knock?" He shivered. "Shut the door."

She handed him a protein shake. It was chocolate and banana, his favorite. He tasted it and turned away so she wouldn't see his reaction. He felt like he had chewed on broken glass.

His mouth, his teeth, the back of his throat—every delicate surface burned.

"I don't know if you've heard . . . Brendan Keegan died yesterday," she said. "Jack just rang me."

Cliff swung away from his desk to look at her. Her expression was impassive, the way she looked when she spoke to the children's teacher or if they bumped into their GP in the supermarket.

"Who?" he said, and she gave a small smile. "Do they know how he died?"

She placed her hands on his shoulders and gave him a little massage. "Probably a heart attack," she told him. "At our age, we've all got to watch what we eat."

That evening he went to bed at the same time as Kim. He tried to lie still and rest his eyes. Instead he tossed and turned. He switched the radio on, but he could not relax. Most nights he sat in his office watching internet porn. When he had not used for several days the footage calmed him and helped him sleep. Tonight, without the images of slick-skinned women absorbing his thoughts, he fell into a restless sleep. He dreamed he spilled a point of ice on shaggy carpet. He crouched, painstakingly picking the tiny shards of crystal out of the fabric and placing them on a glass tray. He loaded them into a pipe. Frustratingly, he woke up before he got to smoke it.

CHAPTER 22

Tuesday, September 5

Jack

Calendar House

Over breakfast, his mother dictated a text message he should send to Martha.

"Mother," he said, frustrated. "Let me do this."

He typed: Police are about to name a new person of interest in the investigation. The person is known to the family and I would prefer you find out from me rather than via the media.

The simple ruse to get his mother-in-law to call him had been his mother's suggestion. His hands shook as he pressed send.

He had not finished eating his scrambled eggs when the phone rang. It was Martha.

"What is it?" she said.

"A local man, Cliff Gatenby, was seen driving near Myrtle Bridge that night. He's married to one of Celia's friends."

"I know who the Gatenbys are. I understood Cliff is your friend too. And I've not heard a thing about him. Inspector Kanton has kept me well informed."

"Inspector Kanton is not . . . as thorough as I would like her to be."

"She's called me at nine every morning."

"Has she?"

It was as he thought—the pair of them was colluding. He wondered what they had said about him and if Martha had contributed to building Kanton's suspicions by remembering incidents from the past—old arguments, perhaps, or times when Celia had called her mother for marital advice.

"I need the girls to come home," he told her firmly.

"Absolutely not. It's best for the girls that they are kept away from everything. They're happy. I'm looking after them. Until things are resolved."

"How can anything be resolved, Martha?" he cried. "Celia is dead."

He heard her sob.

"I'm coming down. You can't keep me away from my daughters."

"I won't stop you. But, Jack, you should be looking for Celia's murderer. You've just told me that there is a man up there in Vanishing Falls who killed my beautiful daughter. I'm not sending my granddaughters back until they catch him."

"I'm doing my best."

His mother held her hand out. "Give me the phone, Jack."

"My mother wants to speak to you," he told Martha.

Dreading what the two women would say to each other, he gave his phone to Victoria.

"Martha. This is Victoria Lily. Bring those children back, please. Jack needs to see them. They need to see their father. I won't hear any excuse. We all need to behave like adults. You're in Launceston, and I'm here, so I've got a better idea of what is going on, and how we should proceed." Victoria listened for a few minutes, her expression changing from surprise to fury. "It's already a tragedy, Martha. Don't make things worse."

Victoria returned the phone to Jack.

"Martha?" he said.

"I'll tell you what I just told your mother. I've had you clocked from early on, Jack. I don't trust you. Something is not adding up for me."

A huge wave of emotion descended on him. "I know you don't like me," he blurted. "I want my daughters to come home. You have to answer my calls. You have to bring the girls here immediately."

"I don't have to do anything you tell me to."

She hung up.

* * *

Cliff

Gatenby's Poultry Farm

Kim was in his office again, standing over him. He felt so sick he could not bring himself to look at her. He took a sip of water. It was too cold and stung the sores in his mouth. He spat it back in the cup.

"Are you high?" she snapped.

"I wish I was. I'm trying to get healthy."

"Just so you know, they're interviewing everyone in town again."

"So what?"

He tapped at the keyboard, wishing she would leave him alone. He stopped typing and stared at his skin. The veins on his arms were discolored.

"They found a green silk tie," she said. "Like the one I got you for Christmas."

That made him turn around.

"She'd been strangled with it."

His mouth felt dry. He tried to think. He could not remember much about the night Celia disappeared. It felt like ages ago.

"We need to off-load the painting," she said.

He put his finger to his lips and turned up the music on his laptop. He had instructed her to be careful about what she discussed around here. He had not found any bugs yet. He was checking several times a day.

"I need the keys to the concrete shed. I'm going to Launceston," she said.

"I'll come."

"No. It's important for us both to act normal. If anyone asks, tell them I'm going to visit Celia's children." She opened one of his drawers. "Where are the keys?"

He shut the drawer abruptly. "Stop it."

It was hard to separate his increasing irritability from reality. Kim was prowling around his office and it felt like she was calling the shots. He had not looked at his wife properly for ages. There was no longer a gray stripe down the center of her scalp where the color had grown out; now her hair was the same chestnut brown all over. She wore knee-high leather boots and red lipstick. Both looked odd on her, like she was a girl playing at dress-up in her big sister's clothing. He tried to remember what she wanted from him.

"What are you looking for, Kim?"

"The keys to the shed."

They were in his pocket. "What were you saying about a green tie?"

"You were wearing your green tie the night she went missing."

Panic surged up through his stomach. "I did nothing, Kim."

She gave a short nod.

"Brian Smithton . . ." he began.

"Tell the police, Cliff. I'm sick of hearing your theories. I am trying to help you. Do you wonder why I took the goat's skull off your truck? Any minute someone's going to come knocking. We need to get the painting out of here."

Obediently he went to the concrete shed with Kim and helped her put the painting into her car. After she left, he returned to his laptop. He had forgotten what he was working on. On a sheet of paper pinned to his corkboard, someone had written: "Meth is an unfaithful mistress." The words were scribbled—maybe it was his writing, maybe not. He could not remember writing them. He tore the page down and set it on fire in the rubbish bin.

* * *

Joelle

Smithton's Fine Meats

On Tuesday Joelle insisted on coming into work with Brian. The butchery was quiet. The meat sat undisturbed in the trays beneath the plastic wrapping. She polished the glass and when she could stand the silence no longer, she went next door for some company with Nev. They stood by the window, sharing a chocolate bar, and watched the cars moving slowly through the rain.

"Joey," Nev began.

"For the millionth time I'm fine."

"Of course you are, love."

Joelle brightened as she saw Kim striding up the street. She knocked on the window and Kim's face lit up with a big smile. She came straight into the news agency, shaking the rain off her umbrella.

"Darling. I'm on my way to see Celia's children. I've been worried about you." She was dressed up with lots of accessories—a furry scarf, makeup, and bangles on her wrist. "You poor thing. I wish it wasn't you that found her. But at least they can have a proper funeral. Not knowing is worse."

Kim opened her arms and they hugged. It was a wonderful hug and Joelle wished it would never end. Eventually Kim said, "Okeydokey," and stepped away. Kim's fur scarf had a squirrel's face on the end of it. The tail felt soft and fluffy. Joelle rubbed it between her fingers until Kim said, "Stop that."

Nev leaned against his counter and crossed his arms. "Sad news about Brendan Keegan."

"We didn't really know him," Kim said. "What did he die from?"

"They're saying it was a heart attack. I heard someone broke into their house," Nev said. "Drug-addict scum."

"Nothing to steal in that junkyard," Kim said.

"There is. Some of the junk is very valuable," Joelle remembered. "When I was taking the dog food to Karen, she had this old-fashioned painting—"

"He looked like he had health problems," Kim interrupted. "Karen does too."

Nev rubbed his chin, watching her closely. "Someone slaughtered the dogs. All five of them."

"Oh no! Poor Karen Keegan," Joelle said. "Karen says the dogs are her babies. I didn't like those dogs. She says they're big softies, but they always bark at me. Poor Karen and poor Brendan Keegan."

"You didn't know him." Kim's voice was hard. She fluffed her fur stole around her neck. "I don't think he was about to win husband of the year."

"Is that thing real?" Nev pointed at the stole.

"No idea," Kim said. "Joelle, can you walk me to my car, please?"

"Joey doesn't need to be going outside in this weather."

"Joelle, you decide what you can do." Kim smiled. "I need to talk to you privately."

"It's okay, Nev," Joelle said, feeling important.

Kim hooked her arm through Joelle's as they walked down the wet pavement.

"That man doesn't like me."

"Yeah, he would. Nev likes everyone."

They were outside the Rosella Café when Kim stopped walking and took Joelle's hand. "I'm worried about you, Jo-jo."

"Everyone always worries about me. I'm fine."

"Listen. I've seen how your husband is with you. I can tell he's nice. Cliff—my husband—is not. For him, everything is"—Kim closed her eyes tightly—"black and white. Cliff is strong-minded."

It was the kind of thing her mother used to say about Trapper.

"You're scared of your husband," Joelle observed.

Kim gave a tight little laugh. "You need to be careful. Cliff is the kind of man you don't want to get on the wrong side of."

Joelle held herself very still. Her skin crawled with a thousand pinpricks.

"It's none of my business." Joelle's voice sounded like it had been strained through a dirty rag.

Kim gripped her arm. "It is. That's what I'm telling you, Joelle. He thinks it is. I care about you, Joelle."

As Kim drove away, Joelle walked very slowly back to the butchery. Nev was waiting for her on his doorstep.

"What is she up to?" He frowned.

"Her husband is mean."

"She's got his number."

"What?"

"She's not as fragile as she acts. That fur thing, that isn't hers."

"It's Celia's," Joelle agreed.

"So why is she wearing it?"

"In memory." Joelle gave him a cross look. "Nev, you're being annoying. Kim's one of the nicest people in this town. She wants to come over. I'll probably make an apple tea cake or date loaf. Something that ladies like."

Nev held the butchery door open for her. He followed her inside.

"You know, Karen Keegan is going to need a friend."

Joelle grimaced. "We don't have much in common."

Nev nodded. "I get it. She's all right, when she's in a good mood. I knew her when she was a kid. They've done it tough. She'll have to get used to being alone. But I bet she'd love to go to the Rosella Café if you asked her."

Joelle tried to imagine sitting in the Rosella Café, listening to Karen talk about how much she missed her dogs.

"I don't know if I want to be best friends with her."

Nev chuckled. "It's only a coffee."

* * *

Cliff

Vanishing Falls village

He parked in the supermarket car park. In case someone was watching him, he walked around for half an hour.

Everything seemed normal on the main street. There were no uniformed police or undercover cops, as far as he could tell. Brian Smithton stood on the pavement outside his butchery, talking to Nev from the news agency. Brian wore his white shirt, black slacks, and a green tie. Was everyone around here, apart from Cliff, blind? Cliff pulled his cap down and walked in the other direction, toward the housing commission estate and the dealer's flat. He hoped to settle part of his debt and make a small purchase.

No one answered his knock. He knocked harder. Inside an infant screamed. A woman flung open a door and came onto the landing. She was typical of any of the women he saw in these flats—hard done by even though she had probably never worked a day in her life.

"Piss off, you've woken up the baby." She flicked cigarette ash in his direction. "Get going before I call the police."

He hurried away, hating that a woman like her could make him feel stressed. As he passed the damp, narrow service laneway behind the green grocer's, a thin, disheveled boy whistled to him. With his ulcerated lips and bloodshot eyes, he was one of the youths who Cliff thought of as the walking dead. They were growing in number.

"You want this?" The boy tapped his shirt pocket.

"Maybe."

Cliff examined the gear. They agreed on a price and Cliff shoved a fifty-dollar note into his hand.

"You mention my name and you're fucking dead," Cliff said.

For good measure, he punched the kid hard enough in the

guts that he fell to his knees. Cliff left him crawling on the ground.

He began driving toward the falls car park, his usual spot to sort himself out, but as he passed the turnoff to Old Dairy Road, he braked. Halfway along, he hid his car behind the cattle chute and took out his things. It would not be a good look to be seen anywhere in the national park when they were pulling out dead bodies. He was smarter than that.

The hit took less than a minute. It roared inside his skull and his eyes lost focus. On the radio, a one-hundred-piece orchestra was playing Nirvana. He flicked his hands and the music soared; he was the conductor.

He saw Joelle's big yellow wagon driving up the middle of the road. She parked in her driveway and hurried inside her house awkwardly, holding her bag in front of her. The door opened, and she ran back outside, flapping her arms in front of the shrubbery. It confused him for a moment; then he realized she was trying to coax out a cat. She gave up and ran back inside her house.

That poor girl.

Kim was right—Joelle Smithton wouldn't know what was going on. She was naive and trusting and her husband thought he had nothing to worry about. The gall of him, standing there in the main street wearing one of those green ties that he wore every day. The murder weapon was under everyone's nose and they were all too stupid to see it.

It was time to set things right. Cliff stepped out into the cold drizzle.

* * *

Joelle

The Smithtons' house

O n Old Dairy Road the white pickup truck was parked behind the cattle chute. Joelle hurried inside and locked the door behind her. Then she remembered Snowcat was outside and she raced back out and tried to encourage him to come in with her. He refused.

Back inside, she dialed the butchery number but there was no answer. She looked out the window. The pickup was still there. It was barely visible, a bruise in the rain.

There were potatoes to peel. She set them on the sink and began taking off the skins. Her hands were shaking.

Someone knocked at the front door. She didn't want to open it. She ran into the lounge room and looked out through a crack in the curtains. The light had thickened, dimming the front yard, the apple tree, the empty road. There was no one standing on the doormat.

She picked up her car keys and handbag and hurried to the back of the house, planning to run around the side, jump into her car, lock the doors, and drive to the butchery. She could not stay here.

As she opened the back door, a large man rushed at her from outside, almost knocking her down. Cliff Gatenby filled her hallway, dripping water everywhere.

"You need to learn the truth about the butcher," he said.

His eyes frightened her. They were cold and black like they had been at the fair.

"I've worked everything out." Cliff spoke rapidly. "All this land was never the Lilys'. They had no right to change the sign. Brian Smithton never wanted the sign changed. It's Murdering Creek, and the butcher knows why. Brian Smithton killed Celia Lily. Strangled her with his green tie."

He told her he had compiled a timeline of how Brian Smithton broke into the Lilys' house, killed Celia, and disposed of her body off Myrtle Bridge.

"Check his closet and see if a green tie is missing. Stop crying. I'm not going to hurt you. I am trying to help you. You need to get out of here. You might be next. Do you hear what I'm saying?"

Snowcat jumped through the cat flap. The smack of the plastic startled Cliff.

"Fucking cat!" he shouted.

He ran out the door. Thinking quickly, Joelle slammed the door shut behind him and locked it. She burst into tears and pressed Brian's mobile number. It went straight to voice mail. Why wasn't he answering? She tried the butchery. It rang out.

Wind rattled at the roof as she went down the hall and into the bedroom. She looked over the satin-trimmed blue blanket, the posy of winter flowers in the vase on the dressing table, the books about cricket and politics on Brian's bedside table, the appliqué magazine and pink box of tissues on hers. The cozy familiarity usually made her feel glad.

She stood in front of the wardrobe and touched the handle. She opened the left-hand side. On the railing were the green ties. Her hand quivered as she reached out to touch their silky length. There were many. All the same. The tie he wore every day. Only Brian would know if one was missing.

* * *

Cliff

Gatenby's Poultry Farm

There was no point trying to talk sense to Joelle Smithton. She had screeched at him like a banshee. He drove home and played on the Xbox in his office until he heard Kim arrive back from Launceston. He remembered she had been trying to sell the painting and he wondered how rich they were.

In the house she was putting the shopping away with the music blaring. A huge box of fresh fruit and vegetables sat on the table. More bags of food lay around the kitchen. He looked at the groceries. These were luxuries they never usually bought—Arnott's biscuits and packets of chips, cartons of fruit juice, chocolate bars, and toiletries. There was even a carton of beer for him.

"Job done?"

"Not quite. I made them give me some cash up front."

He opened her wallet. There was three hundred dollars in there.

"Where's the rest?" he said.

"That's my deposit. Once it's sold, we get whatever the amount is."

He took two hundred fifty dollars. "I left you fifty."

"Thanks."

The boys were getting ready for footy training. They carried their dirty cleats through the living room. Not one of them said hello to him. He followed his sons outside and watched them get into the station wagon.

"You forgetting something, boys?" he called.

They greeted him without enthusiasm.

The dog was barking. The stupid mutt had trotted in circles around the Hills Hoist, winding her chain up so she was now held tight at the neck.

"Sort that dog out," he told them.

Back in the house, everything looked normal—the school-bags hung from the hooks in the hallway, neat piles of washing lay on the end of each boy's bed, waiting to be put away. Something was not right, and he could not put his finger on it. Maybe it was how Trixie kept barking. When dogs barked, it meant something. Or maybe he was paranoid.

Kim was in the bathroom. He listened outside the door. He couldn't hear running water or any of the usual sounds of someone using the bathroom. Instead it sounded like she was rummaging through the medicine cabinet.

She came out clutching her rose-colored toiletry bag.

"Where are you going?" he said.

"Football training."

He looked his wife over. She was wearing gym gear and he

grabbed her, running his hands over her body: her buttocks, the slenderness of her arms and waist, her breasts. He cupped his hands around her butt and pulled her against him.

"I have to go," she said.

"Stop saying no to me."

"My best friend is dead." Kim lifted his hands off her backside. "I'm not in the mood."

"So I get punished for something Brian Smithton did. I warned Joelle about him."

"Tell me you didn't?"

In the yard outside Trixie was barking. "Can someone stop that noise?"

"I'll loosen her," Kim said.

"No. The boys can. Or she can learn not to . . ." he began, but he started coughing and couldn't finish the sentence.

His cough was getting worse. All day he breathed in the dusty fibers of the feed, chicken shit, and incinerated broilers. He drank some water. By the time he was breathing properly, Kim had gone.

He looked down the empty driveway. At least the dog had stopped barking.

Without the boys and Kim, the house felt hollow. He looked in the mirror. A stranger's eyes stared back. He had a long shower, mulling over the unusual things that were happening. If Kim was trying to leave, wouldn't she wear something different than gym gear? Although, if she was smart, that would be a good way to try to trick him. By the time he made sense of it, reminding himself that he was high and not thinking straight, the water had run cold. He got out, dried himself off, and put on clean clothes.

He checked the wall calendar. Sure enough, Tuesday did say football training.

Rain pummeled the tin roof. Football usually got canceled when the rain fell so heavily. It ruined the field to have spikes digging into the soft grass. He stood on the back doorstep and wondered what was making him anxious. He listened carefully. Past the rain, he heard a distant cow lowing. There was no other sound.

He smelled the blood as soon as he went down the back steps. Trixie lay on the ground at the end of her chain. Cliff's pig-hunting knife was stuck in her neck.

Blood pooled around her.

He felt nothing—no sorrow, no shock, and no guilt.

It was his knife. He had no recollection of using it.

He inspected his hands. They were clean.

* * *

Jack

Calendar House

K im's whispery voice was frantic when Jack answered his phone.

"I don't know what to do," she said. "He's gone crazy. Killed the dog. I'm scared."

"You need to get out of the house."

"I'm not at home. I can't go home. I'm in the car, at footy. The boys are nearly finished. I don't know where to take them. They don't know he's killed Trixie. He's already driven past once to check that I'm here."

In the past months, every time Celia had offered to help, Kim had been defiant and dismissive. He felt sorry for her, but it was frustrating to be asked for advice by someone who never intended to follow it.

"Can you call a friend?"

"I'm calling you, Jack. Listen. There's more. He told me . . ." Her voice broke. He heard her draw a breath. "He said Celia was under Myrtle Bridge. . . . Jack?"

"I'm here."

"He said this on Saturday, when we were up at the lakes. How did he know that? I don't know what to do."

"Tell the police. Right now."

"If he thinks I've contacted the police . . ."

"Go somewhere safe. With the boys. You need to get off the phone and do that now."

"Can I come over?"

"One thing at a time, Kim. Slow down."

He didn't want her here. He would have to make up beds and organize food for the boys, and there was always the threat of her unstable husband turning up.

"Jack, I've got no fuel, no money, where else can I go? Please."

"Haven't you got a cousin in Launceston?"

"Jesus."

"Sorry. Fine, come here. I do want to help you."

Less than fifteen minutes later, Kim's agitated rap sounded on the door. He let her in and told her kids to watch television and help themselves to a snack. He could hear them hunting through the fridge as he took Kim into the lounge room, where a nice fire was burning.

"Start at the beginning," Jack said.

Kim sniffed and wiped her eyes. "He's been getting worse and worse. I used to be able to tell when he was high and when he's sober; now it's impossible. He's delusional. He thinks people are spying on him. A couple of times he said strange things about Celia. I ignored it. I didn't think it meant anything. . . . I didn't think it would come to this. He said he had a dream that her body was in the gorge beneath Myrtle Bridge."

"It might not mean anything, Kim."

"In his dream, he said she'd been strangled with green silk." She shook her head and covered her face with her hands. "He's out of control."

He picked up the phone.

"What are you doing?" she said.

"Calling Inspector Kanton."

He repeated to the inspector everything that Kim had said. Kim watched him closely, spinning her wedding ring, a habit he had never noticed. She barely blinked and it was unnerving. He turned away, positioning himself so he could see her reflection in the window.

Kanton asked a few questions, and then said, "I'm coming over. Is that all right?"

"Of course."

"I want you to ensure your house is secure. Lock the doors, the windows. Keep everyone together, inside obviously."

It was the first time her advice to him carried the assumption that he was innocent. In the reflection, Kim had become still. She no longer turned her ring or wiped her eyes. Her face was blank. He supposed she was in shock.

He hung up the phone and glanced at the shelf where he had hidden the handgun. He truly hoped he would not have to use it.

When he glanced back at Kim, she was staring at him intently.

He reassured her. "You're safe now."

She covered her face with her hands. After a moment she murmured, "Can you make me a coffee?"

"Wait here," he said.

He went into the kitchen and turned the machine on. He placed two cups on the table. He stood there for a moment, trying to digest the information.

Kim came up behind him. "Need help?" she said.

It was like she was checking on him. For once he was glad that his mother was staying. She was upstairs, reading, and he decided he would make her a cup of tea and ask her to sit with them while they decided how to proceed. She would offer Kim some no-nonsense advice and, more importantly, relieve Jack of the awkwardness he was starting to feel about being alone with Kim.

* * *

Joelle

The Smithtons' house

Not knowing what else to do, Joelle began preparing dinner for her family. By the time Brian came home, she had the table set with a bowl of mashed potato, a fresh salad, and four plates waiting for the chicken schnitzel that was turning crispy and golden in the oven. Brian took two of the plates and put them back in the cupboard. He explained that he was late because he had taken the twins to his sister's house.

"No, no, no!" Joelle put her hands over her ears. "That's miles away."

"Darling, you need a break from everything. I'm worried about you."

"I need my children!"

She continued to shout the words as Brian took the chicken out of the oven. He sat down and shook his napkin onto his knee. He scooped potato onto her plate, and then onto his own. Next, he served the salad. Finally, the schnitzel. All the while she yelled for him to bring her children home. She could not be without them.

"Sit down!" Brian commanded.

He had never raised his voice at her before. Shocked, she sat down and cradled her head on the table. When she looked up, he was eating as though nothing bad was happening.

"What did you do with the potato? It's delicious."

"I can't eat my dinner. I want Emily and Baxter to come home. Now."

Brian chewed and nodded. He swallowed and took a sip of water. "They will come home, in a few days. Think of it as a holiday."

She began to cry. "Brian, you said that no one would take my children away and now you have gone and done it."

He put his cutlery down. "Everything I do is in your best interest. If I'm insulating you, or being overprotective, it's for your own well-being."

"I don't know what you mean. Stop using big words to trick me."

"I'm trying to look after you. You make it very hard. Sometimes."

"Go away."

"Joey, there is nothing I would not do for you."

Was it like Cliff said? The night Celia disappeared, Joelle had woken up and Brian was not sleeping beside her. He hated the thought of Celia being mean to her. He hated Jack Lily even more. She thought of that cloudless summer's day when they stood at the lookout above the waterfall, and Brian had told her about the Mountains of the Spirits and the sacred forests stretching as far as the eye could see. Brian had explained that these were the ancestral lands of the Pallittorre. Those people had lost their land in a brutal way and their bones lay in the creek beds, groves, and gullies beneath the ancient mountain range. Some people wanted to pretend the violence never happened. Brian said that was wrong. That was why, the first time they drove along Murdering Creek Road after the Lilys had gotten the council to put up the new sign, Brian made the car screech to a stop. He had run over to the sign and hit it with a long stick.

Her mobile phone was on the table. Next thing she knew, Brian reached over and took her phone. He scrolled through it and then switched it off. He left the room and came back a moment later without it.

"Brian?"

"You don't need it. I want you to rest."

During dinner, Brian's phone rang. He went all the way to the twins' room at the other end of the house before he answered it. She followed him. The door was ajar. She tiptoed closer so she could hear what he said.

". . . The Cutting is this town's lifeline and an escape route."

Her mouth dropped open. She heard Brian tersely thank the person and hang up. She hurried back to the table and picked up her fork, pretending to be eating dinner like he had told her to.

"Good girl."

He was pale, like someone had pulled a plug out of him and his blood had drained away.

"Who was on the phone?"

He looked at her for a long while. "Just Nev. The police put a roadblock on the Cutting this afternoon. No one is leaving, no one is coming in."

"Why?"

"I don't want to talk about things that might upset you."

She took a deep breath, trying to think of the words she

needed to make him understand. "Brian, it makes me more upset when you don't talk to me."

He hesitated. "The Keegans' dogs were poisoned with rat bait. The police think Brendan Keegan died the same way in a robbery gone wrong. A painting was stolen. But I don't want you to worry about these things." Brian pulled her into a big hug and kissed her. "My darling. Tomorrow I'm taking you away for a few days."

"To your sister's?" she asked hopefully.

"Farther away than Nicky's place. It's not good for you to be exposed to this drama."

The thought of being sent away filled her with horror. She ran into the lounge room and lay on the couch and cried for a while. Brian did not care. She could hear him stacking the dishwasher. After a while, he poked his head into the lounge room and told her to get ready for bed while he finished washing the pots.

It was too early for bed. She put her nightie on and sat on the bed, picking at her fingernails, wondering what to do. Brian came into the bedroom with the pink tablets. He popped one out of the foil tray.

"Take one or you'll be tossing and turning all night," he said.

"Not doing that anymore."

"It will help you."

"I'll go to sleep, I promise. But I need to tell you something first."

"No." He shook his head. "We're not talking about this anymore."

Her thoughts rose and scattered in her mind, like the

pigeons hungry for the food she and Alfred threw to them. Each individual thought was captured in her head—the skull-and-crossbones symbol she saw on the package in Kim's car, the green tie, the painting Karen was minding for Jack Lily, the speech made by Cooper Gatenby in the grade-three class-room, Mr. Keith's stories about the old days—but together they formed a frantic swirl of confusion that could not be put into words.

She tried to explain but Brian did not want to listen. "Don't work yourself up, Joey."

"If the dogs and Mr. Keegan were poisoned . . . how come Karen is still alive?"

"I told you to stop talking about it." His voice cracked.

"Can you call Jack Lily, Brian? I want to tell him some-thing."

"No, I won't! The man is a criminal, and criminals belong in jail."

"But, Brian—"

"You have to stop, darling. Please. I can't handle it any-more."

Frustrated, Joelle clenched her fists. Without his patience the words blew away. Fatigue twisted around her. She closed her eyes. "I'm trying to do the right thing."

When she opened her eyes, he held his hand out. The sleep-ing pill lay in the cup of his palm. Reluctantly, she plucked it from him. She put the pill in her mouth and pushed it be-tween her gum and cheek. He handed her a glass of water.

"Swallow," he said, watching her closely.

Brian loomed over her and she felt very small. She slapped her hand over her mouth and looked up at him. Part of her felt like she had no choice. She had to do what he said. But there was someone inside her, a small strong person, a girl with wild, unbrushed yellow hair and chubby legs, standing on a train track being pelted with pebbles from all directions.

That little girl said no.

She pushed past him, ran into the bathroom, and spat the melting tablet into the sink.

"I told you. I'm not doing it anymore!" she shouted. "I don't like it."

She returned to bed and pulled the blanket around her, hiding her face. The rain shook the tin roof. The leatherwood branches scratched at the side of the house. She thought of how the birds must have felt when black cloud belched its way up the valley's low sky: dread, and an understanding that there was nothing you could do except shelter and hope you came out unscathed at the end.

* * *

Cliff

Vanishing Falls village

The first time he drove past the football oval the team was running around the field in a tight pack, throwing balls between them as the rain poured down. He spotted

Kim's station wagon, one of many cars lined up on either side of the goalposts. The third time he drove past everyone was clearing out.

He could not go home. It was possible the dead dog was an ambush. This technique was used in warfare to draw the enemy in—a dead body left in the open, forcing people to be curious, to make mistakes.

Cliff would not make a mistake tonight. He drove into the falls car park, scoping the perimeter to ensure no one was hiding in the forest spying on him. It was a miserable place. Fog hung in the trees like cobwebs. Wet mud flicked up his legs with each step as he strode through the small ferns growing along the edge of the car park. Confident the area was secure, he rang Kim's phone, and then Jack's. Neither answered, and that told him exactly where Kim would be.

On the drive to Jack's farm, he noticed a long-limbed, thin man riding a horse in the paddock, keeping pace with his car. A hard-faced woman rode behind him. These were the shadow people. He reminded himself they were not real. Still, his attention was riveted by the evil pair. It made driving dangerous. There was a better chance of evading them if he moved on foot. He veered and braked hard in the grass on the side of the road.

He followed the bridle path beside the river. It felt like he was starring in an action film outrunning the bad guys. He jogged athletically, swinging his arms, his legs like pistons. He saw the scene how the audience would—a fit, strong man, running easily across the uneven tussocks. Adrenaline pumped through him. It was good to be alive.

With a huge jump, he vaulted over a wooden fence and crossed the paddock toward Jack Lily's mansion. At the edge of the lawn he stopped. The monolithic house rose up, the spotlights illuminating the pillars and trees and the glistening white driveway where the cars were parked. He had hoped he was wrong about Kim and Jack plotting, so it was a shock to see his wife's car parked next to Jack's Jaguar.

He stared at the house. He thought he saw a curtain shake and he crouched down low. Turning up at Jack's place meant showing his cards. They would know he knew. There was, however, a play in poker called a double bluff. You told the truth about your cards, letting everyone think you were lying. Jack, as always, would think he was the smart one. This time that arrogant bastard would be wrong. Cliff laughed a loud, cracking laugh.

Behind him, in the direction of the river, something was coming in from the rain. The shadow people had followed him. He could see the man on a horse, wearing a top hat. The lady was now sitting on a tree branch reading a book. The sight filled him with terror. Without caring if he was spotted by Jack, Cliff hurried toward the house yard. The first shelter he reached was Jack's hothouse. It was locked. Cliff broke the window with a rock. He managed to stick his arm inside and unlock it without cutting himself on the jagged glass.

It was warm and dry and the orchids smelled sweet. He took out his pipe. From here, he could keep an eye on the house, and on the shadow people, while he prepared a twirl. He searched through the rain for the shadow people. They had gone.

* * *

Jack

Calendar House

As Jack had hoped, the presence of his mother diluted some of the tension. By the time Inspector Kanton and her colleague arrived, Victoria, Kim, and he were sitting quietly at the kitchen table. Victoria listened attentively as Kim repeated to the police, almost word for word, the details that she had told Jack. Occasionally, Victoria asked Kim to clarify a point. Jack was surprised that Inspector Kanton did not seem to mind the interference.

Kim paused constantly, picking up her coffee cup and putting it down without drinking any. It was clear she was struggling to cope with her torment, and she was a stronger woman than Jack had thought.

"You have to understand that he rambles. He speaks quickly and he jumps from topic to topic. I'll summarize. Before her body was discovered by Joelle, Cliff told me that Celia would be found in the river beneath Myrtle Bridge Road, strangled with a green silk men's tie. He believed our local butcher, Brian Smithton, murdered Celia over a land rights issue. He's deluded. He thinks there is a conspiracy, led by the police, to cull certain people. He thinks he's being spied on. Our house is a fortress with CCTV everywhere. Isn't it, Jack?"

He nodded, wary of being cast a part in her unsavory narrative.

Kanton listened to Kim with an expression that gave nothing away—no sympathy, no surprise.

Fergus rose from his fireside bed and stretched. He came over and put his snout on Kim's leg and she patted him. He sniffed her hand. Jack saw a stain on the back of her hand, a small red smear that she had tried to rub off. The dog slid its tongue over her skin.

Kim noticed him looking and she pulled her hand back. She moved her seat closer to Jack's. "Brian Smithton wears a green tie to work. This is something Cliff mentioned many times."

"Well, there was a green men's tie found on Celia's body. The forensics team has managed to take a DNA sample from it." Kanton spoke slowly and carefully. "There will be Celia's DNA, of course, and hopefully someone else's. We'll have those results soon."

"Wouldn't the river destroy DNA?" Kim said.

"Almost. The tie had been submerged for a week and water erodes DNA. In summer, we would be lucky to obtain a full DNA profile after a day in a warm pond or lake. But it's cold in this part of the world. They tell me they're confident of obtaining DNA up to a fortnight after submersion."

Jack interrupted. "I'm furious that you kept this information from me."

"We always keep stuff back. You know how it works. The green tie, for example, is something we considered keeping confidential." Inspector Kanton eyed Jack steadily. "Now, I have to ask. Were Cliff and Celia in a relationship?"

"No," Jack said. "We were all friends. If anything, she didn't like him."

Kim murmured, "There were a few odd things."

"There was nothing. I disagree with that," Jack said. "Absolutely."

"It's late," Victoria intervened, and Jack gave her a grateful look. "Perhaps this conversation can be finished tomorrow."

"Sure." Inspector Kanton read a message on her phone and typed a response. She stood up. "I'll be honest with you, Kim, we don't know where Cliff is right now. We sent a car to your house, but he's not at home. We'll keep an eye on things, but I think you're safest to remain here tonight."

"Are you going to arrest Cliff for murdering Celia?" Kim asked.

Kanton frowned. "No one is getting charged with anything tonight. We don't want to make any mistakes."

"Shouldn't Kim go into protective custody?" Jack asked.

"Not right now. It's nearly midnight," Kanton said. "This house is secure. The walls are two feet thick—better than the jail."

"Measures made to keep out bushrangers a hundred and fifty years ago aren't going to stop a man having a psychotic episode."

"If he turns up, call us. We have people on duty." Kanton was annoyingly calm. "Before I go, Kim, I'm curious, does Cliff have any wild theories on what happened at the Keegan farmhouse?"

She shook her head. "We were up at the lakes that weekend, fishing."

"Do you think it's linked?" Jack asked.

"No idea." Kanton glanced at her colleague, who was making copious notes. "It appears that Keegan was exposed to rat poison. We're still working out what happened."

"That's horrible," Victoria said. "I remember a boy dying from that when I was young. A painful way to die."

"As I said, we're still working out what happened," Kanton said. "I'll speak with you all tomorrow."

Jack frowned at her dismissive manner. "You better take care to tick every box, file every report, because when this is over, I'm going through your case with a fine-tooth comb."

"Jack," Kim said, and the warning sounded like something Celia would say. "They're doing their job."

Together, Jack and Kim stood on the doorstep as the police returned to their vehicle. Kim kept her hand on the dog's collar. She shivered and pressed herself against Jack, wedging Fergus tightly between their legs.

"I'm freezing," she said.

Reluctantly, he put his arm around her shoulders. She leaned even closer into him as they watched the police car disappear into the rain. The wifeliness of her gesture was discomforting. He didn't know how to extricate himself without upsetting her.

"I appreciate all you're doing for me," she said.

"We should go inside," he said weakly.

His mother was waiting in the entrance hallway. "Kim, you should check on your children," she said. "Jack, would you walk me to my room? I don't feel well."

Once they were alone, she turned to him. "That woman is an actress."

"Mother, she's frightened."

"I don't like how she's dragging you into her mess. What does she want?"

"I don't know," he conceded. "But she will be gone first thing in the morning."

* * *

Joelle

The Smithtons' house

Hours after going to bed, she could not sleep. Gruesomely, she wondered what would be worse, to die by strangulation or from rat poison. Death by rat poison meant you died of internal bleeding. Your vital organs shriveled and collapsed, a claw squeezed your brain like it was a sponge, and your tongue swelled up and you choked. Cooper Gatenby had quoted statistics about how much you needed to eradicate the rodents and how potent the poison was to humans. Cooper said one of the advantages of rat poison was that when the rats were dying, they left their home to search for water. The dead rats didn't pile up under your floorboards; instead they died near the trough.

Karen always made sure there was fresh water in the cages. Joelle had seen her fill the troughs. The dogs barked and snapped their jaws at the stream of running water coming from the hose. Karen was careful with water because they only had that one small, rusty corrugated-iron tank that piped water to the house and to the kennels. Karen wished they were on town water, like everyone else.

Joelle's thoughts were like watching the children do a giant floor puzzle. The puzzle made no sense until the final piece was slotted into place. Even when they were missing a few pieces at the end, it was enough to stop the picture from properly emerging.

She thought of that day last week when Kim brought her the little pink soap as a gift. She had seen the skull-and-crossbones picture on a package on the floor of Kim's car. Why was it just lying there? Cooper Gatenby had been very clear in his speech—all poisons had to be locked in a secure shed. They were deadly.

It was confusing. These were things she needed to tell Jack Lily. He would know what to do with the information. She owed that much to Karen. And she needed to do it before Jack was sent away to jail. She tried to think what to do. Brian had hidden her phone. Tomorrow he was taking her away from here.

Outside it was raining and cold.

On the night Wendy Field disappeared, Joelle had done nothing. She would not do nothing again.

Quietly, she slipped out of bed. She put on her raincoat and gum boots, unlocked the door, and started walking toward the Calendar House.

CHAPTER 23

Jack

Calendar House

The dog's bark woke him up.

Jack pressed his forehead against the windowpane, trying to see what had set Fergus off. His outdoor lighting system illuminated the highlights—knotted oak tree branches and reeds swaying beside the dark lake—but not places an intruder might favor, such as the orchard or the stables. His car and Kim's were the only vehicles on the driveway. Nothing looked unusual. He went into the hallway and walked past his mother's room, and then the adjoining guest rooms where Kim and her sons slept. All was quiet. Fergus heard him and loped up the stairs. The dog pressed his warm snout comfortingly onto Jack's hand.

Knowing he would not be able to get back to sleep tonight, Jack went downstairs to make a cup of tea. In the kitchen, he stared at the rain falling on the vegetable garden and waited for the kettle to boil. It was a surprise, but not a shock, to see Joelle Smithton walking down the garden path in her yellow raincoat. His hands brushed over his dressing gown and pajamas. But really, what did it matter who saw him looking like this now?

He opened the door.

"Hello, friend." She beamed.

"It's not safe out there." He took her arm and ushered her quickly inside.

She watched him lock the door and said, "It's not safe anywhere, Jack. Cliff Gatenby burst into my kitchen today."

Water ran off her raincoat as she blurted a confusing story. He listened carefully. It was a list of small observations: a child's classroom presentation on industrial rodent eradication; the green tie Cliff wore to the Apple Queen Tribute Evening; the grocery-shopping habits of Celia, Kim, and even Karen Keegan; Cliff's surveillance of Old Dairy Road and the Smithtons' house; and a mysterious package that was lying on the floor of Kim's car when she popped over to gift Joelle a cake of rose-scented soap.

"We saw Karen in the supermarket buying soda by the mega pack," Joelle concluded. "Celia said it wasn't good for Karen to drink so much sugary soda."

All those evenings Jack had visited the farmhouse, Karen had never drunk anything except Coke. Keegan made cups of tea for himself, but Jack had never seen Karen with a teacup in her hand.

"Was the teapot laced with poison?" Jack speculated. "Unless Karen poisoned him, it seems unlikely."

Jack thought of Keegan, filling up that heavy iron kettle that he heated on the gas stove. He thought of the dogs and that horrific scene—twisted, tortured creatures. He imagined the route an intruder would take when approaching the Keegans' farmhouse. You would cross the rear paddocks, disable the dogs first, then enter the house to retrieve the painting.

"Maybe he poisoned the tank water," he speculated.

Had Brendan Keegan, the poor bugger, been murdered for the misfortune of seeing Cliff Gatenby's white truck on Myrtle Bridge Road that night? Was the antique painting the accidental spoils of a cold-blooded crime, or was it the reason for both Keegan's and Celia's deaths? Were the chickens that had been fed to the dogs baited with whatever type of poison Joelle had seen on the floor of Kim's car? This trail of bread crumbs might lead to Gatenby's Poultry Farm.

Joelle continued in her melodic voice. "Rats eat the bait when it's covered in peanut butter or honey. People don't eat rat poison because it tastes bad. People might breathe it accidentally and die. Mr. Keith told me that. Still, you should never touch it. That's why Kim slapped my hand away when I wanted to have a look at the skull-and-crossbones package. She said you have to wear gloves."

"Oh my God," Jack said as the answer came to him with sudden clarity.

There had been a hose in the kennels when he inspected the dead dogs. The smell in the air was of rotten seafood, rather than poultry. Perhaps the smell was from a chemical, rather than the meat. The meager amount Jack knew about rodenticide included a rough understanding that the pellets or dust converted into a toxic gas when they got wet. Usually, this occurred in the rat's stomach. Hypothetically, Keegan had gone outside on Sunday morning and discovered his sick dogs, lying in a kennel strewn with baited meat and poisonous pellets, and he had tried to hose it out. Once he entered the unventilated sheds at the rear, the fumes could have overwhelmed him. He managed to reach the driveway, but by then, it was too late. Throwing baited meat was one thing; scattering deadly pellets was murderous. The Gatenbys would know that.

"I need to get you out of here," he told Joelle. "I'm assuming Brian doesn't know you're here."

"No. He's going to be cross."

"I know you're trying to help, but I wish you hadn't come." He scrolled through his phone, looking for Brian's number.

"A long time ago I lived at Pieman's Junction. Something bad happened and I did not try to stop it. I don't want to do that again." She puffed her cheeks out and exhaled loudly. "Brian says not speaking the truth is the same as telling a lie."

"Does he?"

"Sure. Like how you changed the name of Murdering Creek to Hollybank Creek. It's telling a lie," she said matter-of-factly.

Jack felt ashamed. He knew the truth about the massacre that happened at the creek all those years ago. Since the confrontation with Brian Smithton, he had reminded himself that the name change was not about revising history; it was about bestowing a beautiful name onto a beautiful place. Lately it was getting harder to believe his own rhetoric.

"You've got a good man in Brian."

"I know it."

He nodded. "I'm going to call him now."

Brian Smithton would not appreciate a call from Jack Lily in the middle of the night. He might not even answer. Certainly he would be surprised that his wife was almost solving a case the police had appallingly mishandled. Jack thought of what he knew about Joelle and her past. He suspected that the trauma she had survived—whether it was her involvement in the notorious murder at Pieman's Junction, or a neglected childhood—had exacerbated a blockage in her development. It was through her broad social network that she had been exposed to vital pieces of information that she was now piecing together. These were things the police, and Jack himself, had simply failed to consider.

Brian was terse on the phone, but Jack could tell he was grateful. It was a short phone call. He thought of Kim, nestled in the guest room, and he hoped Brian would hurry.

"He's on his way," Jack told Joelle. He lowered his voice. "Can you remind me what led you to look at Myrtle Bridge Road for Celia?"

She pressed her fingers to her temples. "Kim rang me. She didn't know Celia would be there. She just thought the police had not looked there yet. I looked on Brian's map, and Myrtle Bridge was one of the places he had circled."

"What is Brian's map?"

"Brian and Nev sat up late one night. It was card night, but they weren't playing cards. They were trying to work out where Celia might be."

"He was trying to help."

"Are you kidding? Everyone in the town wanted to help find her."

"And you did. Thank you. You are an amazing person."

"I know." She smiled, shyly.

He recited the timeline of events for Joelle. On Friday, before the Gatenbys went fishing for the weekend, Kim had told Joelle to go up to Myrtle Bridge. Yet Kim reported that Cliff had described his dream about the green tie and Myrtle Bridge while they were up at the lakes.

The discrepancies had no impact on Joelle. "Yeah," she said brightly.

Jack leaned toward Joelle. "Think about what this means."

"I don't know."

"Yes, you do."

Joelle's eyes widened. "It's not just Cliff, is it? Kim . . . helped him?"

"Maybe Kim did it herself," Jack said quietly.

Footsteps sounded on the staircase. Jack touched Joelle's hand and put his finger to his lips. Hush. She nodded.

"Act normal," he added in a whisper.

Stricken, he lowered his head and waited. He had always imagined that in an emergency he would be heroic and calm. Tonight there was nothing heroic about him. He felt leaden. He stood up, using the table to steady himself.

Kim entered with a blanket wrapped around her shoulders. Joelle offered a bright, disarming greeting. She seemed to have forgotten the gravity of the situation.

"I saw your car outside, Kim, and I thought you might be here."

"What are you doing visiting in the middle of the night?" Kim asked.

"Cliff turned up at her house," Jack said quickly.

Kim cut him a hard look. "Really." She turned to Joelle. "I'm sorry, darling. He shouldn't have done that. Does Brian know you're here?"

"He's coming to get me."

"Kim, you should go back to bed," Jack said. "You need your rest."

"I'll wait up with Joelle," she said. "You go to bed."

"I need to talk to Brian," he said.

"It's cold in here," Joelle said. "Why don't we make a cup of hot chocolate to warm up. Sometimes I make Baxter and Emily a hot chocolate before bed. They love it."

Jack turned on the stove and poured milk into a saucepan. Joelle measured cocoa and sugar into the pan. She was shivering. He fetched her a mohair blanket from the hallway cupboard. He glanced at Kim, who was seated on one of the kitchen stools. Her legs were tucked under her, and she kept herself very still, like a lizard on a rock. She followed his every movement with her eyes. A streak of anxiety rushed through him.

"Do you want an extra blanket, Kim?"

"I'm fine."

Her lack of emotion concerned him. "Everything will be better in the morning," he said.

"I feel like you wish I was gone," Kim said.

"You and the boys are welcome to stay here as long as you need to," he lied.

Kim softened. Her smile reminded him of the quiet, patient, unassuming woman she had been when Celia was alive, and they were all sitting in this kitchen happily whiling away yet another afternoon, with nice champagne and good food.

Joelle whisked the chocolate mixture. She poured the drinks carefully into mugs.

"Cheers," she said, raising her mug to Kim.

Jack sipped the warm, delicious milk and checked the time. Five long hours remained until dawn.

* * *

Joelle

Calendar House

There were lilies in a vase on the counter. These were not local; they were tropical flowers, probably sent from a well-wisher. The orange pollen had fallen onto the oak. It was the kind that stained, and Joelle wiped it up with a tissue. She noticed a card attached. It said simply, "All my best, Kimmy."

"I didn't know people called you Kimmy," Joelle told Kim. "That's a cute name."

Kim gave a small, tight smile but she wouldn't look at Joelle properly. It felt like Kim was cross with her. Joelle sipped her drink and thought about this. She was almost certain that she had not done anything to bother Kim. If she had done something annoying, it was an accident.

Joelle knew that Jack wanted her to act normal. Acting normal was not easy in tonight's unusual circumstances.

"I hope you don't have a cat," she told Jack. "Lilies can kill cats. I don't know how. Mr. Keith told me."

Kim looked annoyed. Joelle tried to change the subject.

"Here we are," she told Kim. "Locked inside. It's a bit creepy inside this house at nighttime, don't you think? I've never been here at nighttime. I do the tour every year but that's during the day. Old houses smell funny. The carpet smells like oily wool and tea and potatoes and a kind of dirty smell like people who don't have a regular shower or bath."

They both seemed interested now. No one was interrupting, like people often did when Joelle spoke. Jack gave her a tiny, almost imperceptible nod. It was the kind of nod Nev liked to give, if they were gossiping and a customer came into the shop. It meant something like, *Let's keep this conversation between us.* Joelle gave Jack a big wink to show she knew exactly what was going on.

"This house was attacked by bushrangers once," Joelle recalled. "It was a long time ago. No one got hurt but—"

Fergus-the-dog stood up in his bed and started barking. He ran to the kitchen door, yapping and growling. No one had knocked, but someone was out there.

"Flip!" Joelle jolted. "Dog, you scared me."

Upstairs, a boy cried out for his mother. Kim ran into the entrance hallway and called out, "Stay in the room."

Kim raced back into the kitchen. She was breathing rapidly, rushing from one window to the next. "He's coming for us. What are you going to do, Jack? We need the gun."

"I don't keep weapons in the house."

"I know you do."

"He's probably telling the truth, Kim," Joelle said. "I have heard farmers say they don't keep their guns in their house."

"Stop prattling," Kim snapped.

Joelle's feelings were hurt. They were supposed to be friends. She looked at the lilies and at the way Kim was standing so close to Jack. Kim's sons shouted out for her again. An elderly lady called for Jack to come upstairs. Kim touched Jack's chest.

"I'm scared," Kim whimpered.

Fergus barked at the door.

"That's just Brian, coming to get me," Joelle tried to reassure Kim. "I'm going home."

Joelle yanked open the door. Kim screamed.

There was no one there.

Outside, in the garden, a mist was floating through the fruit trees like smoke. Rain and wind rushed the doorway, twisting Joelle's nightgown around her legs.

"Brian will come to the front entrance," Jack said, closing the door.

He announced that he wanted everyone to go upstairs, including Joelle.

"Good plan," Kim said. "By the way, I took the gun you left on the bookshelf and put it under the kitchen sink. It's wrapped in a tea towel. I was glad to see you loaded it."

"Jesus." Jack opened the cupboard. "How did you find this?"

"You kept glancing up at the bookshelf. You know, I've had a lot of practice in detecting when a person is hiding something from me."

Joelle saw a blue-and-white tea towel wrapped around something. Kim shoved past and took out the bundle, carefully unwrapping the swath of fabric. Joelle was frozen at the sight of the dull black metal.

"That is a bad thing to have," she said. "Guns can hurt people, Kim."

Kim gave her a little push, urging her to hurry up the stairs. "We need to be quiet, Joelle. Stop talking in that loud, honking voice if you want to see your husband and kids again."

"Why would you say something like that?" Joelle asked, shocked.

"Come on, let's go upstairs like Jack suggested," Kim said more softly. "I don't want anyone to get hurt."

* * *

Jack

Calendar House

From the upstairs window, he could see Cliff appearing and disappearing into the mist. It seemed he was walking laps of the house.

He looked at the people standing around in the second-floor hallway. The boys were silent, cowed. He feared for them, and for Joelle. His mother was seated in a chair, and they locked eyes.

"What do we do now?" Joelle said.

"We should pray," Victoria said.

"Praying doesn't do any good," Joelle advised. "Brian thinks it does but only if you do it enough. I said to him, if praying is helpful, why didn't anyone ever pray for the Vanishing Falls cricket team—"

Glass exploded downstairs. Fergus scampered to the conservatory door. He was hunched low and growling. The conservatory was a room designed to catch the sun, and many beautiful potted plants lived in there. Jack could hear smashing sounds. Presumably Cliff was in there kicking over the elegant pots.

Kim rushed to Jack's side. She slid her arm through his. They stood at the top of the stairs and watched as Cliff came out of the conservatory. Fergus lunged at him, snarling.

Cliff halted. "Fuck off, Fergus."

"Fergus, sit," Kim commanded.

Fergus obeyed.

"Your dog never liked me." Cliff walked across the foyer. "I'm trying to help you all."

The familiarity of Cliff's gravelly voice was strangely comforting, and Jack had to remind himself of the precarious situation they were all in. "How's it going, mate?"

"I don't know." Cliff stared up at him, taking in the gun and Kim's arm hooked through Jack's. "Looks like I'm missing the party."

Jack freed himself from Kim.

"Line him up." Kim placed the gun in Jack's hand.

"Don't," Chris, her eldest boy, pleaded. "He's trying to get better."

"Mate, go home and get some rest," Jack told Cliff.

"Ha!" Cliff began climbing the stairs. There was a psychotic emptiness in his eyes. "And leave my wife here so you can treat her the same as you treat Keegan's wife?"

"No." Jack glanced at his mother. She had her hands folded in her lap, and her eyes were closed. He felt a surge of protectiveness for her.

Kim was now pressing up behind him and making everything worse. The firearm was slippery with his sweat. Cliff paused on the first landing.

"Shoot him," Kim said. "He killed Celia. He poisoned Brendan Keegan. He killed our dog. Do it. Or we'll all die. It's self-defense."

"He's not armed," said Chris.

"Don't hurt my dad," Cooper said.

"Cliff, I need you to leave," Jack said weakly.

Cliff began moving up the staircase again. Kim slapped Jack on his shoulder and shouted, "Shoot him before he kills us all."

Jack steadied the gun. One of the Gatenby boys began sobbing. Cliff raised his hands and laughed maniacally.

"Don't shoot," he said sarcastically. "You're a pussy, Jack."

Jack fingered the trigger. He had shot rabbits and roos, wild pigs and ducks. Sport was easy. This was nothing like that. He felt feverishly hot.

"I'm not going to hurt anyone," Cliff said. "I didn't kill the dog. I know I didn't."

"Who did, Cliff?" Jack said, frustrated. "If not you, then who, mate?"

Slowly Cliff sank to the floor and sat, midway up the staircase. He appeared subdued, holding his head in his hands. Jack thought of the blood he had seen on Kim's hand.

Dog blood.

He lowered the gun.

"Everything is going to be okay," he said.

Kim grabbed the gun from Jack. It happened quickly.

There were two shots. The second one shattered the chandelier. On the staircase, Cliff screamed as blood poured out of him.

* * *

Joelle

Calendar House

After the shooting, Jack quickly took the gun from Kim. She sat on the ground hugging herself, repeatedly mumbling, "Oh my God."

Jack didn't even look at her. He went downstairs with the gun.

No one seemed to know what to do. Joelle tried to think of something to say but nothing came to mind.

The boys huddled around each other. Mrs. Lily beckoned Joelle to come and sit beside her. The older lady put her arm around Joelle. A moment later, a police siren screamed up the driveway.

Two police officers strode into the vast entrance hallway with Brian and Jack. When Brian saw Joelle, he ran up the stairs two at a time and hugged her so hard she had to wiggle away from him.

"Let me go," she said. "You're squeezing me to death, Brian."

"I woke up and I didn't know what had happened to you,"

he said, gently cupping her face in his hands. "I was so worried, Joey."

"Kim shot at her husband," Joelle said. "Twice."

"It was self-defense," Kim murmured. "I had no choice."

Brian pressed his lips onto Joelle's head. "If it's okay with everyone, I'm taking my wife home."

* * *

Cliff

Calendar House

He wasn't dead. He could move one leg and both his shoulders. There was blood on his face and on the carpet and he was pretty sure it was his. Somewhere, he could hear his children calling his name.

They didn't understand that he had come to help them. Everything he had done was for their own safety. More shadow people had followed him inside and they were multiplying. One of them blocked the doorway, holding her hand out for him to follow her. He wasn't crazy. From a wide window he could see the tall, thin man riding circles around the house on his horse and the lady floating in the sky above the lake.

He knew the drugs could make him delusional. With no sleep, his brain kept trying to trick him. He needed to trust himself and no one else or everyone he loved would be dead before dawn. The shadow people were evil. Their intention was to kill him and everyone else in the house.

He tried to get up and realized he was handcuffed. He let out a huge scream and the shadow people smiled their toothless grins.

* * *

Jack

Calendar House

Inspector Kanton took control, instructing her partner to organize the paramedics. Jack was glad she was such a bossy person. He sank onto a chair beside his mother. For once he could not think how to handle the crisis at hand.

Kanton rounded up the Gatenby boys. She directed them to show her where they had been sleeping. Jack and Kim followed her into the boys' bedroom. Once Kanton had confirmed that the children felt safe enough to remain in the house, she told them to stay in the room while she spoke to the adults.

"Make yourselves at home, darlings," Kim said, kissing each of the boys. "We might be staying here for a while."

Next they gathered in Victoria's room. Inspector Kanton explained the evening's events. "Gatenby rang us himself. They do that. We were driving around when we got the call. He told us you were here and that you were all in danger. Fortunately, we intercepted Brian at the gate. I was worried that the night would end with more casualties."

"Cliff told you we were in danger?" Kim asked.

"He was hallucinating. He claimed there was a mysterious fatal threat to everyone."

"He needs medical help," Victoria said.

Kanton agreed. "I wouldn't mind having a chat with you, Mrs. Lily. Alone."

"Of course." Victoria perked up.

"Actually, I might take a moment with you first, Inspector," Jack said.

"You'll have a turn next, thank you, Jack," she said tersely.

Jack returned to the hallway. He stood with Kim by a wide window that had a view of the driveway. Presently, the medics stretchered Cliff out of the house and placed him inside the ambulance.

"I can't believe this," Jack said. "You didn't have to shoot him."

"No. I could wait until his next episode and let him have a crack at me. You have no idea what it's like, Jack."

"No."

"I'm damned if I do; I'm damned if I don't."

Emboldened by the police presence in his house, he said, "I feel sorry for you. But everyone has choices, Kim. You need to be honest about everything that's happened."

She pressed her face to the glass and watched the ambulance roll down the driveway. She turned to him with a horrible smile and said, "I've got the letter that your mother wrote to you."

"What letter?"

"Blue envelope, old-fashioned writing. Celia showed it to me. We had a little laugh about it. Fancy telling your son that he will inherit everything, but only if he is a widower. And then your wife dies in mysterious circumstances. It's terrible timing."

"Give it back."

"I don't know, Jack. Don't you think we should show it to the police?"

"Burn it. You understand—my mother is ill."

"I do understand." She feathered her fingers across his arm, a gesture that was suggestive in its lightness. "Your mother knows she can rely on you. I hope I can too."

Later, in the kitchen, they gave their statements to Inspector Kanton. Jack tried to say as little as possible. Kim elaborated, detailing her fear and how brave Jack had been in letting her family shelter here when her abusive husband was hunting them. After Kanton left, Kim leaned against Jack and whispered, "Finally I feel safe."

He thought of the analogy he had given her, that a snake was under her porch. It wasn't. It was here, trying to curl up beside him. If he moved away, it would strike.

CHAPTER 24

A week later

Joelle

A fter the shooting at the Calendar House, things were not great for Joelle. Inspector Kanton had told Brian that the information she provided had opened many new lines of inquiry. Her friends kept saying she was amazing, but it was not as fun being a hero as she thought it would be. She felt tired. It was a struggle to get out of bed in the mornings.

When Brian was at work, Miss Gwen kept her company. Miss Gwen made them endless cups of tea and cooked meals for the freezer and tidied things that didn't need to be tidied. Joelle had tried to describe to Brian the things that he had done these past few weeks that needed to stop. It was hard to explain the problems without getting upset. She didn't like criticizing a beautiful, kind man like Brian. Miss Gwen thought it would be a good idea if they wrote down the issues.

"Don't lock me in the house. Don't make me take sleeping tablets. Don't send my children away without talking to me first. Don't hide my phone. Don't tell me I have to go on a holiday when it's not really a holiday."

Brian went pale when he read the list. He placed it in the

top drawer of his bedside table. "If I do any of those things ever again, I want you to remind me to look in this drawer." He swore quietly and then apologized for cursing. "There is no excuse. All I can say is, these past few weeks have been unusual. Have I ever treated you wrongly like this in the past twelve years?"

She shook her head. "I don't even have to think about it. I love being your wife. And I love being independent. That's why it breaks my heart that you have been so controlling lately, Brian."

"You deserve to be treated like a princess," he said.

"Not a princess locked in a tower, Brian."

He didn't get the joke.

One afternoon, in the hour after Miss Gwen departed and before Brian and the kids were due home, Kim texted Joelle and asked her to come over. Joelle decided to take some frozen meals to Kim. She had not seen her since that terrifying night.

Kim seemed agitated when she opened the door. She thanked Joelle brusquely for the casserole and soup and put them in the fridge.

"I need a favor," Kim said. "You can't tell anyone."

"Sure thing, Kim. My lips are buttoned and zipped."

Joelle had barely begun miming a button and a zip motion on her lips when Kim headed to her bedroom. Joelle followed. Kim dragged Jack's painting out from under the bed. There were the children, their faces glowing with innocent beauty, and the women with the decorations and the Vanishing Falls rock pool water in all its shades of blue and white that made it

look like it might gush off the canvas. Kim didn't bother trying to show it to her, like Karen had. She wrapped it up in the
actual sheet that was on the bed.

"How did you get this?" Joelle asked.

"Don't worry. Remember, I consider you to be a good friend.
Help me get this to your car."

Numbly, Joelle nodded. Her cheeks ached from smiling.
Together they carried the painting out through a side door
and lay it in the back seat of Joelle's car.

"Take this." Kim handed her a piece of paper and a single
key. "I've written down the address and number for a storage
shed about an hour along the coast road. I want you to leave
that thing there."

"I can't, Kim."

"I have no choice. Everything here is 'proceeds of crime.'
They've taken my car on a truck to search it for evidence.
They'll be back to seize anything of value. That painting is
worth a million dollars and legally it doesn't belong to anyone.
Jack found it in the Keegans' junkyard. He should have let
them keep it—he does not need the money. I do though. For
my children. Everything I have done is for my children. You
understand that."

Joelle couldn't find the words she needed. She shook her head.

"Why are you here?" Kim said. "Why did you come?"

"I wanted to go to the Rosella Café with you."

"No." Kim sounded frustrated. "We can't be seen together
anymore."

"Oh." Joelle looked at the ground. Her sneakers were muddy
from the driveway.

Kim softened. "I never intended to hurt Celia. I just wanted the painting. When she interrupted me in the hallway, she was so drunk she didn't realize I had gone home and come back. We argued. I suggested that we sit in the truck, so we didn't wake up her kids. She was incredibly rude, especially about my marriage. Believe me, I wish it didn't happen."

"Oh no, Kim." Joelle covered her mouth with her hands. "Please, no."

"I am sorry. Afterward, what could I do? I drove up to Myrtle Bridge Road in a panic. When Keegan saw Cliff's truck up there, it was easy for me to let Cliff take the blame. And then Cliff was running around accusing your husband of killing Celia. I'm sorry for that. I probably should have tried harder to stop him. I didn't really think anyone would pay attention to Cliff's ramblings. I wanted Cliff to obtain the painting for me, which he did. Cliff didn't mean for Keegan to die. But I have no sympathy for Brendan Keegan. He got what he deserved. What kind of man asks his wife to prostitute herself?"

"I don't know." Joelle felt herself turning numb.

"All my life I have tried to do the right thing. It would break your heart, Joelle, if I told you the things I have given up for the sake of other people. A beautiful baby girl grew up without her mother. And you know what? Everyone lets me down. Why? Why?" Kim swiped a tear from her cheek.

"I don't know that either." Joelle wrung her hands, sick with fear.

"It's all right." Kim's voice cracked with sadness. "You're a good woman. We all must take control of our lives. I'm doing that now. I'm going to take my children far from here, and we will be safe."

Kim thrust a ziplock bag into her hand. Inside was a blue envelope. "Don't lose this—store it with the painting. It's my insurance policy. Now go."

They hugged. Joelle's boobs pressed down on Kim, who felt bony and small.

"I feel really sorry for you, Kim."

"I know you do. Thank you for helping me."

With the painting in her car, Joelle left the chicken farm. As directed, she drove along the road that led to the Cutting. As she approached the turnoff to Marsh End, she slowed down. She thought of Karen, lonely for her husband, missing her dogs. Anxiously, worried that Kim might be watching her, she turned left. The steering wheel was slippery with her perspiration. Outside Karen's house, she honked her horn and waited. It took a while, but Karen came out.

"What am I supposed to do with trotters?" Karen shouted from the stoop. "Haven't you heard?"

"I don't have trotters, Karen," Joelle called back, climbing out of the car. "That's yours, in the back seat."

Karen came down the steps, complaining that she was in no mood for visitors. Joelle opened the car door and pulled back the cotton sheet. Karen fell silent.

"This is what it's all about, isn't it?" she said.

"You know it's worth a million bucks. Kim says it was on your property. So it's probably yours."

"I'd trade it for Brendan any minute."

"Do you want it?"

"I guess. It's true; it was found here."

Joelle smiled brightly. "Sell it and you could go on a holiday to New York or London or Coles Bay."

"I always wanted to go on a cruise."

"Great. All-you-can-eat buffet," Joelle enthused.

"You having a go?" Karen's eyes narrowed.

Joelle felt confused. "I don't think so."

Karen laughed, a pretty, pealing sound. It was the first time Joelle had heard her laugh. She couldn't help but smile right back.

A month later

Cliff

Launceston Reception Prison

Cliff had a plastic mattress on a steel bench, a toilet with no seat, a washbasin, a television, and a jug. That was it. He was on remand, waiting for his case to be mentioned. When he didn't hear from her, he had hoped that Kim was staying one step ahead of the police. She would use the money from the painting to hire him a powerful lawyer from the mainland who would get him out of here.

She had not returned any of his calls. Apart from his legal aid solicitor and the medical staff helping him detox, he had received one visitor. Kane, his mate from Wallaby Rocks, was not as hopeless as Cliff had thought. He sat with Cliff and went over the events that had led to Cliff being incarcerated. Kane explained that Cliff was ill. He was suffering from the terrible disease of addiction and Kane believed there was a cure.

Kane joined him for a meeting with the legal aid solicitor. They agreed Cliff would plead guilty to the manslaughter of Brendan Keegan and to the animal cruelty offenses, as well as the misuse of a controlled substance.

Kane believed that Cliff had been set up by Kim. It was Kim who had supplied the aluminum phosphide bait, and four slaughtered chickens, by bringing them to Wallaby Rocks. As they had sat by the campfire that night, Cliff could recall Kim urging him to feed the dogs baited chicken and scatter the remaining pellets through the cage. Kane questioned why Kim had selected that particular bait. From what Cliff had told him, there were other baits that did not convert to poisonous vapor when hosed. If another chemical had been used, Keegan would probably be alive.

During questioning, the police had asked Cliff why he had removed the goat skull from his vehicle. In the days following the Marsh End farmhouse robbery, Kim had casually admitted she had taken the skull off with wire cutters and thrown it on the farm rubbish dump. Cliff wondered if she did this to draw attention to him, to make people suspect he had something to hide.

"Do you think I'm being paranoid?" he asked Kane.

"Not this time, I'm sorry to say."

Kane thought Kim should face manslaughter charges too. But Cliff wanted to take responsibility. It was the first step in his recovery. Kane could not argue with that.

It was Kane who offered to look after the boys when he heard that Kim had been charged with Celia's murder. In the hours before her arrest, she had physically attacked Jack Lily in the supermarket, accusing him of stealing a million-dollar painting from her. Kane told Cliff that the case against her was strong. Under interrogation, she admitted to killing Trixie and then blaming Cliff for the cruel act. It was a relief to Cliff to know he was not responsible for hurting the family dog.

When Cliff had served his time, Kane promised there was a cabin waiting for him. Meditation and fresh air were key to recovery from addiction, Kane advised, as well as hard work. Fortunately, there were a lot of handyman jobs that needed doing at Wallaby Rocks.

* * *

Joelle

Vanishing Falls village

The day of the Apple Festival was a beautiful spring day with acres of blue sky. The Apple Float was a grand apple steamer that had been built on a car. It was decorated with apple blossoms and local artists had painted murals of orchards and fairies along the sides. Miss Gwen declared it the crown jewel of the parade.

There had been a rigorous debate about whether to hold the Apple Festival. Miss Gwen said that lots of people thought it wasn't right to be celebrating so soon after two people were murdered. In the end, it was decided that since Celia had worked so hard on the committee, the celebration should go ahead.

A lump rose in Joelle's throat when she saw the Lily girls waving from the float. They looked beautiful in their pastel-colored dresses. Across the street, Jack Lily stood with Celia's mum. She was tall and athletic, but she didn't have Celia's beautiful smile. She looked sad.

Joelle and her family, including Brian's sister, followed the crowd pushing down the main street toward the old jetty and the few remaining apple trees. People were splashing cups of cider on the grass beneath the trees—an old-fashioned health blessing—and the air was fragrant with cloves, ginger, and cinnamon.

Outside the packing shed was a row of tents where you could buy sweet and savory apple delicacies. Jack Lily emerged holding four toffee apples. Joelle waved to him. He came over to say hi. It turned out that Brian's sister, Nicky, knew him.

"Hello, Nicola," Jack said. "I didn't make the connection: you two are related."

"Small world," Nicky said. "How did you go with that painting?"

"I was only holding it for a friend," he said.

"I hope they've got it under lock and key," Nicky said. "It's worth more than what we thought."

Jack looked pained.

"Have you got a tummy ache?" Joelle said. "Maybe you ate too many toffee apples."

Jack laughed politely, and after a brief exchange with Brian, he excused himself to rejoin his mother-in-law. Across the paddock, near the drinks bar, Joelle noticed Karen Keegan sitting by herself at a picnic table. She had plaited her hair and twisted it up into a big bun on the top of her head. She looked quite nice. Her face lit up when she saw Joelle, and she gave a little wave.

Joelle went over and sat across from her.

"I'd like to buy you a drink," Karen said.

"No, thanks. I don't like the taste of alcohol. Disgusting."

Karen shrugged like she didn't care one way or the other, but she looked how Joelle felt when she saw the mums from school having coffee in big noisy groups at the Rosella Café. She felt sorry for Karen, so she said, "Do you want to buy me an apple juice?"

Karen told the bartender to bring over two apple juices. The juice was sweet and thick. Joelle drank until the cup was empty. They sat peacefully for a while, watching people walk past, including Mr. Keith, who came in with Matron and sat at the bar. Joelle called out a friendly greeting to everyone she knew.

"I guess I won't be seeing you anymore, since you won't be coming over with the dog food," Karen said.

Joelle thought about what Nev had said.

"Do you ever go to the Rosella Café?" she asked. "Rosella Café is the best place to have coffee with a friend."

"I love a good coffee."

"Are we making a coffee date?"

Karen gave her a small smile. "Lock it in."

The kids were calling Joelle, so she told Karen goodbye.

She was grinning, not enough to make her cheeks hurt, but enough that Brian was going to want to know what was going on. Near the old jetty, Alfred was running an apple-packing competition, and Nev had children lining up to try the apple-bobbing game. Emily and Baxter grabbed Joelle's hands. They wanted her to join in and they wouldn't take no for an answer.

ACKNOWLEDGMENTS

Heartfelt thanks to my agent, Julia Kenny from DCL Literary Agency, for her encouragement, thoughtful and talented editing, persistence, and friendship. Special thanks to Arielle Datz for all your help.

My wonderful editor, Carrie Feron, scrupulously shaped this novel and I'm so glad to have worked with her. My gratitude also to the tremendous team at William Morrow and HarperCollins who worked so hard behind the scenes, including Stephanie Evans, Rachel Weinick, Rachel Meyers, Andrea Molitor, Allison Draper, Kaitie Leary, Bianca Flores, and especially Asanté Simons.

The novel owes a debt to the following friends and professionals who contributed their expertise: A'ishah Amatullah, Nathan Castle, Tara Castle, Clare Forster, Kaye Gee, Lucy Hyde, Eleanor Limprecht, Dr. Margaret Robin, Matthew Searle, and Writerful Books.

Deepest thanks to Sabrina Scrogie, the constant ray of sunshine in our lives.

I wish to acknowledge the Traditional Owners of the land on which this novel was written and researched, and recognize their continuing connection to land, waters, and culture.

And lastly, to Mum and Dad, my wider family, and William, Scarlett, Miles, and Teddy . . . much love.

About the author

About the book

Insights,
Interviews
& More . . .

Meet Poppy Gee

Tara Castle

Poppy Gee was born in Tasmania and moved to Brisbane to attend university when she was eighteen. In Brisbane, she was working behind the bar in the beer garden at the Royal Exchange Hotel when she met her future husband, a carpenter named William. They now have three young children and two cats. Poppy has worked in hospitality, childcare, and journalism, and is currently focusing on raising her children and writing. In her spare time, she likes taking her children to the beach, hiking alone in the forest, snow-skiing with her family, exploring historical places, gardening, and reading. ⟋

Behind the Book Essay

In this novel, I have imagined a village located in a fictional valley, somewhere near the Gog Range and Mole Creek in the Meander Valley in northern Tasmania. There are, however, real historical events, people, and places weaved into the story. Here are some:

The Apple Blossom Celebration

Apple growing in Tasmania has a romantic history. The first apple tree was planted in 1788 when Captain William Bligh anchored near Bruny Island. Apple trees thrived in the cool climate, producing hard rosy fruit that was highly sought after. In the Mersey Valley, apples were transported initially on the Mersey River, then trucked by road to the apple port at Beauty Point wherethey were shipped to the world. The peak of the apple boom was in the 1950s and '60s, when bountiful orchards covered more than 25,000 acres of land. Festivals were held to bless the blossoming apple trees in spring, and to celebrate the harvest in autumn. There were float parades, balls, crownings of apple queens, and competitions held to showcase the skills of the orchardist. These festivals are being revived for fun in the Huon Valley and Spreyton.

The Convict Cannibal

The name for Pieman's Junction, the fictional town of Joelle's youth, was inspired by a chilling Tasmanian tale.

In 1822, Tasmania was a brutal penal colony called Van Diemen's Land. Alexander "Pieman" Pearce, an Irish farm laborer, was serving a seven-year sentence for stealing six pairs of shoes. He was imprisoned on Sarah Island, a jail in Macquarie Harbour, on the rugged west coast. Convicts arrived by ship via Hell's Gates, a treacherous harbor entrance. Cold, wet, thick forest surrounded the harbor; the jail was thought to be inescapable.

Pearce was part of a work-gang cutting pine logs on the edge of the harbor when he and seven men overpowered the overseer. Ill-equipped except for one ax, and unskilled in surviving in the wild Tasmanian bushland, they attempted to hike across the mountains to settled areas of the island. After fifteen days without food, the men began to kill and eat each other. As the party was depleted, it became a game of cat and mouse, with no one willing to fall asleep. ▸

Behind the Book Essay *(continued)*

Eventually, Pearce seized the ax and killed his last companion.

Pearce knew he had reached the settled farmlands when he saw sheep grazing. Assisted by sympathetic convict shepherds, he achieved 111 days on the run before he was captured. Upon his arrest, no one believed his farfetched story of survival and he was sent back to Sarah Island. He escaped a second time, with a young convict named Thomas Cox. Pearce was captured alone after ten days. He claimed the pair reached a river and Cox refused to swim across. Pearce admitted to killing him. This time the authorities believed him: pieces of human hands and fingers were found in his pockets.

He was hanged at the Hobart Town Gaol in 1824. The *Hobart Town Gazette* reported a large crowd gathered to watch the spectacle and that right before Pearce dropped, he told the crowd: "Man's flesh is delicious. It tastes far better than pork or fish."

Nicknamed the "Pieman," the self-confessed cannibal-murderer is one of Tasmania's most notorious criminals. After his death, Pearce's body was sent to surgeons for dissection. His skull was sold to an American phrenologist, Dr. Samuel George Morton. The skull remains at the

University of Pennsylvania Museum
of Archaeology and Anthropology.

Tasmanian Massacres

Tasmania is a beautiful island with a
terrible history. After settlement in
1803, the conflict between British
colonists and Aboriginal Tasmanians
peaked during the Black War, a violent
period running from the 1820s until
1832. It was prompted by the rapid
spread of the colonists' farms and
livestock over traditional hunting
grounds and their abduction of
Aboriginal women and girls for
sexual purposes. Aboriginal warriors
retaliated with theft and murder,
and roving parties of convicts and
colonists were ordered to attack
the Aboriginal people in their bush
camps to suppress the native threat.

It is only in recent times that some
of these events are being acknowledged.
One horrific example was the Cape Grim
massacre. In Tasmania's northwest,
the Van Diemen's Land Company
was given prime Aboriginal kangaroo
hunting grounds to turn into sheep
farms. In 1827, the Peerapper clan was
gathering muttonbird eggs and hunting
seals when convicts working for the ▶

VDL Company abducted and raped several Aboriginal women. In the skirmish that followed, a shepherd was speared in the leg and an Aboriginal chief was shot dead. Later that month, a party of Peerapper returned and killed 118 sheep belonging to the VDL Company.

Retribution was merciless. On February 10, 1828, thirty Aboriginal men were murdered by VDL Company convict shepherds. The stockmen threw the men's bodies over a sixty-meter coastal cliff and fired upon their families who were camped on the beach below. The VDL Company attempted to cover up the massacre, officially acknowledging that only three Aboriginal people had been killed. Years later, the diaries of George Augustus Robinson were revealed. Robinson, the controversial "conciliator" of Aboriginal tribes, documented in detail his travels around the island. His diaries contained interviews with two of the convict perpetrators who were open about their role in the event, and several Aboriginal witnesses. By comparing the journal with the official VDL Company records, historians have been able to confirm what happened that day. The Cape Grim massacre was one of many atrocities committed against the Aboriginal inhabitants of the island.

Historic Houses

Tucked between Tasmania's farms and forests are a variety of convict-built, historic sites—stone bridges, roadside jails, old stores, and churches. Particularly impressive are the grand houses built by the pastoralists throughout the 1800s.

The country homestead closest to the fictional Vanishing Falls village would be Old WesleyDale, located near Mole Creek in the central north. In 1829, the land was granted to Lieutenant Travers Hartley Vaughn, a retired Irish army officer. He built a compound with high, thick walls which are still standing today. Inside is a stone barn with gun-slit windows, a relic of the volatile relationship between colonists and the traditional landowners. The compound also provided protection from bushrangers. In 1837, Vaughn sold the property, then known as Native Hut Corner, to Henry Reed, a Yorkshire farmer who made his fortune in shipping and whaling. Reed completed the eleven-room, two-story house using ▶

the labor of probationary convicts
from the government depot at Deloraine.
Reed was a devout Wesleyan Methodist,
and for forty years he preached to
the locals under a wattle tree on his
property. The house currently operates
as an upmarket bed-and-breakfast.

The inspiration for my fictional
Calendar House came from Mona Vale
House, near Ross in the central island.
The palatial mansion has a window for
every day of the year, fifty-two rooms,
twelve chimneys, seven entrances,
and four staircases for the four seasons.
Built from stone quarried on the
property, it is three stories high and
has an Italianate tower with sweeping
views. This mansion was built by Robert
Kermode in 1868 and it hosted Queen
Victoria's son, the Duke of Edinburgh,
on the first royal visit to Tasmania.
The land was originally granted to
Robert's father, William Kermode,
in 1821. He was a successful farmer,
although his wealth is thought to have
come from the slave trade. In 1822,
William Kermode took a nine-year-old
Aboriginal boy named George Van
Diemen to England to be educated.
George was one of the few Aboriginal
people to travel to England at that time.
He contracted tuberculosis in smog-
filled Liverpool and died upon return
in 1827, aged fourteen.

Since the Duke of Edinburgh paid the

first royal visit to Tasmania, Mona Vale House has hosted dignitaries including the future King George VI and Queen Elizabeth II, military strategist Lord Kitchener, and Sir Noel Coward.

Mona Vale remains a private residence.

Historic Villages

I grew up in Launceston, an old river city of elegant parks and stately buildings, noted for its well-preserved colonial architecture. A short drive away are several villages which came to mind as I was writing: Westbury, a classic Georgian garrison village; the historic village of Chudleigh; and Mole Creek, with its brick hotel that once hosted hunters and fur trappers. The quaint row of cottages that sit along Mole Creek's pretty stream inspired the homes of Joelle and Miss Gwen. Nearby is Mole Creek Karst National Park, an underground network of limestone caves, streams, and springs nestled beneath spectacular scenery.

Vanishing Falls

There is a waterfall in Tasmania called Vanishing Falls, located in the south. Deep in dense forest, the Salisbury ▶

River cascades over a dolerite sill and drains into a limestone cave system. The falls are inaccessible—there is not even a walking path.

Colonial Painter

John Glover was a landscape painter who, in 1831, at the age of sixty-four, moved from England to northern Tasmania with his wife and sons. They farmed at Patterdale, Mills Plains, in the state's north. He produced atmospheric paintings of nature, Aboriginal people, and farming life. In 1835, four crates of his paintings were loaded onto the ship *Protector* along with wool, 2,175 kangaroo skins, 300 opossum skins, bark, hides, seal skins, and whalebone. These sixty-eight paintings appeared in a selling exhibition on New Bond Street, London, that same year. Five of these paintings have turned up in recent years, in private collections. It is unclear what happened to the remainder of the paintings. ༄

Poppy Gee's Ten Favorite Novels Set in Tasmania

The Roving Party by Rohan Wilson

Lost Voices by Christopher Koch

The Hunter by Julia Leigh

Poet's Cottage by Josephine Pennicott

The Potato Factory by Bryce Courtenay

Wanting by Richard Flanagan

Bruny by Heather Rose

Wintering by Krissy Kneen

Past the Shallows by Favel Parrett

The Alphabet of Light and Dark by Danielle Wood ⟡